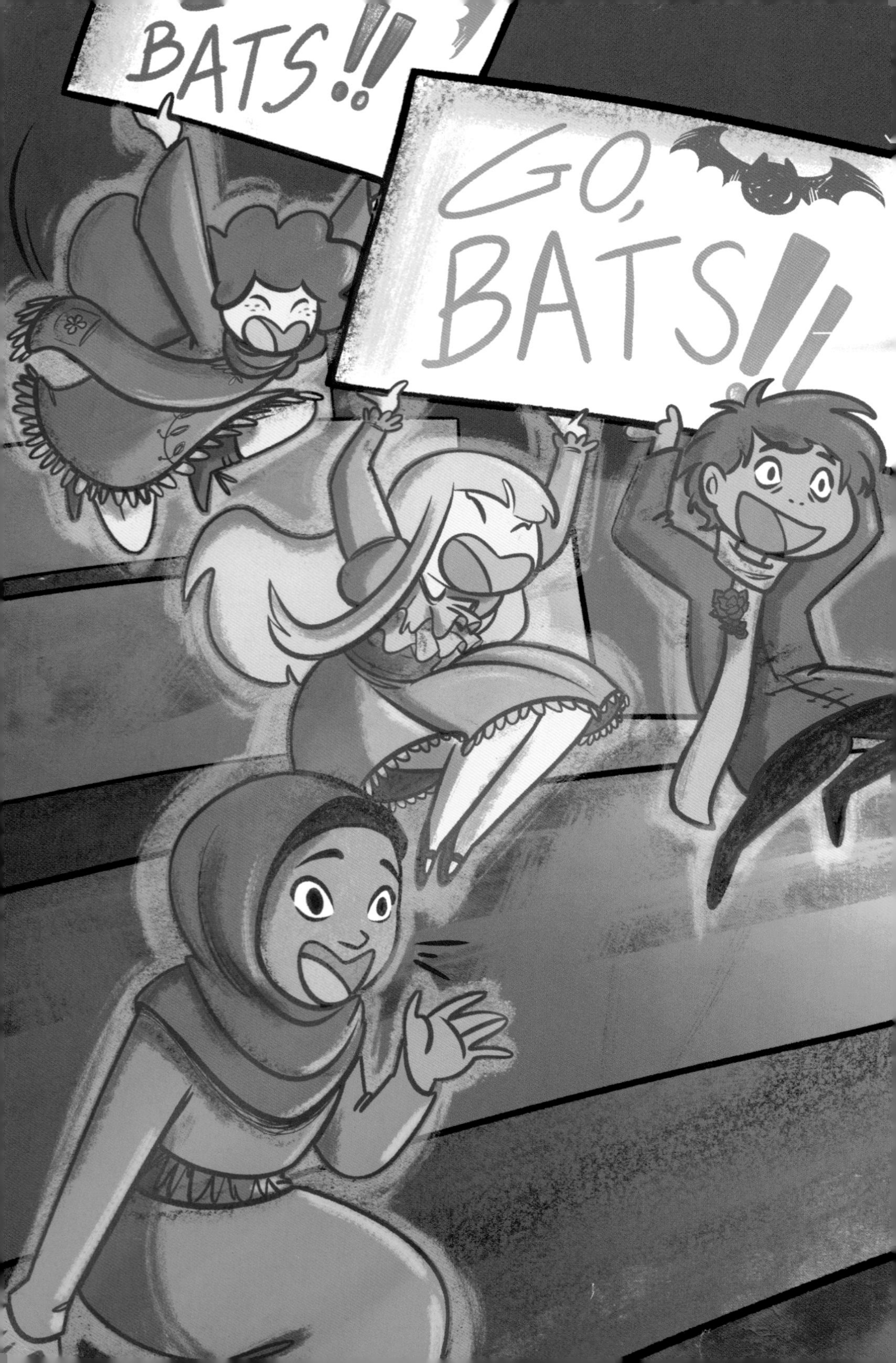
BATS!!
GO, BATS!!

Graphic Novel

Spirited

GO, GHOUL, GO!

By Liv Livingston

Illustrated by Anna Volcan at Glass House Graphics

LITTLE SIMON

New York   London   Toronto   Sydney   New Delhi

This book is a work of fiction. Any references to historical events, real people, or real places are used fictitiously. Other names, characters, places, and events are products of the author's imagination, and any resemblance to actual events or places or persons, living or dead, is entirely coincidental.

LITTLE SIMON
An imprint of Simon & Schuster Children's Publishing Division
1230 Avenue of the Americas, New York, New York 10020
First Little Simon edition March 2024

Simon & Schuster: Celebrating 100 Years of Publishing in 2024
For information about special discounts for bulk purchases, please contact Simon & Schuster Special Sales at 1-866-506-1949 or business@simonandschuster.com.
The Simon & Schuster Speakers Bureau can bring authors to your live event. For more information or to book an event, contact the Simon & Schuster Speakers Bureau at 1-866-248-3049 or visit our website at www.simonspeakers.com.
Cover by Manuel Preitano. Illustrated by Anna Volcan at Glass House Graphics. Assistant on layouts Giulia Balsamo. Colors by Natalyia Torretta, Antonino Ulizzi, and Vanessa Costanzo. Lettering by Giovanni Spadaro/Grafimated Cartoon. Supervision by Salvatore vDi Marco/Grafimated Cartoon.
Designed by Brittany Fetcho
Manufactured in China 1123 SCP
2 4 6 8 10 9 7 5 3 1
Library of Congress Cataloging-in-Publication Data
Names: Livingston, Liv, author. | Glass House Graphics, illustrator.
Title: Go, ghoul, go! / by Liv Livingston ; illustrated by Glass House Graphics.
Description: First Little Simon edition. | New York : Little Simon, 2024.
Series: Spirited ; book 2 | Audience: Ages 5–9 |
Summary: Now that she is better settled into her new life at Gloomsdale, eight-year-old Liv Livingston feels like she has adjusted to this town of ghosts and supernatural beings, so she soon has the confidence to try out for the Ghoul Squad, the school's cheerleading team.
Identifiers: LCCN 2023017458 (print) | LCCN 2023017459 (ebook)
ISBN 9781665942300 (paperback) | ISBN 9781665942317 (hardcover)
ISBN 9781665942324 (ebook)
Subjects: CYAC: Graphic novels. | Supernatural—Fiction. | Cheerleading—Fiction. | Schools—Fiction. | Friendship—Fiction. | LCGFT: Paranormal comics. | Graphic novels.
Classification: LCC PZ7.7.L596 Go 2024 (print) | LCC PZ7.7.L596 (ebook) |
DDC 741.5/973—dc23/eng/20230517
LC record available at https://lccn.loc.gov/2023017458
LC ebook record available at https://lccn.loc.gov/2023017459

Contents

CHAPTER 1

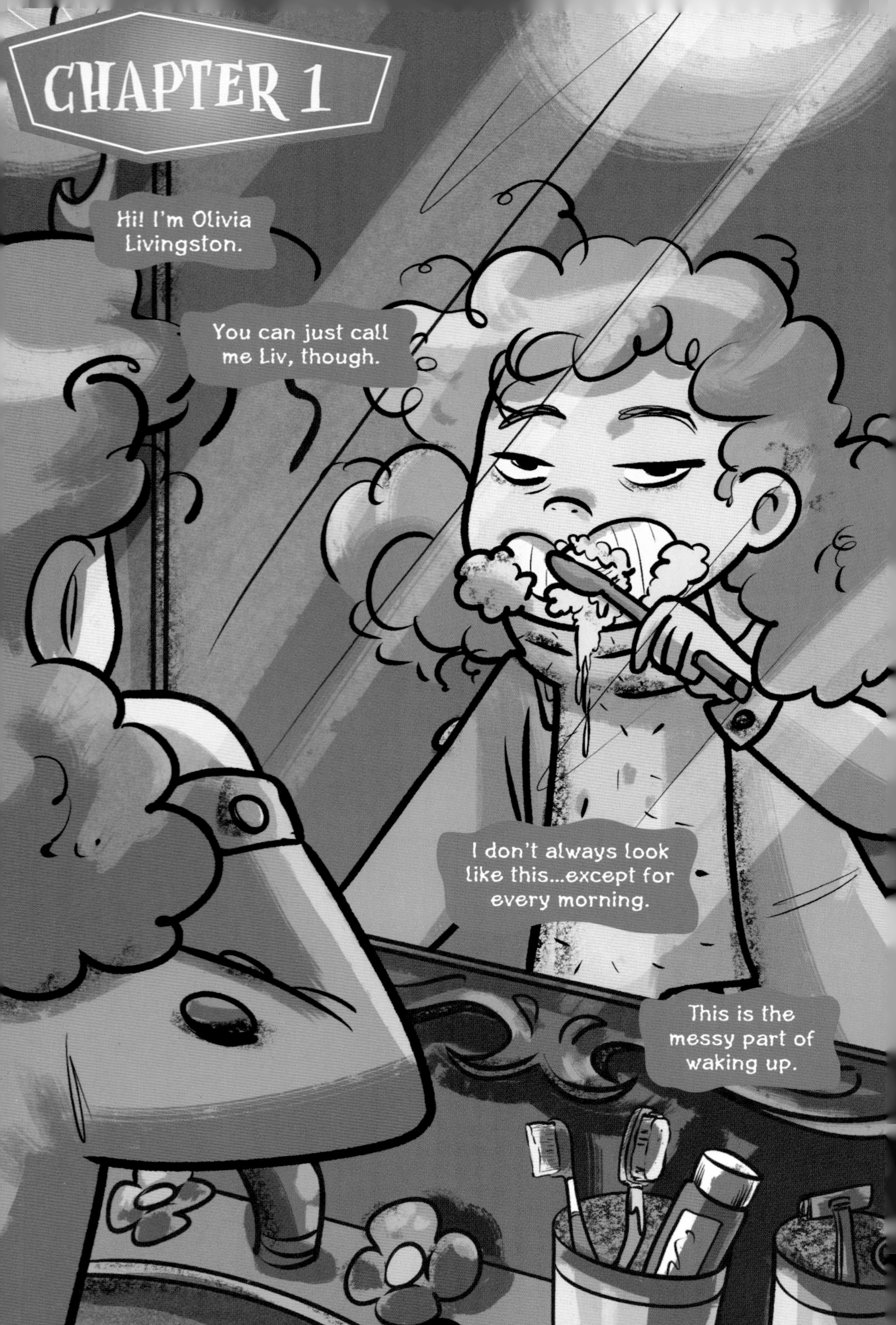
Hi! I'm Olivia Livingston.
You can just call me Liv, though.
I don't always look like this...except for every morning.
This is the messy part of waking up.

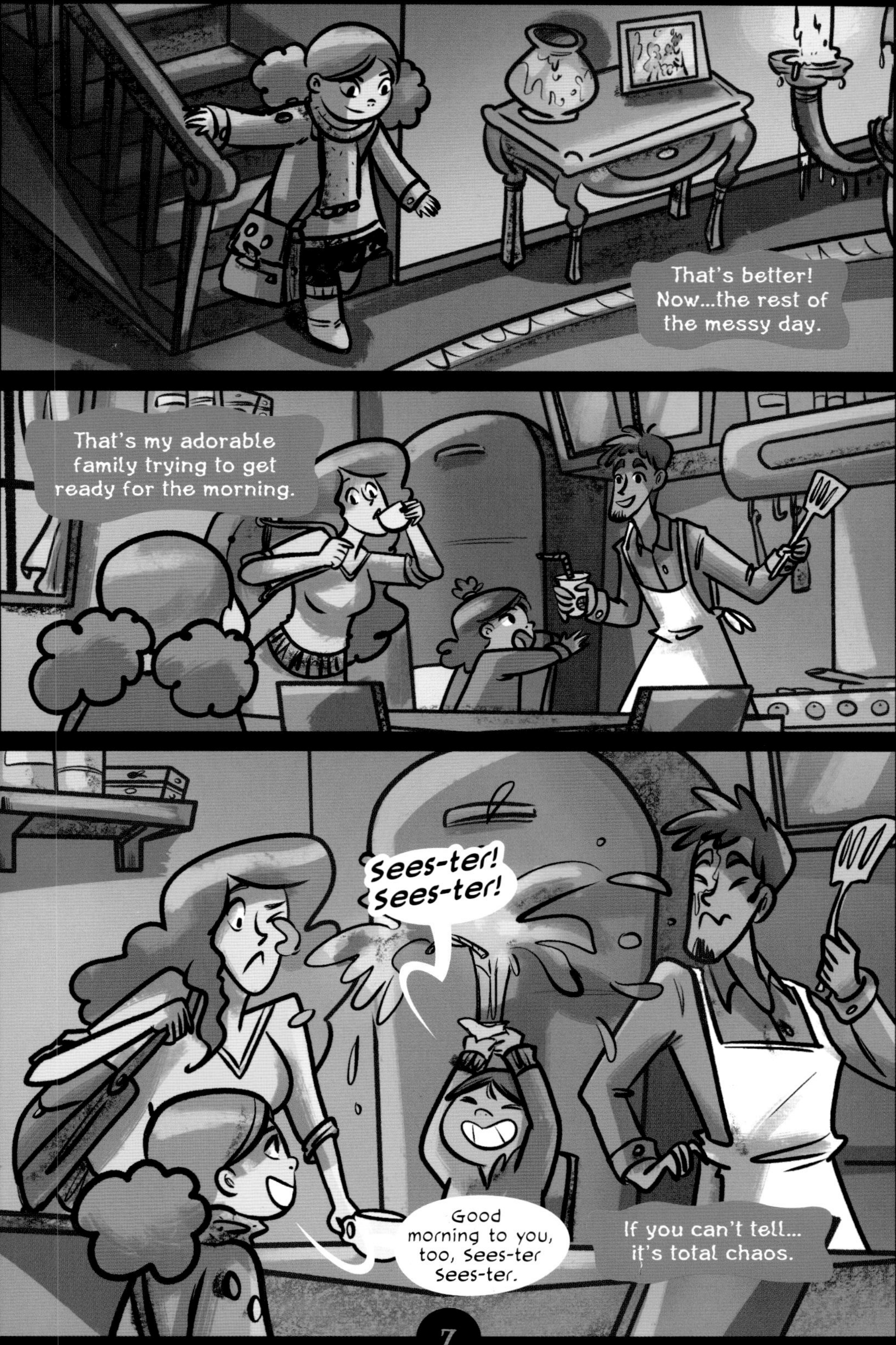
That's better! Now...the rest of the messy day.
That's my adorable family trying to get ready for the morning.
Sees-ter! Sees-ter!
Good morning to you, too, Sees-ter Sees-ter.
If you can't tell... it's total chaos.

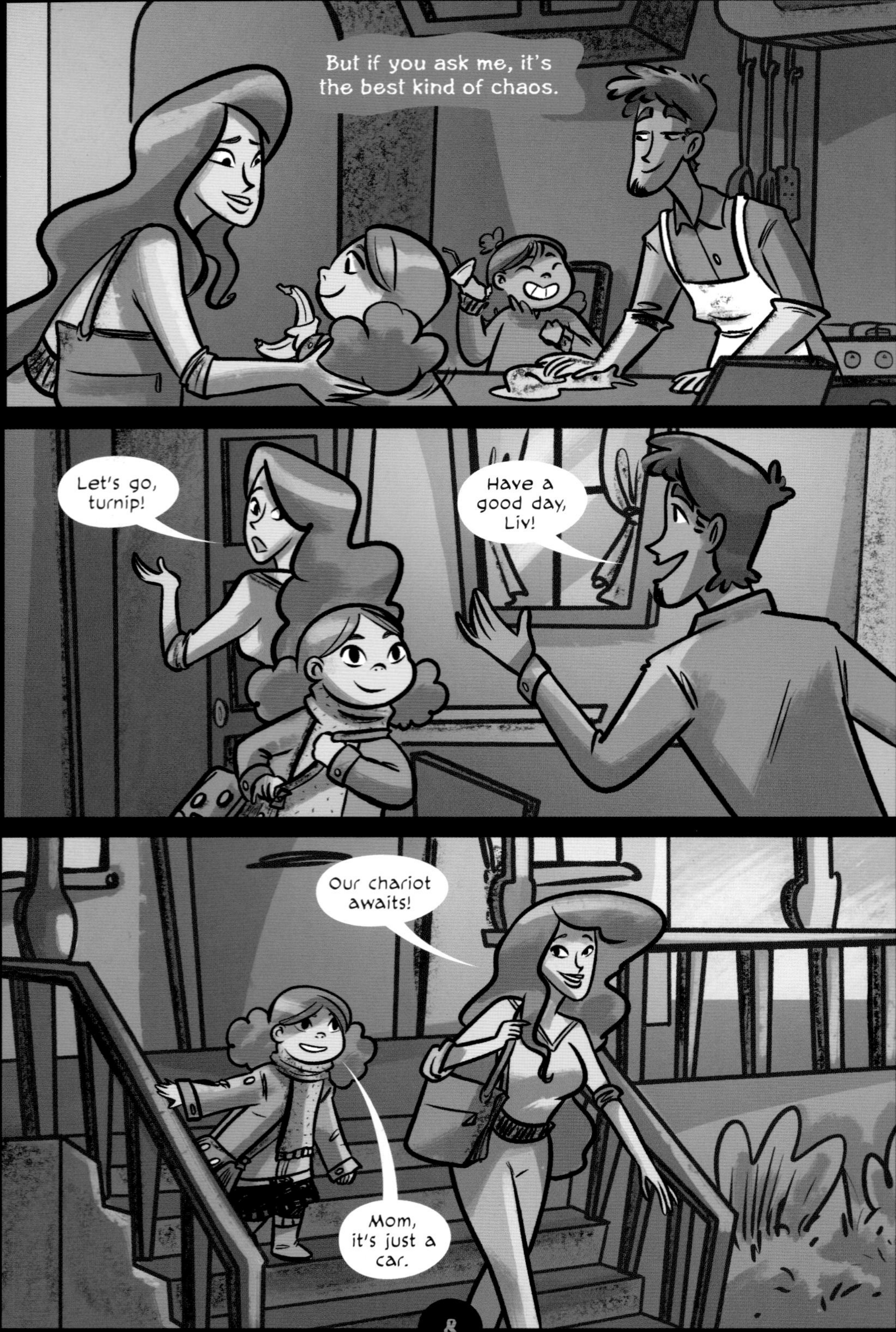
But if you ask me, it's the best kind of chaos.
Let's go, turnip!
Have a good day, Liv!
Our chariot awaits!
Mom, it's just a car.

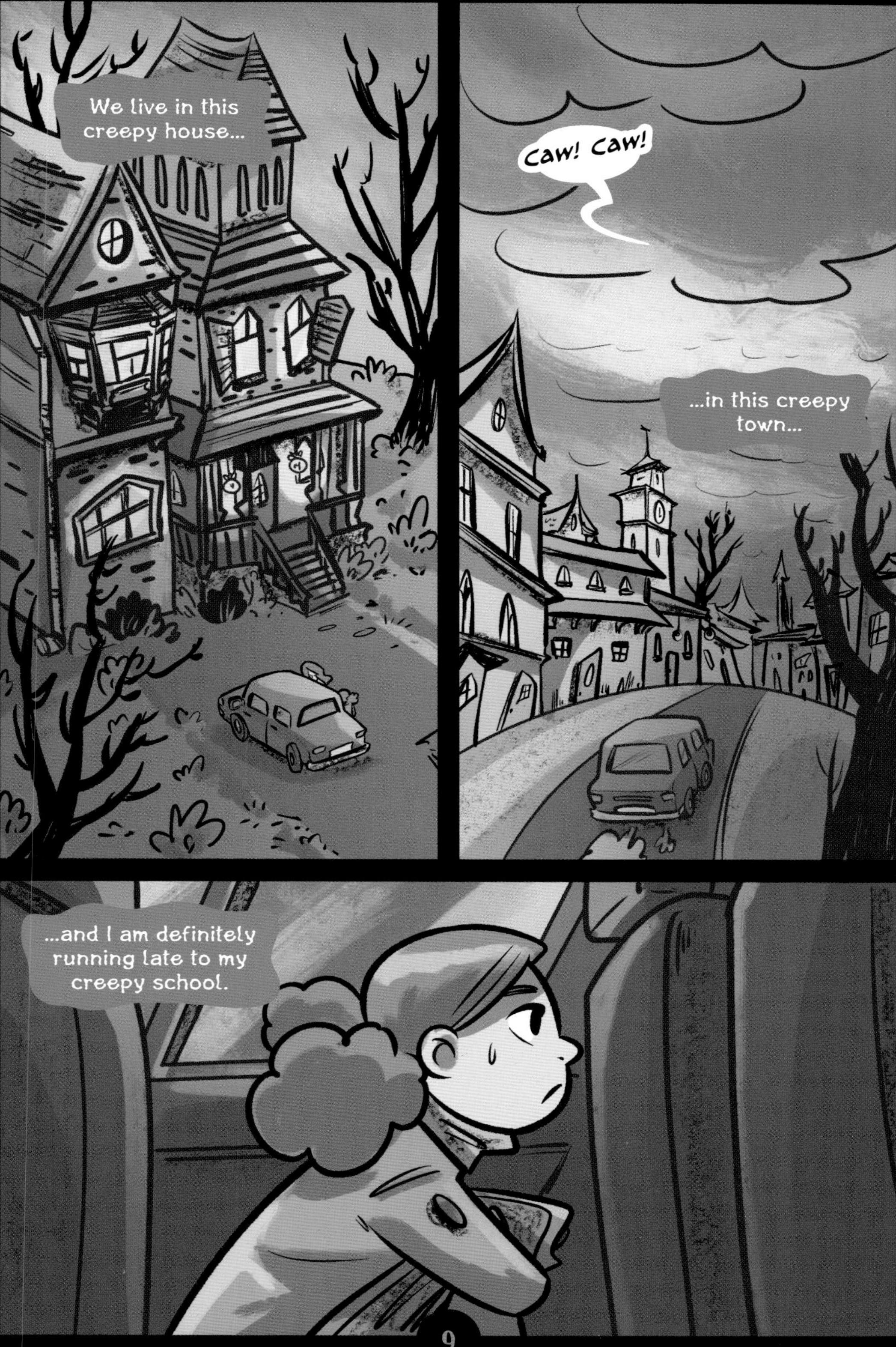
We live in this creepy house...
CAW! CAW!
...in this creepy town...
...and I am definitely running late to my creepy school.

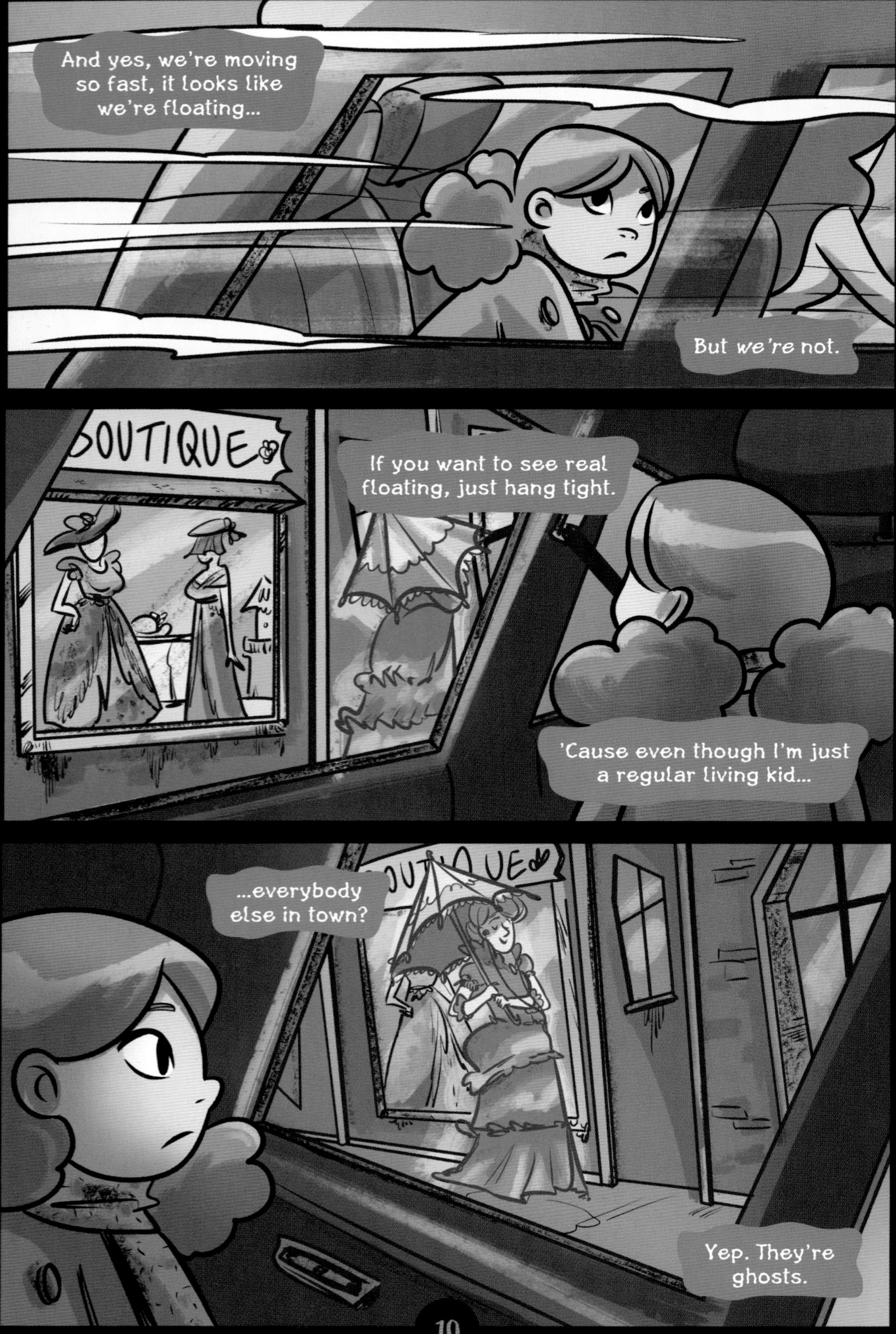
And yes, we're moving so fast, it looks like we're floating...
But *we're* not.
OUTIQUE
If you want to see real floating, just hang tight.
'Cause even though I'm just a regular living kid...
...everybody else in town?
Yep. They're ghosts.

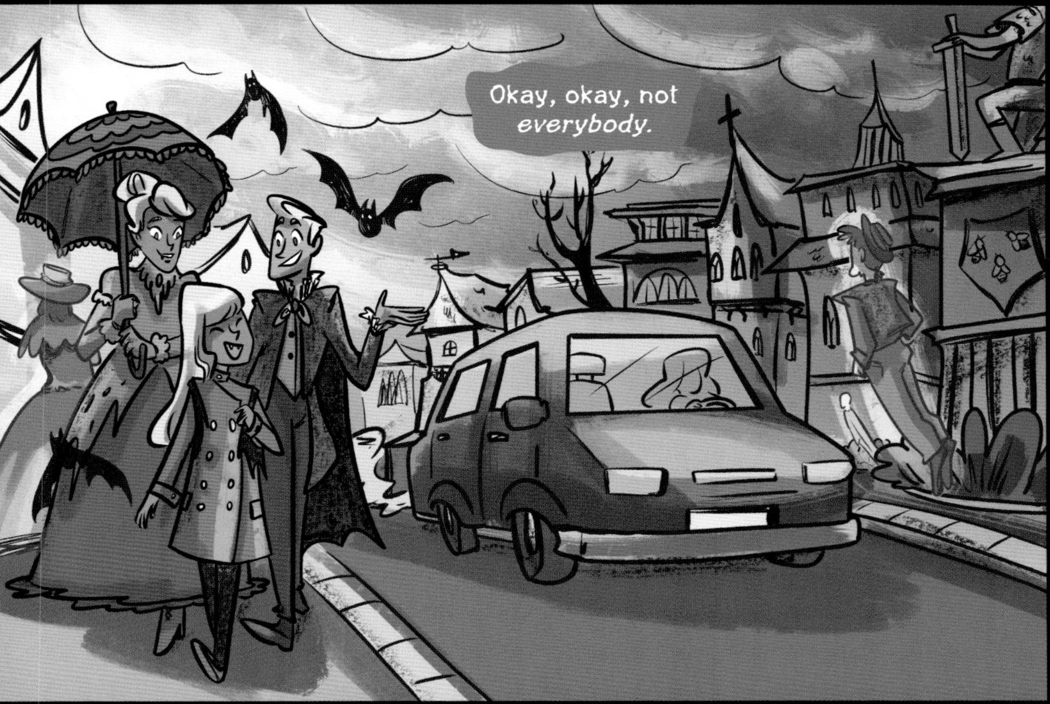
Okay, okay, not *everybody*.

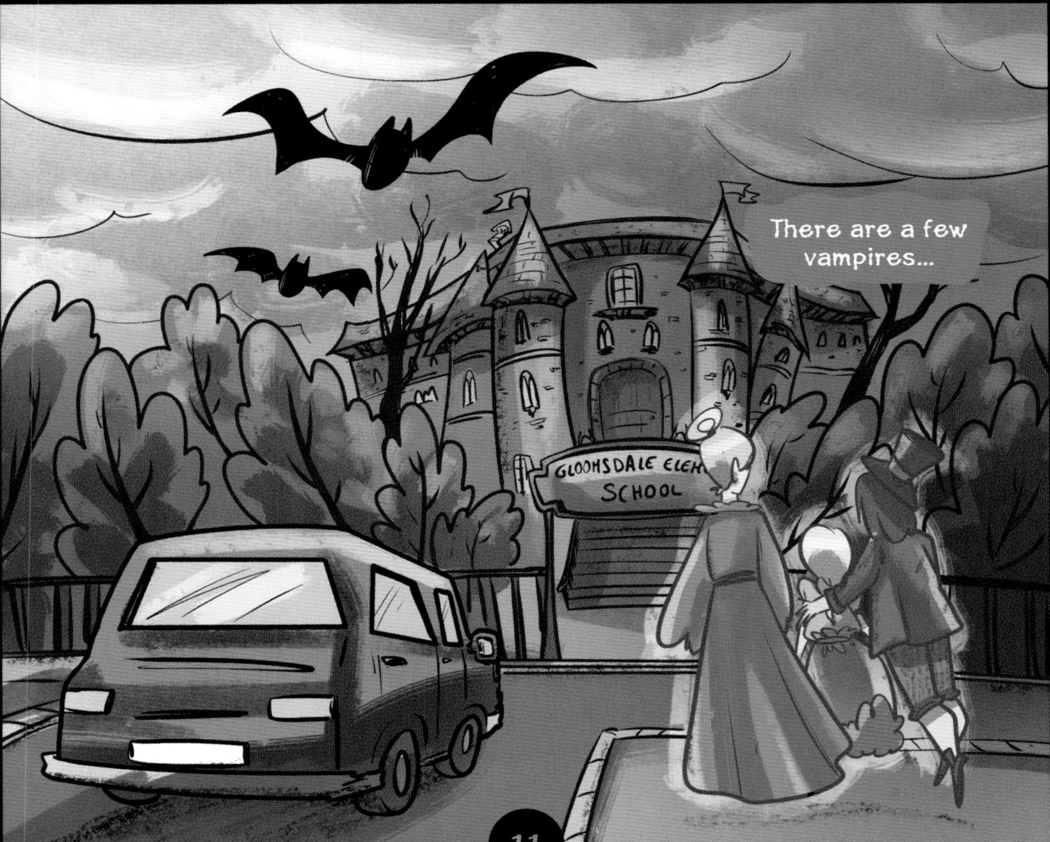
There are a few vampires...
GLOOMSDALE ELEM
SCHOOL

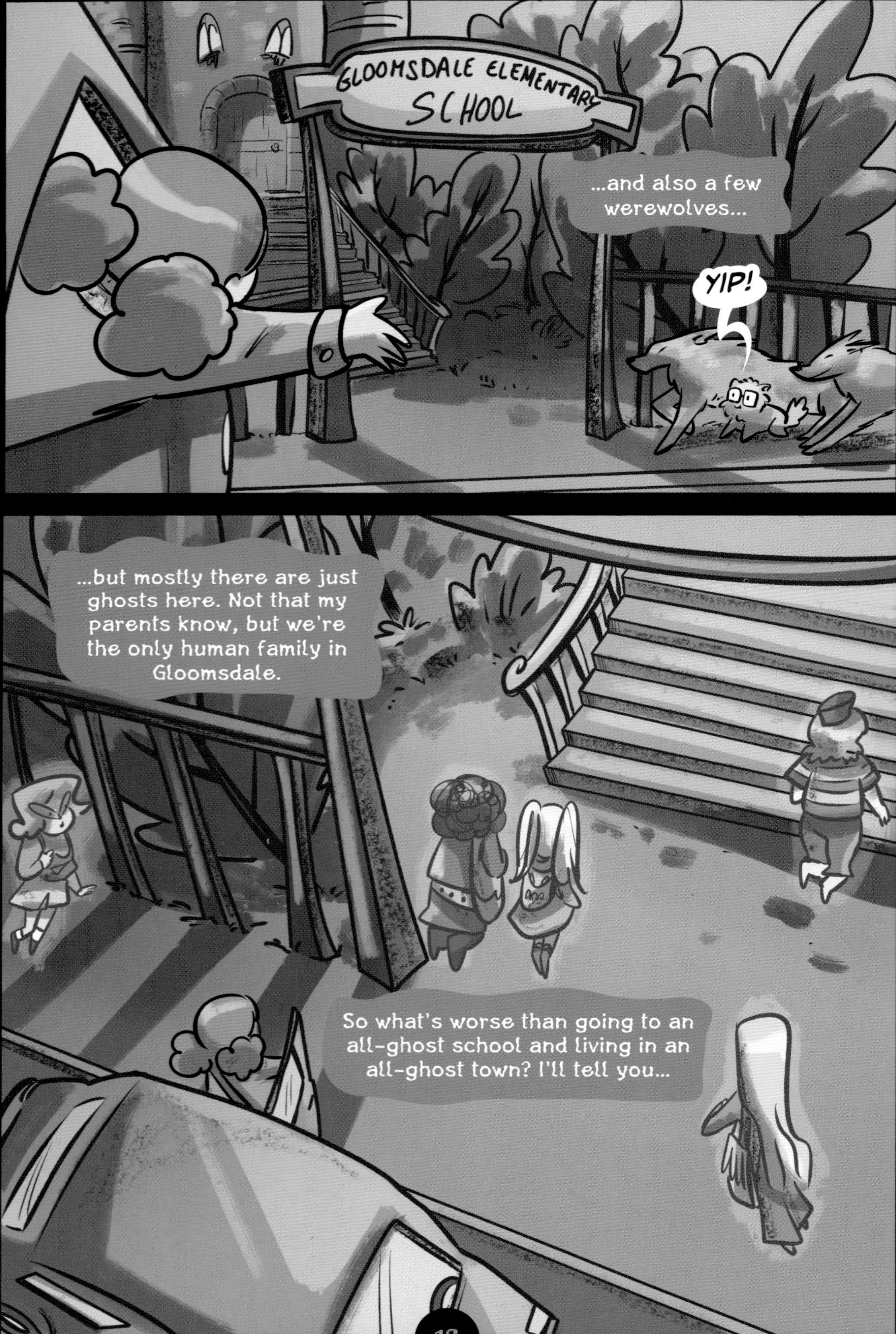
GLOOMSDALE ELEMENTARY SCHOOL
...and also a few werewolves...
YIP!
...but mostly there are just ghosts here. Not that my parents know, but we're the only human family in Gloomsdale.
So what's worse than going to an all-ghost school and living in an all-ghost town? I'll tell you...

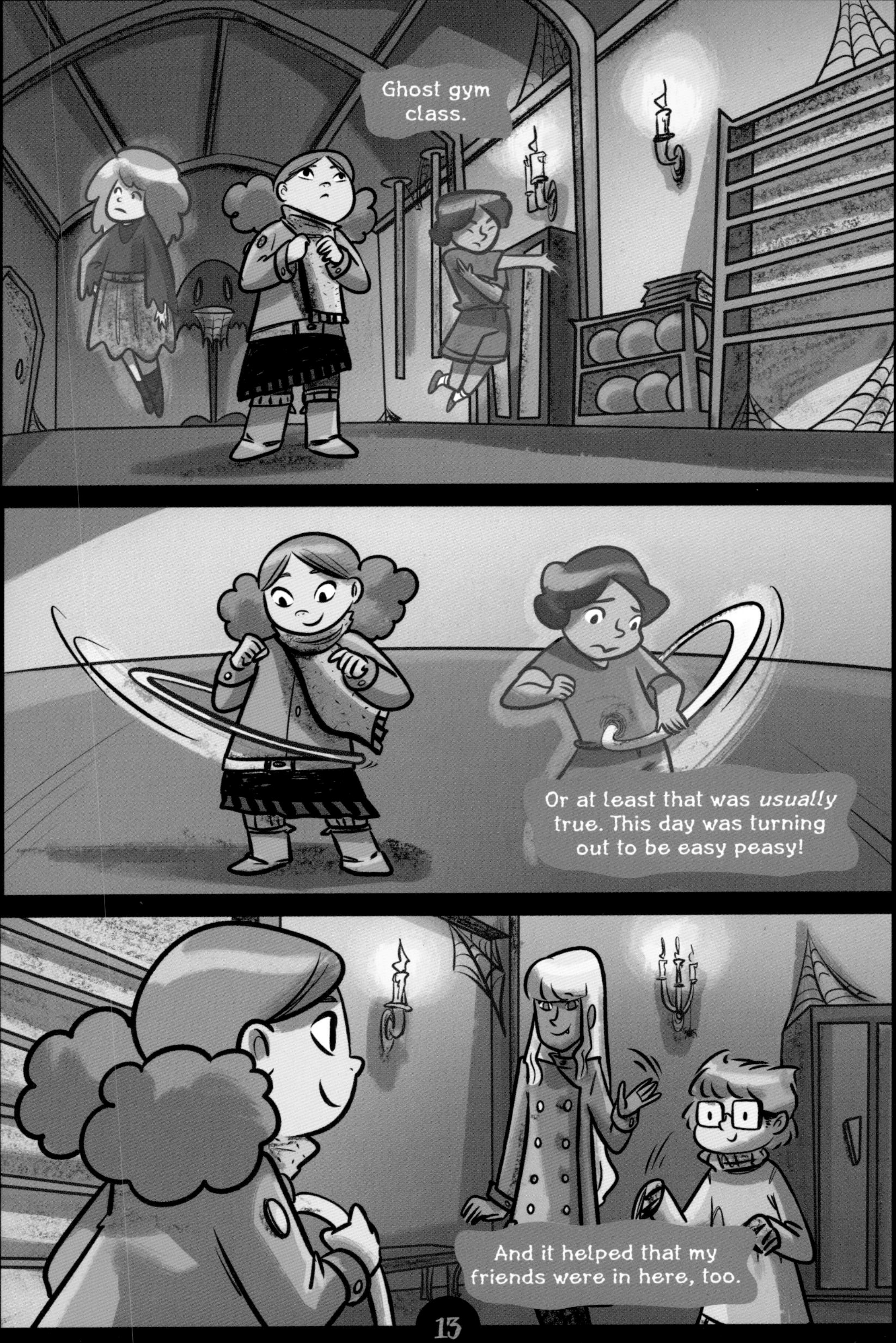
Ghost gym class.
Or at least that was *usually* true. This day was turning out to be easy peasy!
And it helped that my friends were in here, too.

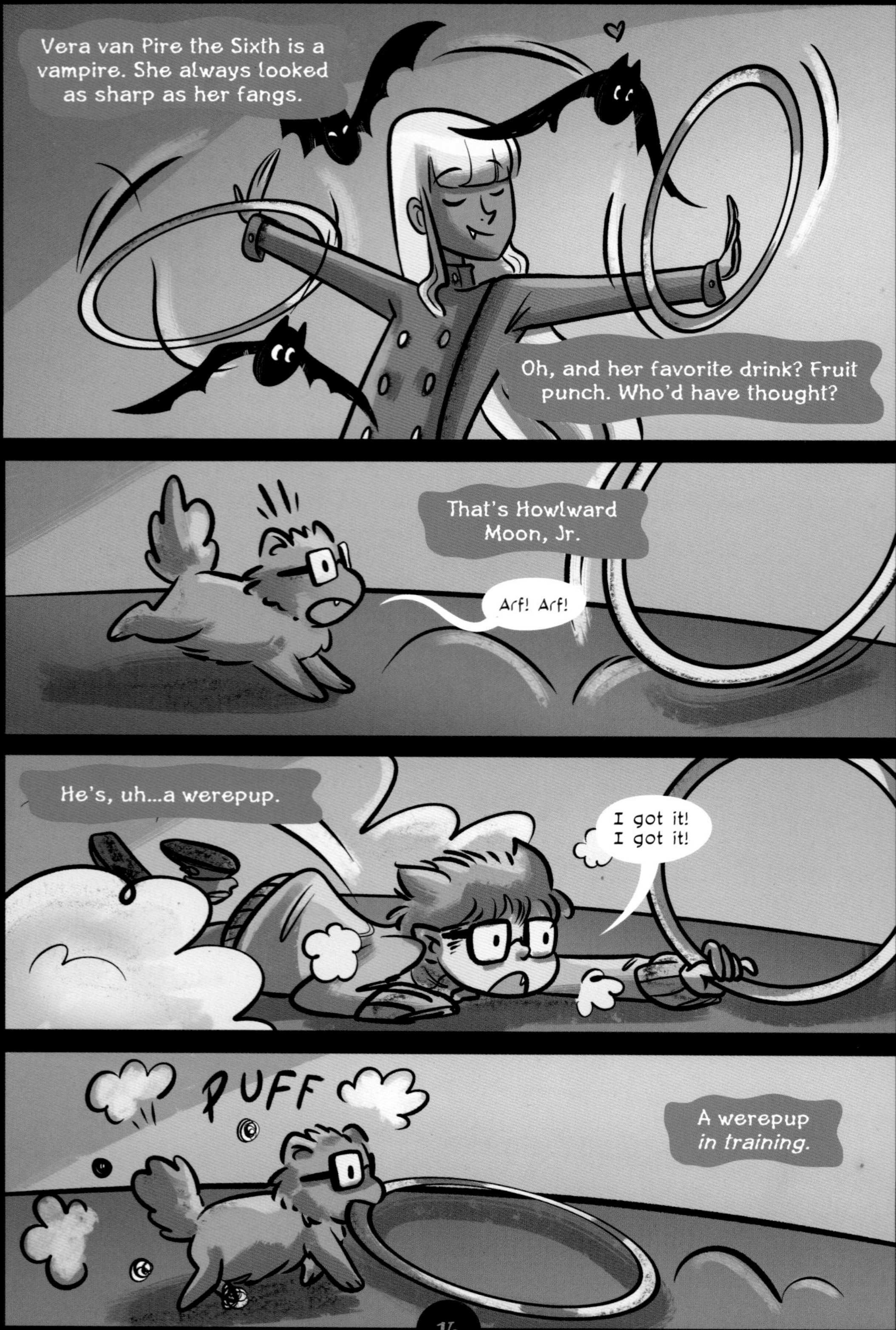

Vera van Pire the Sixth is a vampire. She always looked as sharp as her fangs.
Oh, and her favorite drink? Fruit punch. Who'd have thought?
That's Howlward Moon, Jr.
Arf! Arf!
He's, uh...a werepup.
I got it! I got it!
PUFF
A werepup *in training.*

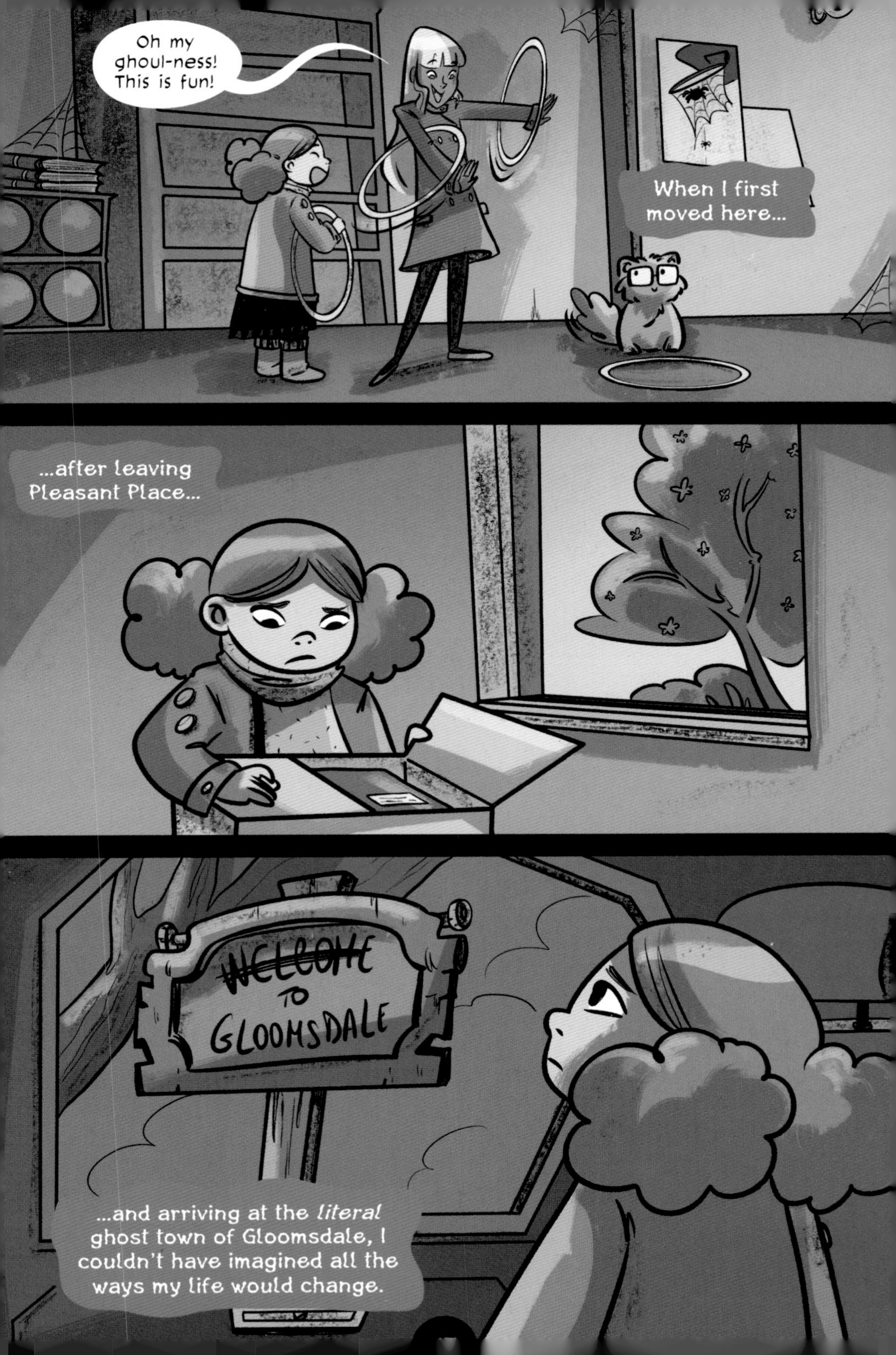
Oh my ghoul-ness! This is fun!
When I first moved here...
...after leaving Pleasant Place...
WELCOME TO GLOOMSDALE
...and arriving at the *literal* ghost town of Gloomsdale, I couldn't have imagined all the ways my life would change.

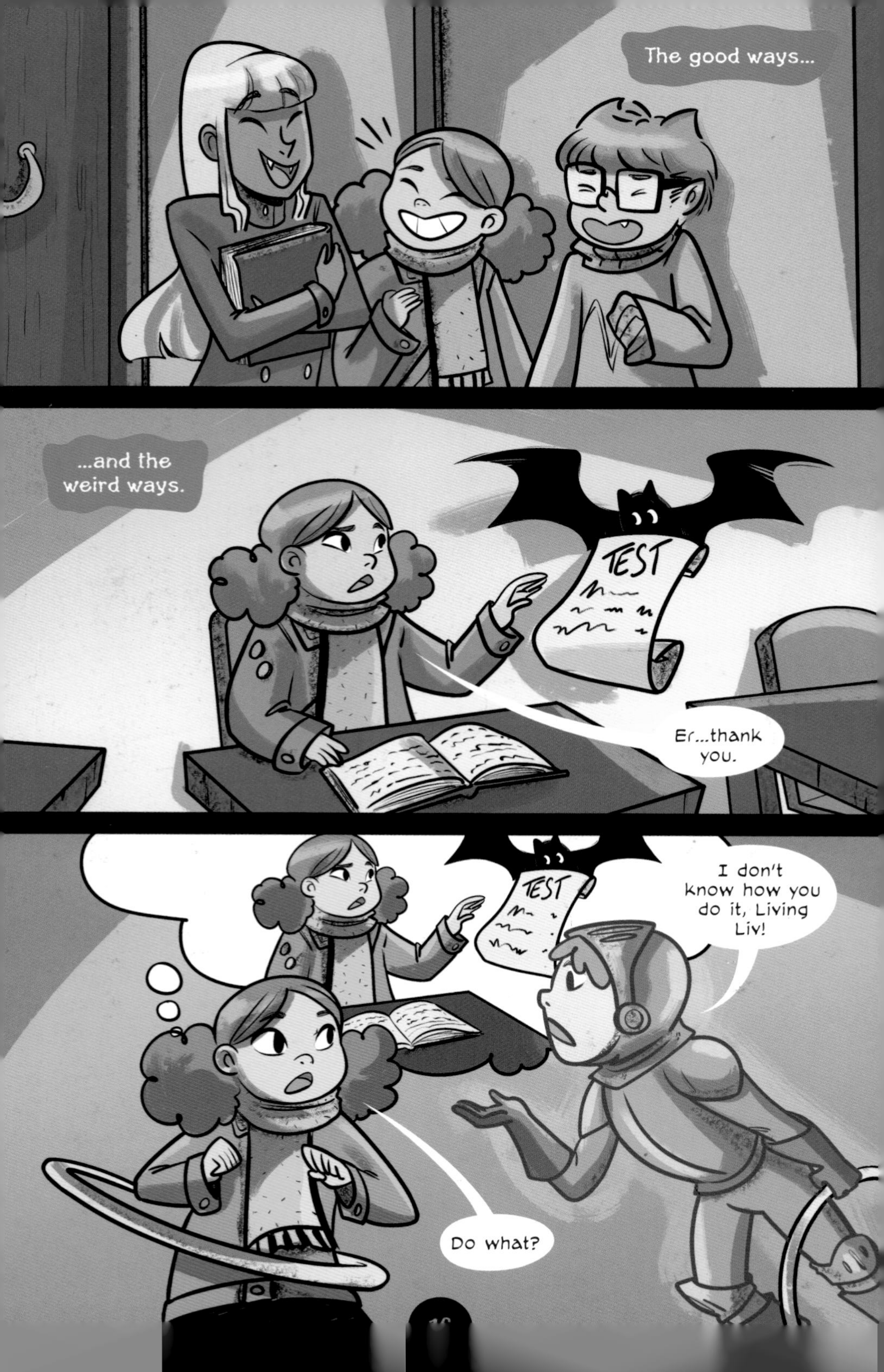
The good ways...
...and the weird ways.
TEST
Er...thank you.
TEST
I don't know how you do it, Living Liv!
Do what?

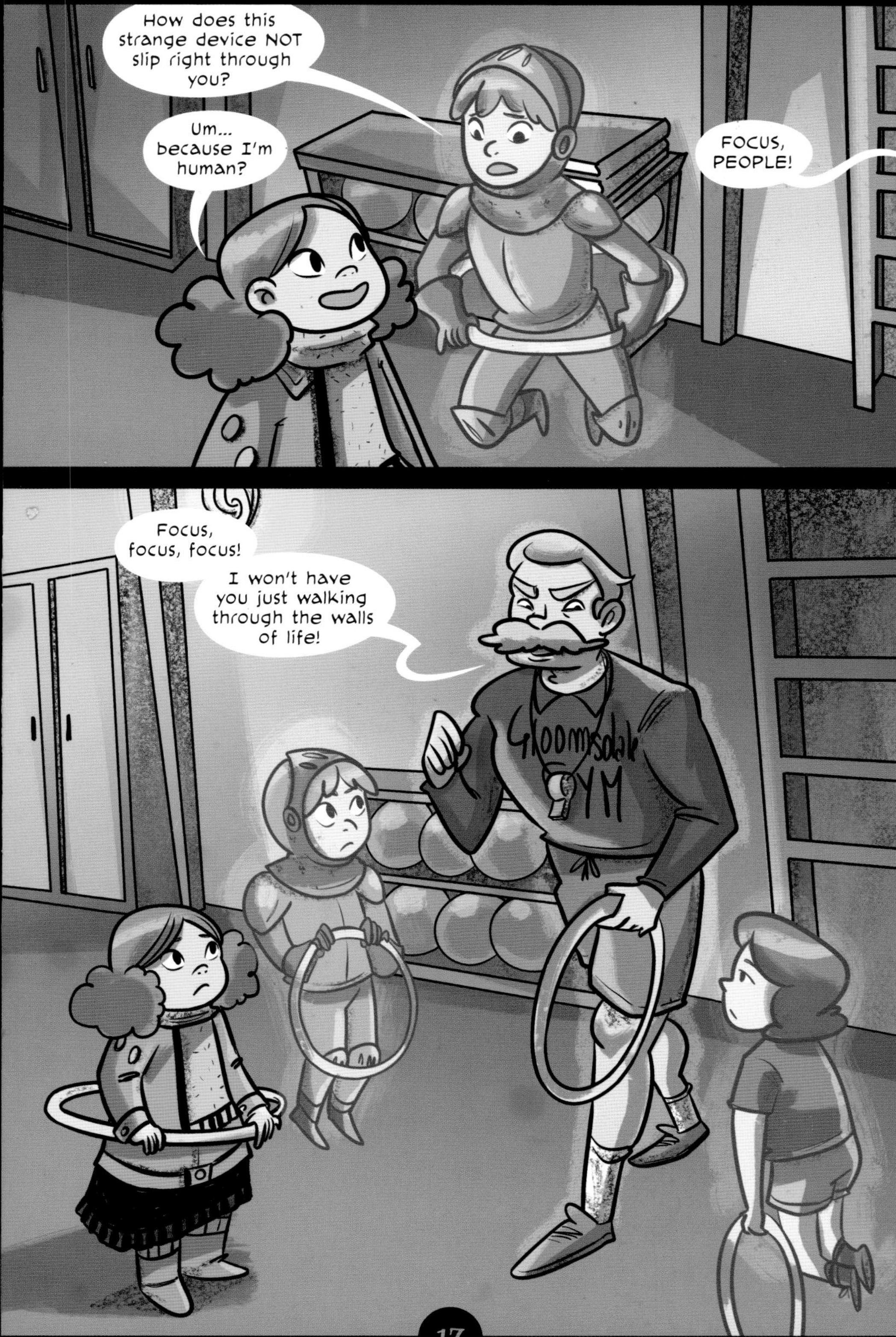
How does this strange device NOT slip right through you?
Um... because I'm human?
FOCUS, PEOPLE!
Focus, focus, focus!
I won't have you just walking through the walls of life!
GYM

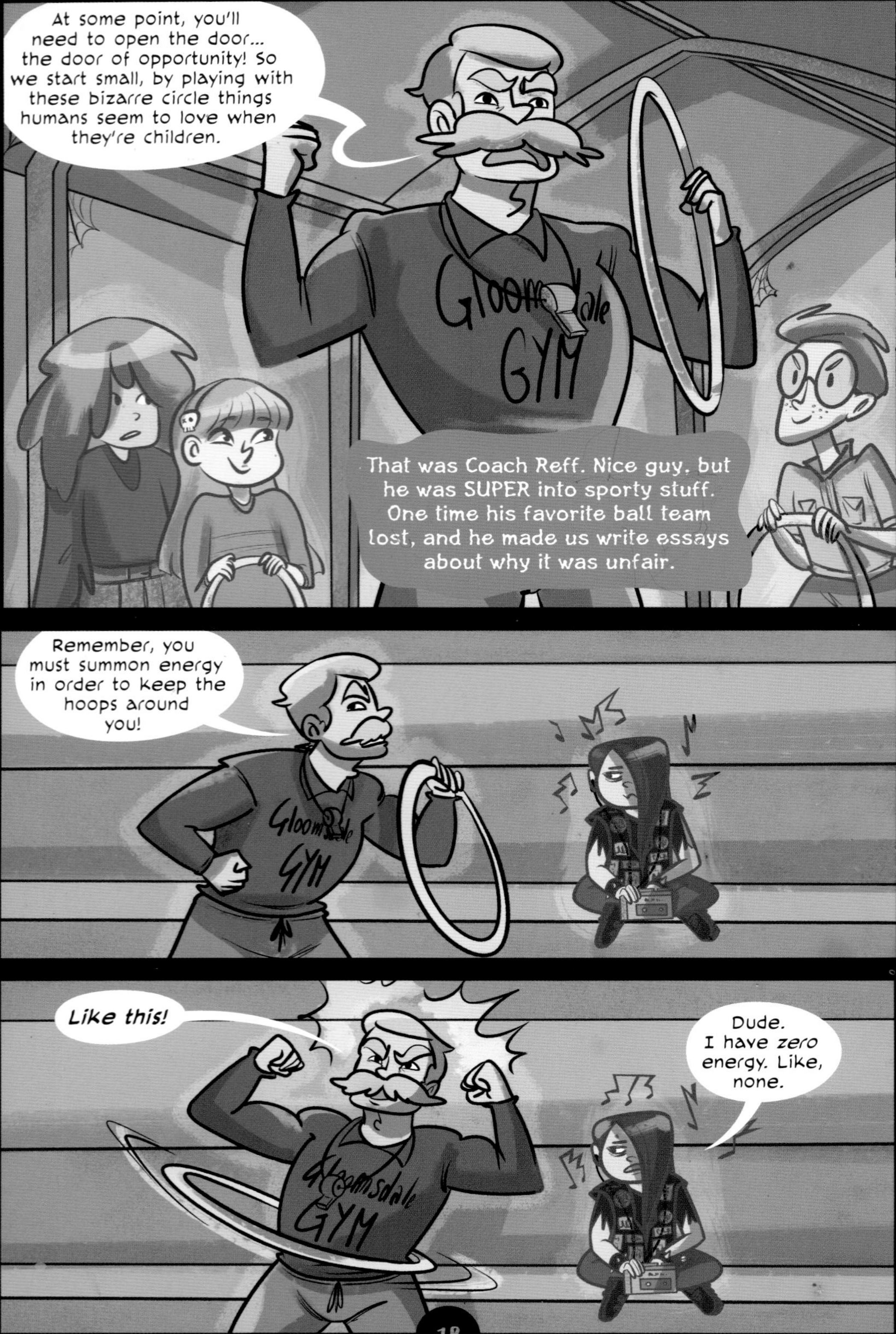
At some point, you'll need to open the door... the door of opportunity! So we start small, by playing with these bizarre circle things humans seem to love when they're children.
Gloomsdale GYM
That was Coach Reff. Nice guy, but he was SUPER into sporty stuff. One time his favorite ball team lost, and he made us write essays about why it was unfair.
Remember, you must summon energy in order to keep the hoops around you!
Like this!
Dude. I have *zero* energy. Like, none.

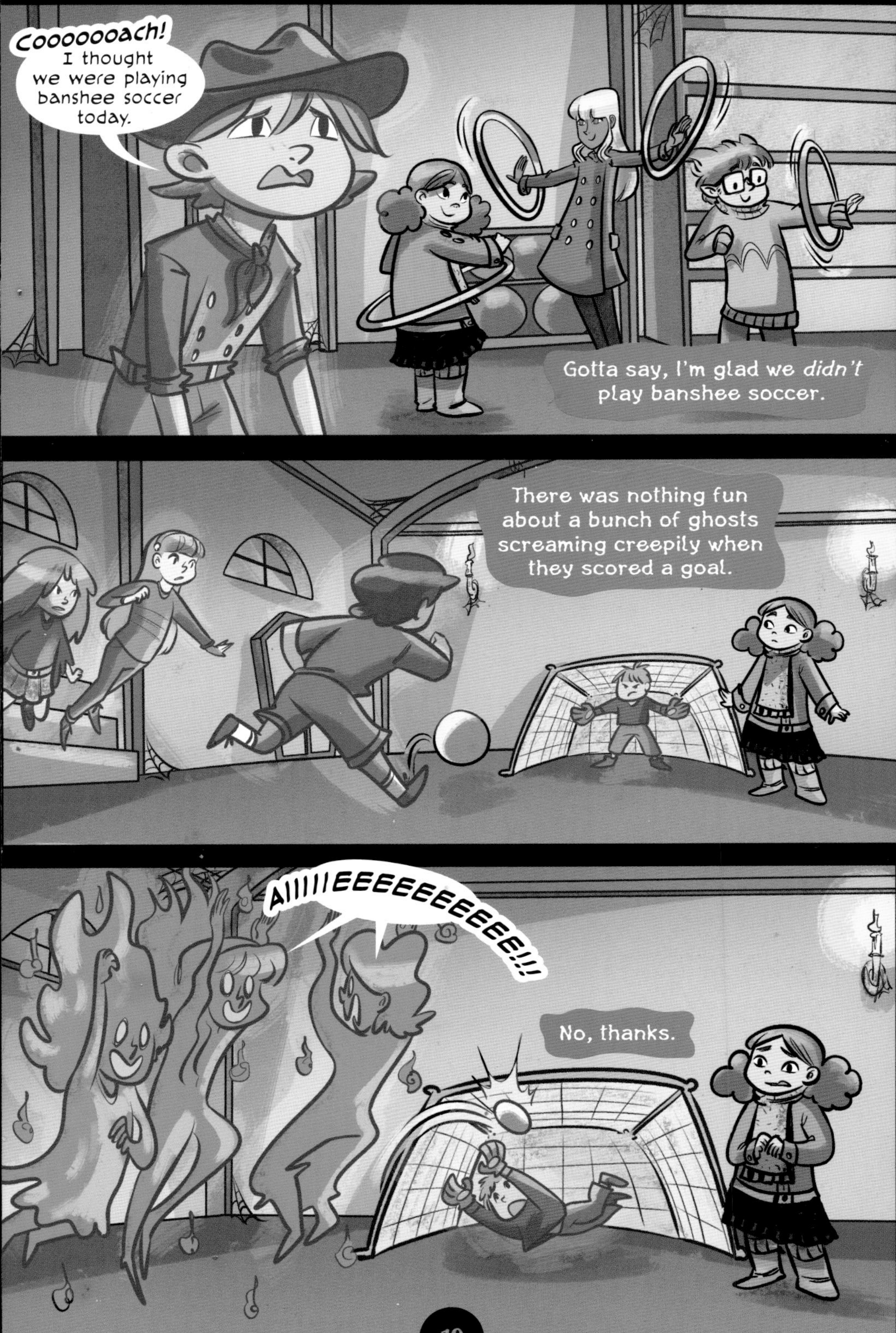
Cooooooach! I thought we were playing banshee soccer today.
Gotta say, I'm glad we *didn't* play banshee soccer.
There was nothing fun about a bunch of ghosts screaming creepily when they scored a goal.
AIIIIIEEEEEEEEEEEE!!!
No, thanks.

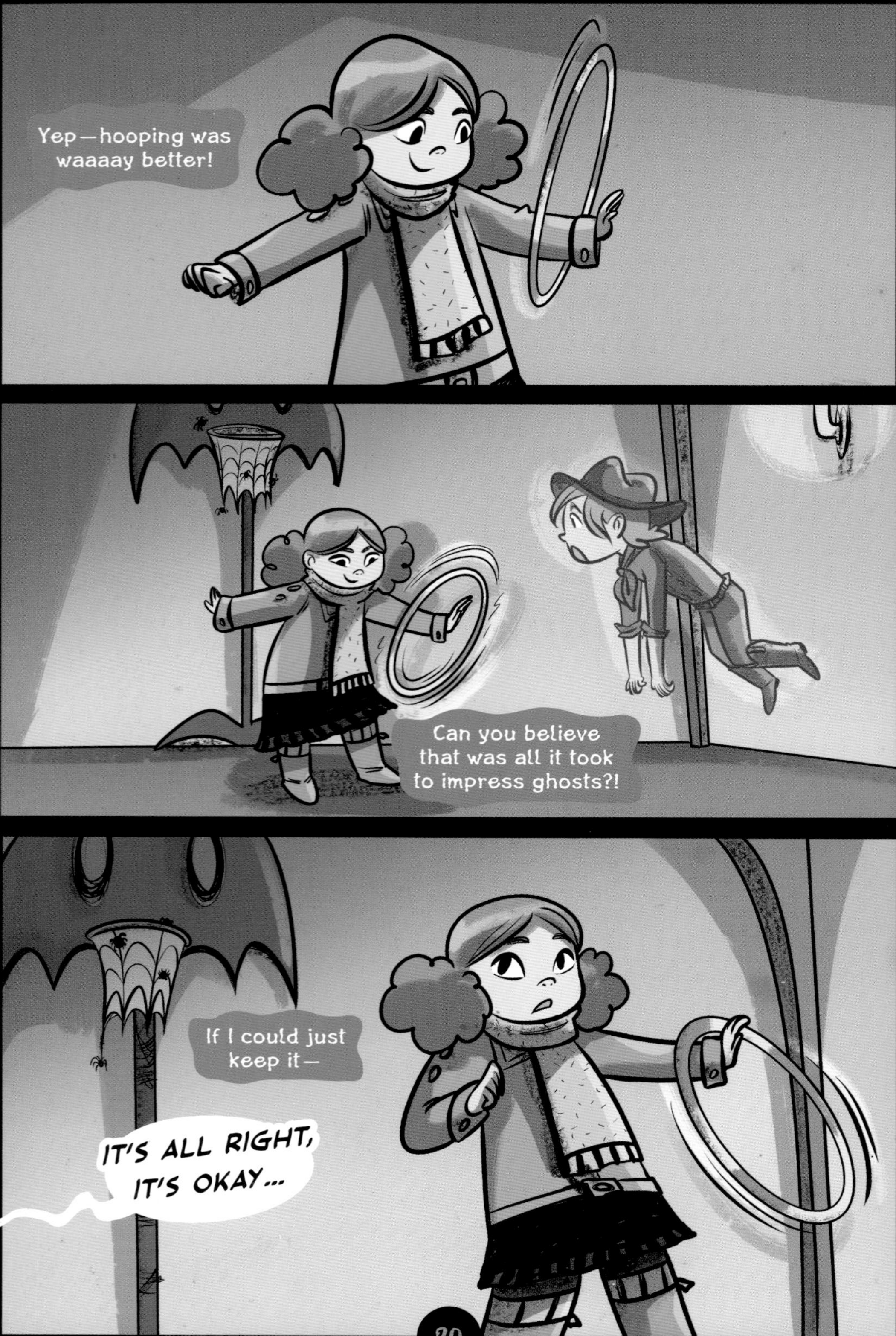
Yep—hooping was waaaay better!
Can you believe that was all it took to impress ghosts?!
If I could just keep it—
IT'S ALL RIGHT, IT'S OKAY...

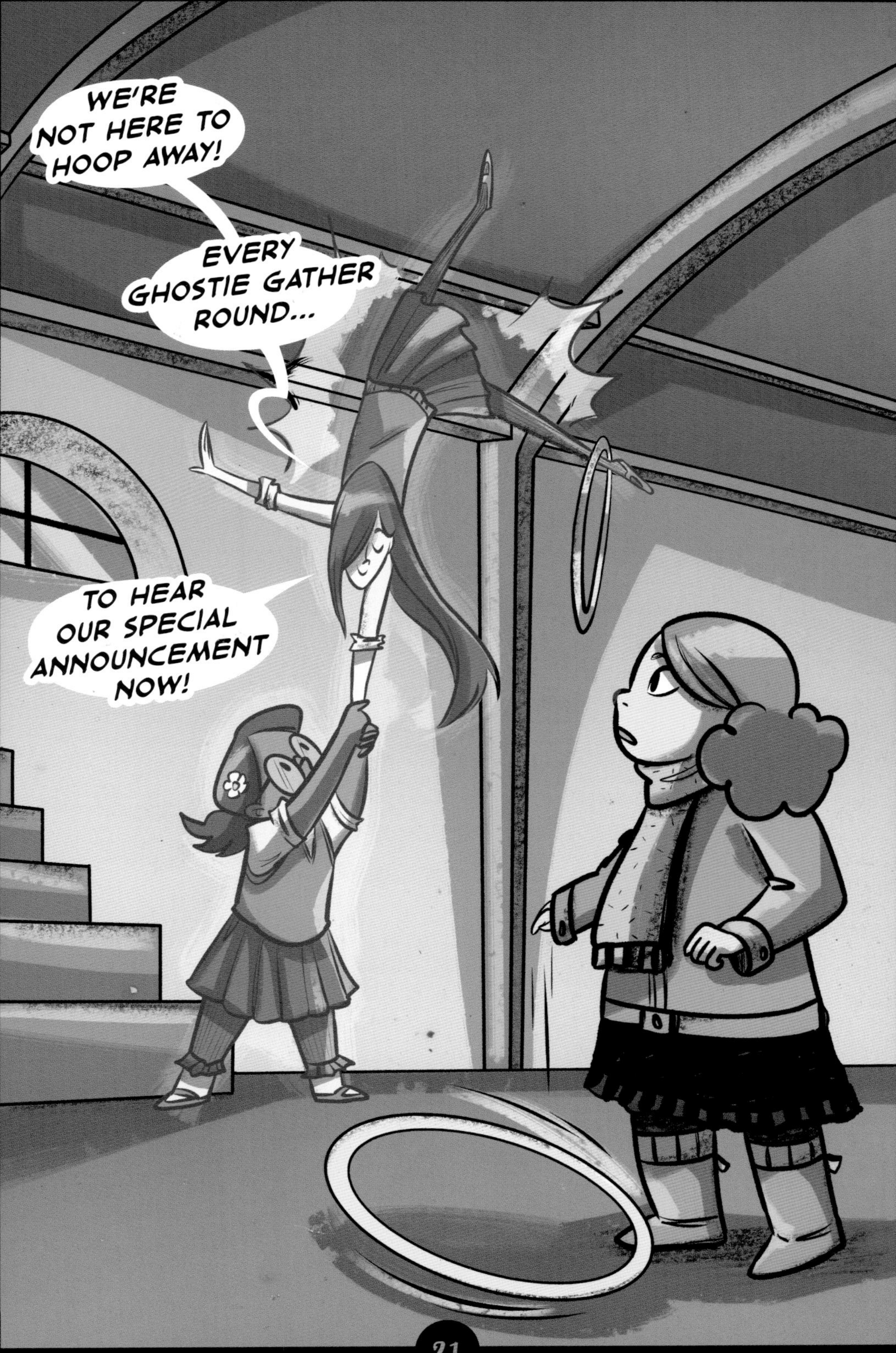
WE'RE NOT HERE TO HOOP AWAY!
EVERY GHOSTIE GATHER ROUND...
TO HEAR OUR SPECIAL ANNOUNCEMENT NOW!

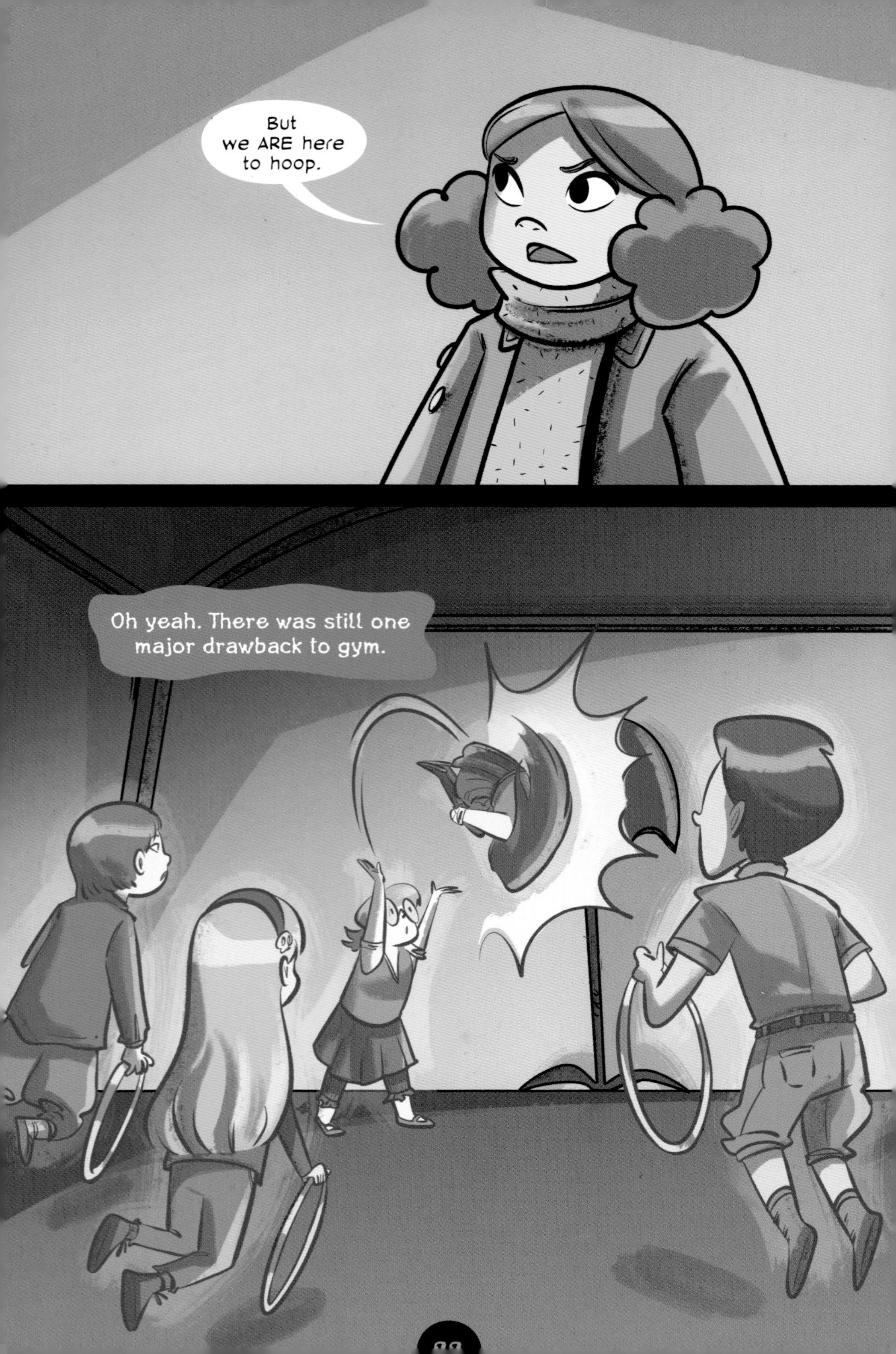
But we ARE here to hoop.
Oh yeah. There was still one major drawback to gym.

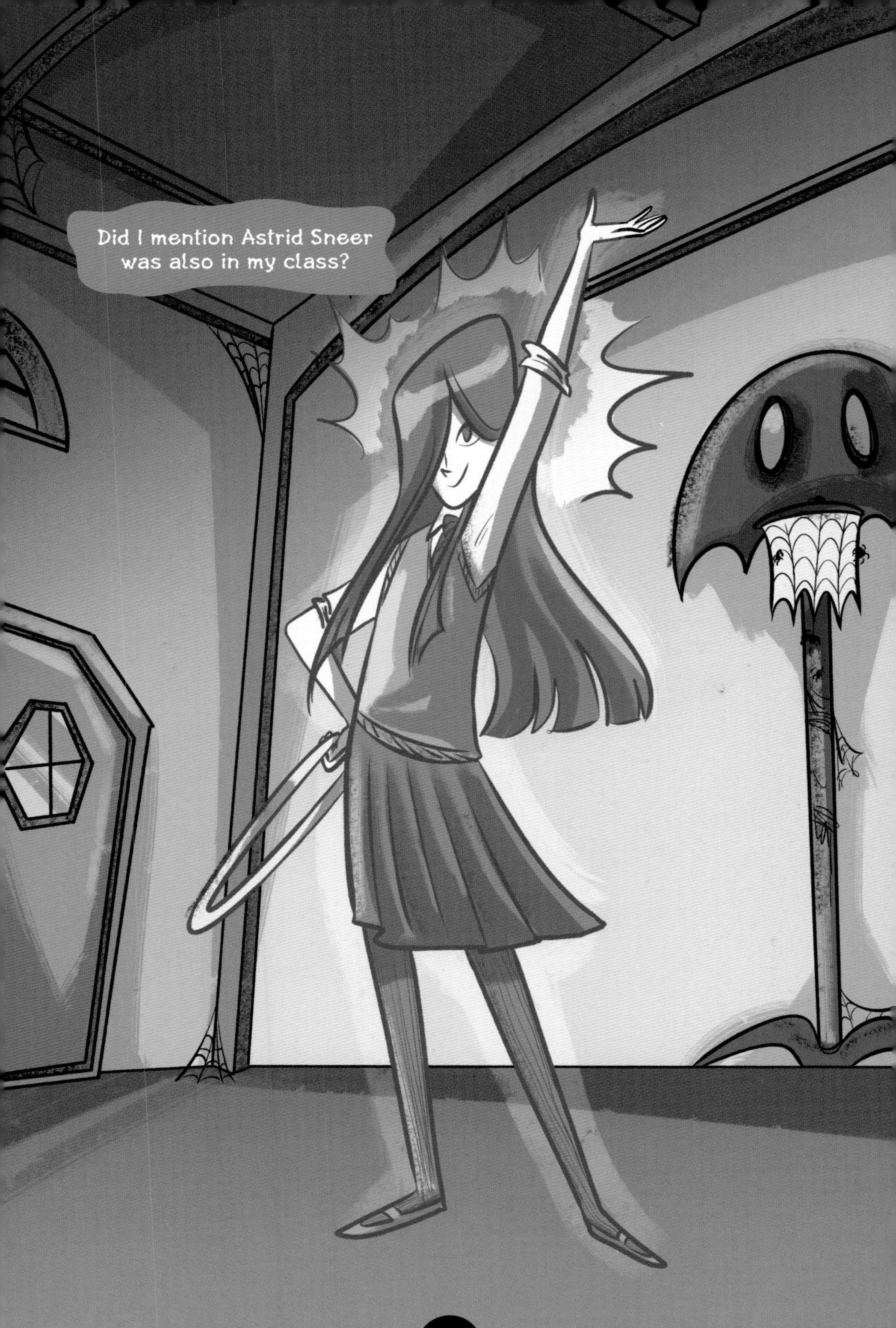
Did I mention Astrid Sneer was also in my class?

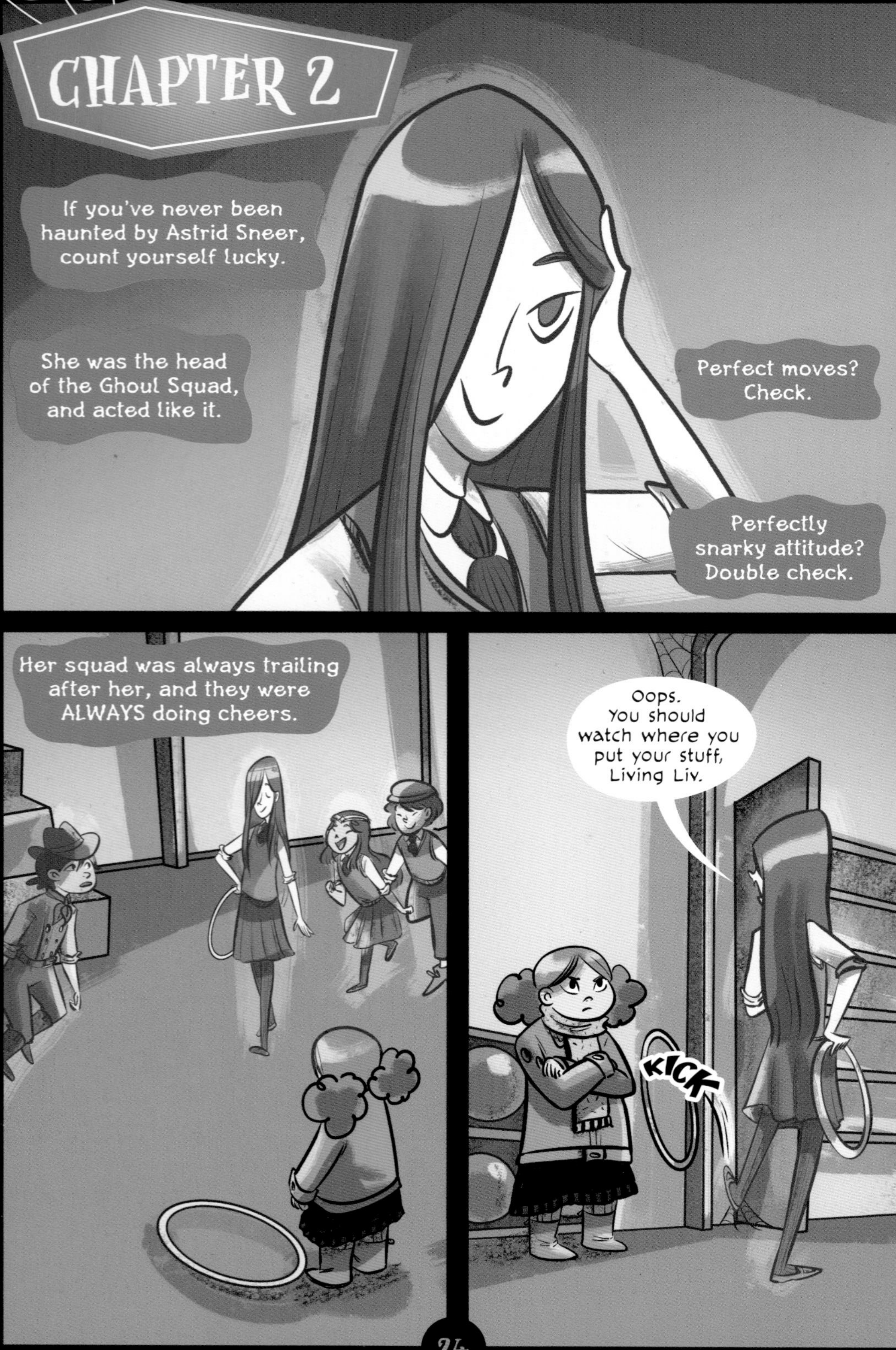
CHAPTER 2
If you've never been haunted by Astrid Sneer, count yourself lucky.
She was the head of the Ghoul Squad, and acted like it.
Perfect moves? Check.
Perfectly snarky attitude? Double check.
Her squad was always trailing after her, and they were ALWAYS doing cheers.
Oops. You should watch where you put your stuff, Living Liv.
KICK

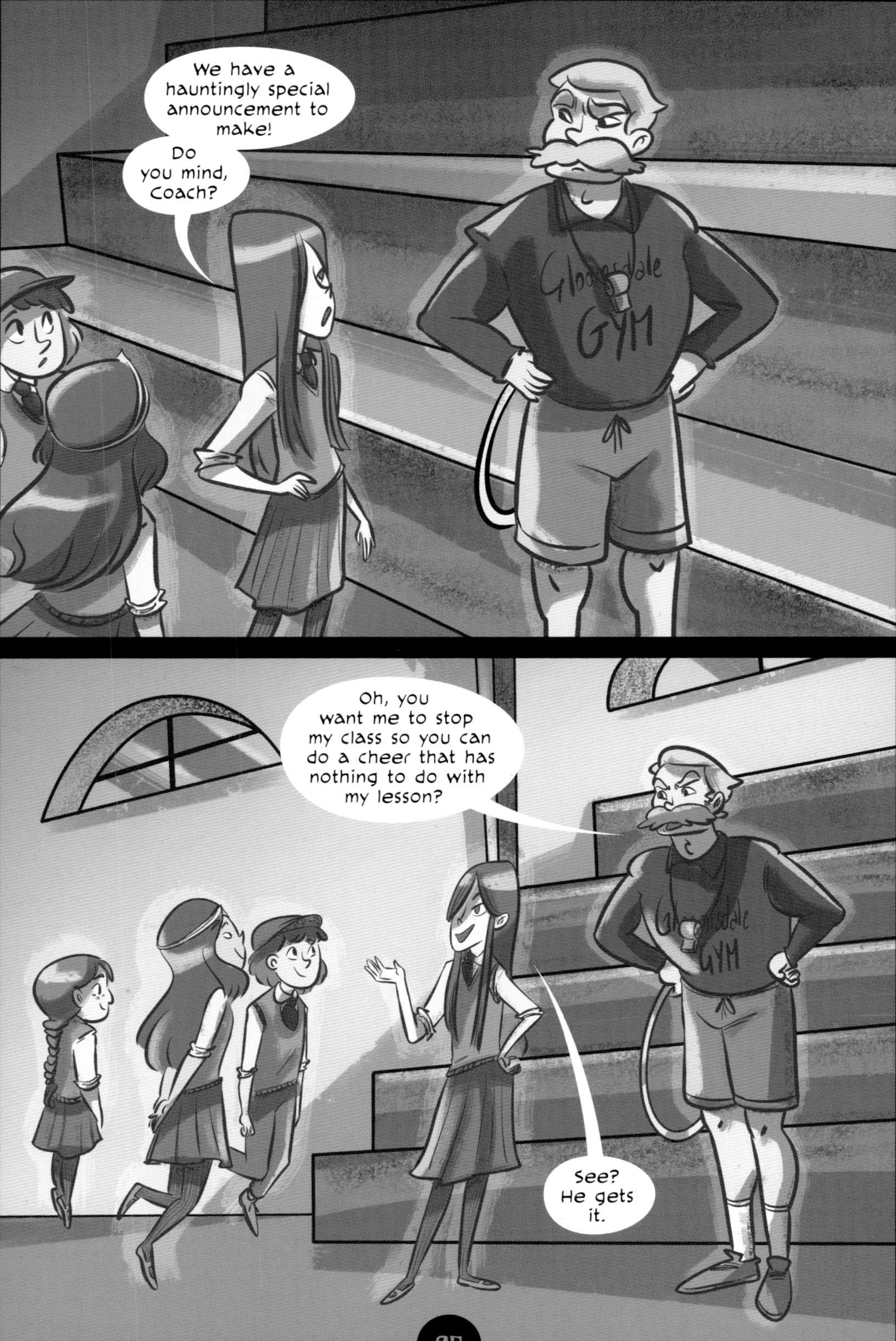
We have a hauntingly special announcement to make!
Do you mind, Coach?
Oh, you want me to stop my class so you can do a cheer that has nothing to do with my lesson?
See? He gets it.

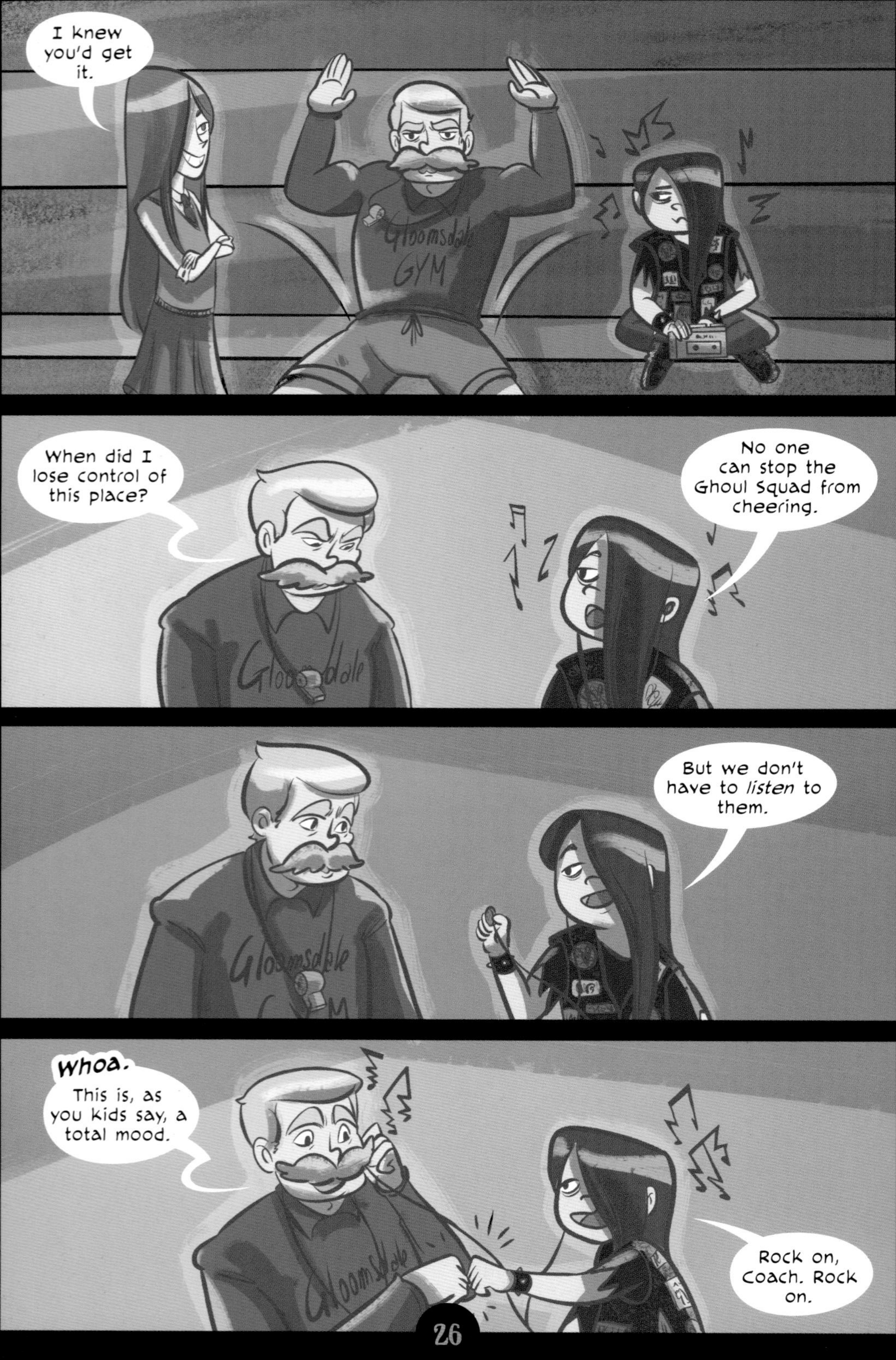
I knew you'd get it.
Gloomsdale GYM
When did I lose control of this place?
No one can stop the Ghoul Squad from cheering.
But we don't have to *listen* to them.
Whoa.
This is, as you kids say, a total mood.
Rock on, Coach. Rock on.

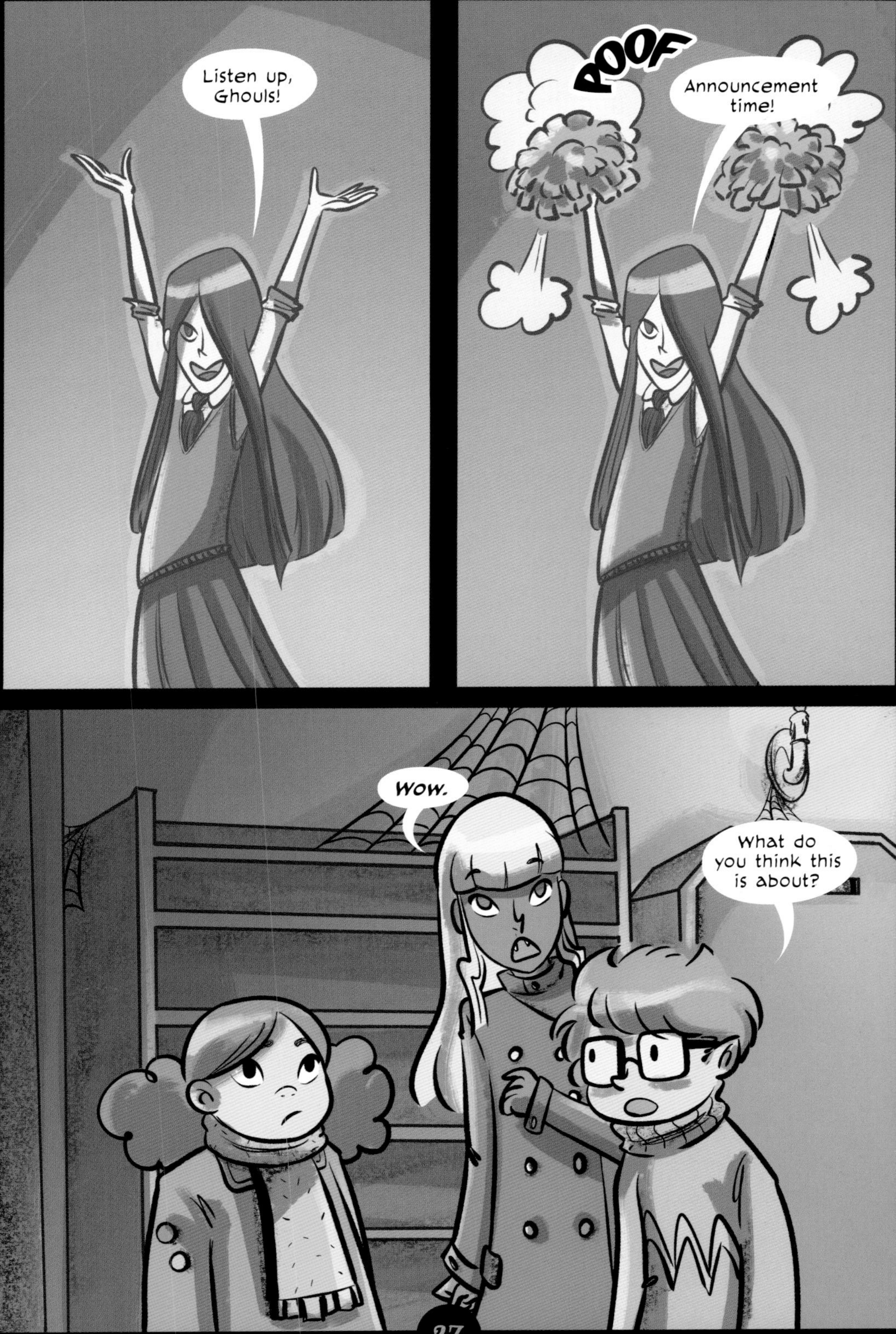
Listen up, Ghouls!
POOF
Announcement time!
Wow.
What do you think this is about?

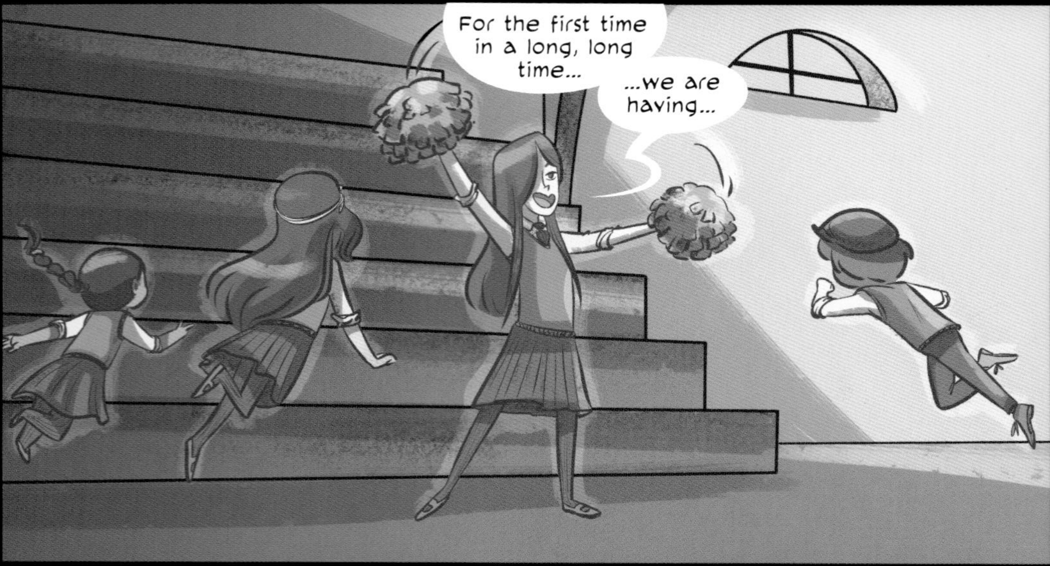
For the first time in a long, long time...
...we are having...

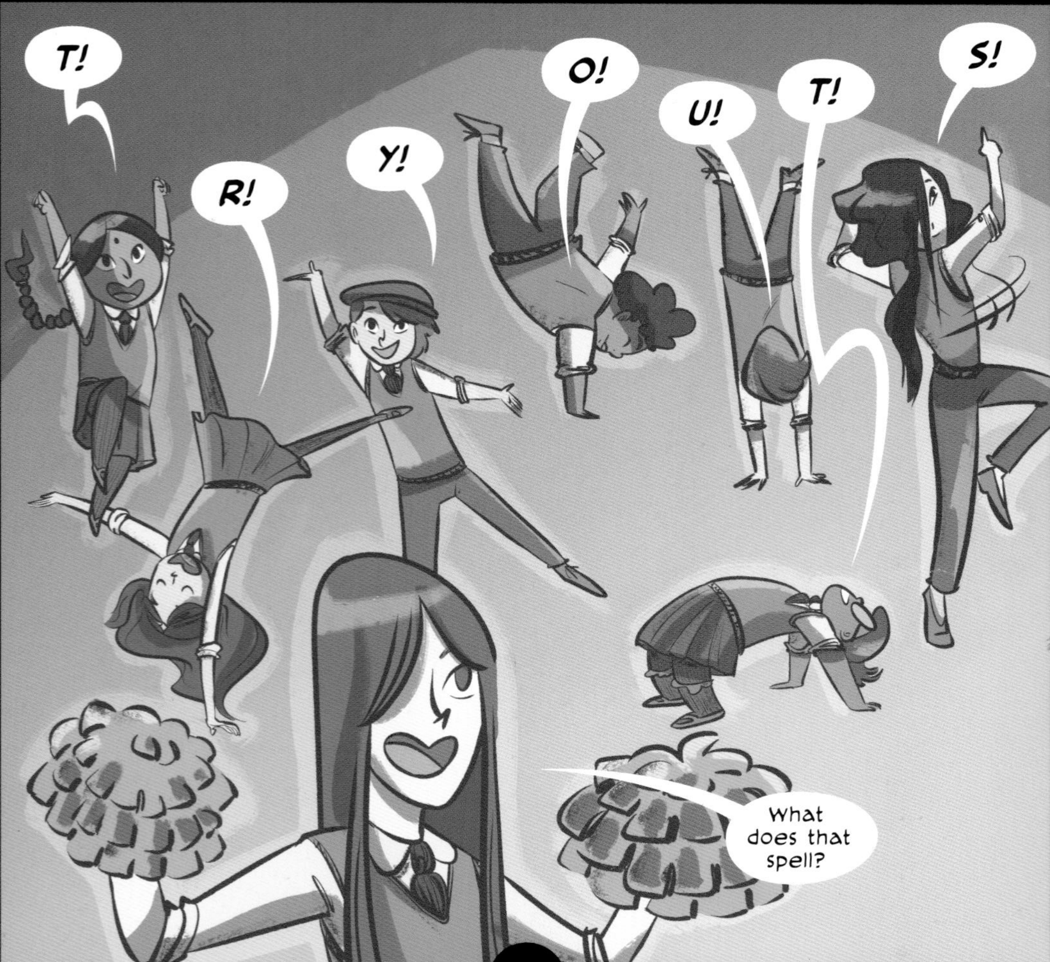
T!
R!
Y!
O!
U!
T!
S!
What does that spell?

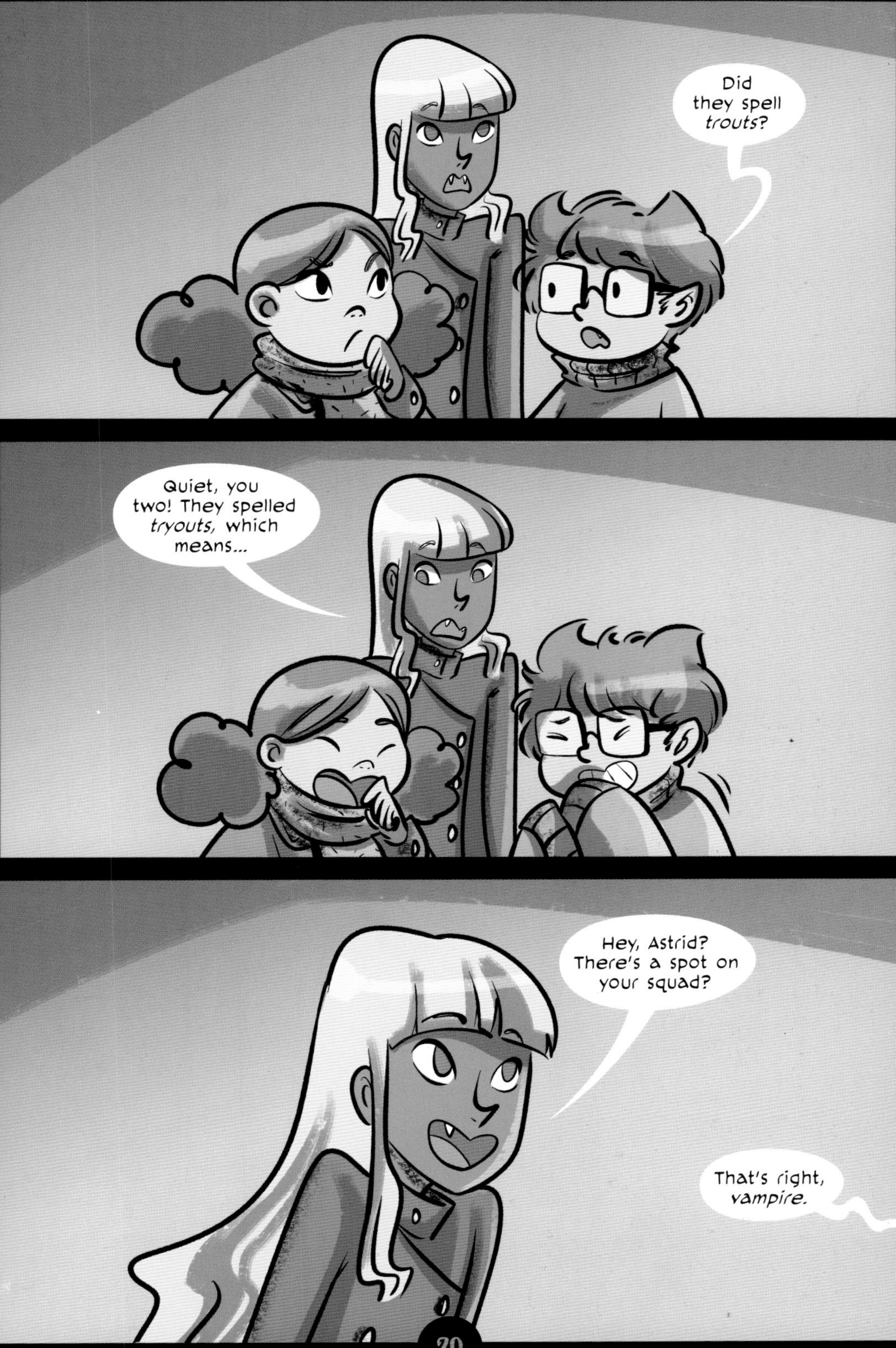
Did they spell *trouts*?
Quiet, you two! They spelled *tryouts,* which means...
Hey, Astrid? There's a spot on your squad?
That's right, *vampire.*

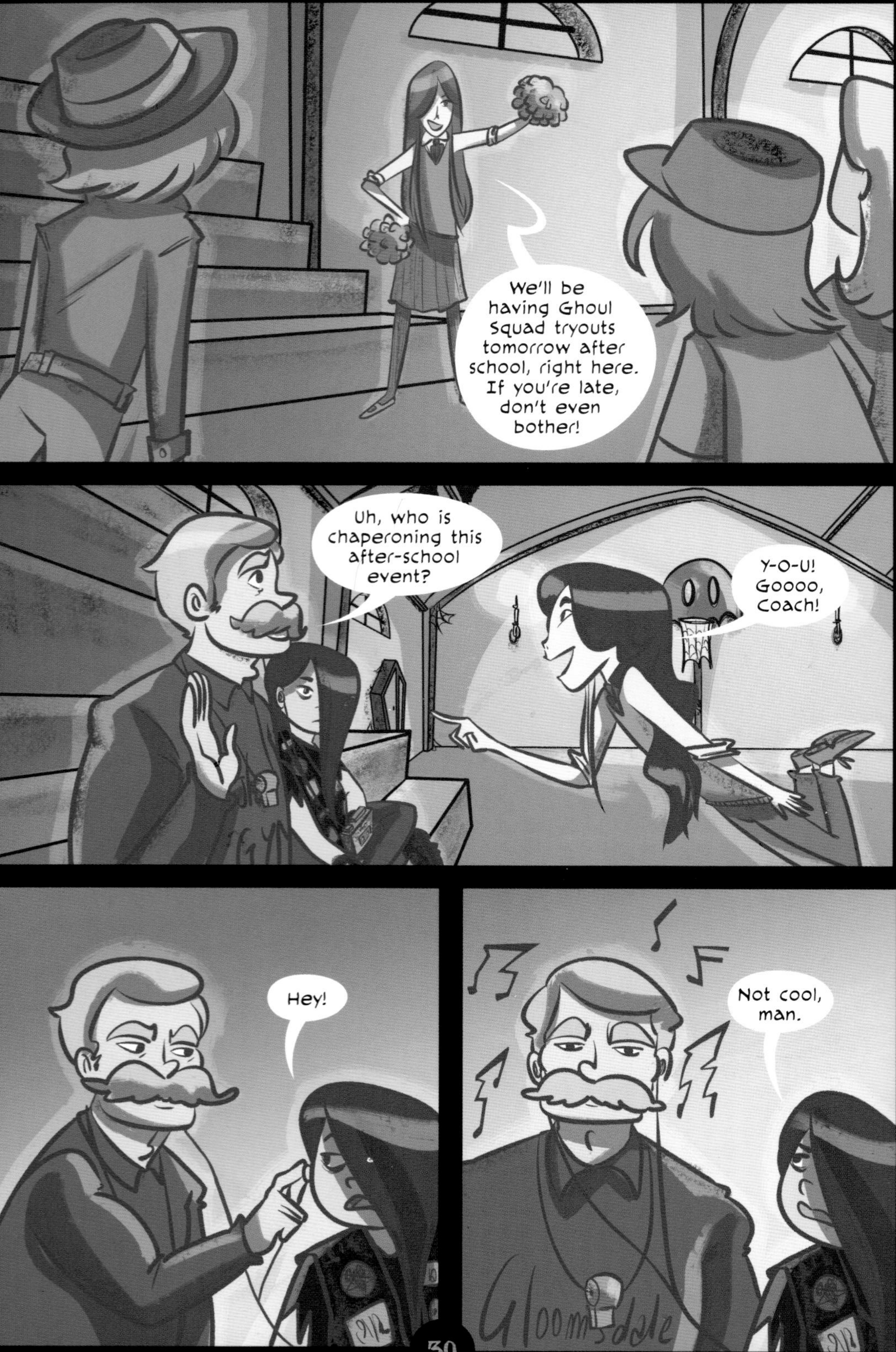
We'll be having Ghoul Squad tryouts tomorrow after school, right here. If you're late, don't even bother!
Uh, who is chaperoning this after-school event?
Y-O-U! Goooo, Coach!
Hey!
Not cool, man.
Gloomsdale

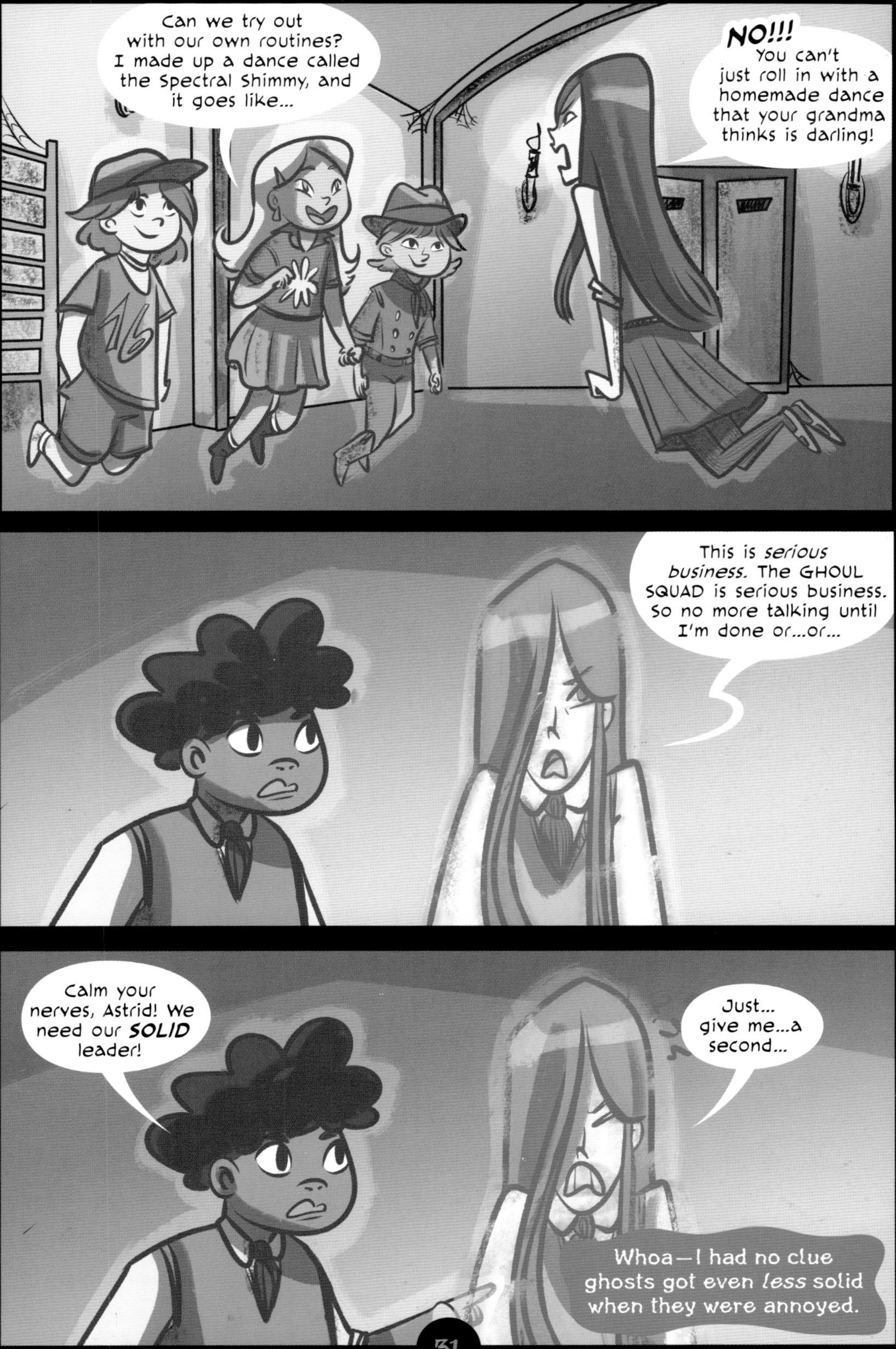
Can we try out with our own routines? I made up a dance called the Spectral Shimmy, and it goes like...
NO!!! You can't just roll in with a homemade dance that your grandma thinks is darling!
This is *serious business.* The GHOUL SQUAD is serious business. So no more talking until I'm done or...or...
Calm your nerves, Astrid! We need our ***SOLID*** leader!
Just... give me...a second...
Whoa—I had no clue ghosts got even *less* solid when they were annoyed.

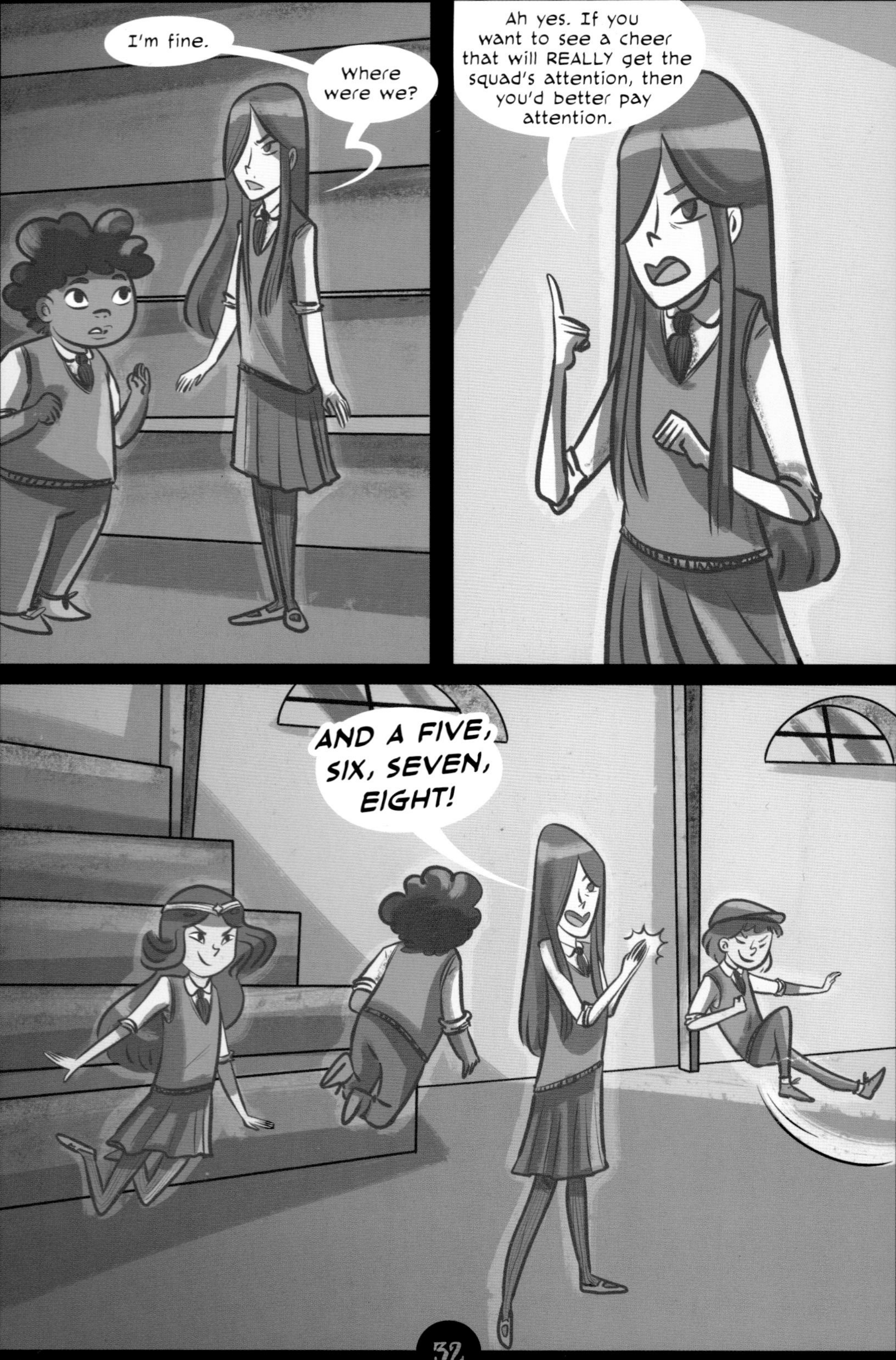
I'm fine.
Where were we?
Ah yes. If you want to see a cheer that will REALLY get the squad's attention, then you'd better pay attention.
AND A FIVE, SIX, SEVEN, EIGHT!

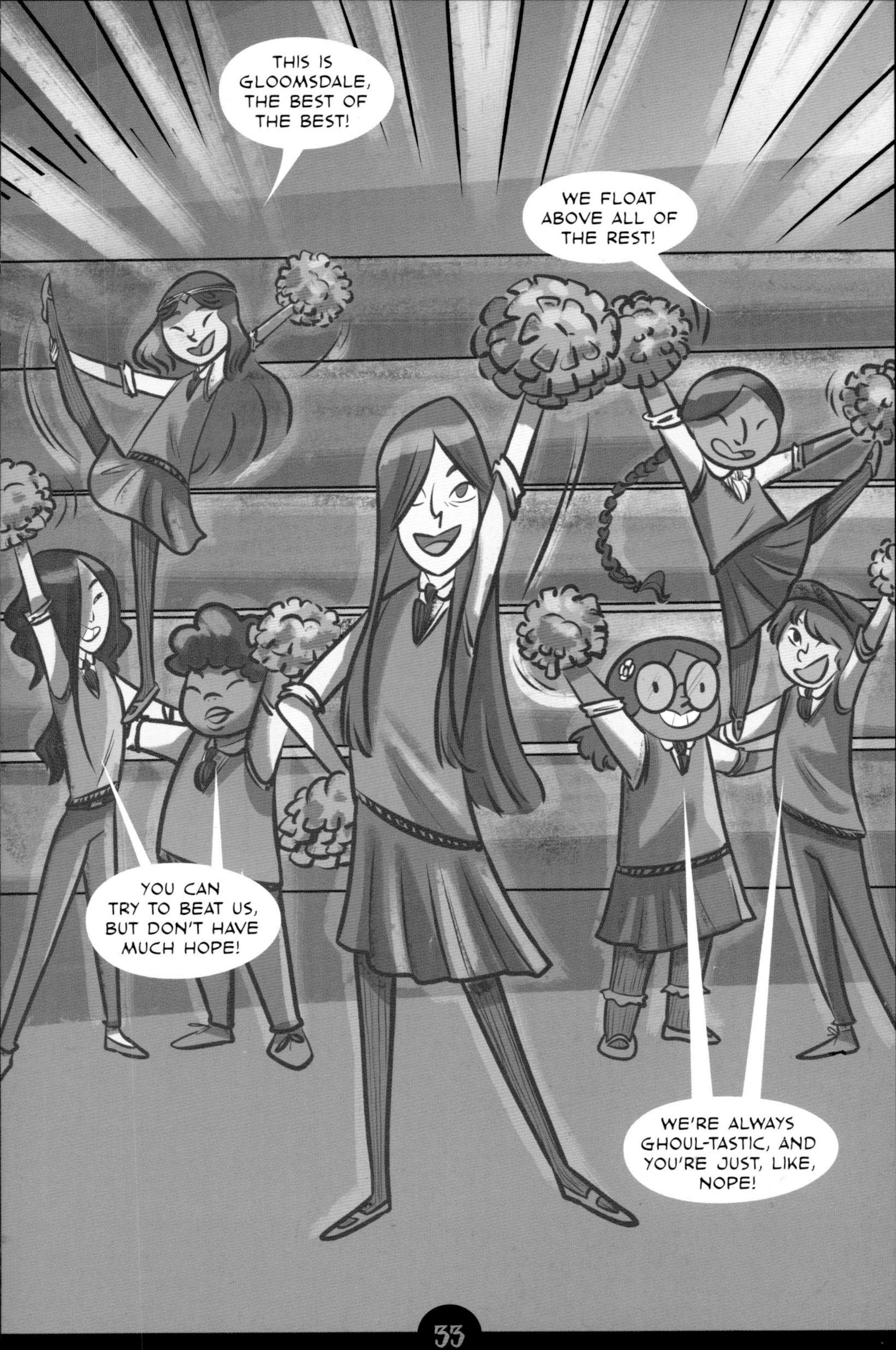
THIS IS GLOOMSDALE, THE BEST OF THE BEST!
WE FLOAT ABOVE ALL OF THE REST!
YOU CAN TRY TO BEAT US, BUT DON'T HAVE MUCH HOPE!
WE'RE ALWAYS GHOUL-TASTIC, AND YOU'RE JUST, LIKE, NOPE!

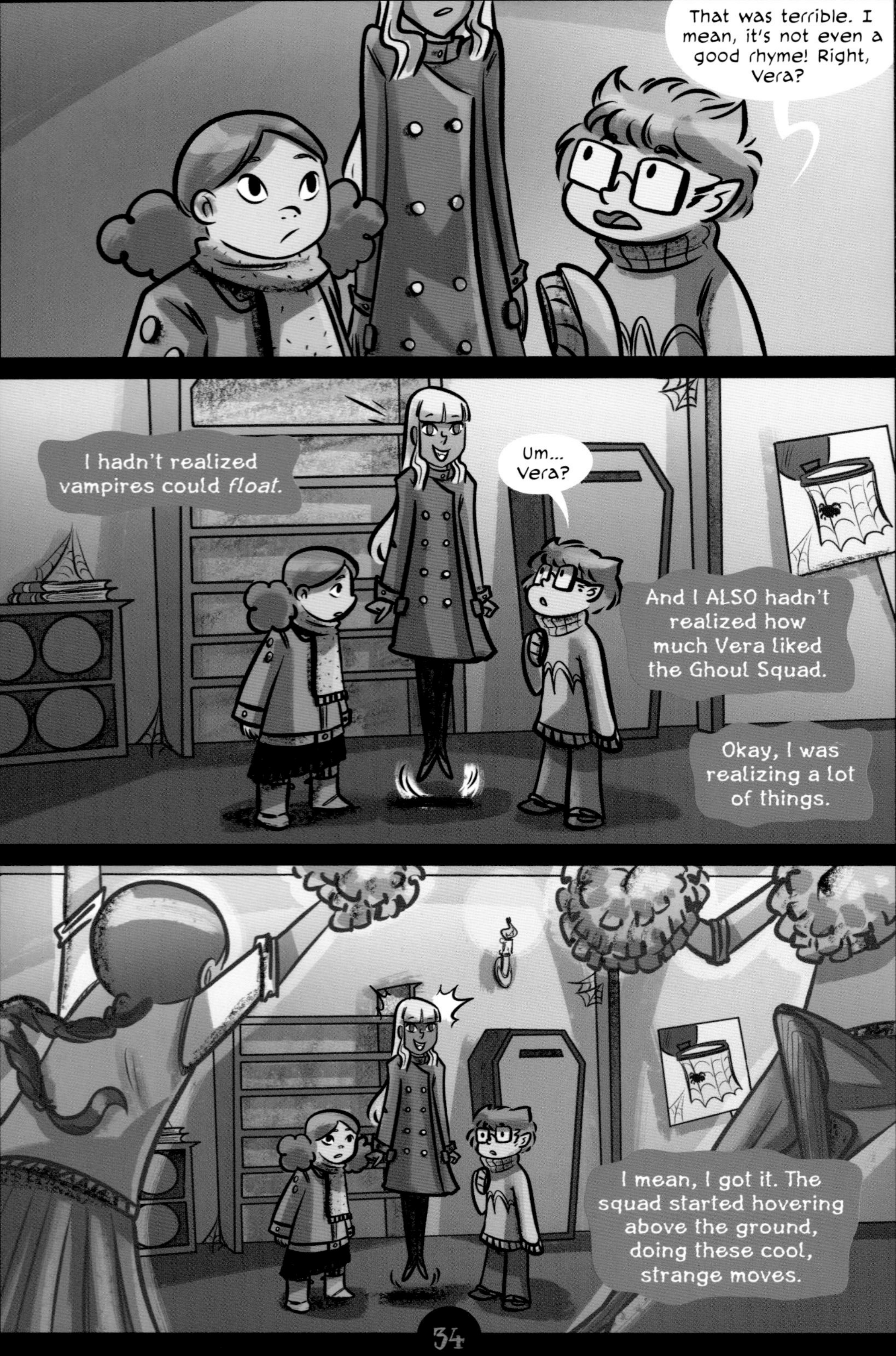
That was terrible. I mean, it's not even a good rhyme! Right, Vera?
I hadn't realized vampires could *float.*
Um... Vera?
And I ALSO hadn't realized how much Vera liked the Ghoul Squad.
Okay, I was realizing a lot of things.
I mean, I got it. The squad started hovering above the ground, doing these cool, strange moves.

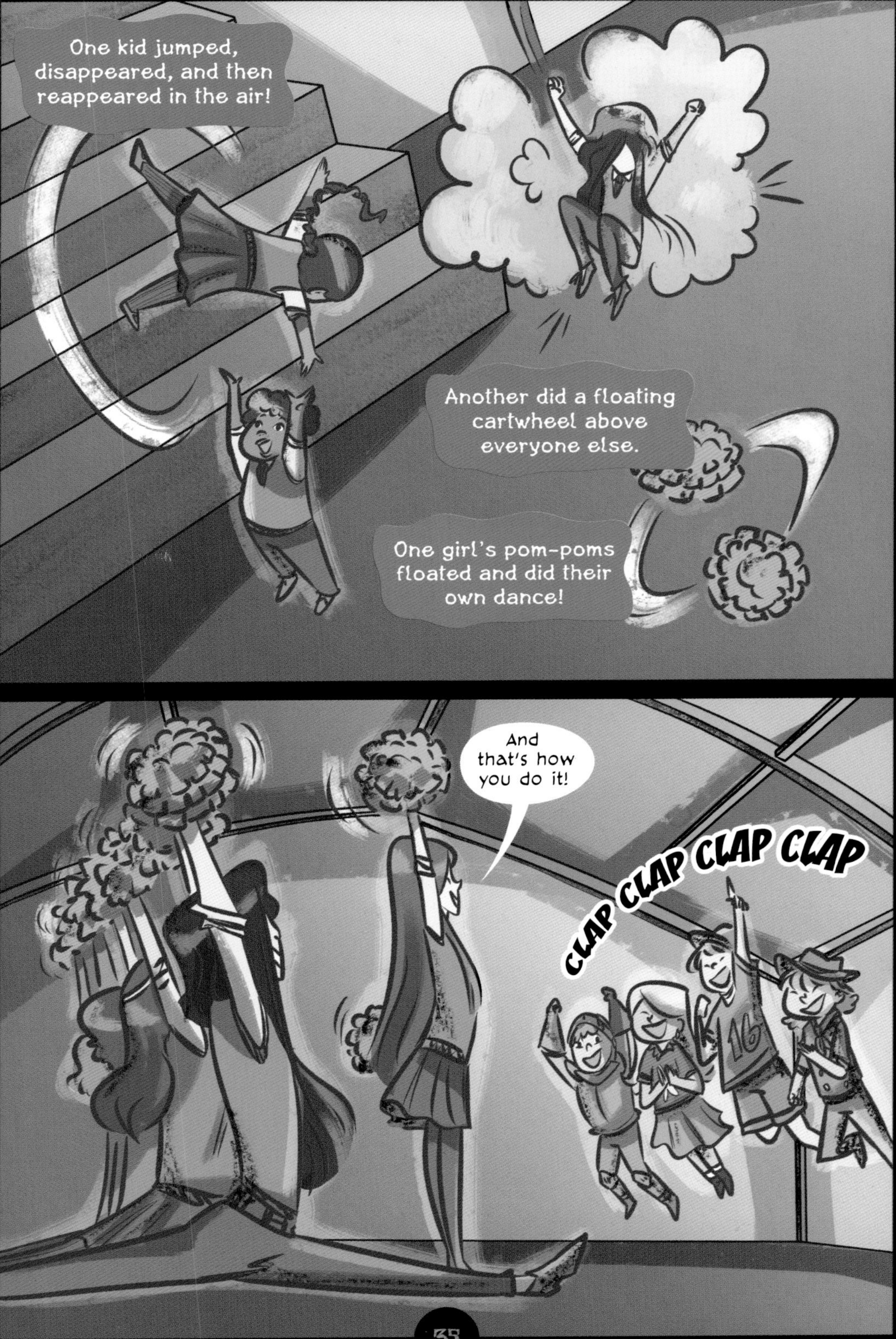
One kid jumped, disappeared, and then reappeared in the air!
Another did a floating cartwheel above everyone else.
One girl's pom-poms floated and did their own dance!
And that's how you do it!
CLAP CLAP CLAP CLAP
16

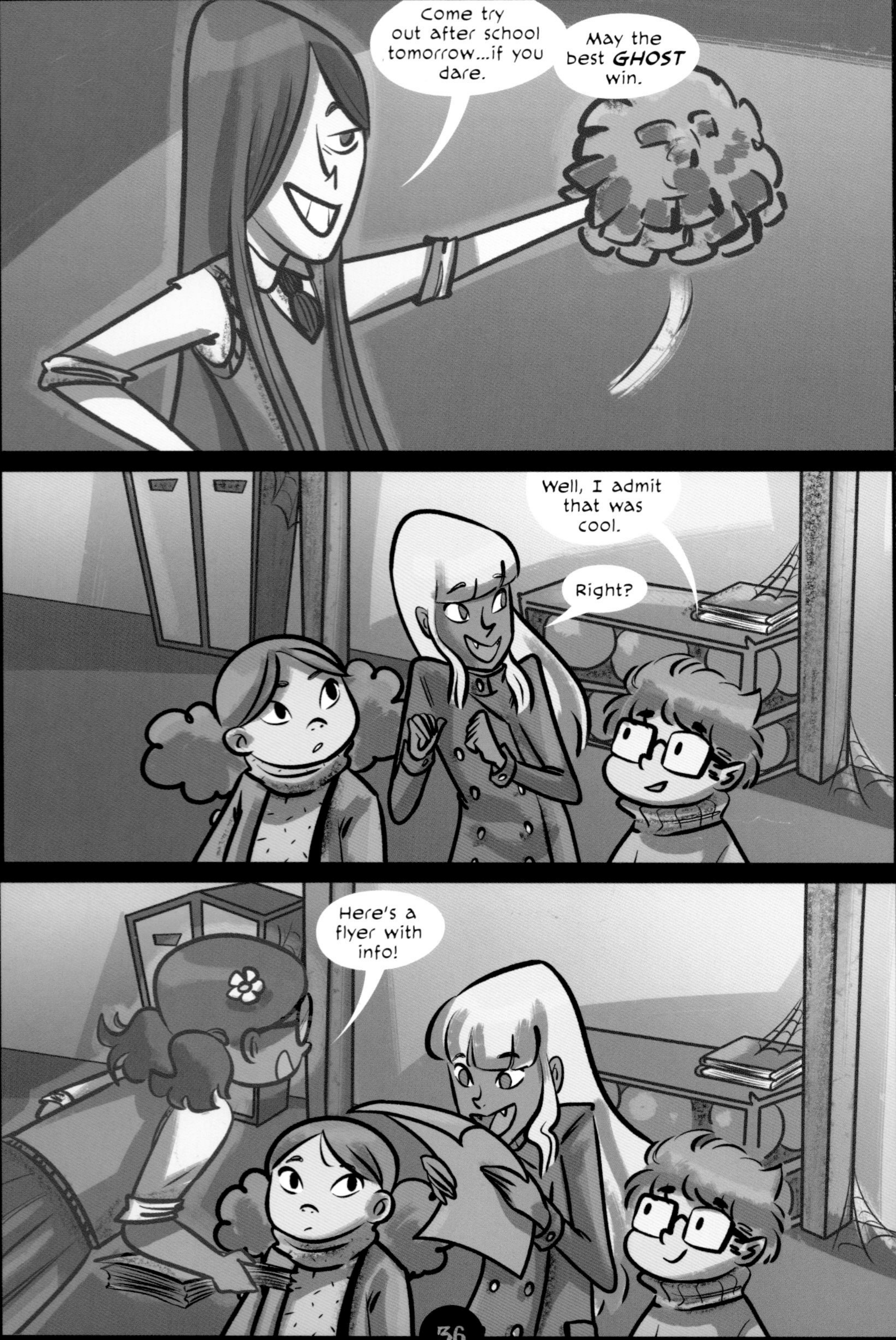
Come try out after school tomorrow...if you dare.
May the best **GHOST** win.
Well, I admit that was cool.
Right?
Here's a flyer with info!

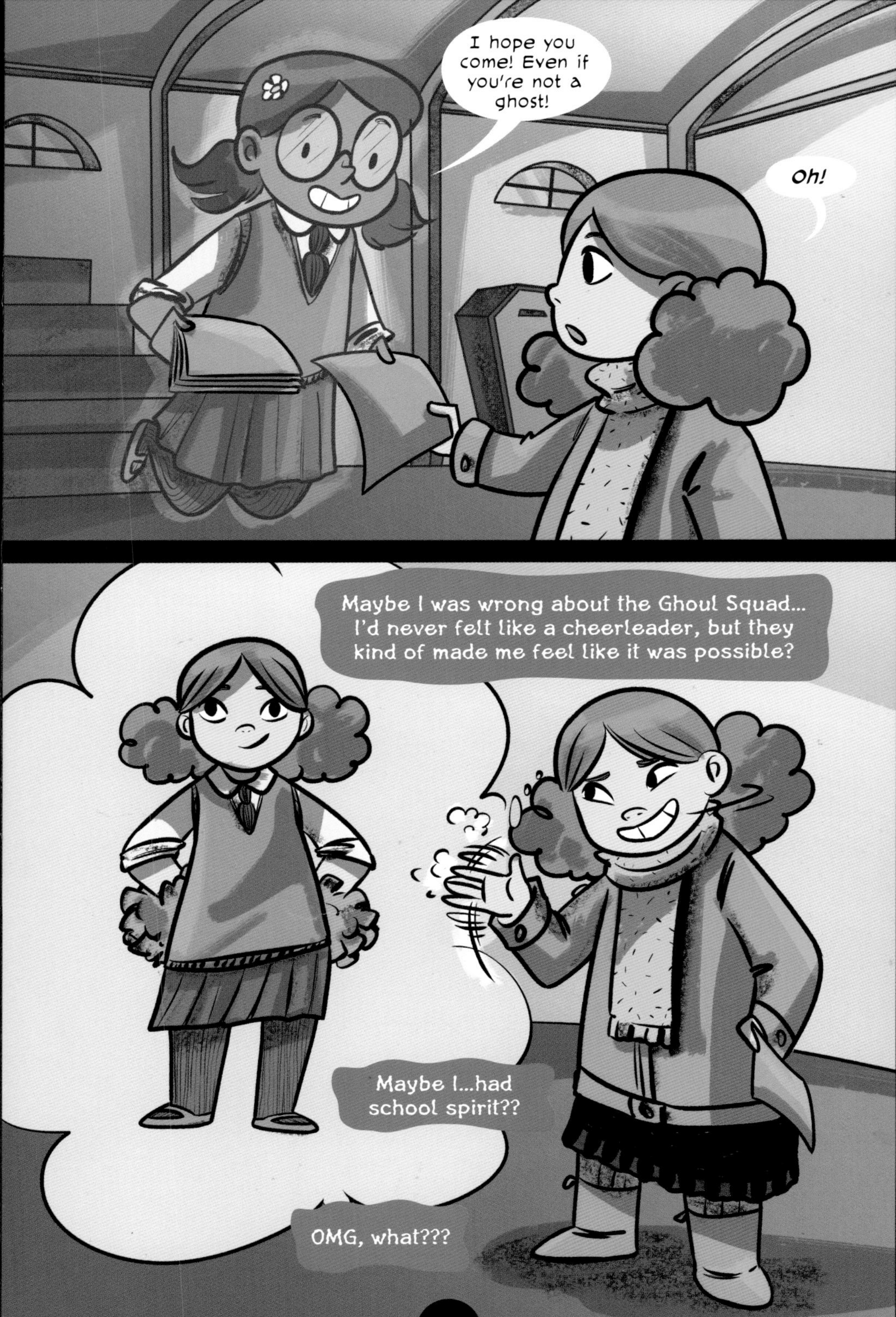
I hope you come! Even if you're not a ghost!
Oh!
Maybe I was wrong about the Ghoul Squad... I'd never felt like a cheerleader, but they kind of made me feel like it was possible?
Maybe I...had school spirit??
OMG, what???

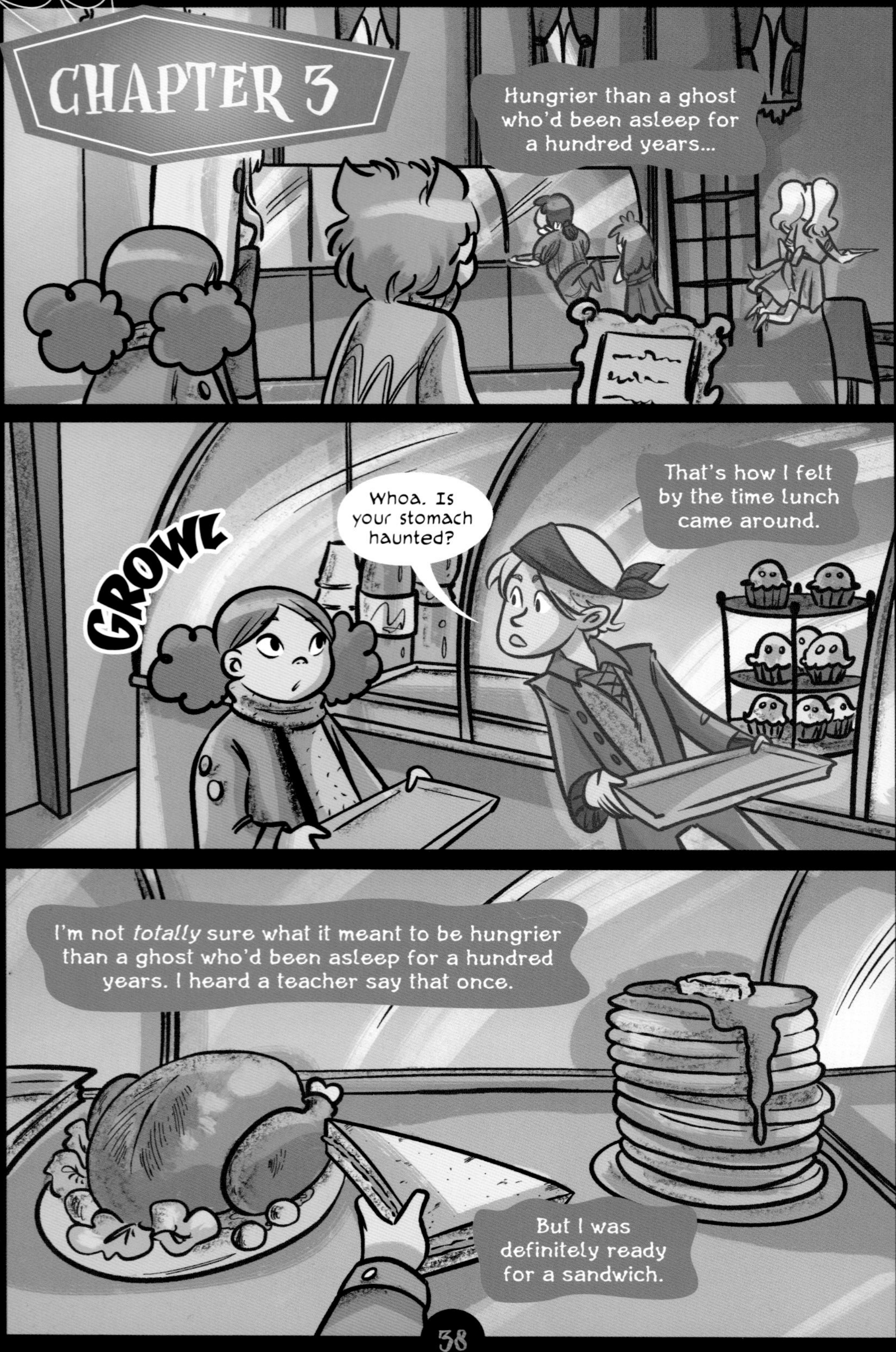
CHAPTER 3
Hungrier than a ghost who'd been asleep for a hundred years...
That's how I felt by the time lunch came around.
GROWL
Whoa. Is your stomach haunted?
I'm not *totally* sure what it meant to be hungrier than a ghost who'd been asleep for a hundred years. I heard a teacher say that once.
But I was definitely ready for a sandwich.

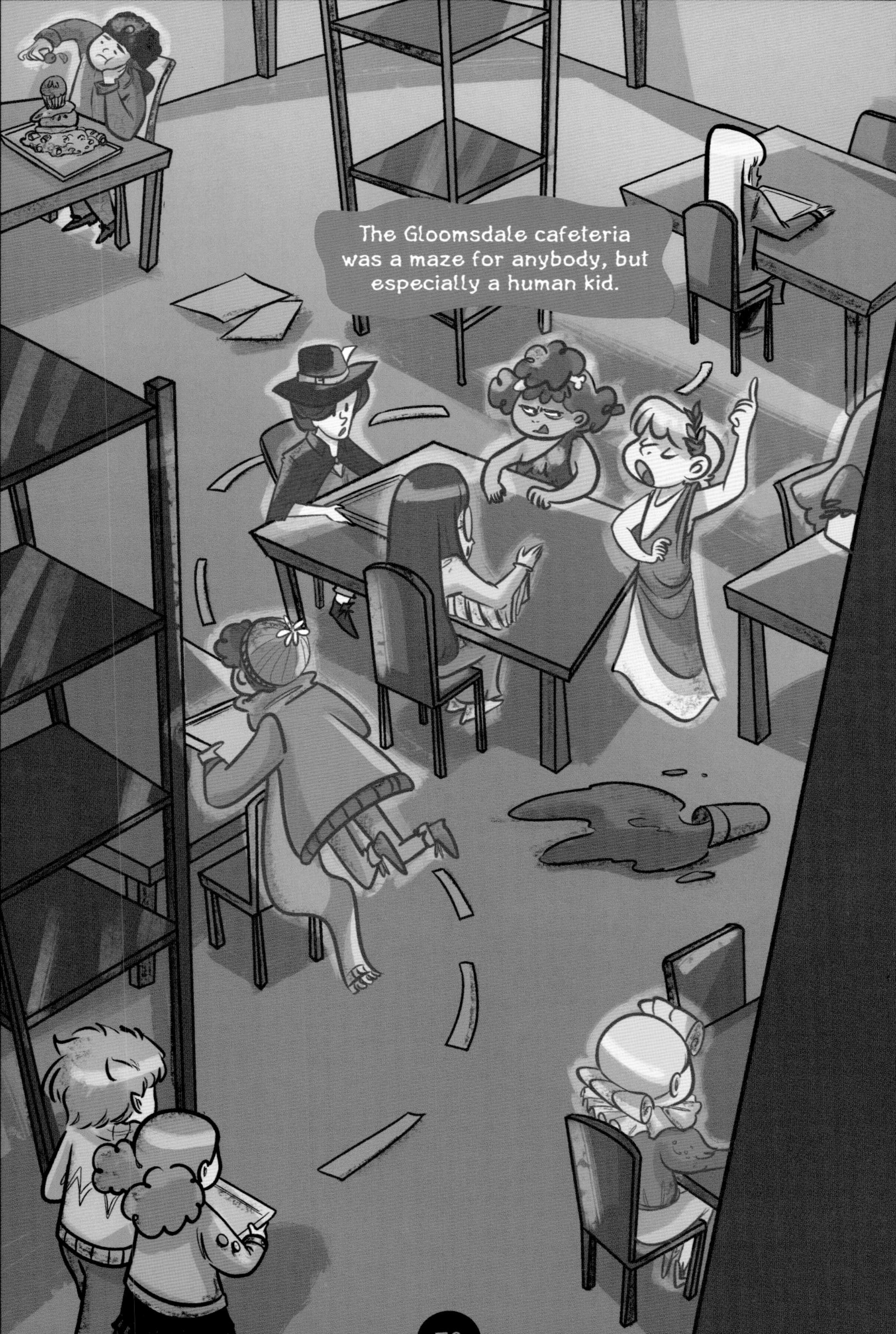
The Gloomsdale cafeteria was a maze for anybody, but especially a human kid.

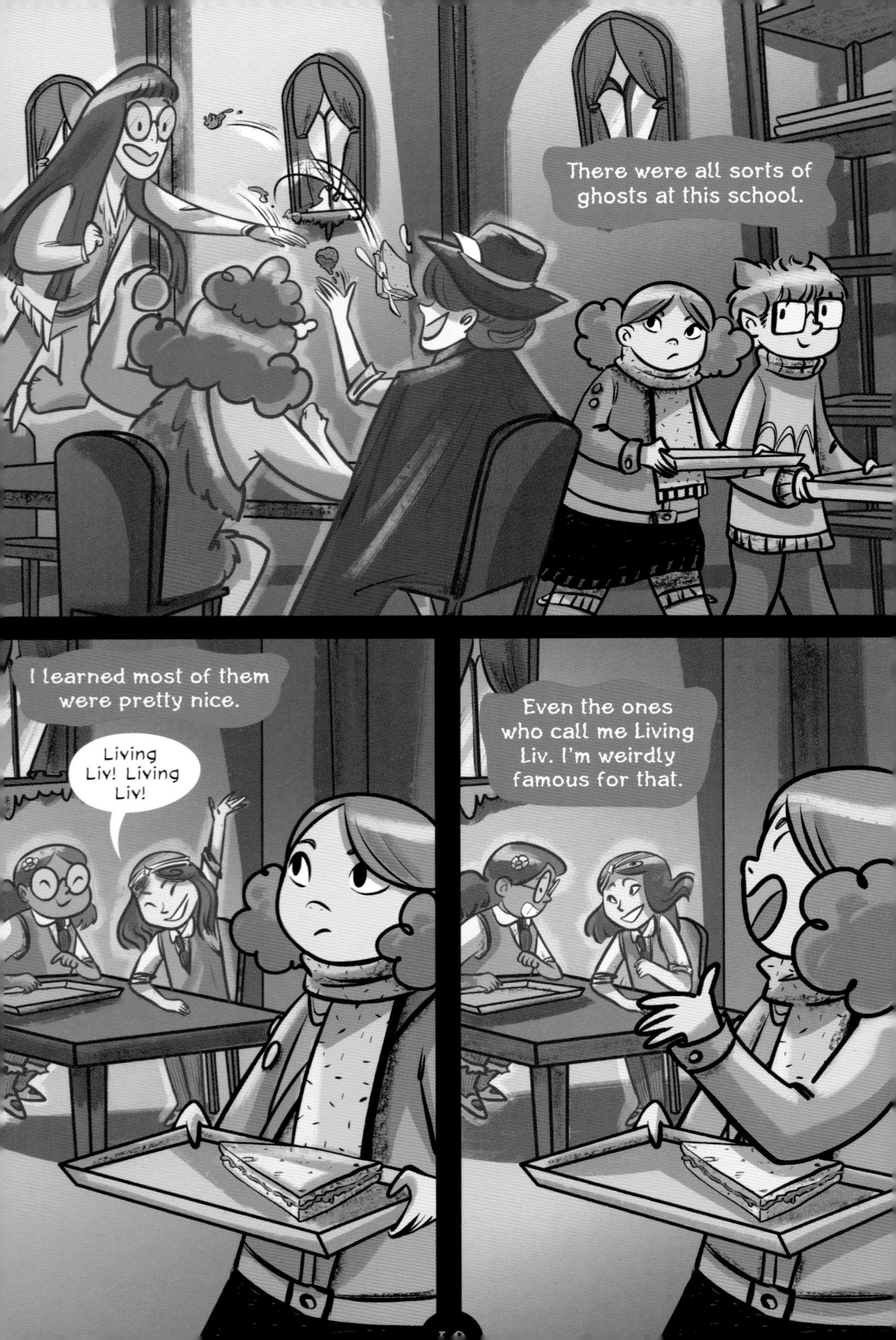

There were all sorts of ghosts at this school.
I learned most of them were pretty nice.
Living Liv! Living Liv!
Even the ones who call me Living Liv. I'm weirdly famous for that.

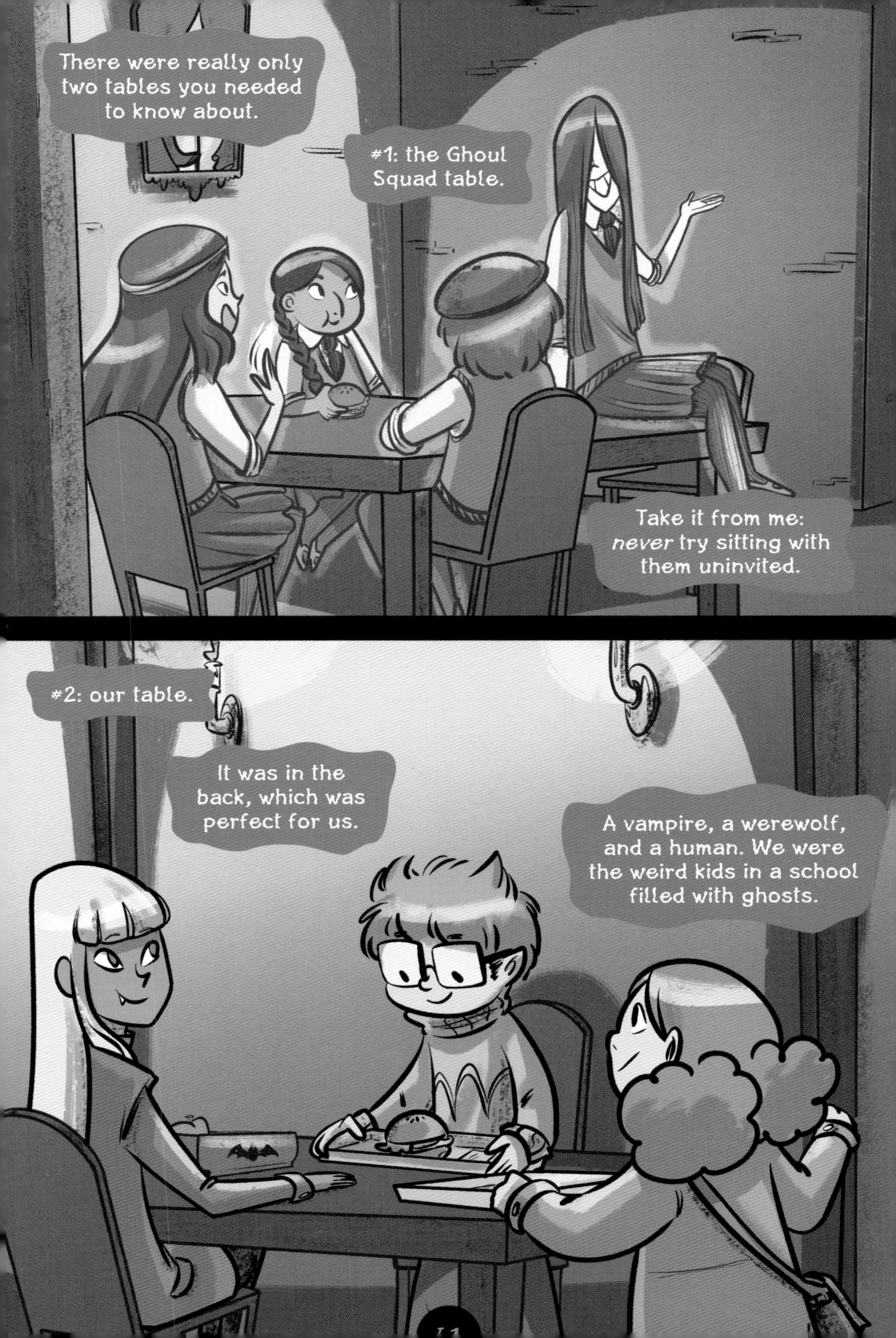
There were really only two tables you needed to know about.
#1: the Ghoul Squad table.
Take it from me: *never* try sitting with them uninvited.
#2: our table.
It was in the back, which was perfect for us.
A vampire, a werewolf, and a human. We were the weird kids in a school filled with ghosts.

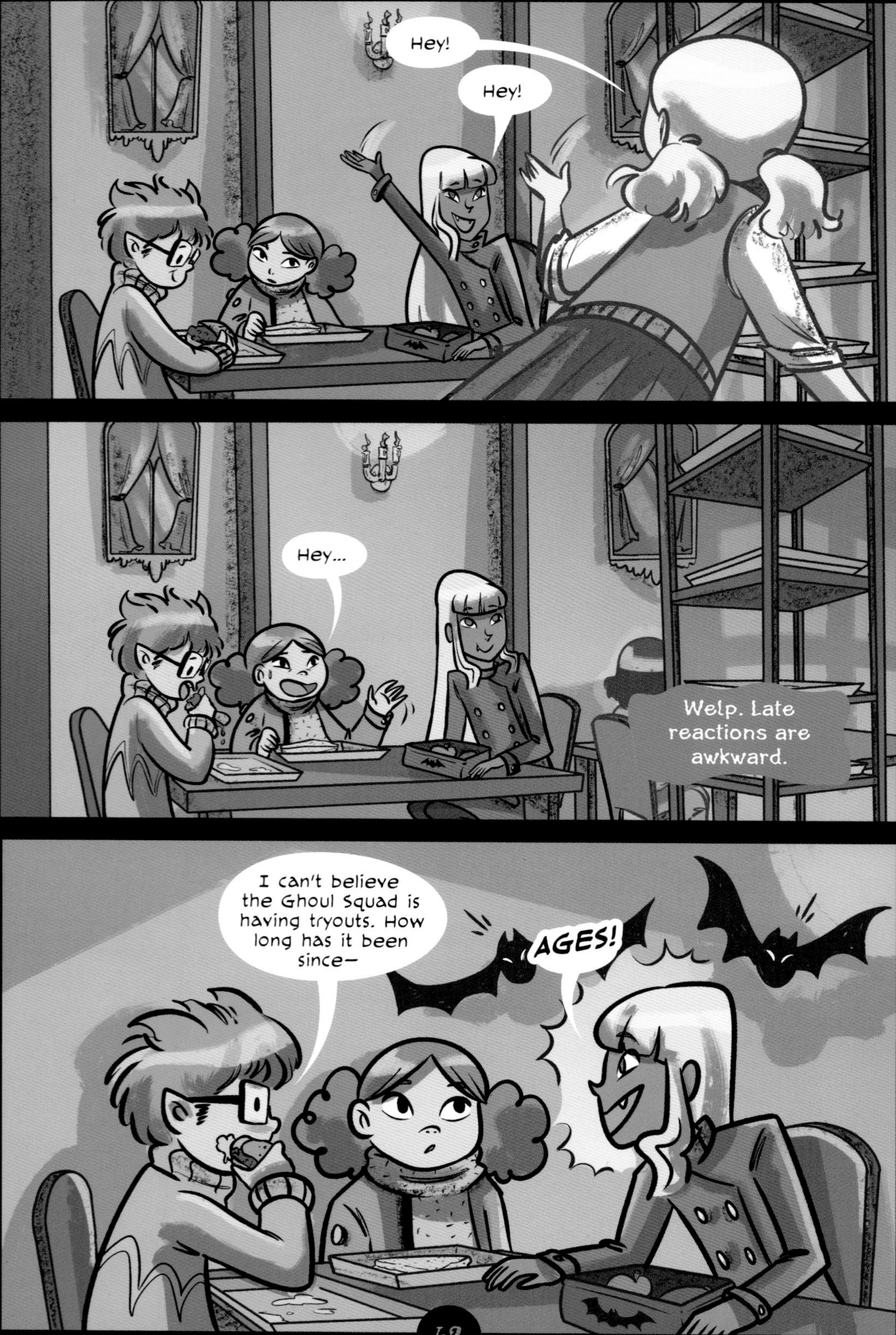

Hey!
Hey!
Hey...
Welp. Late reactions are awkward.
I can't believe the Ghoul Squad is having tryouts. How long has it been since—
AGES!

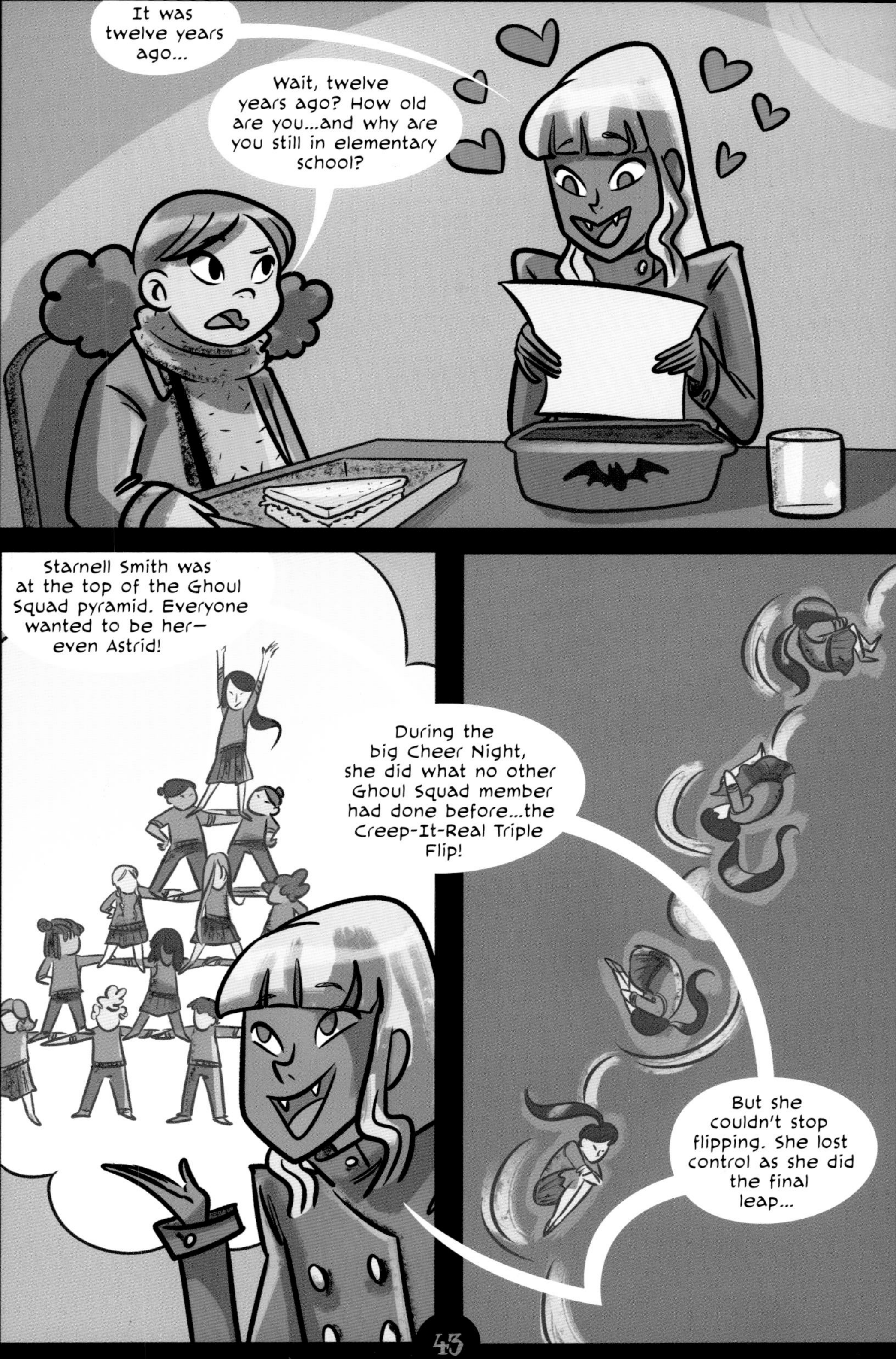

It was twelve years ago...
Wait, twelve years ago? How old are you...and why are you still in elementary school?
Starnell Smith was at the top of the Ghoul Squad pyramid. Everyone wanted to be her—even Astrid!
During the big Cheer Night, she did what no other Ghoul Squad member had done before...the Creep-It-Real Triple Flip!
But she couldn't stop flipping. She lost control as she did the final leap...

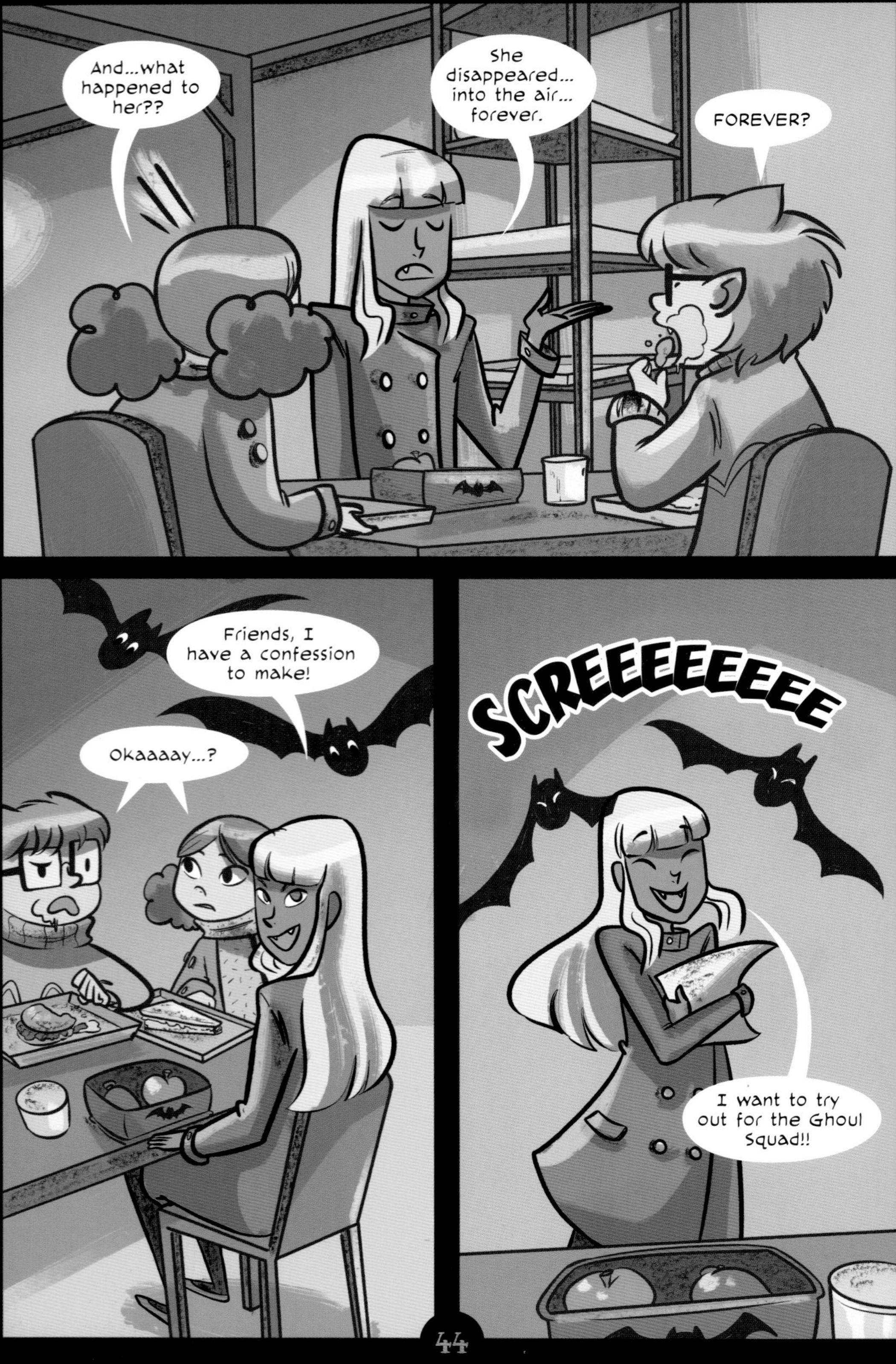
And...what happened to her??
She disappeared... into the air... forever.
FOREVER?
Friends, I have a confession to make!
Okaaaay...?
SCREEEEEEEEE
I want to try out for the Ghoul Squad!!

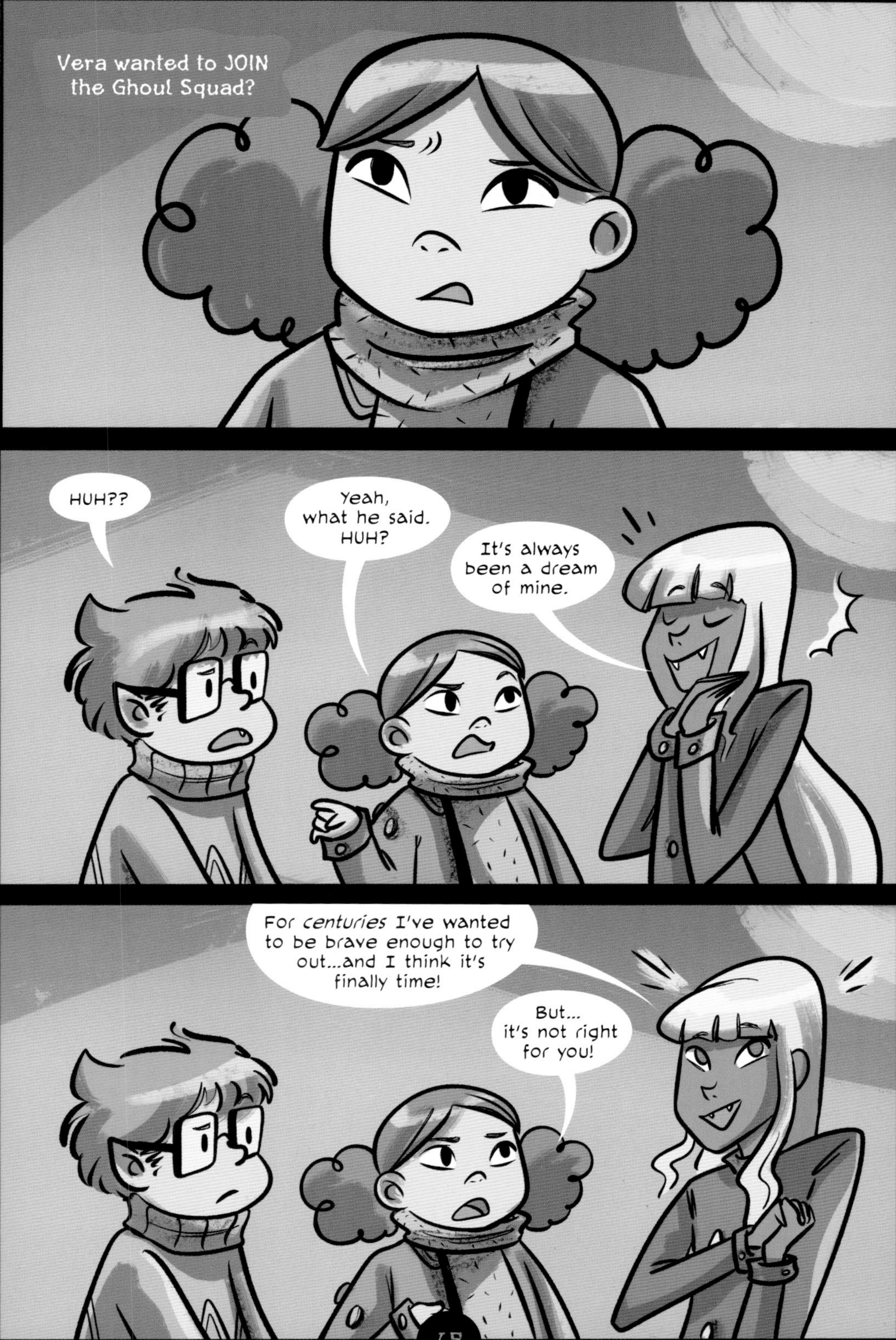
Vera wanted to JOIN the Ghoul Squad?
HUH??
Yeah, what he said. HUH?
It's always been a dream of mine.
For *centuries* I've wanted to be brave enough to try out...and I think it's finally time!
But... it's not right for you!

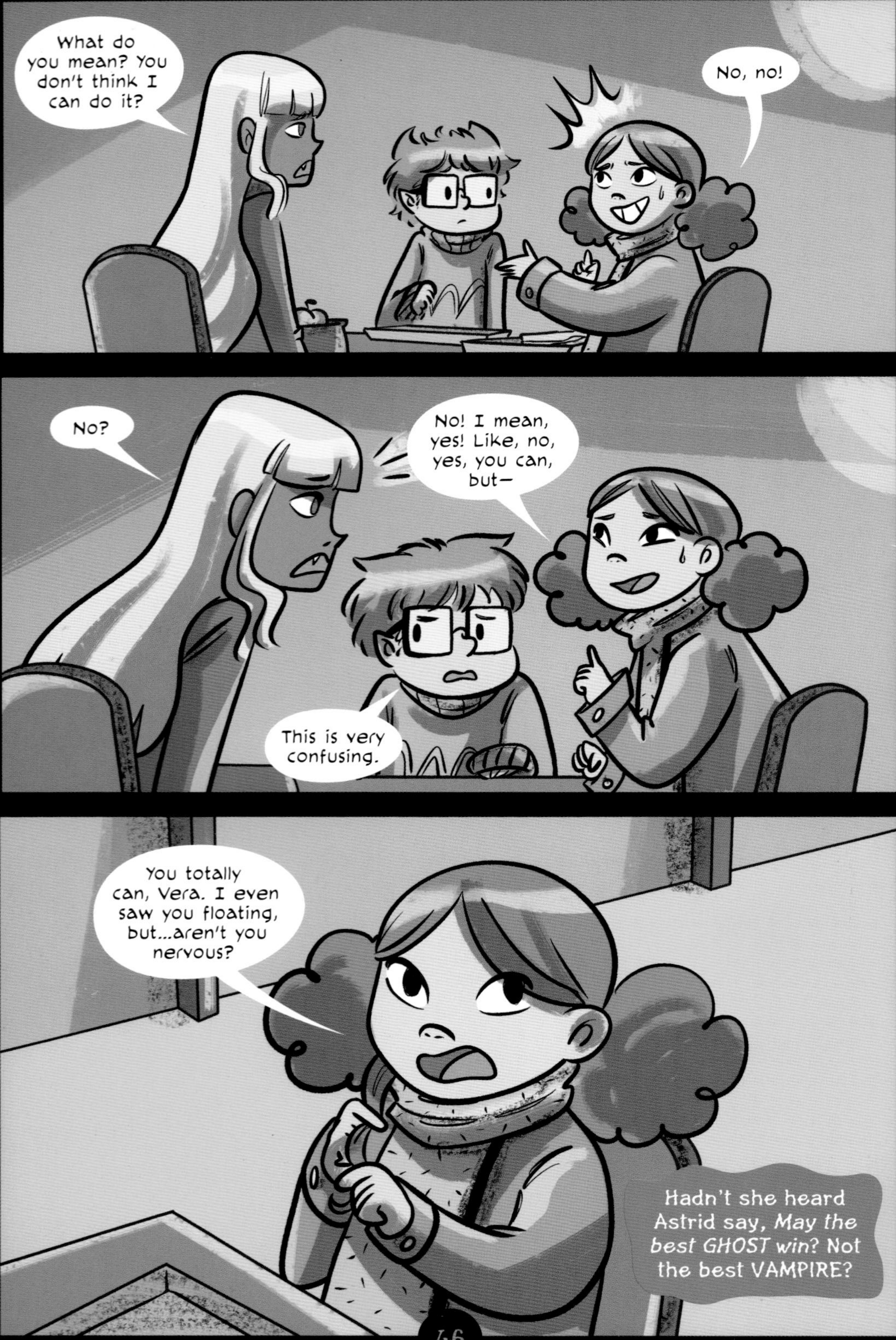
What do you mean? You don't think I can do it?
No, no!
No?
No! I mean, yes! Like, no, yes, you can, but—
This is very confusing.
You totally can, Vera. I even saw you floating, but...aren't you nervous?
Hadn't she heard Astrid say, *May the best GHOST win*? Not the best VAMPIRE?

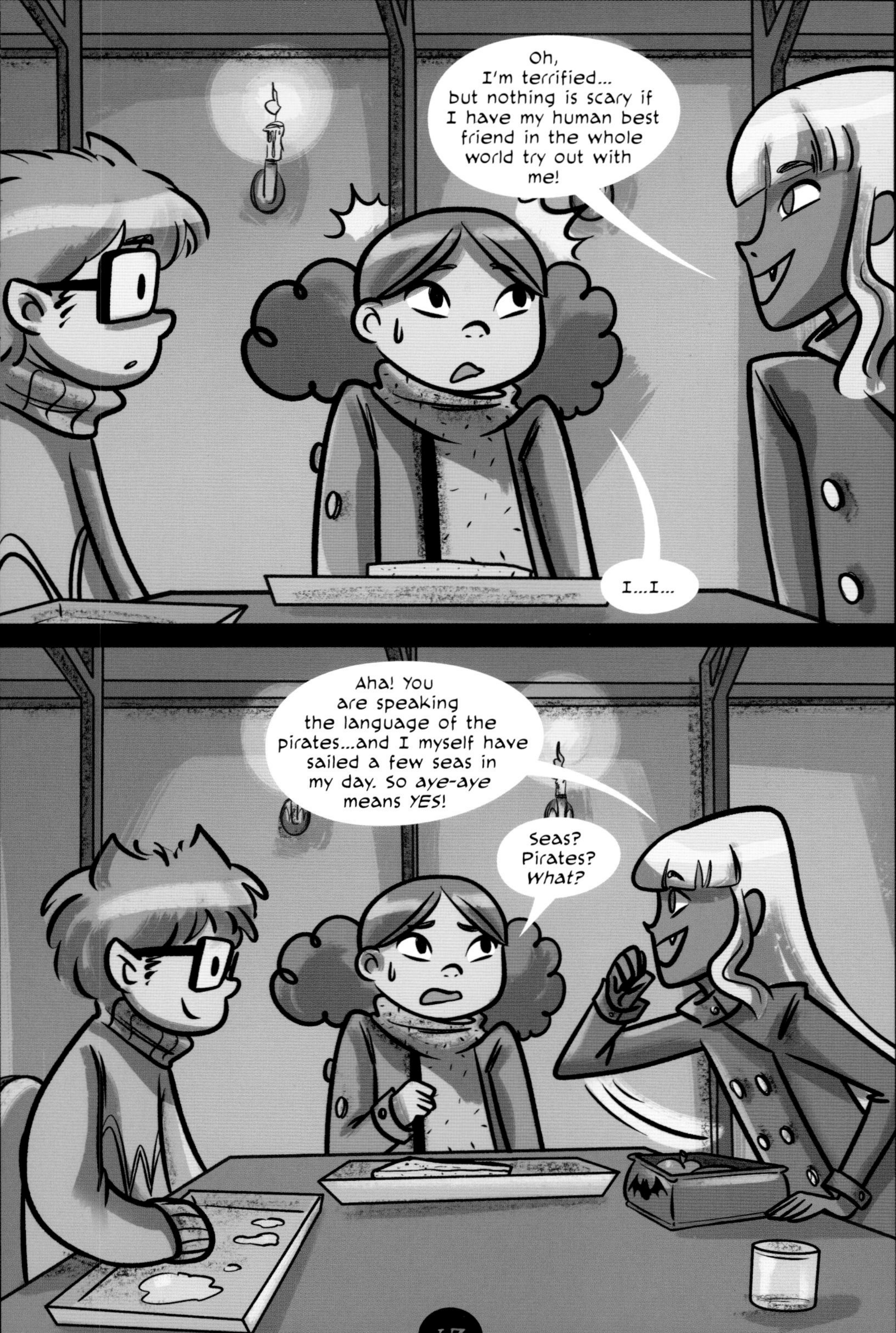
Oh, I'm terrified... but nothing is scary if I have my human best friend in the whole world try out with me!
I...I...
Aha! You are speaking the language of the pirates...and I myself have sailed a few seas in my day. So *aye-aye* means *YES*!
Seas? Pirates? *What?*

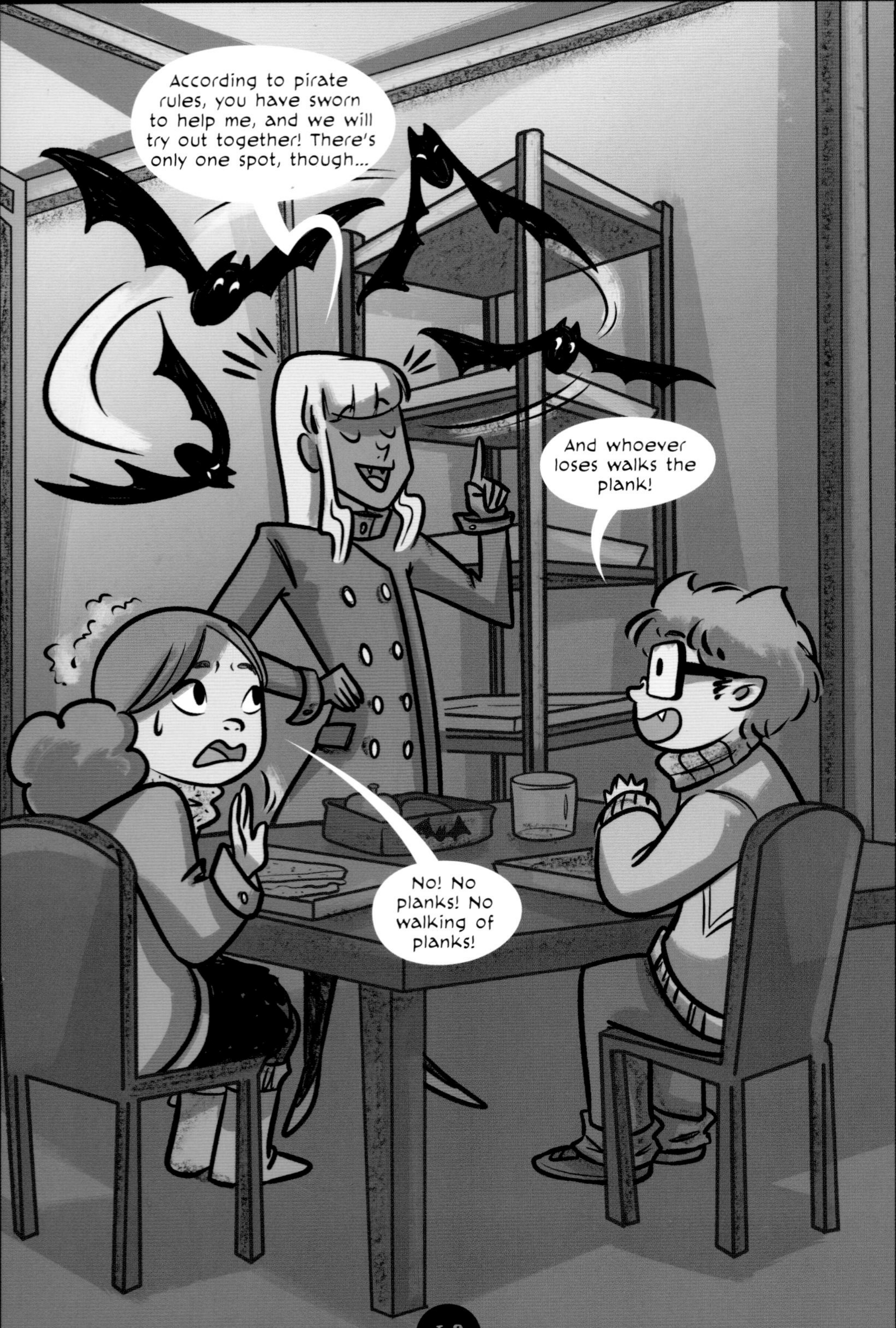
According to pirate rules, you have sworn to help me, and we will try out together! There's only one spot, though...
And whoever loses walks the plank!
No! No planks! No walking of planks!

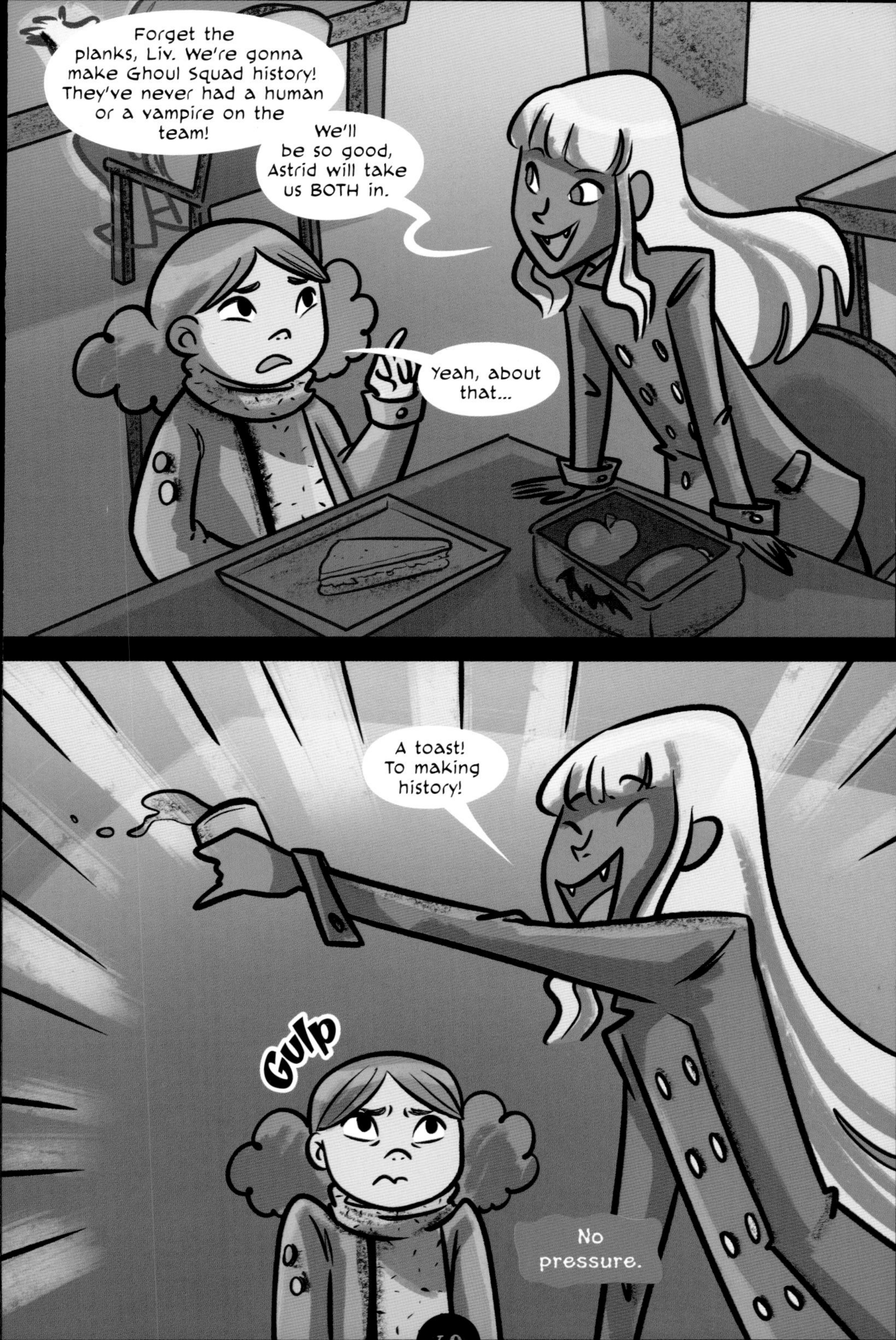

Forget the planks, Liv. We're gonna make Ghoul Squad history! They've never had a human or a vampire on the team!
We'll be so good, Astrid will take us BOTH in.
Yeah, about that...
A toast! To making history!
Gulp
No pressure.

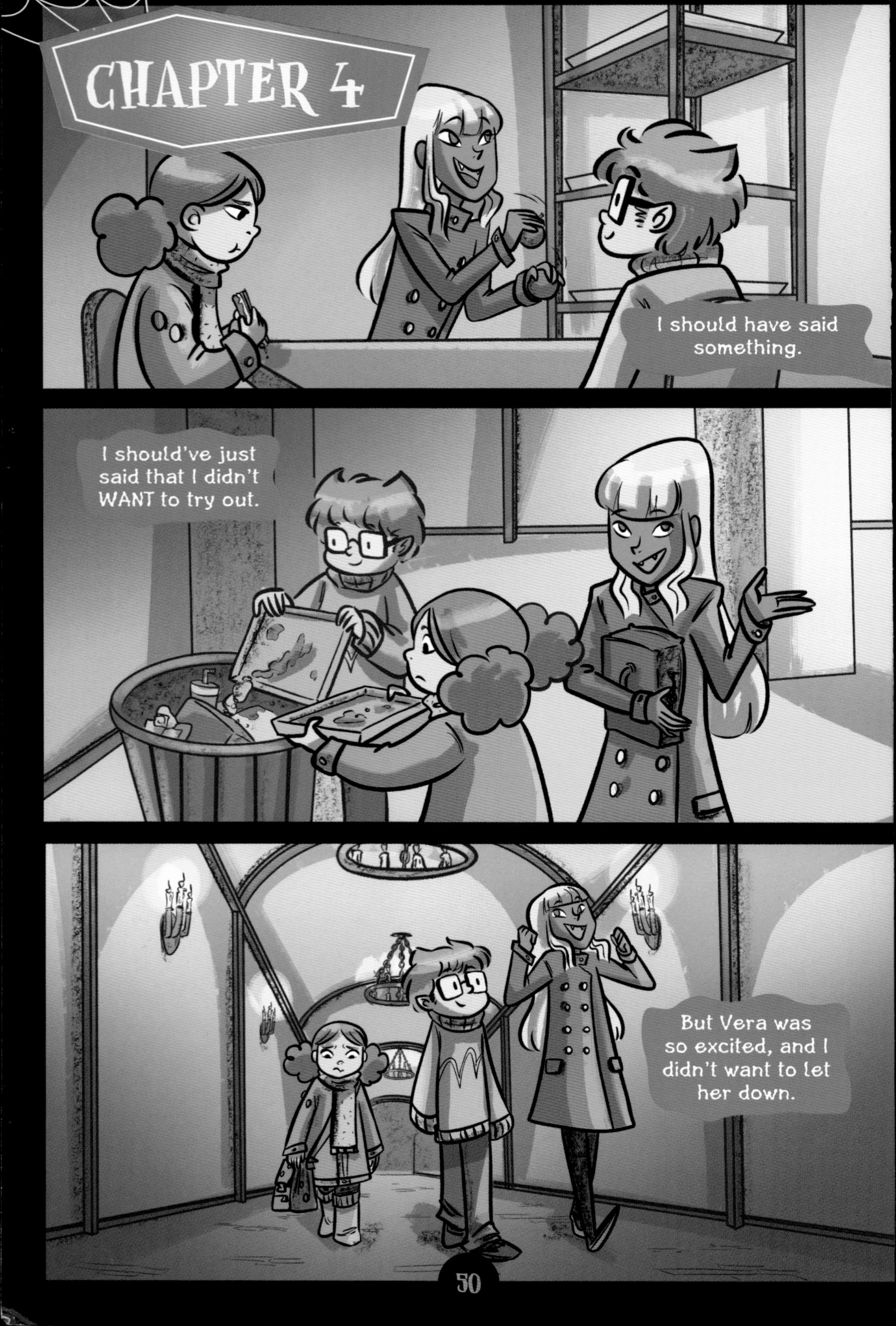
CHAPTER 4
I should have said something.
I should've just said that I didn't WANT to try out.
But Vera was so excited, and I didn't want to let her down.

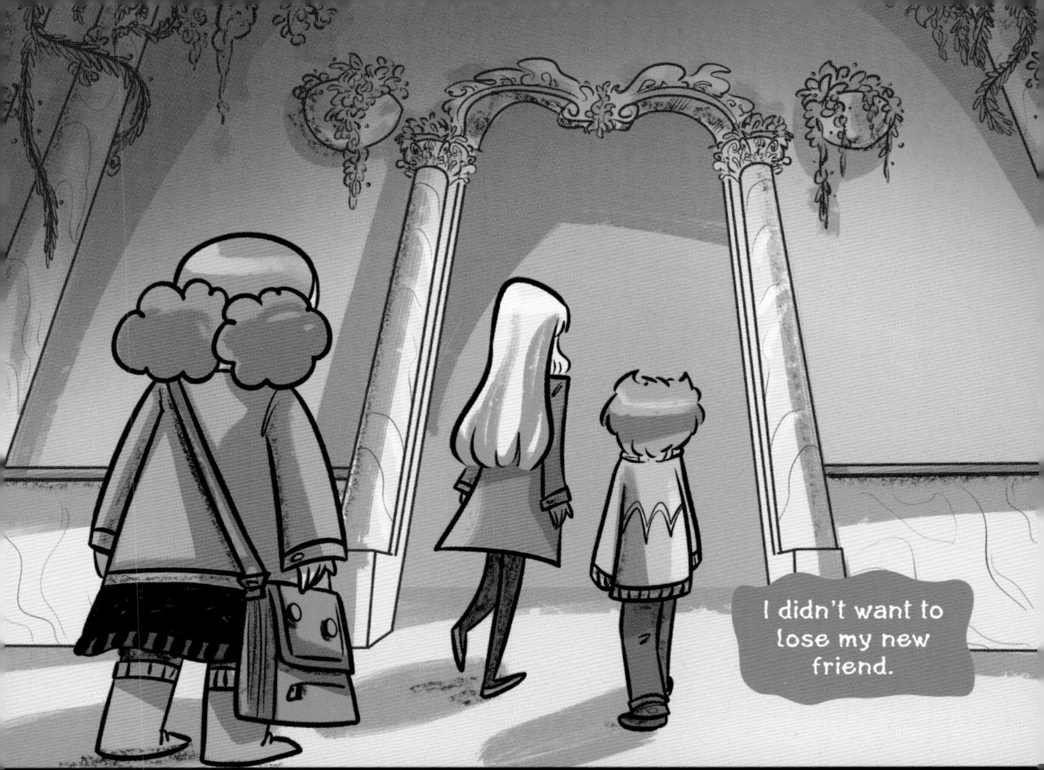
I didn't want to lose my new friend.

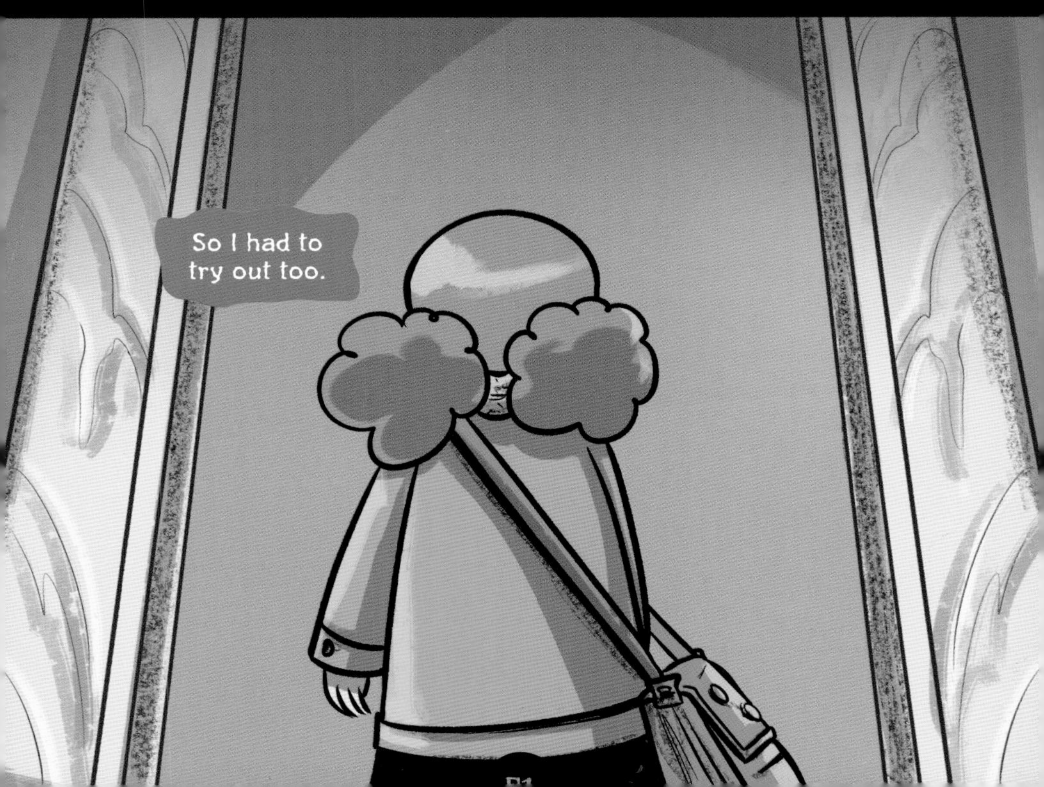
So I had to try out too.

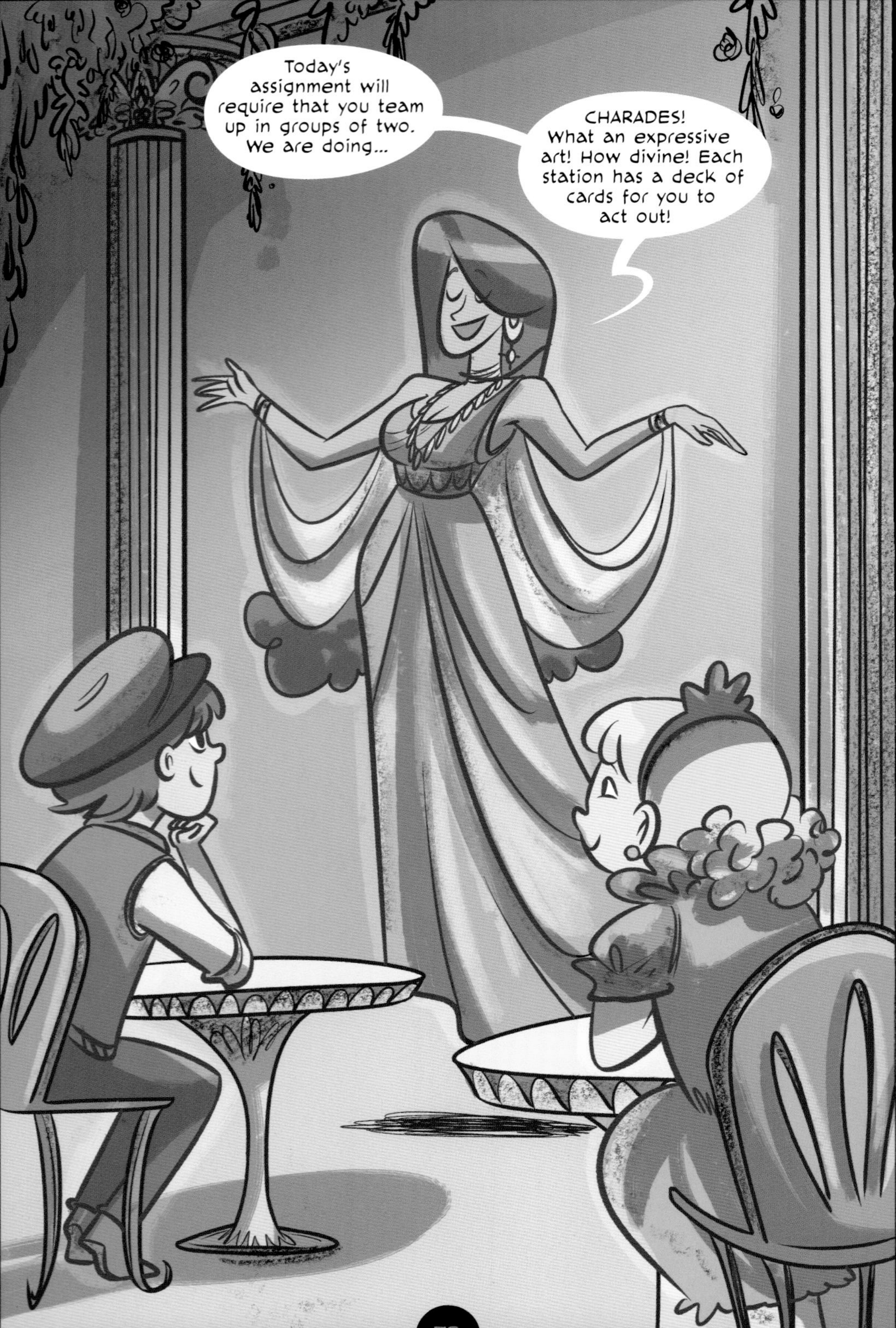
Today's assignment will require that you team up in groups of two. We are doing...
CHARADES! What an expressive art! How divine! Each station has a deck of cards for you to act out!

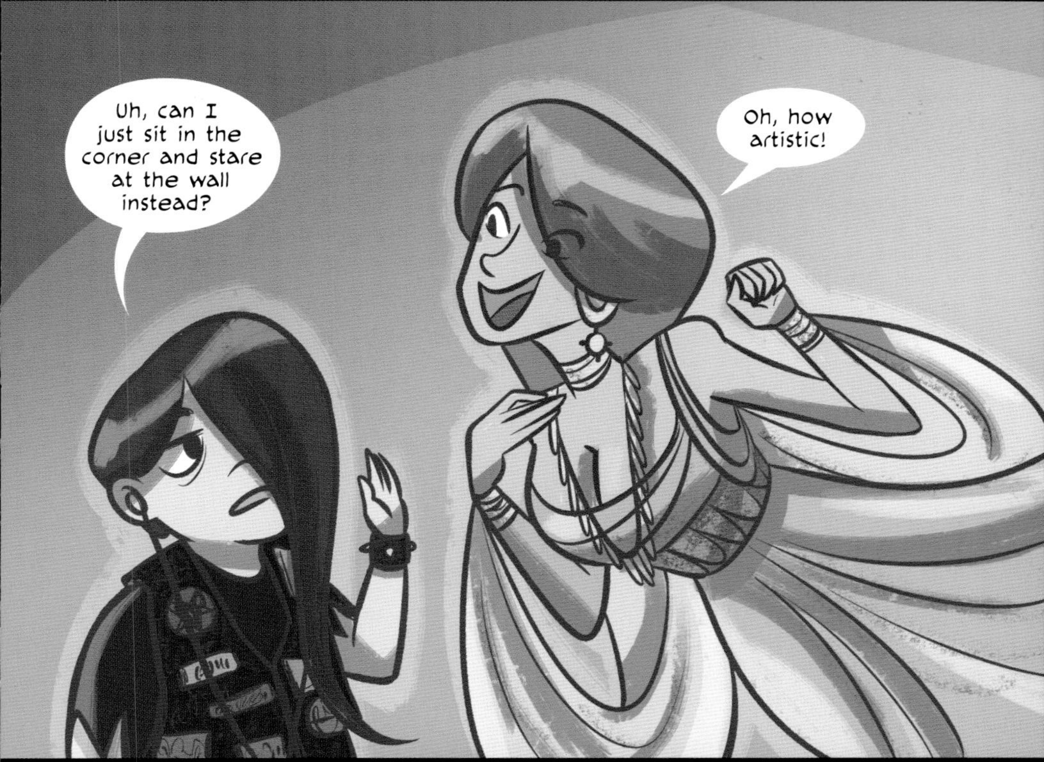
Uh, can I just sit in the corner and stare at the wall instead?
Oh, how artistic!

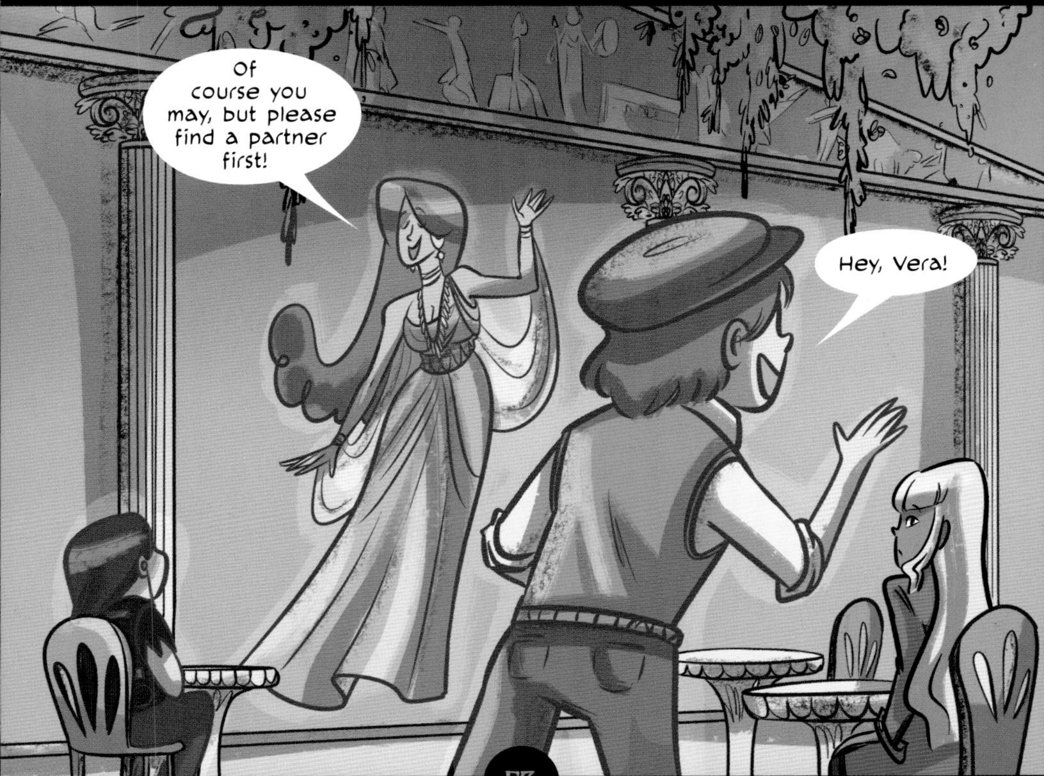
Of course you may, but please find a partner first!
Hey, Vera!

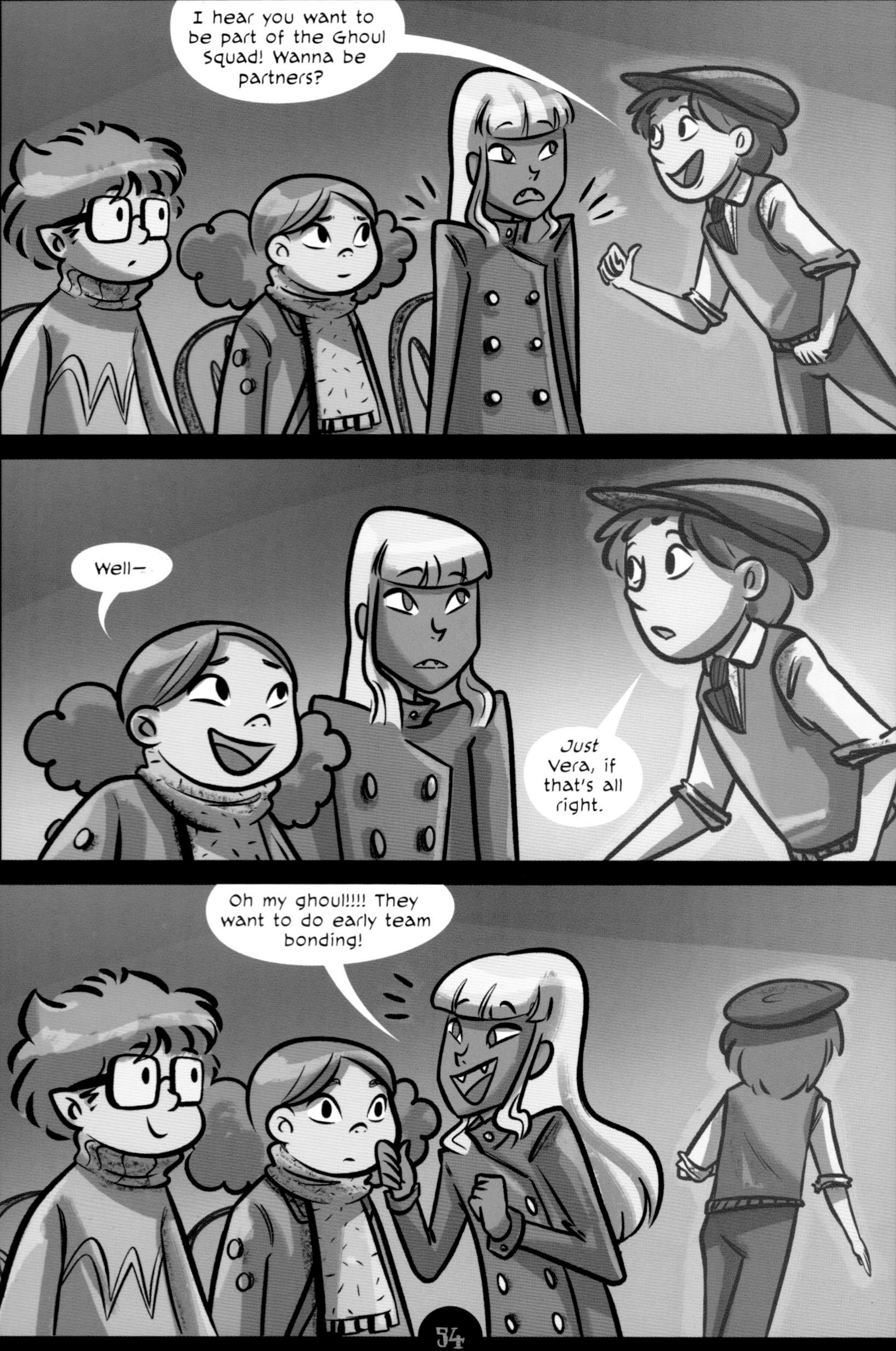
I hear you want to be part of the Ghoul Squad! Wanna be partners?
Well—
Just Vera, if that's all right.
Oh my ghoul!!!! They want to do early team bonding!

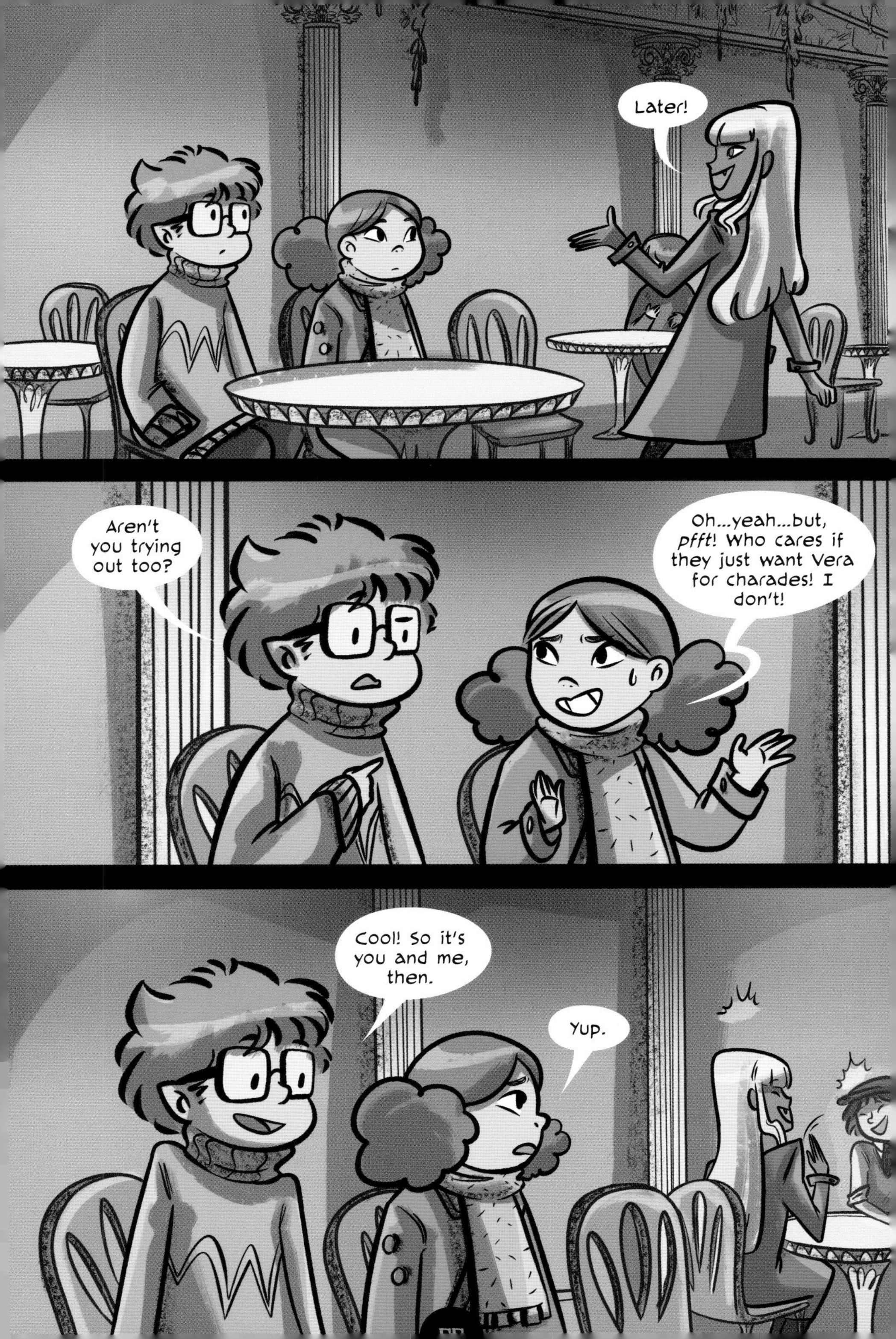
Later!
Aren't you trying out too?
Oh...yeah...but, *pfft*! Who cares if they just want Vera for charades! I don't!
Cool! So it's you and me, then.
Yup.

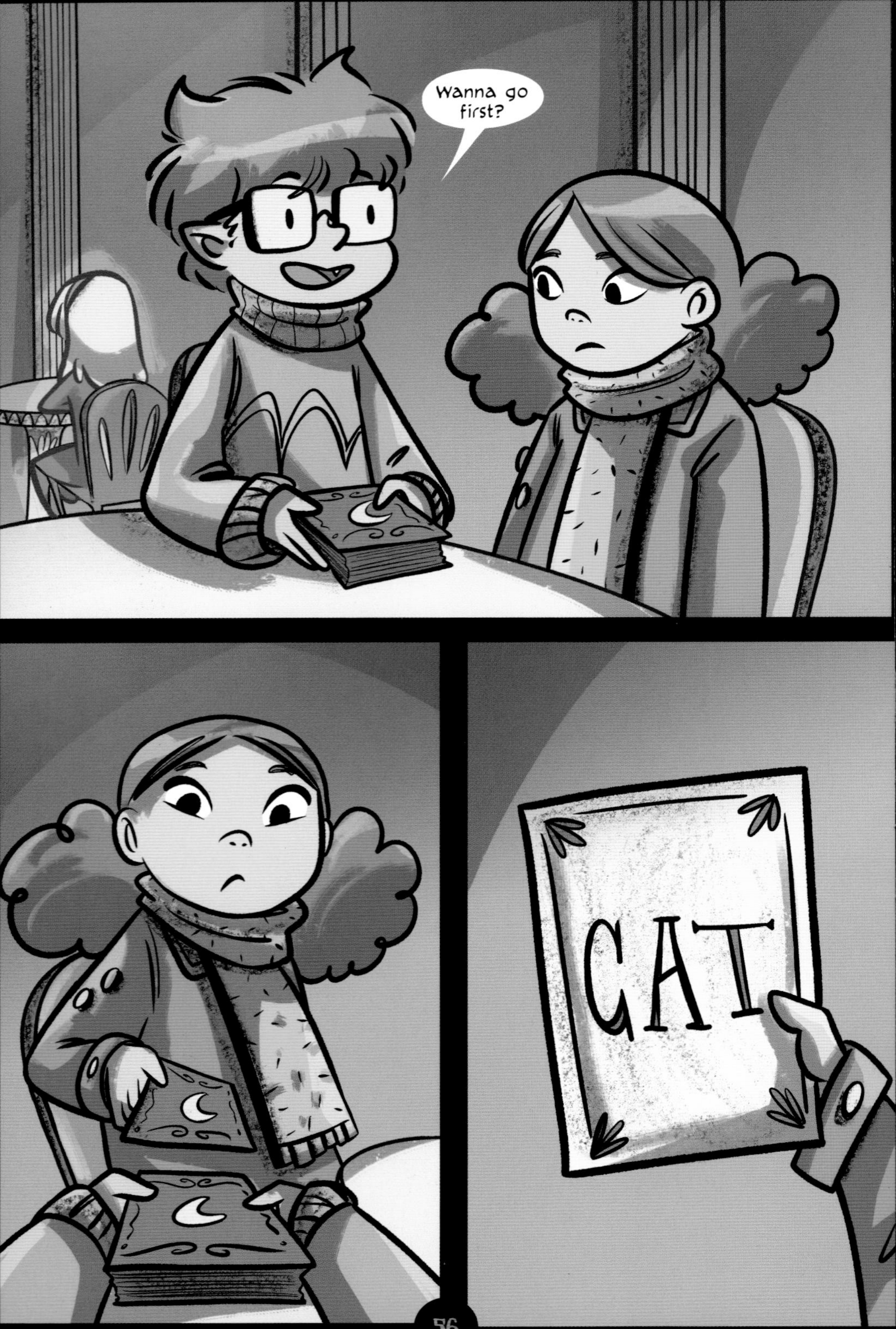
Wanna go first?
CAT

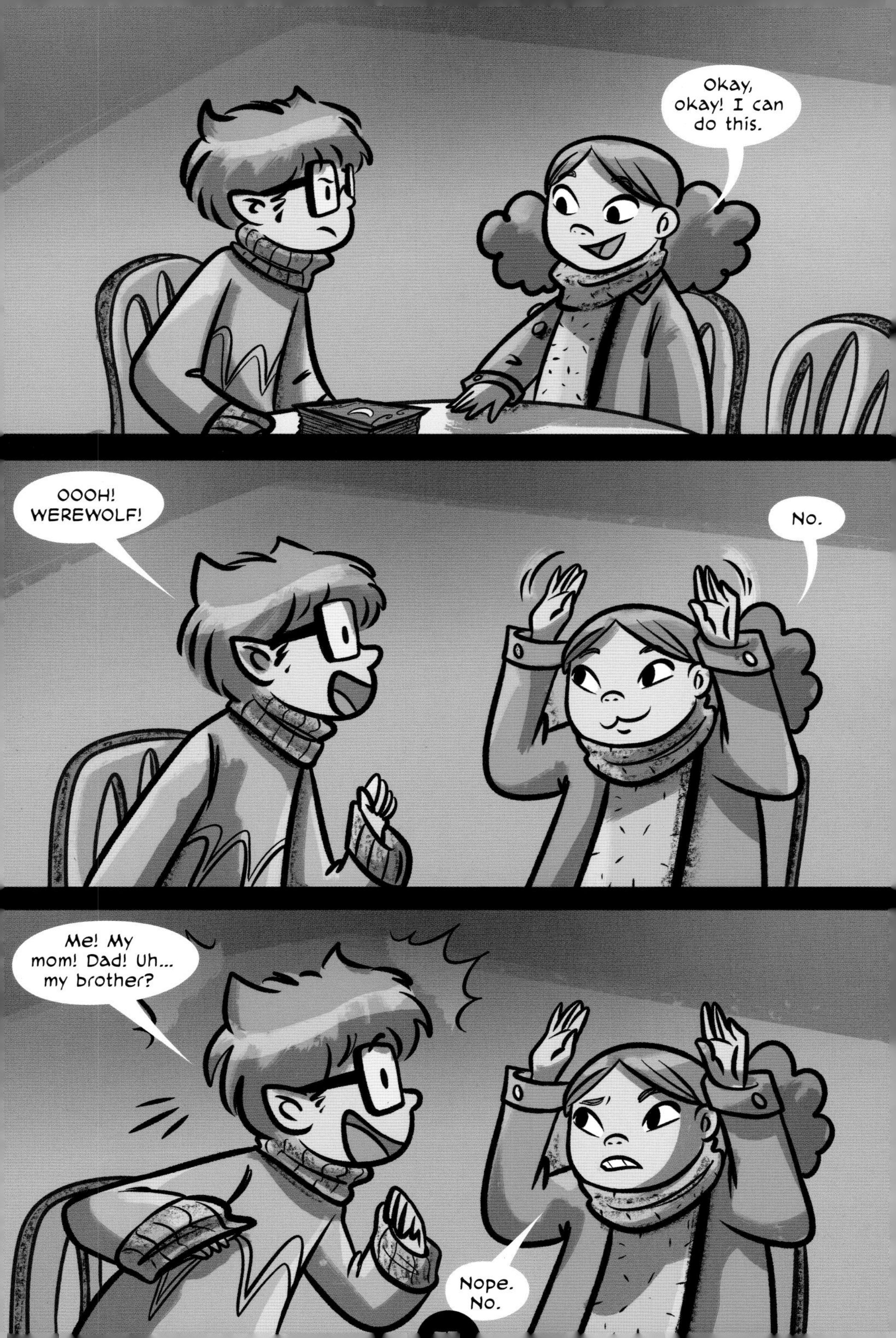
Okay, okay! I can do this.
OOOH! WEREWOLF!
No.
Me! My mom! Dad! Uh... my brother?
Nope. No.

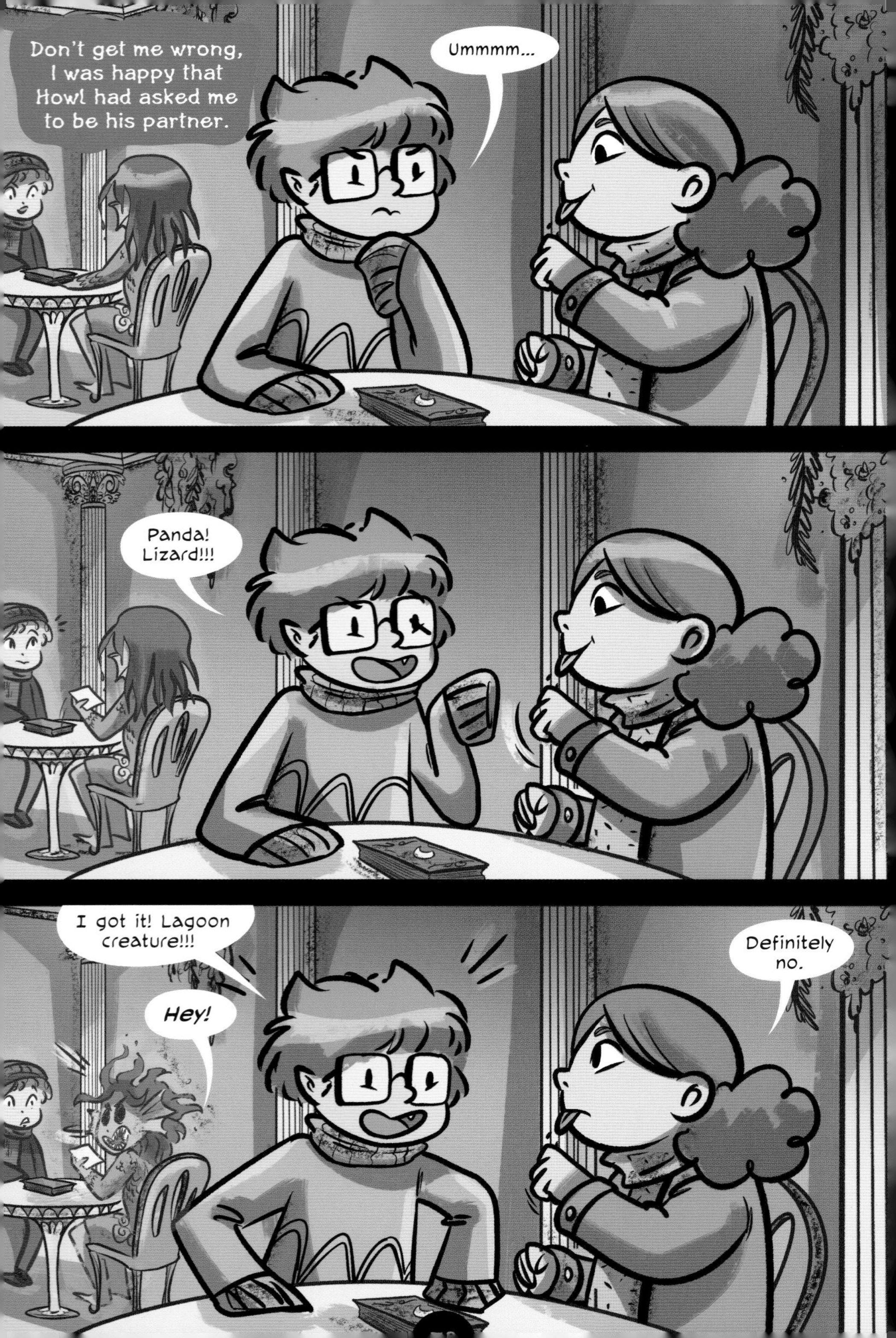
Don't get me wrong, I was happy that Howl had asked me to be his partner.
Ummmm...
Panda! Lizard!!!
I got it! Lagoon creature!!!
Hey!
Definitely no.

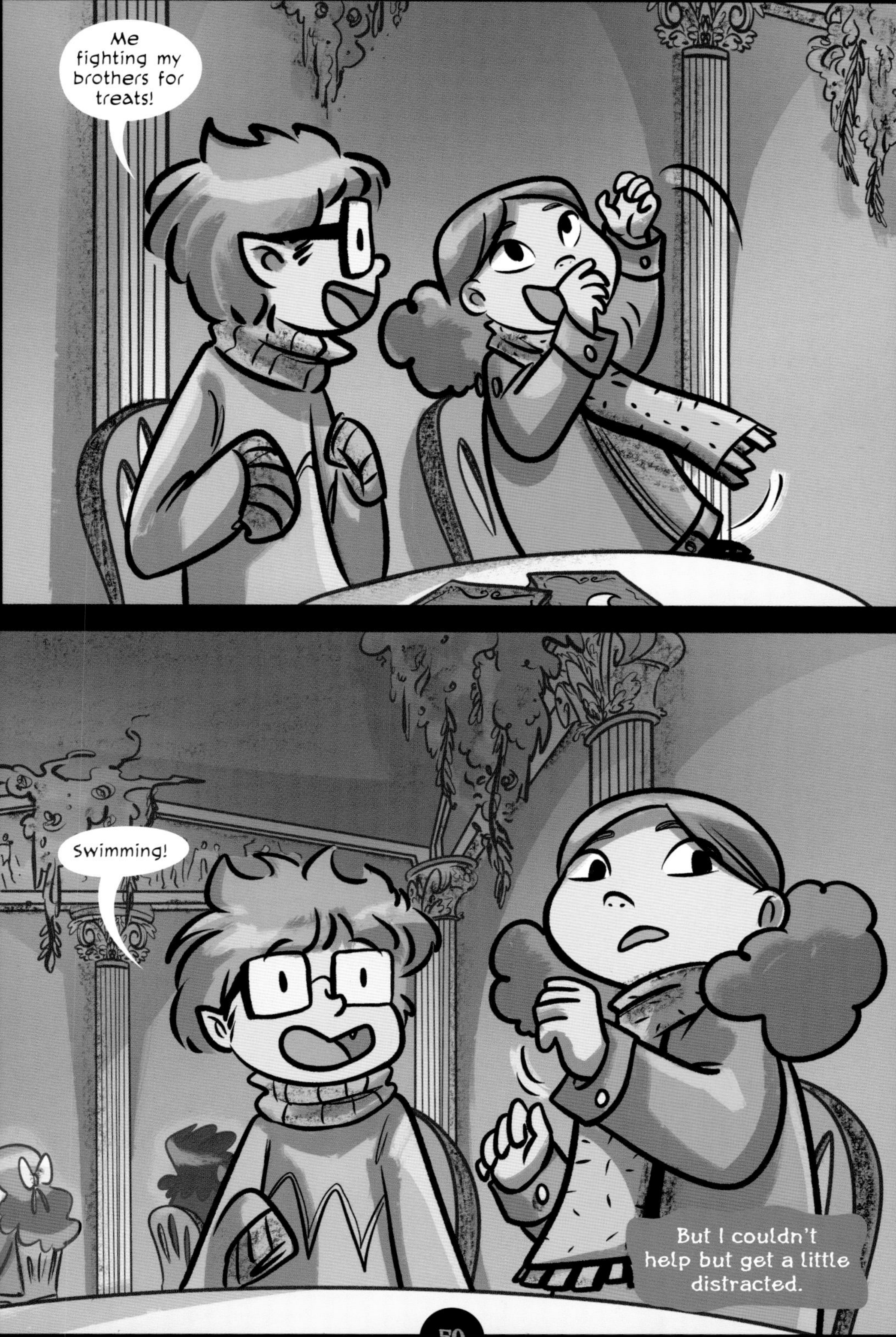
Me fighting my brothers for treats!
Swimming!
But I couldn't help but get a little distracted.

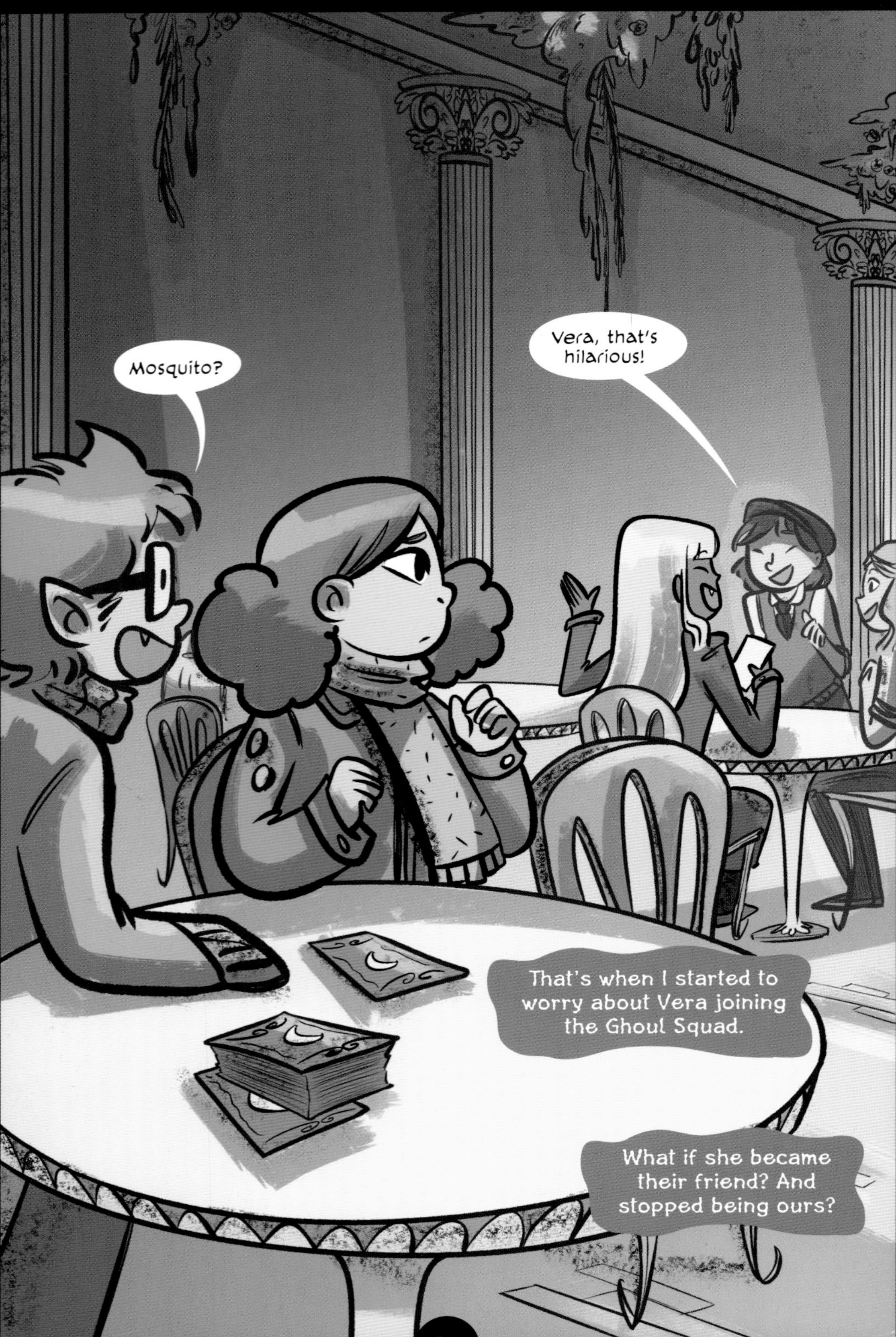
Mosquito?
Vera, that's hilarious!
That's when I started to worry about Vera joining the Ghoul Squad.
What if she became their friend? And stopped being ours?

CHAPTER 5

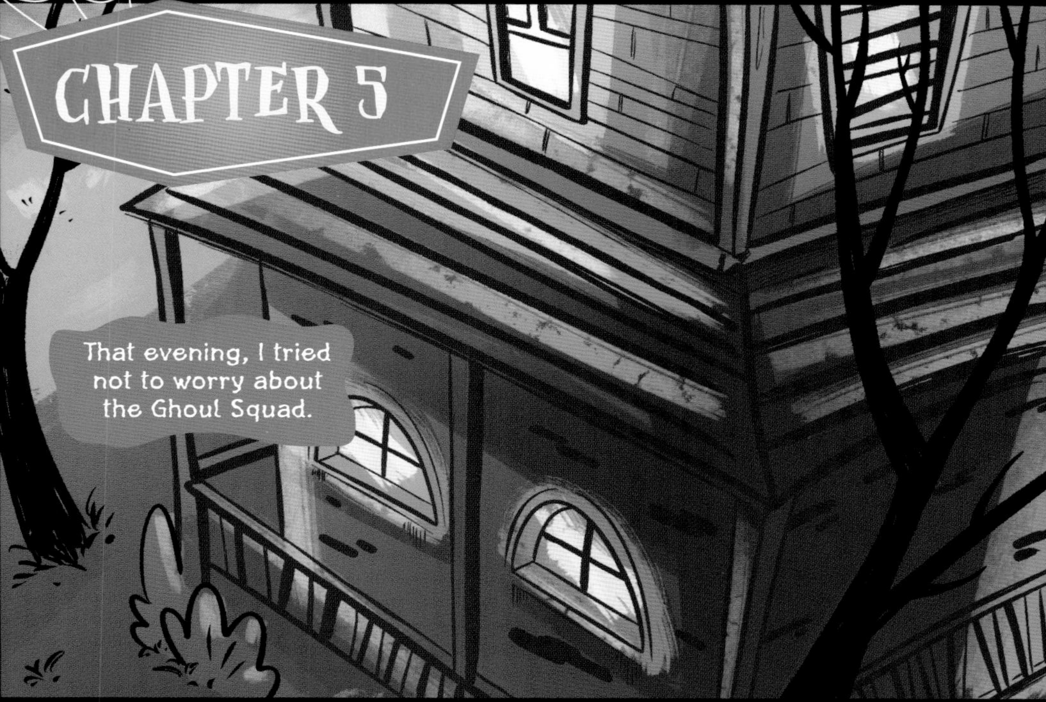
That evening, I tried not to worry about the Ghoul Squad.

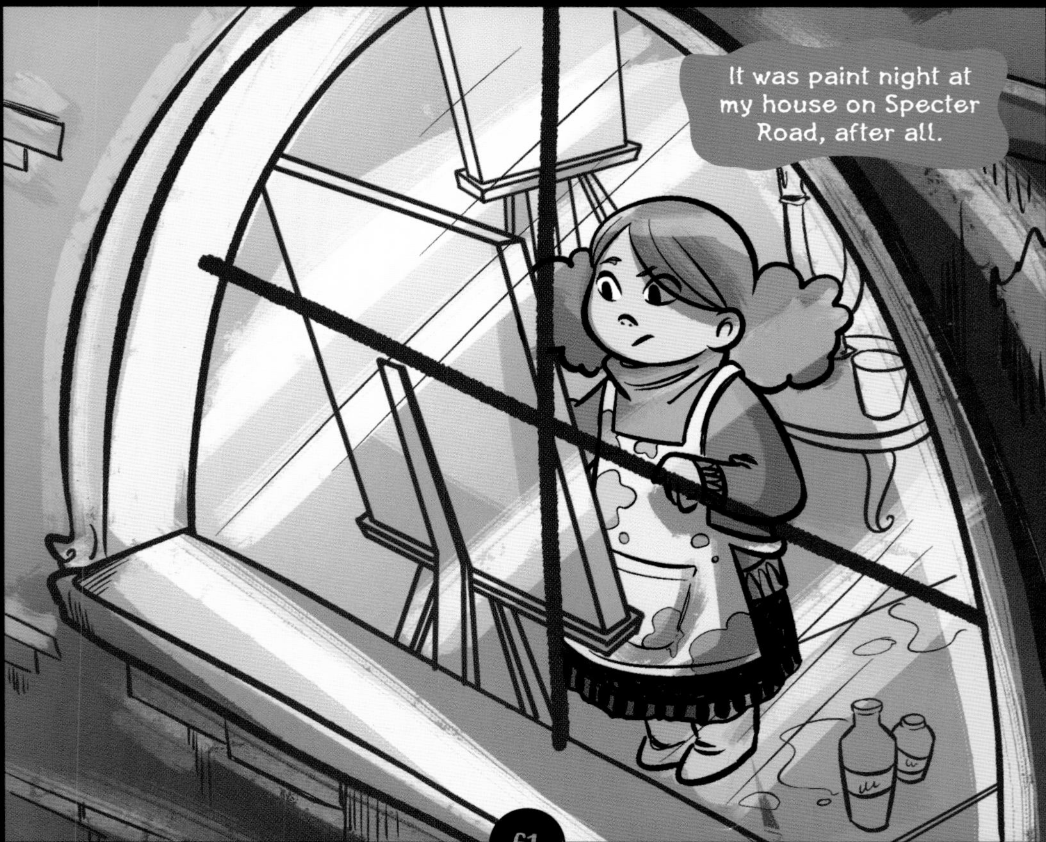
It was paint night at my house on Specter Road, after all.

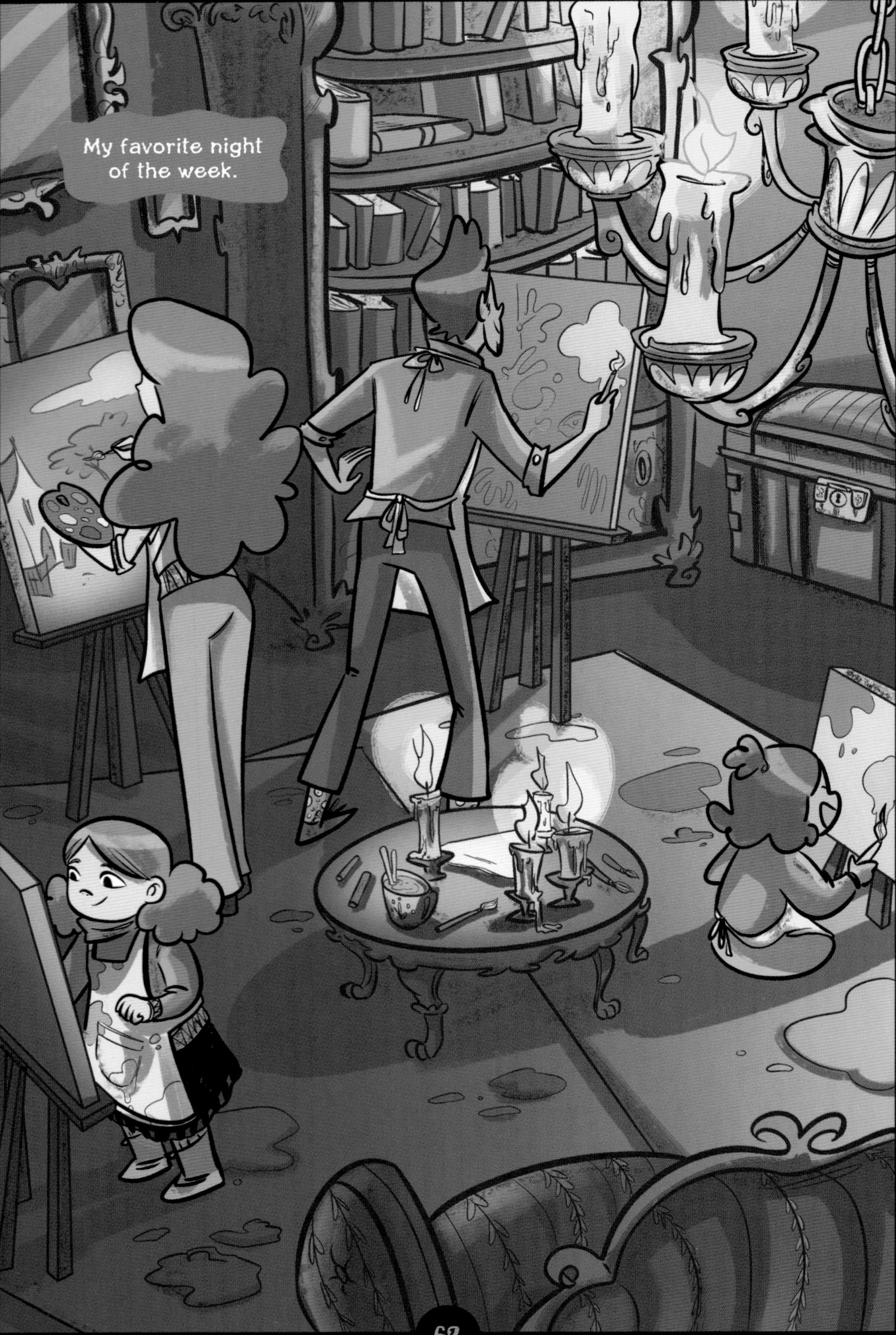
My favorite night of the week.

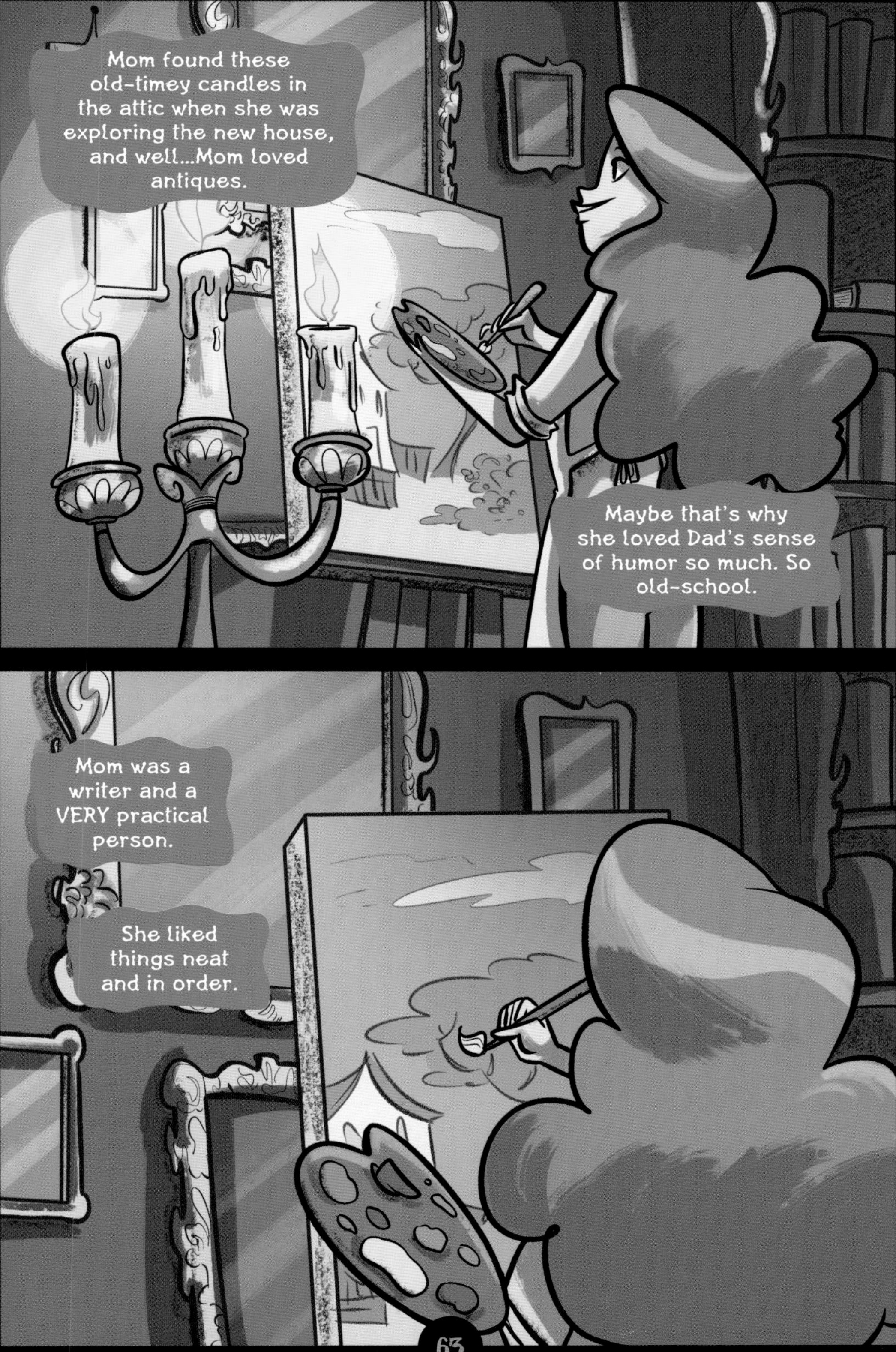
Mom found these old-timey candles in the attic when she was exploring the new house, and well...Mom loved antiques.
Maybe that's why she loved Dad's sense of humor so much. So old-school.
Mom was a writer and a VERY practical person.
She liked things neat and in order.

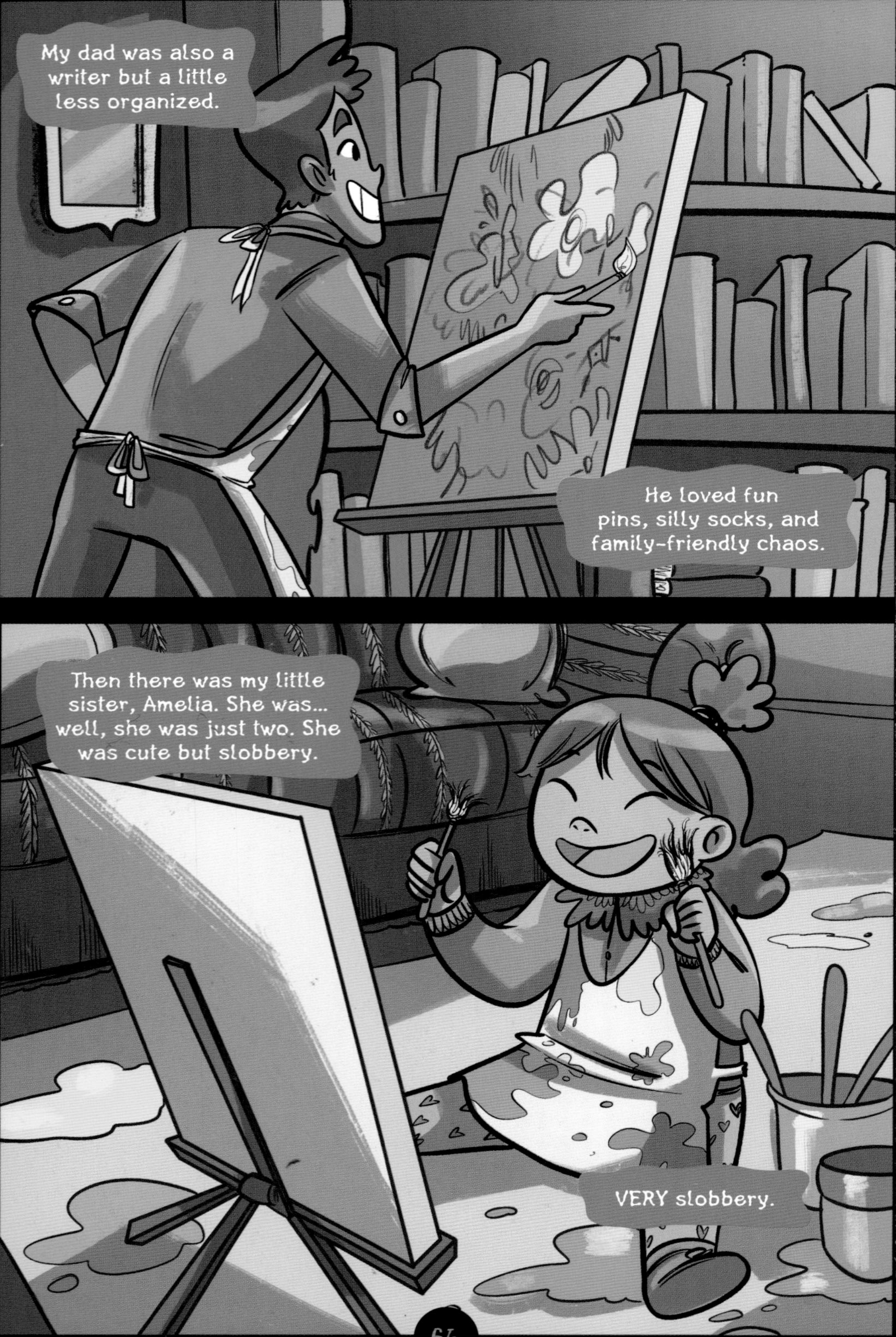
My dad was also a writer but a little less organized.
He loved fun pins, silly socks, and family-friendly chaos.
Then there was my little sister, Amelia. She was... well, she was just two. She was cute but slobbery.
VERY slobbery.

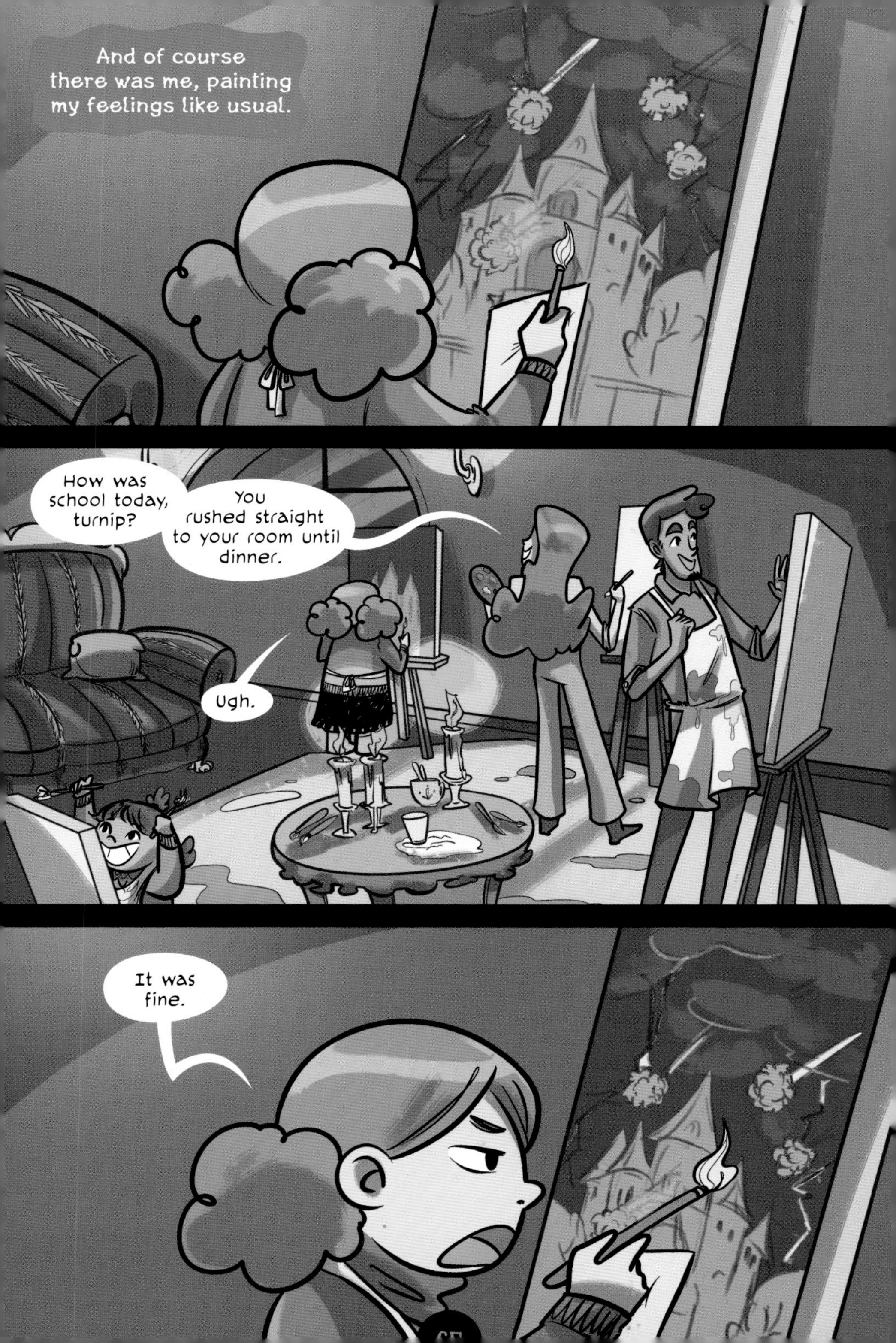
And of course there was me, painting my feelings like usual.
How was school today, turnip?
You rushed straight to your room until dinner.
Ugh.
It was fine.

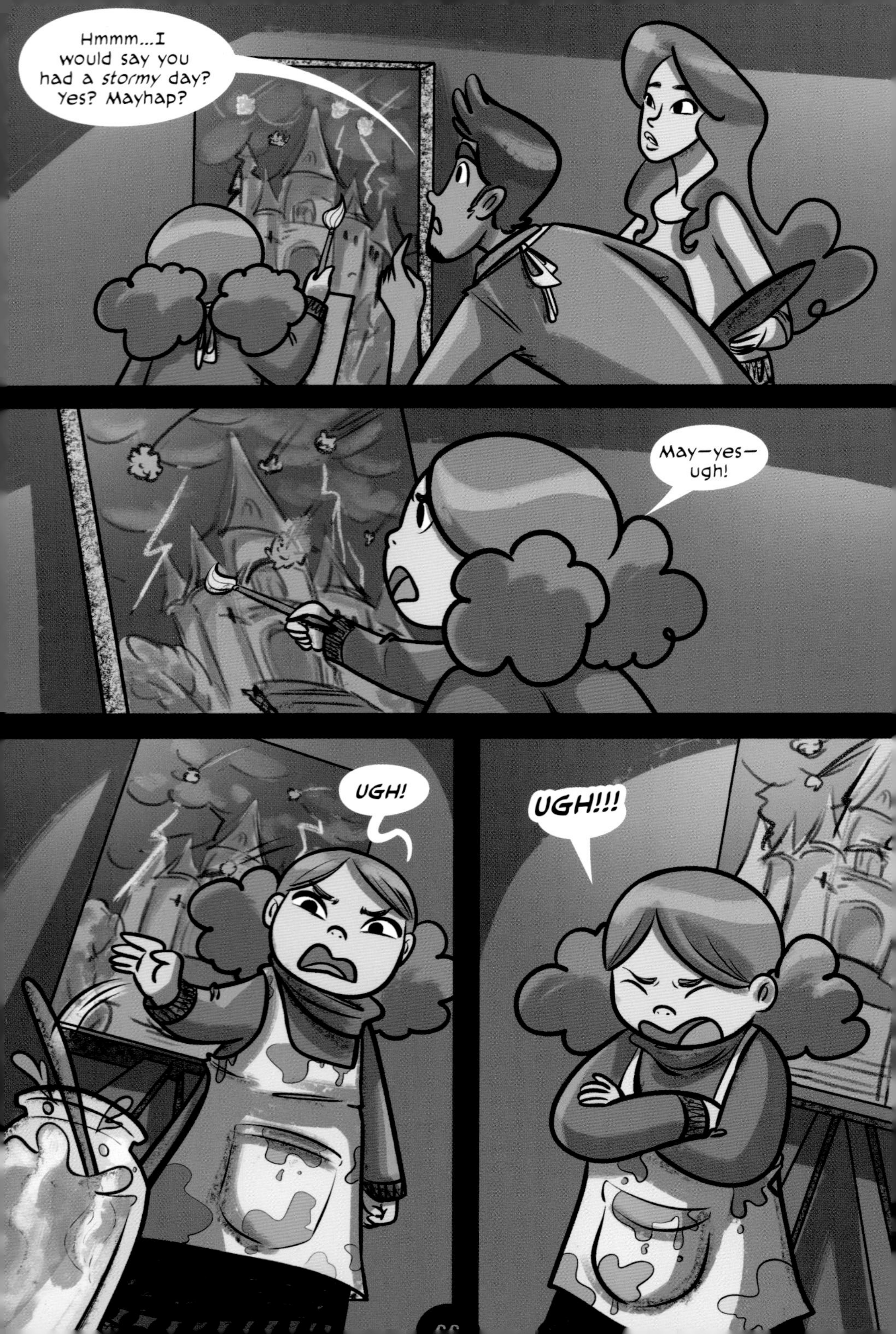
Hmmm...I would say you had a *stormy* day? Yes? Mayhap?
May—yes—ugh!
UGH!
UGH!!!

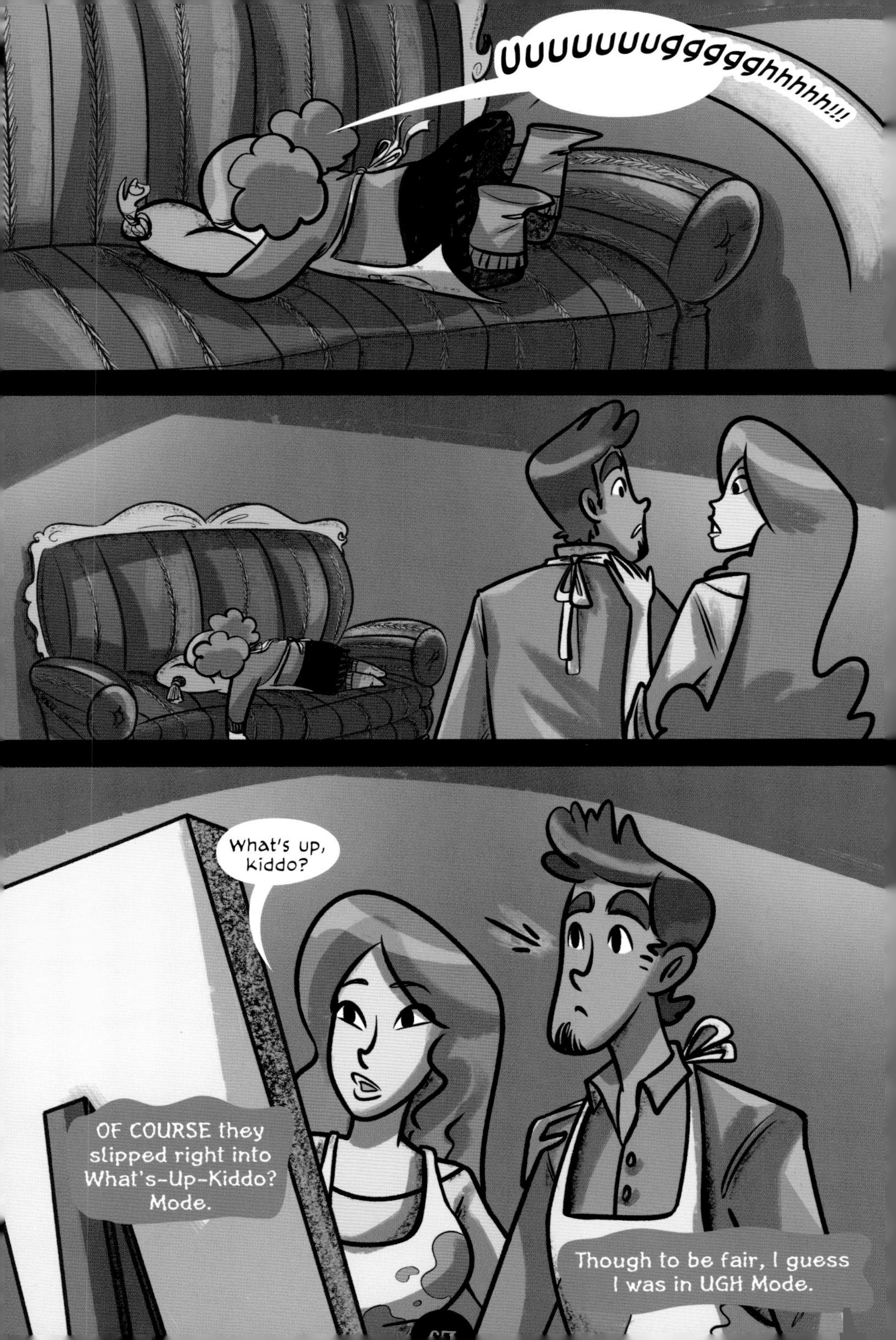
UUUUUUUGGGGGHHHHH!!!
What's up, kiddo?
OF COURSE they slipped right into What's-Up-Kiddo? Mode.
Though to be fair, I guess I was in UGH Mode.

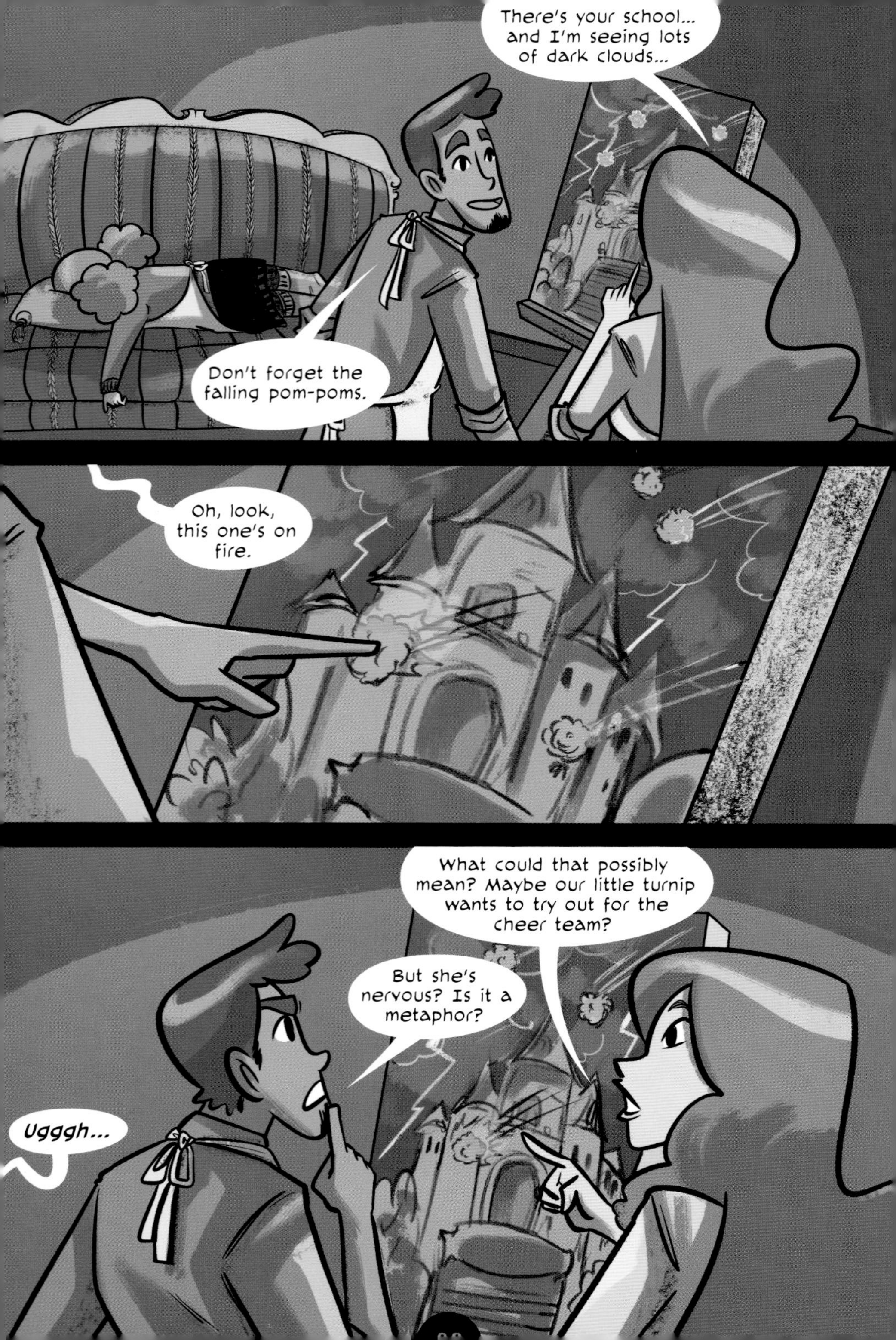
There's your school... and I'm seeing lots of dark clouds...
Don't forget the falling pom-poms.
Oh, look, this one's on fire.
What could that possibly mean? Maybe our little turnip wants to try out for the cheer team?
But she's nervous? Is it a metaphor?
Ugggh...

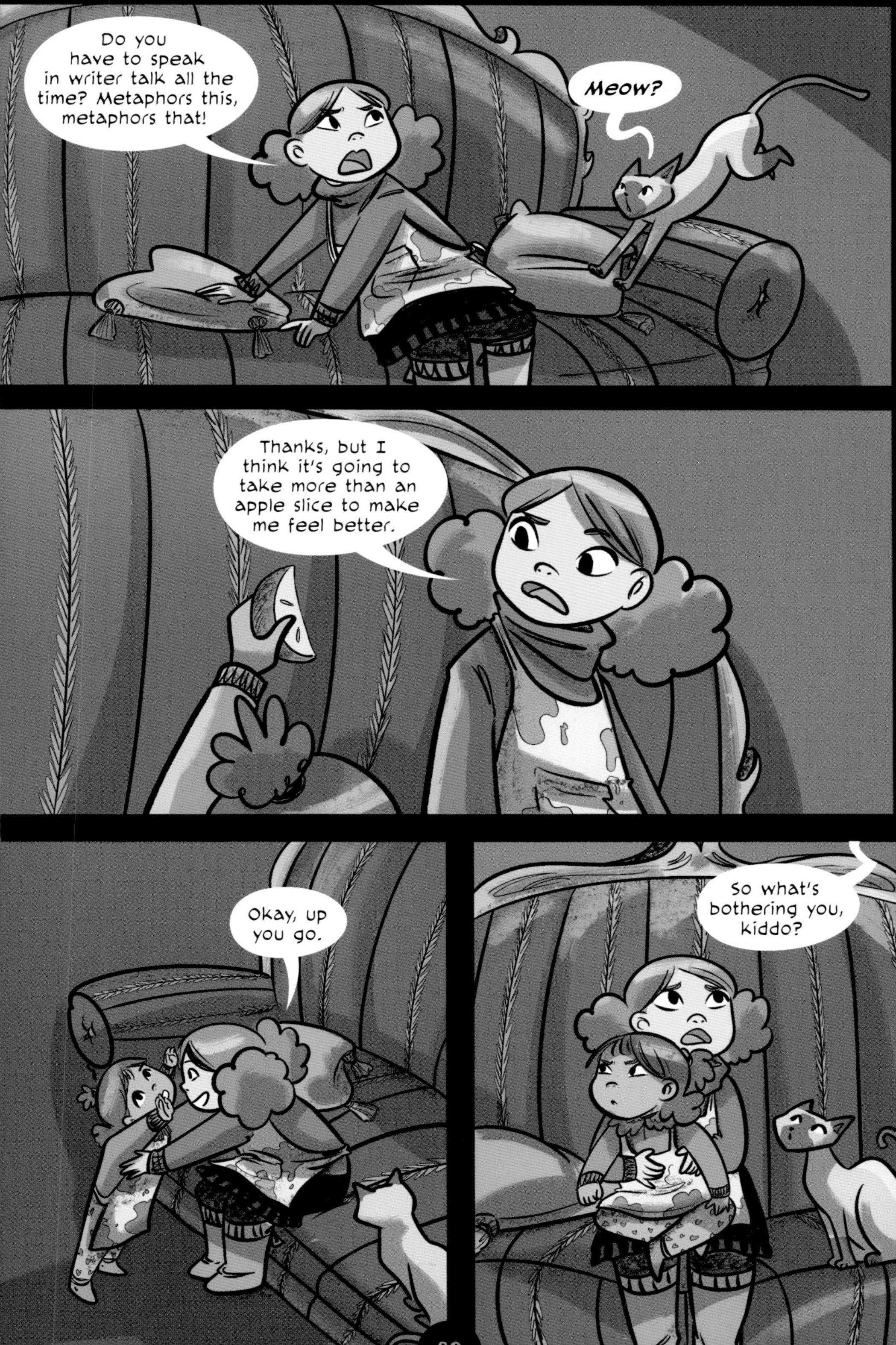
Do you have to speak in writer talk all the time? Metaphors this, metaphors that!
Meow?
Thanks, but I think it's going to take more than an apple slice to make me feel better.
Okay, up you go.
So what's bothering you, kiddo?

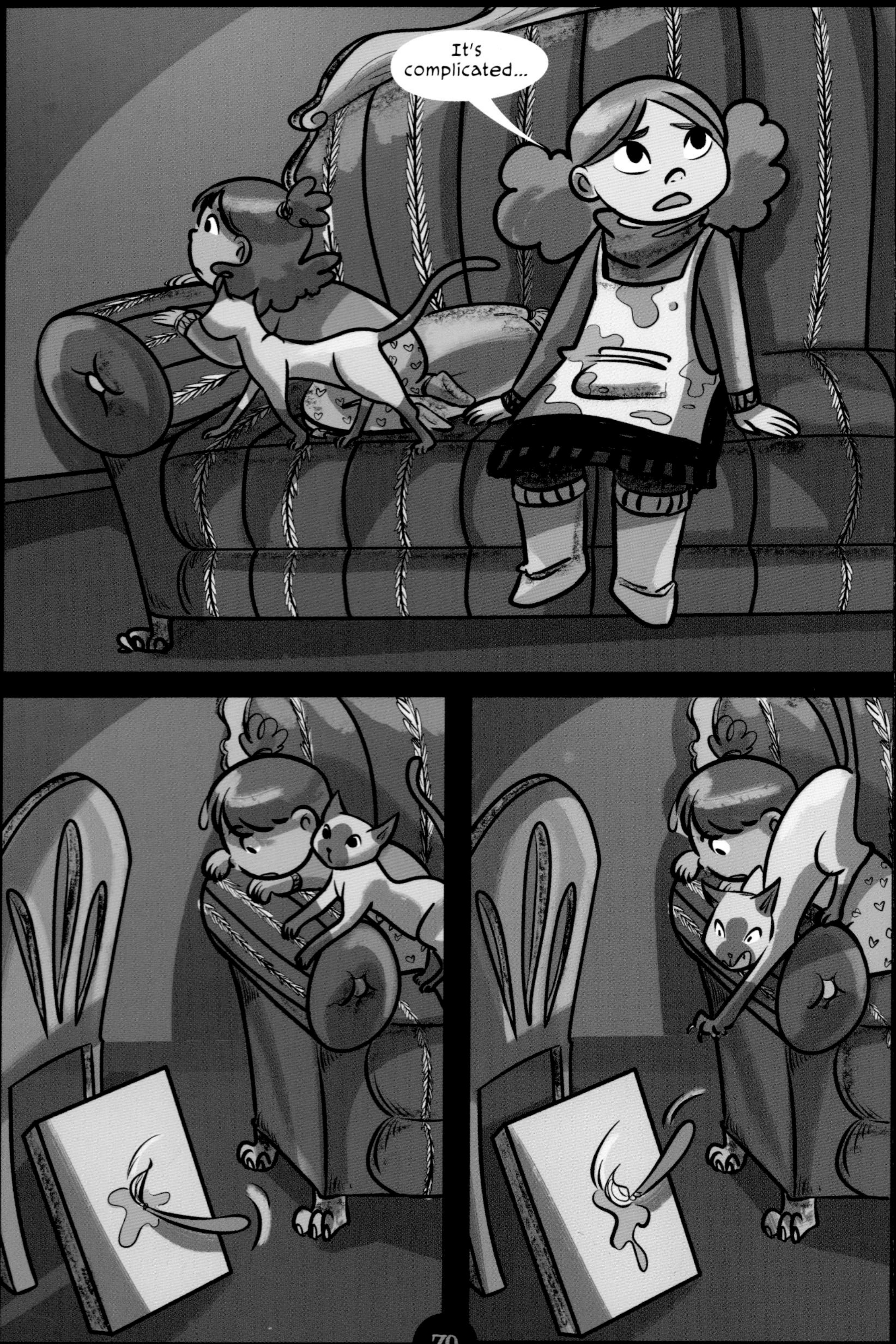
It's complicated...

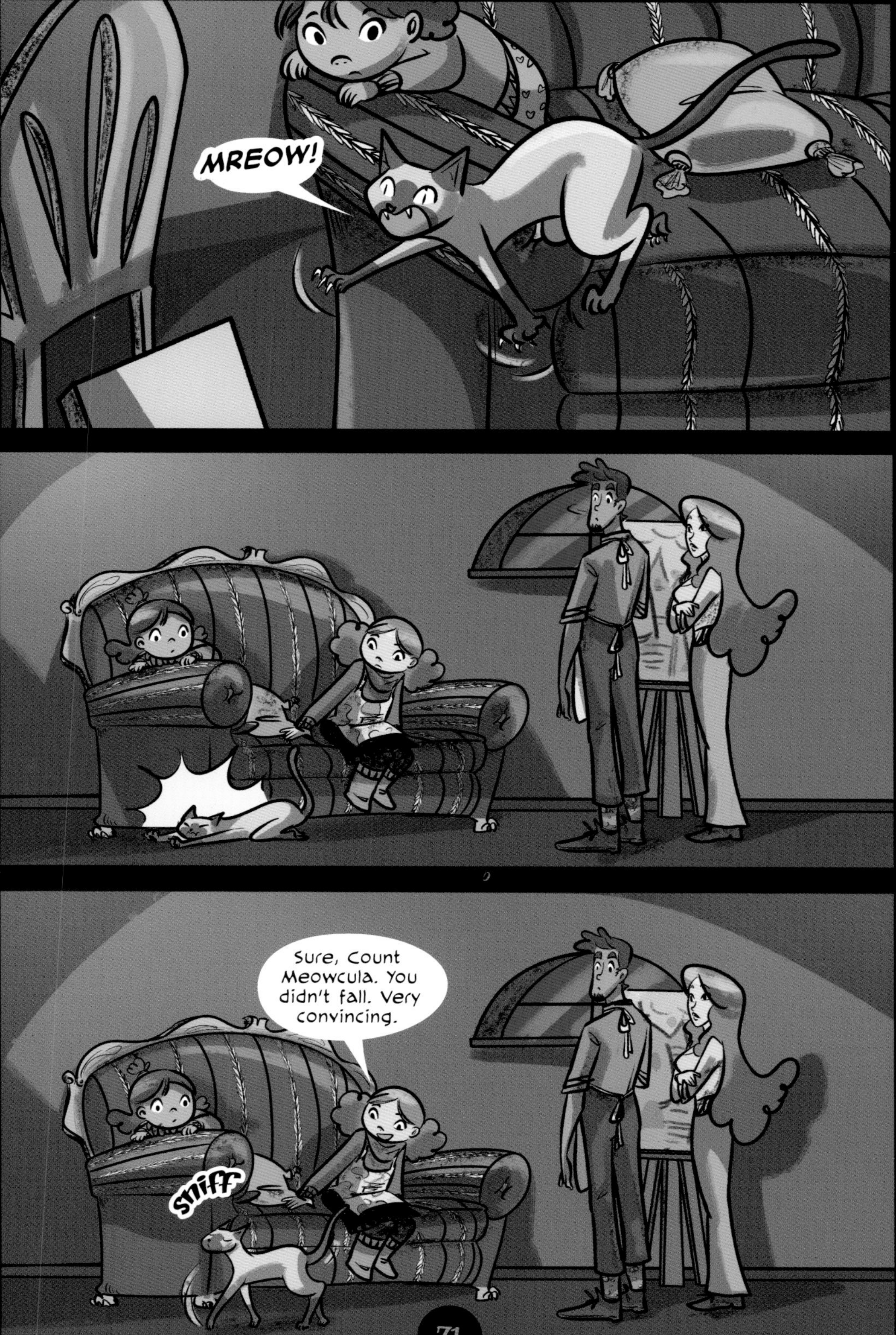
MREOW!
Sure, Count Meowcula. You didn't fall. Very convincing.
sniff

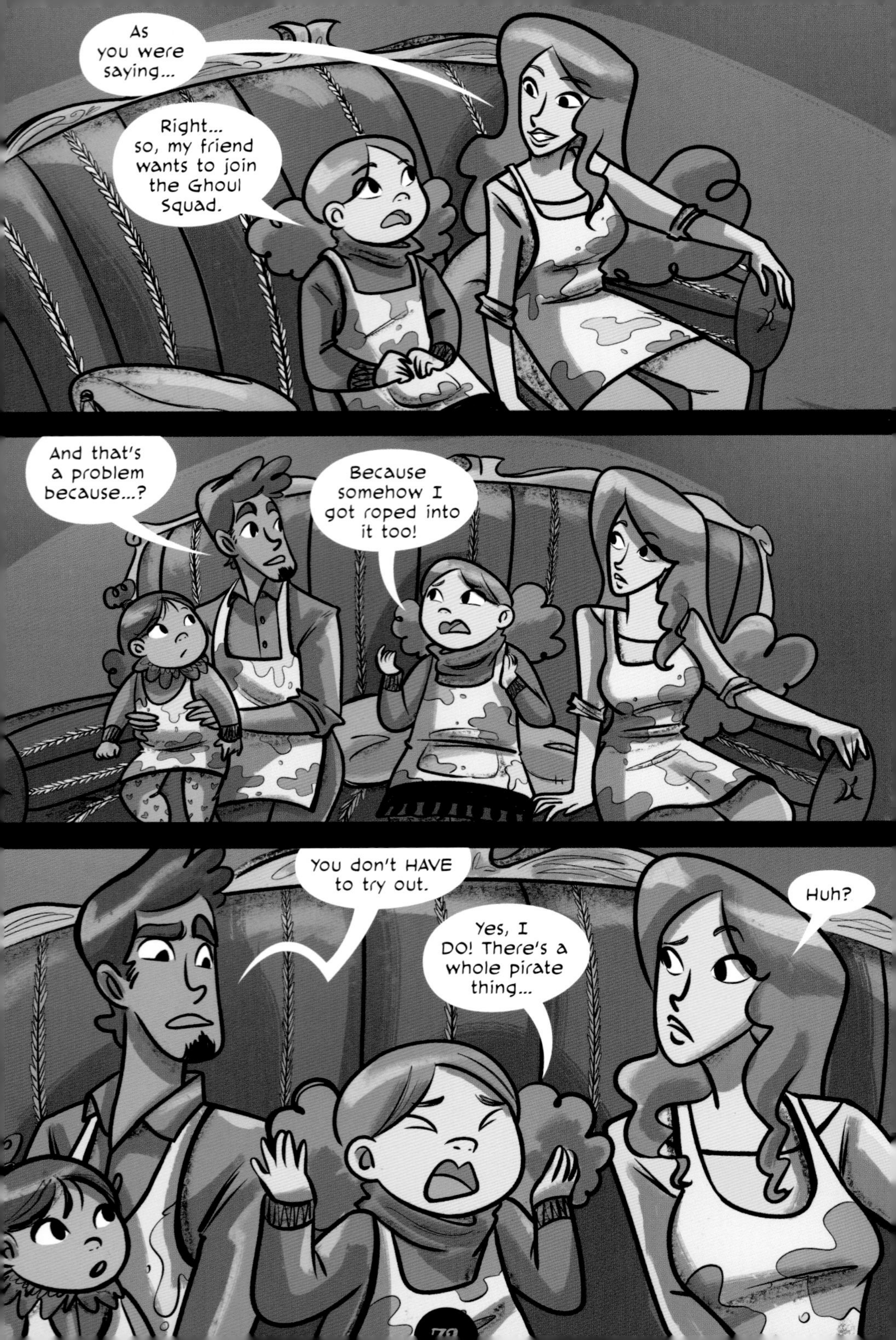

As you were saying...
Right... so, my friend wants to join the Ghoul Squad.
And that's a problem because...?
Because somehow I got roped into it too!
You don't HAVE to try out.
Yes, I DO! There's a whole pirate thing...
Huh?

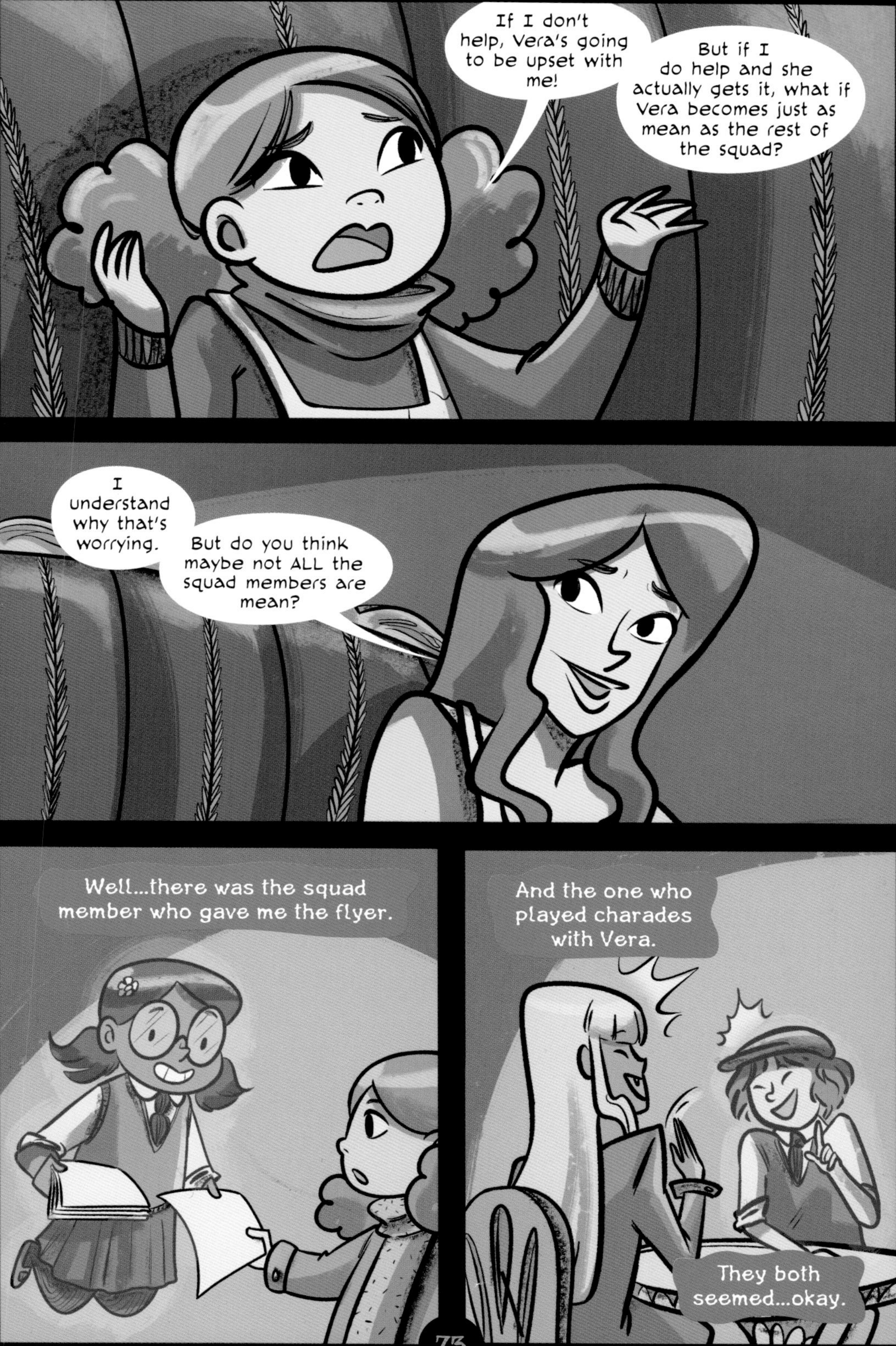
If I don't help, Vera's going to be upset with me!
But if I do help and she actually gets it, what if Vera becomes just as mean as the rest of the squad?
I understand why that's worrying.
But do you think maybe not ALL the squad members are mean?
Well...there was the squad member who gave me the flyer.
And the one who played charades with Vera.
They both seemed...okay.

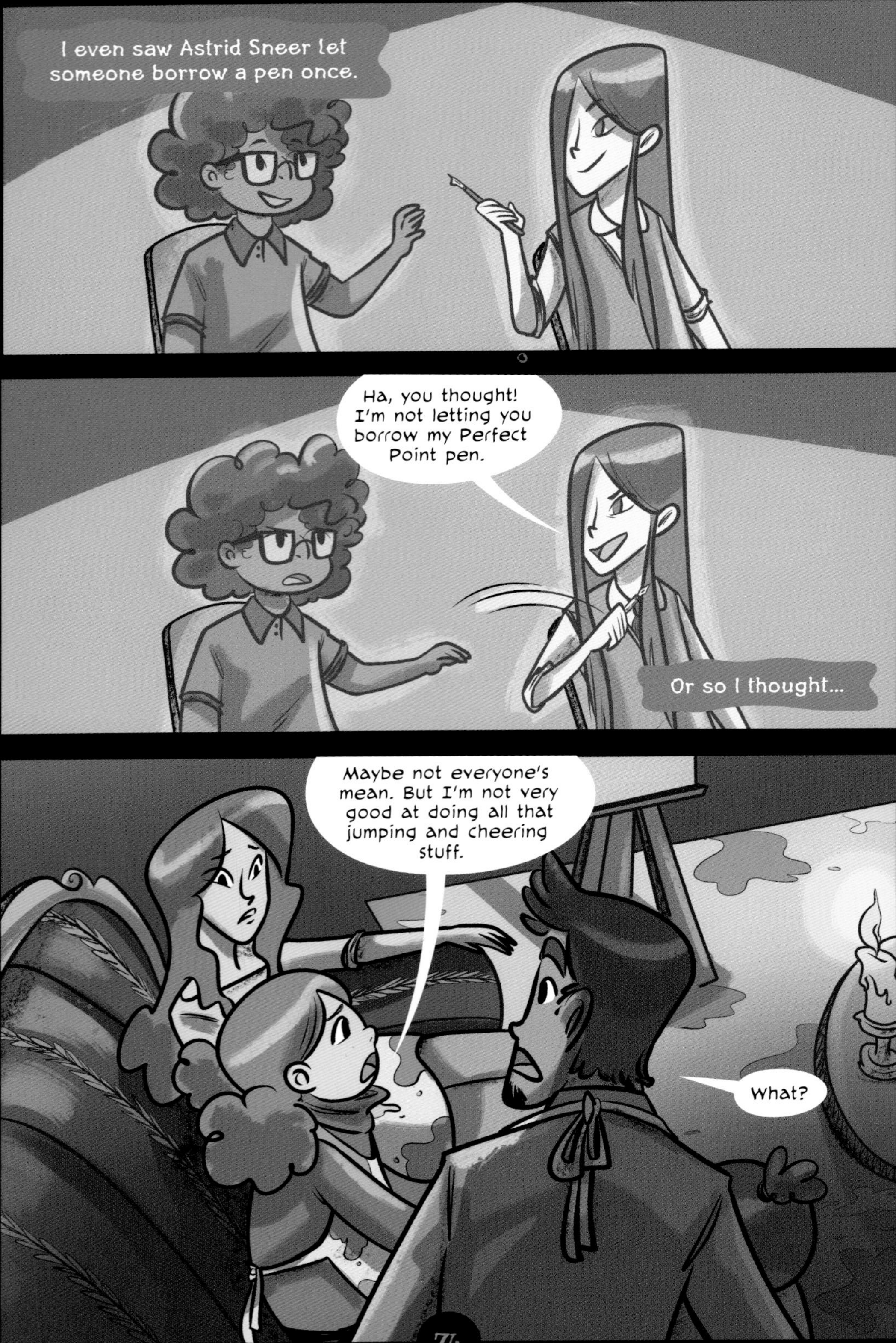
I even saw Astrid Sneer let someone borrow a pen once.
Ha, you thought! I'm not letting you borrow my Perfect Point pen.
Or so I thought...
Maybe not everyone's mean. But I'm not very good at doing all that jumping and cheering stuff.
What?

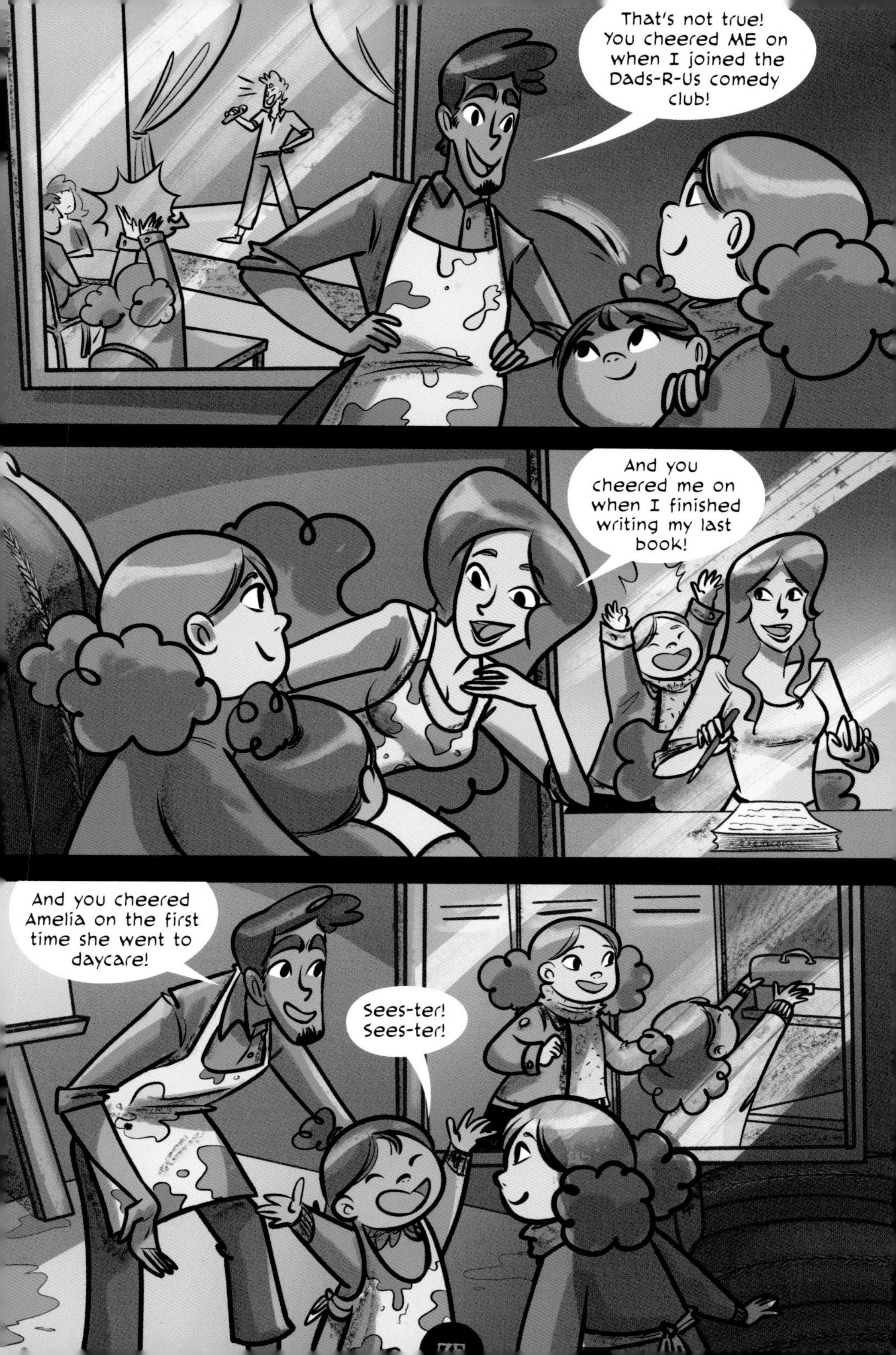

That's not true! You cheered ME on when I joined the Dads-R-Us comedy club!
And you cheered me on when I finished writing my last book!
And you cheered Amelia on the first time she went to daycare!
Sees-ter! Sees-ter!

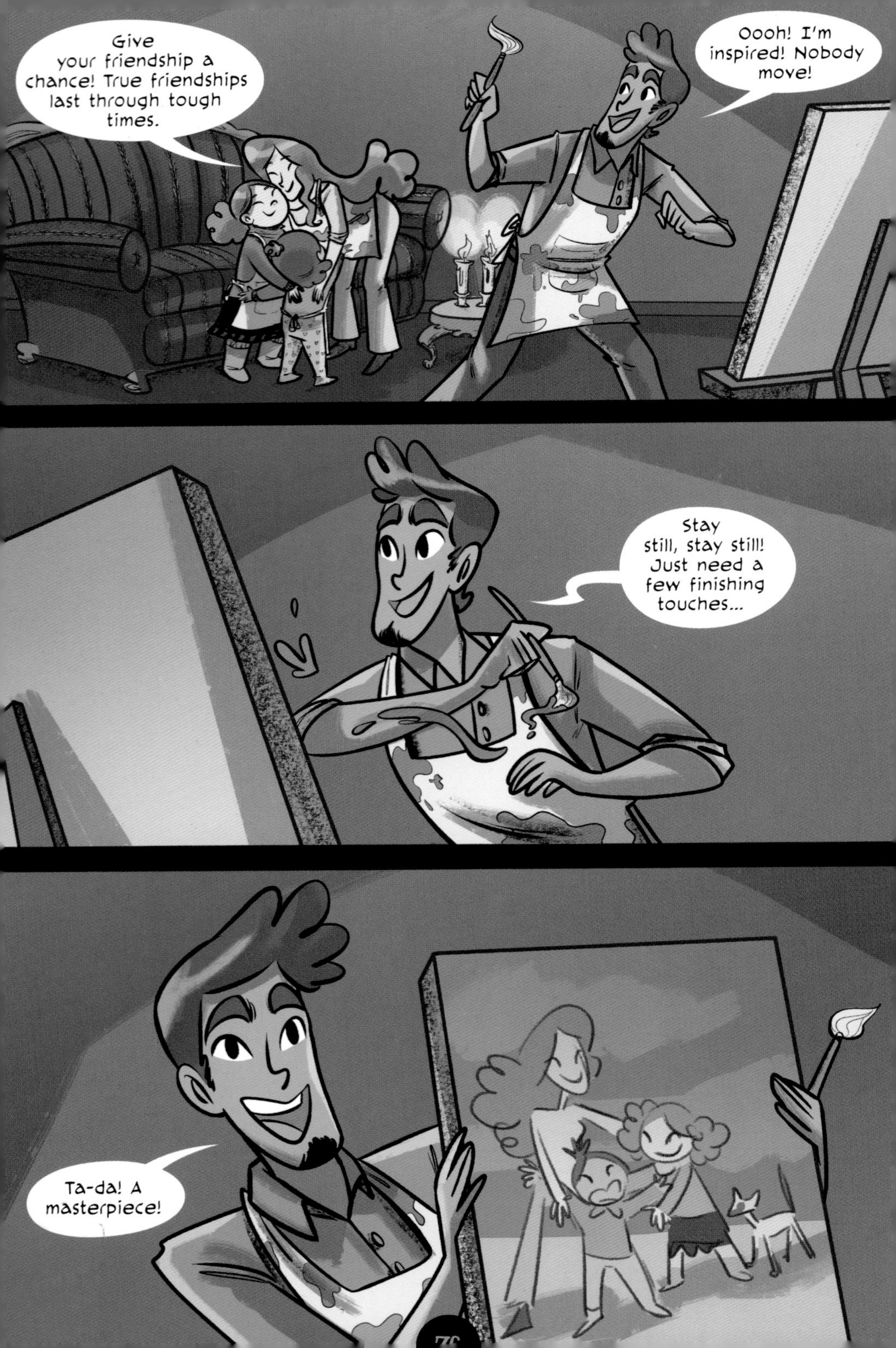

Give your friendship a chance! True friendships last through tough times.
Oooh! I'm inspired! Nobody move!
Stay still, stay still! Just need a few finishing touches...
Ta-da! A masterpiece!

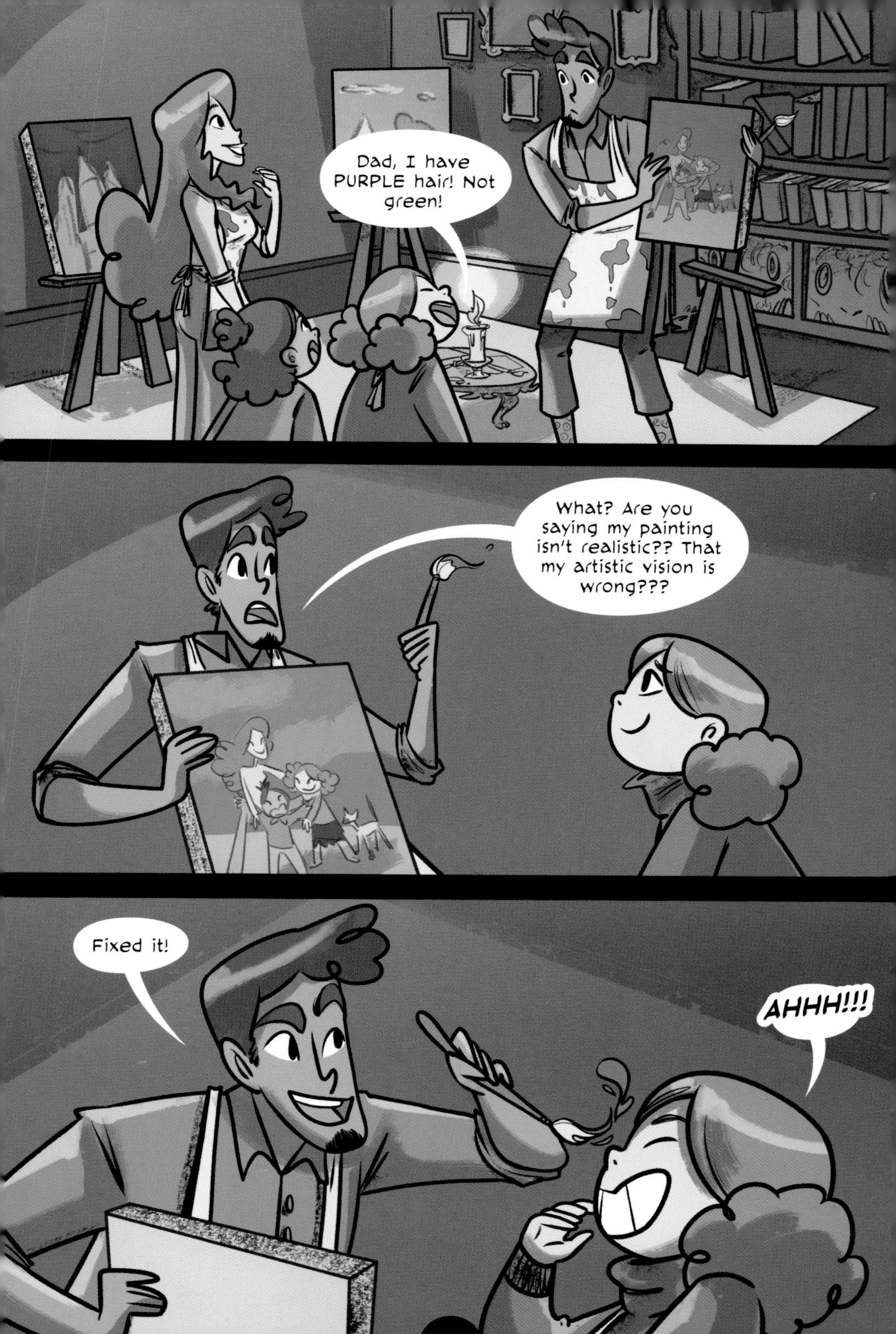
Dad, I have PURPLE hair! Not green!
What? Are you saying my painting isn't realistic?? That my artistic vision is wrong???
Fixed it!
AHHH!!!

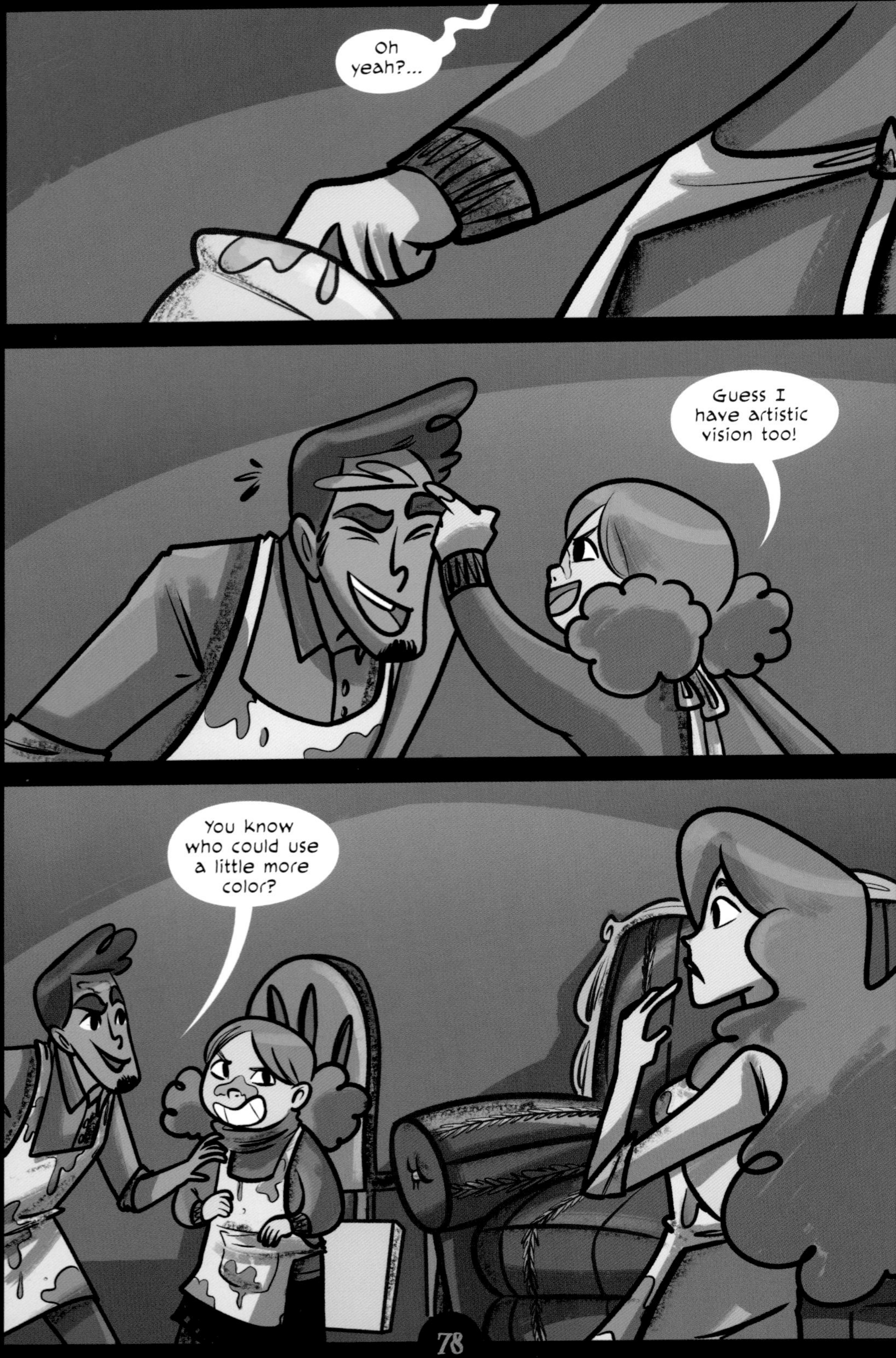

Oh yeah?...
Guess I have artistic vision too!
You know who could use a little more color?

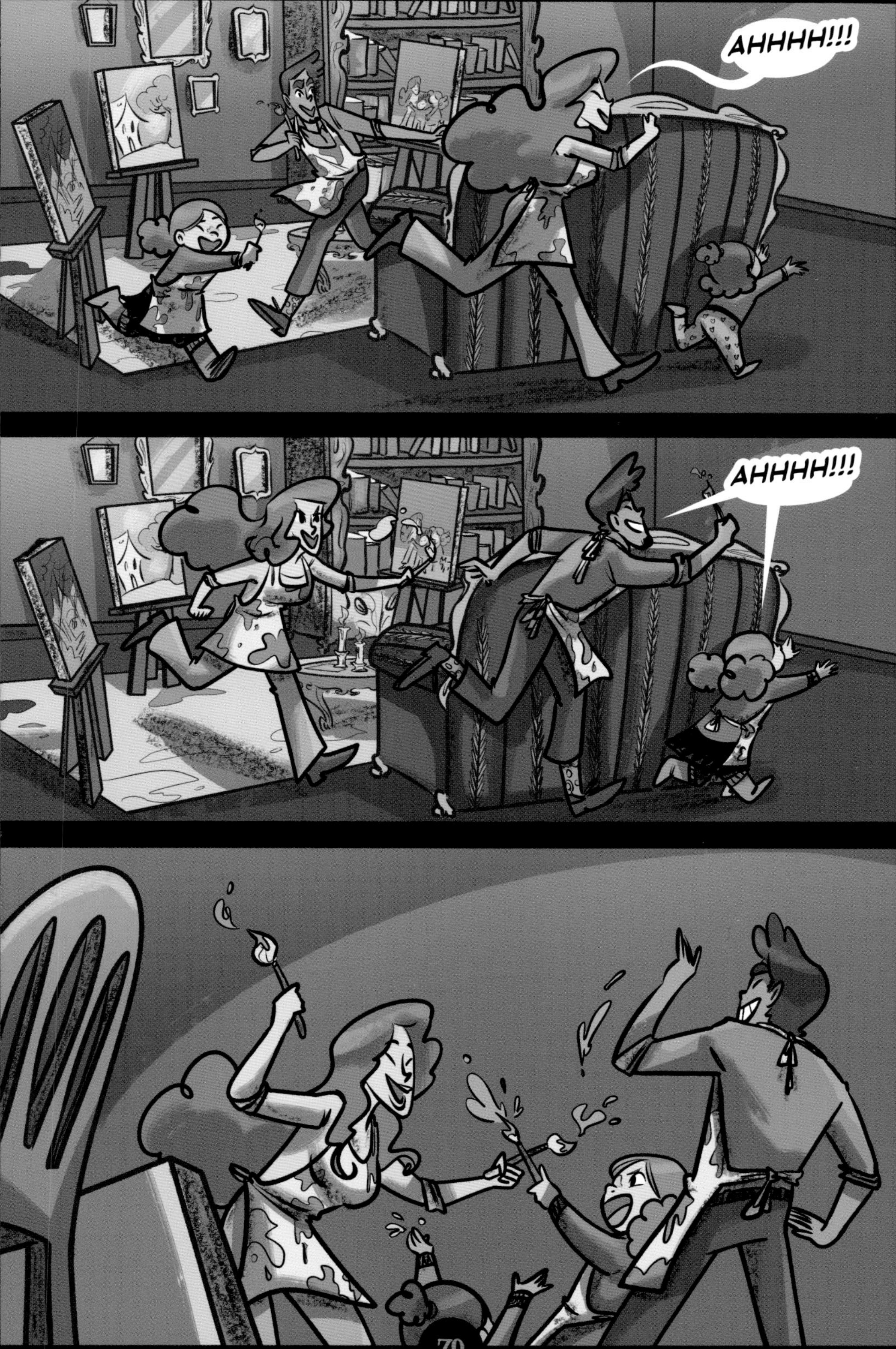
AHHHH!!!
AHHHH!!!

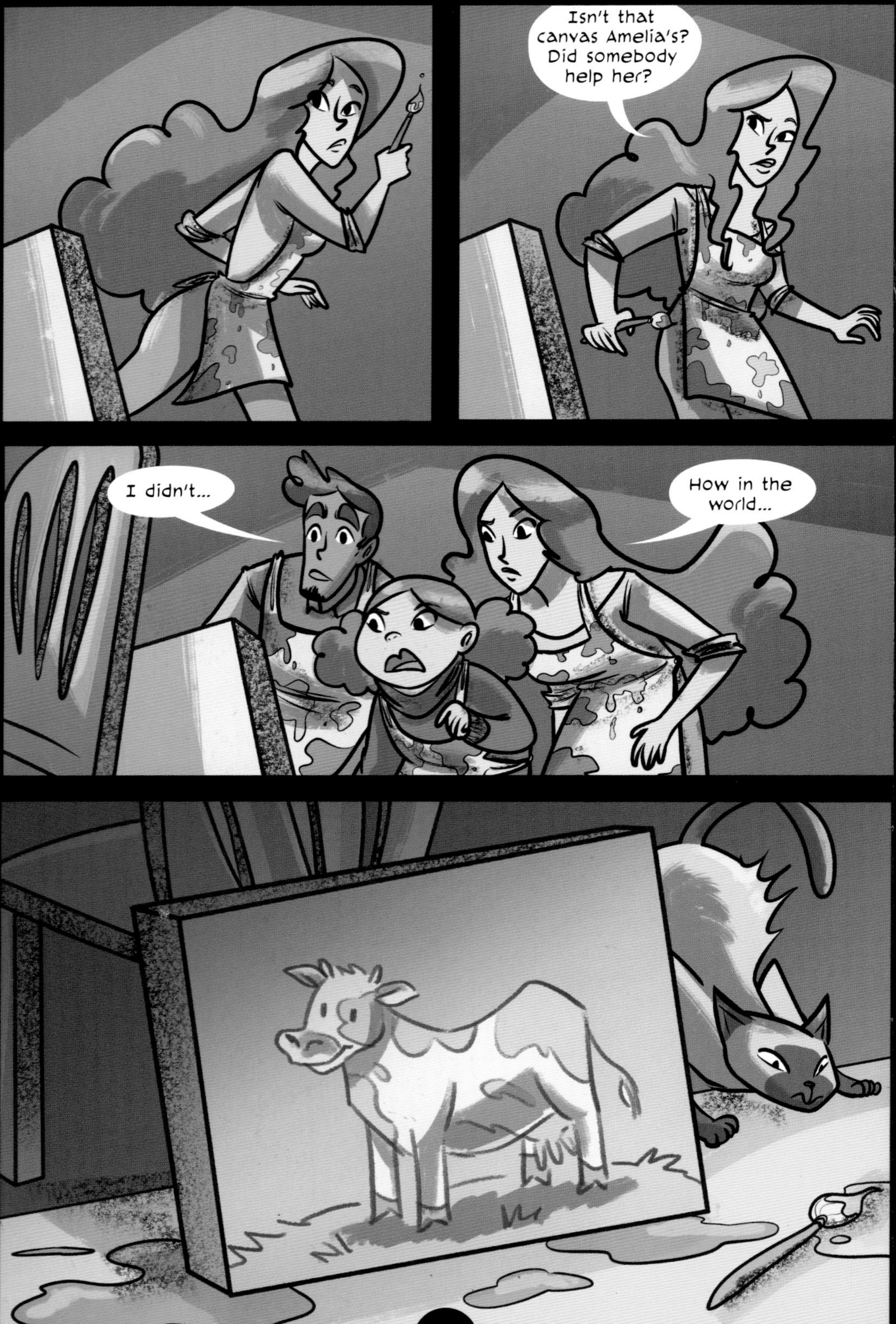

Isn't that canvas Amelia's? Did somebody help her?
I didn't...
How in the world...

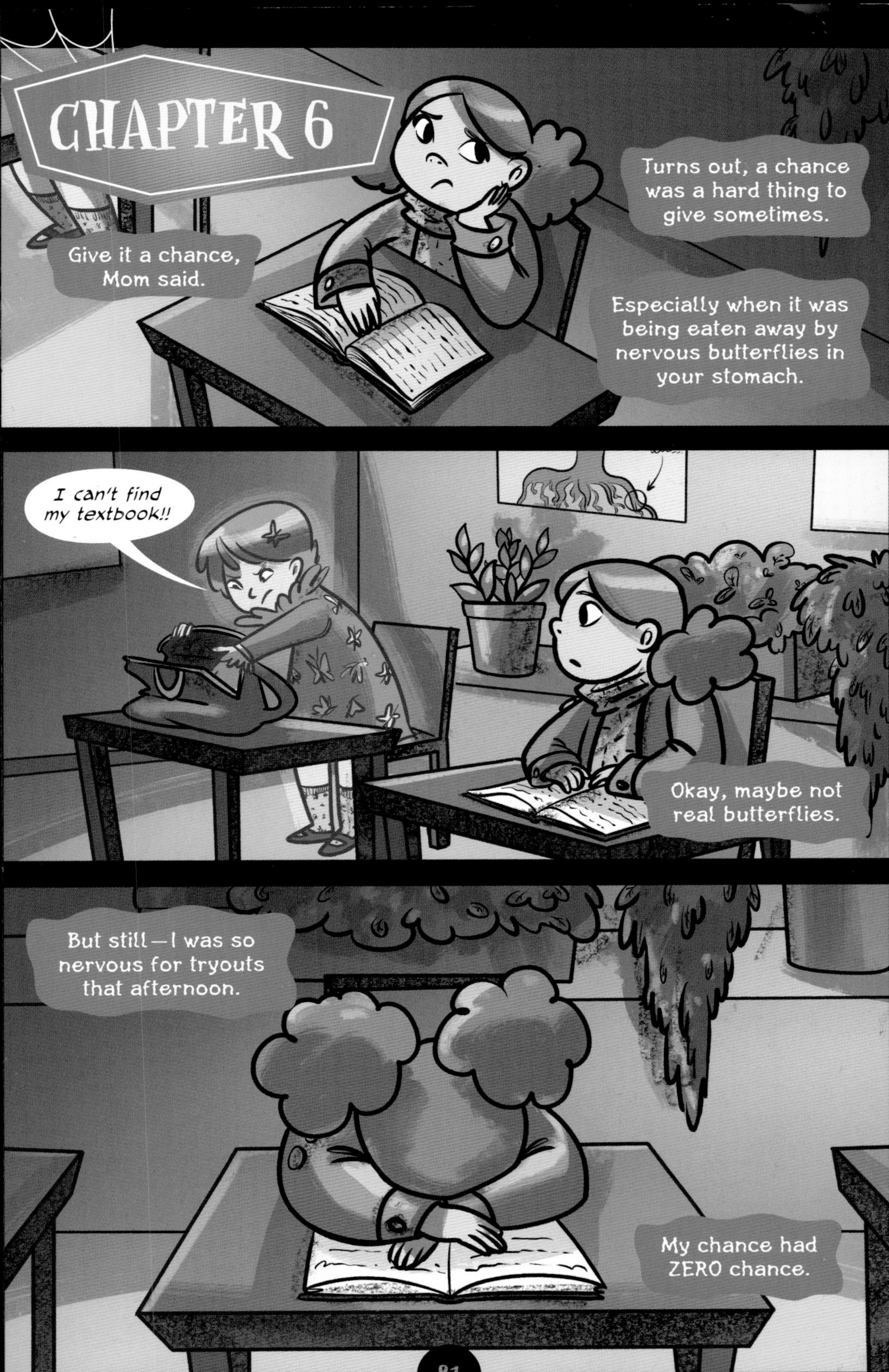
CHAPTER 6
Give it a chance, Mom said.
Turns out, a chance was a hard thing to give sometimes.
Especially when it was being eaten away by nervous butterflies in your stomach.
I can't find my textbook!!
Okay, maybe not real butterflies.
But still—I was so nervous for tryouts that afternoon.
My chance had ZERO chance.

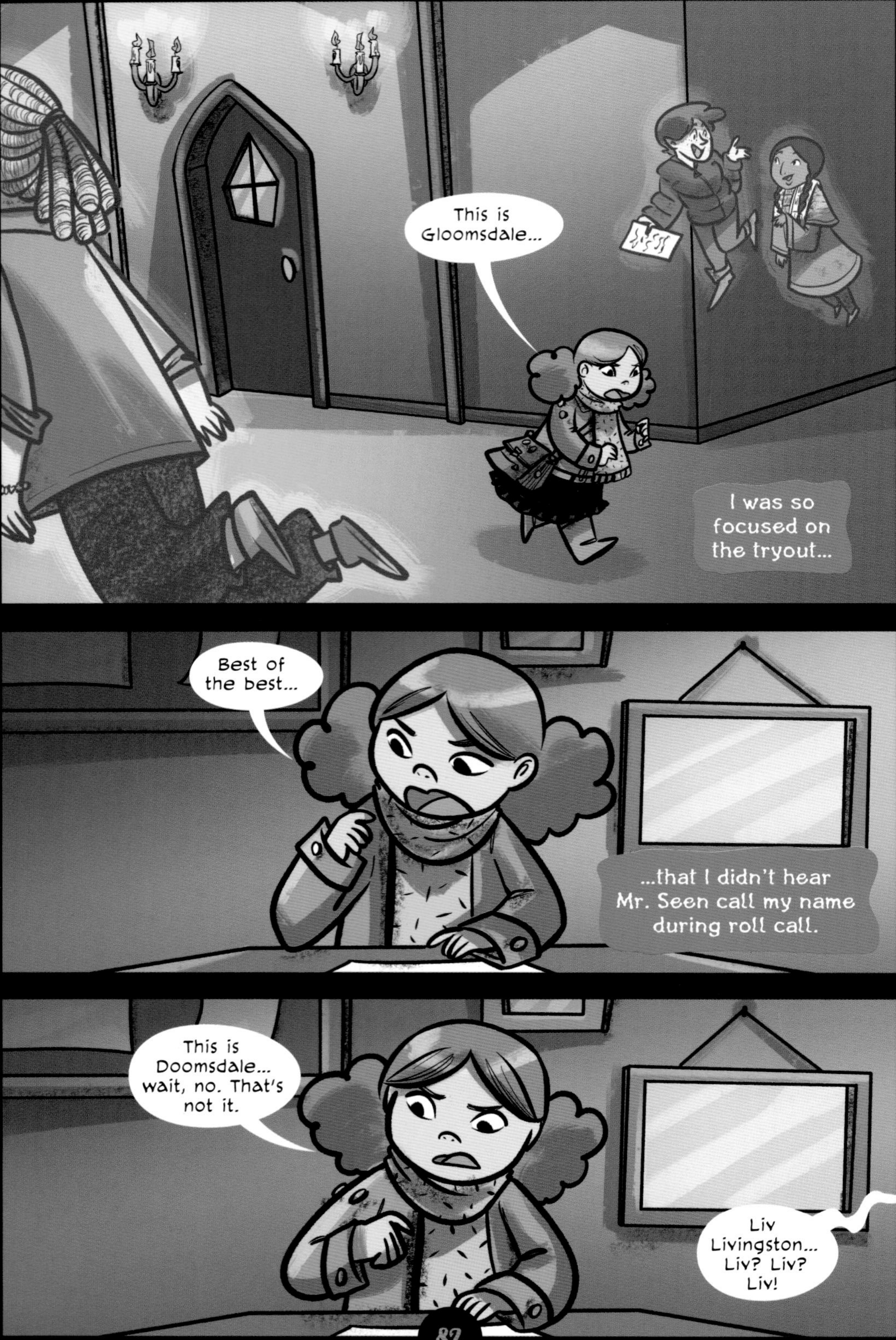
This is Gloomsdale...
I was so focused on the tryout...
Best of the best...
...that I didn't hear Mr. Seen call my name during roll call.
This is Doomsdale... wait, no. That's not it.
Liv Livingston... Liv? Liv? Liv!

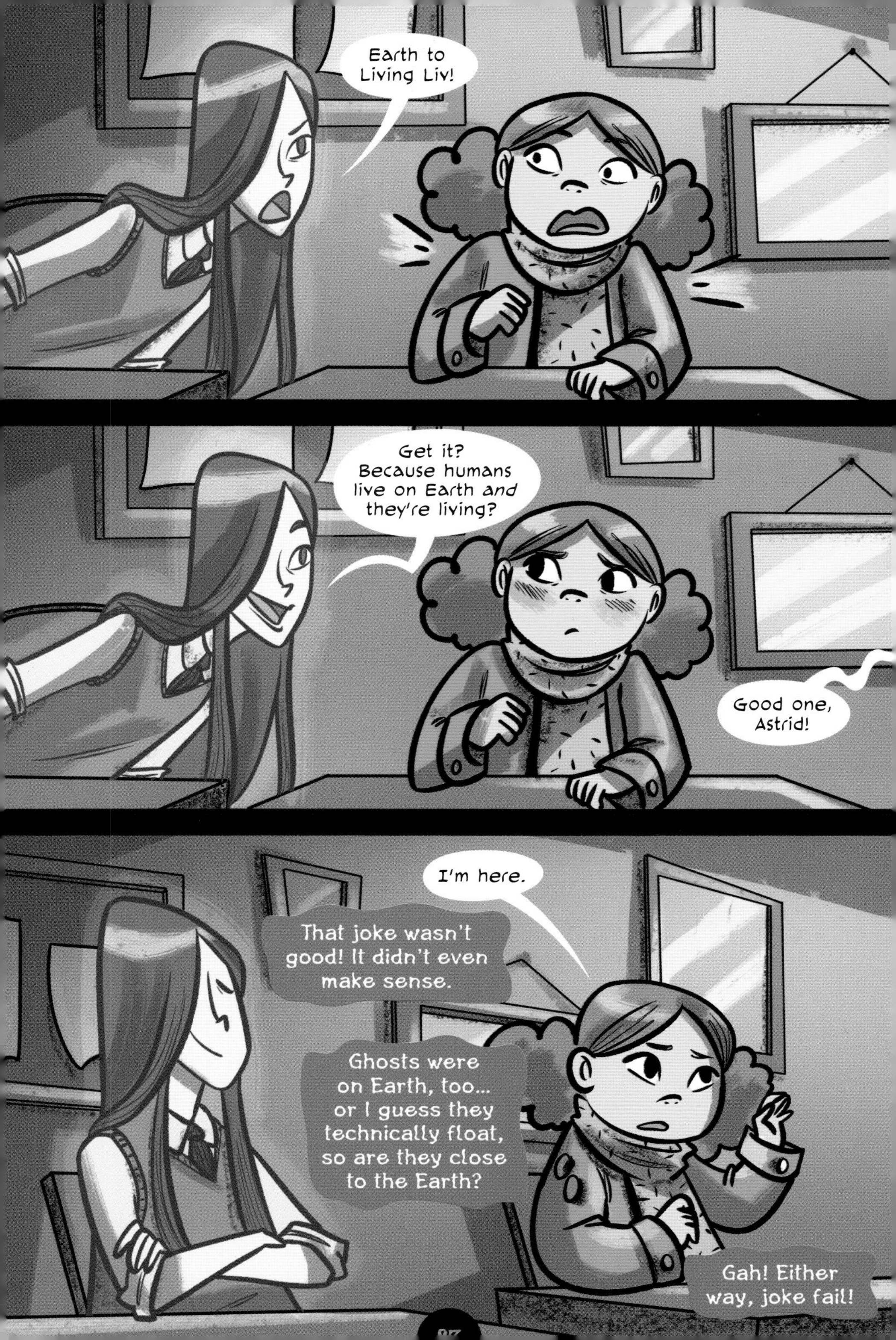
Earth to Living Liv!
Get it? Because humans live on Earth *and* they're living?
Good one, Astrid!
I'm here.
That joke wasn't good! It didn't even make sense.
Ghosts were on Earth, too... or I guess they technically float, so are they close to the Earth?
Gah! Either way, joke fail!

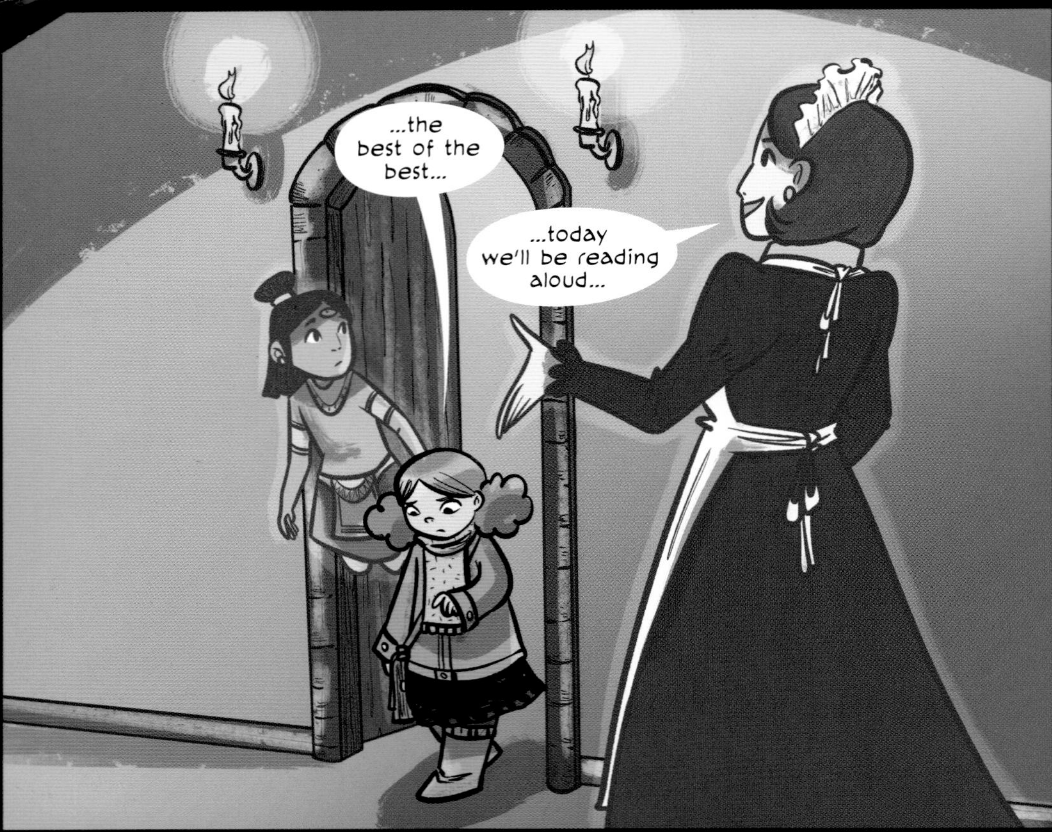
...the best of the best...
...today we'll be reading aloud...

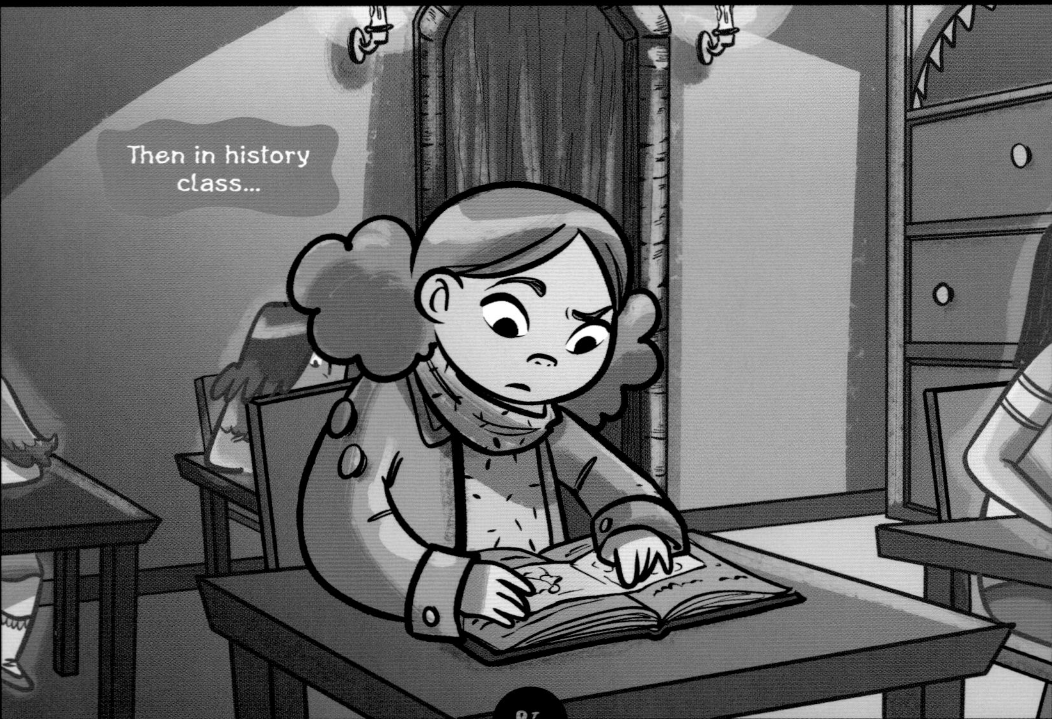
Then in history class...

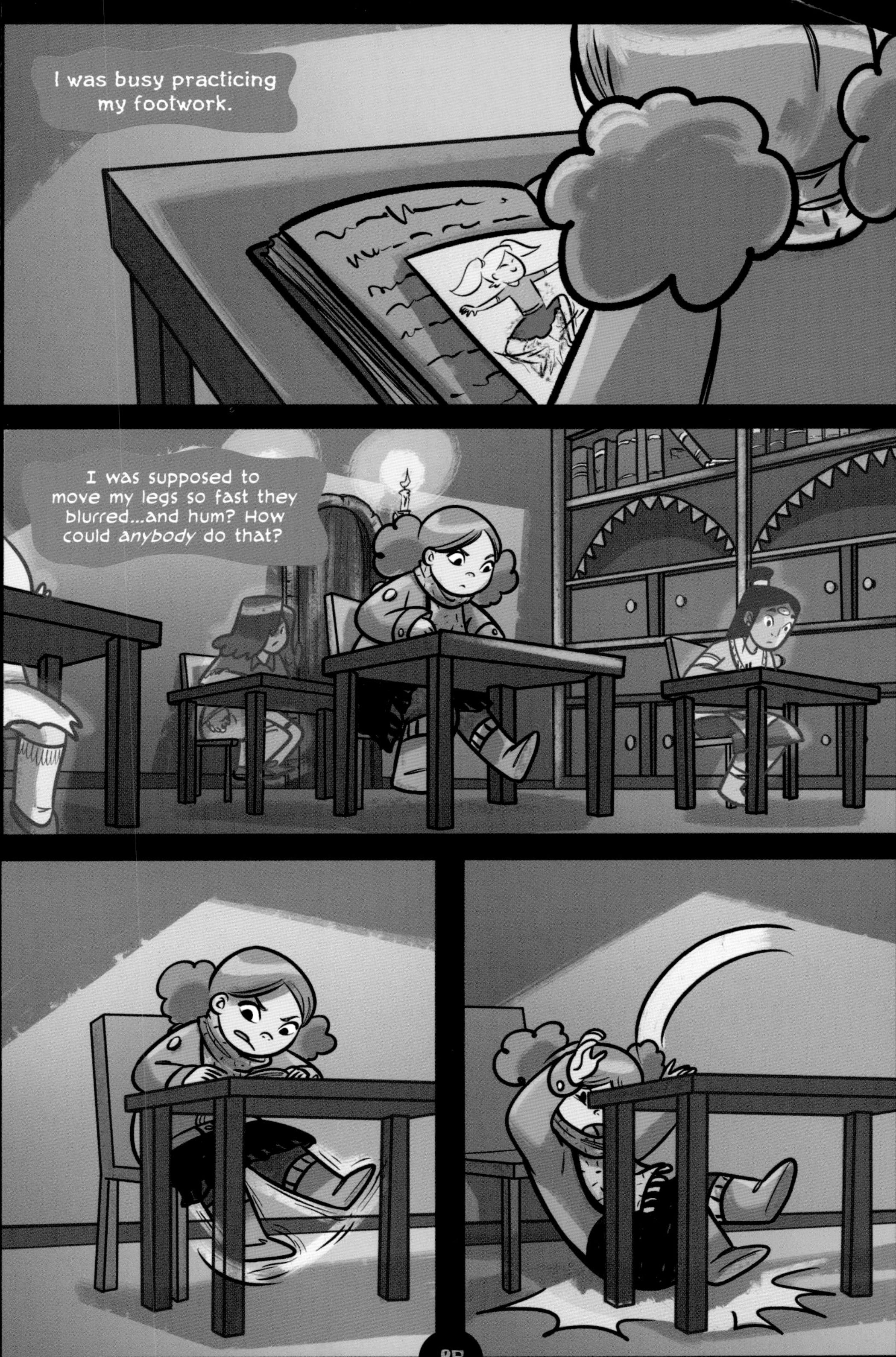
I was busy practicing my footwork.
I was supposed to move my legs so fast they blurred...and hum? How could *anybody* do that?

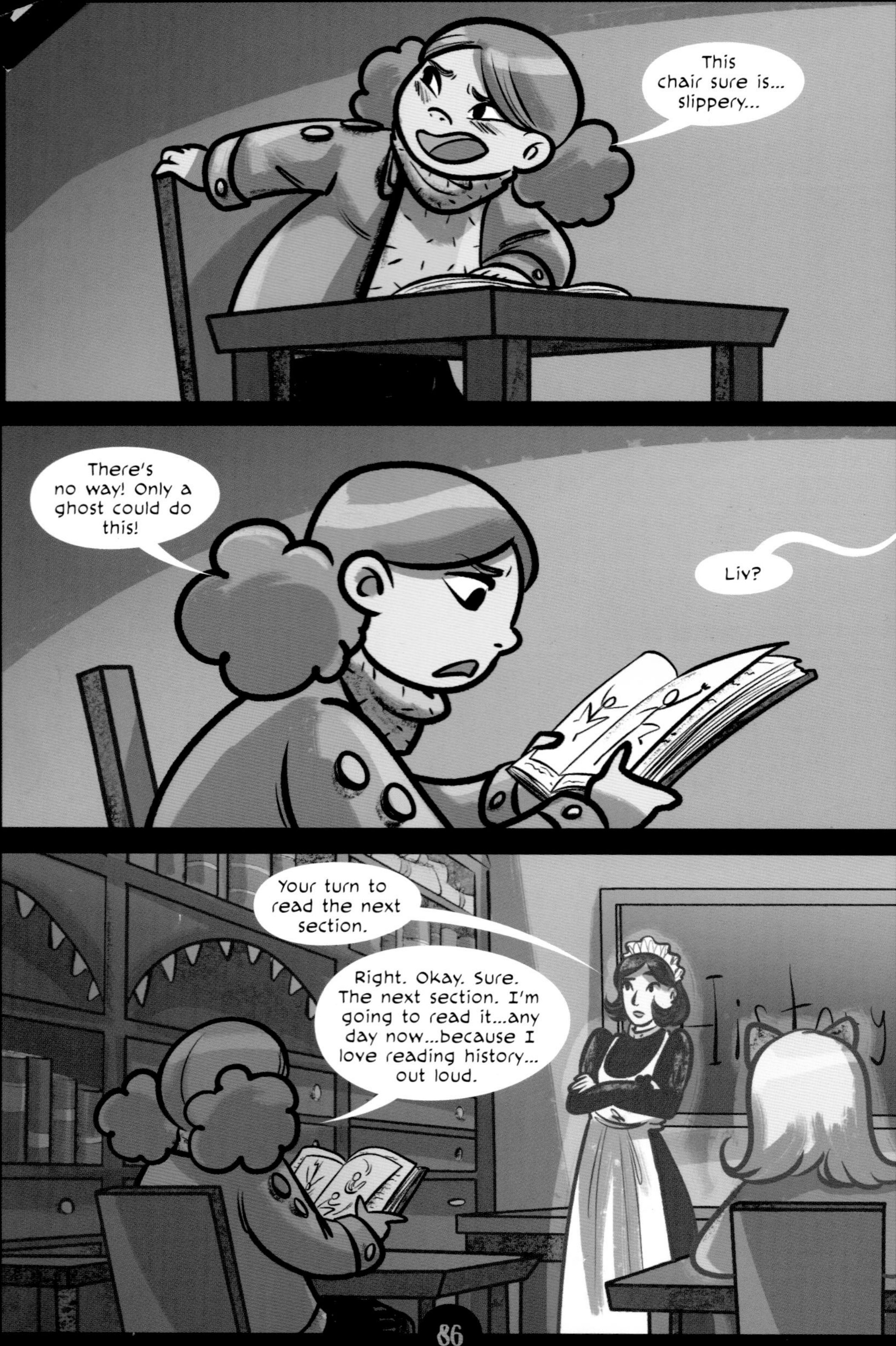
This chair sure is... slippery...
There's no way! Only a ghost could do this!
Liv?
Your turn to read the next section.
Right. Okay. Sure. The next section. I'm going to read it...any day now...because I love reading history... out loud.
History

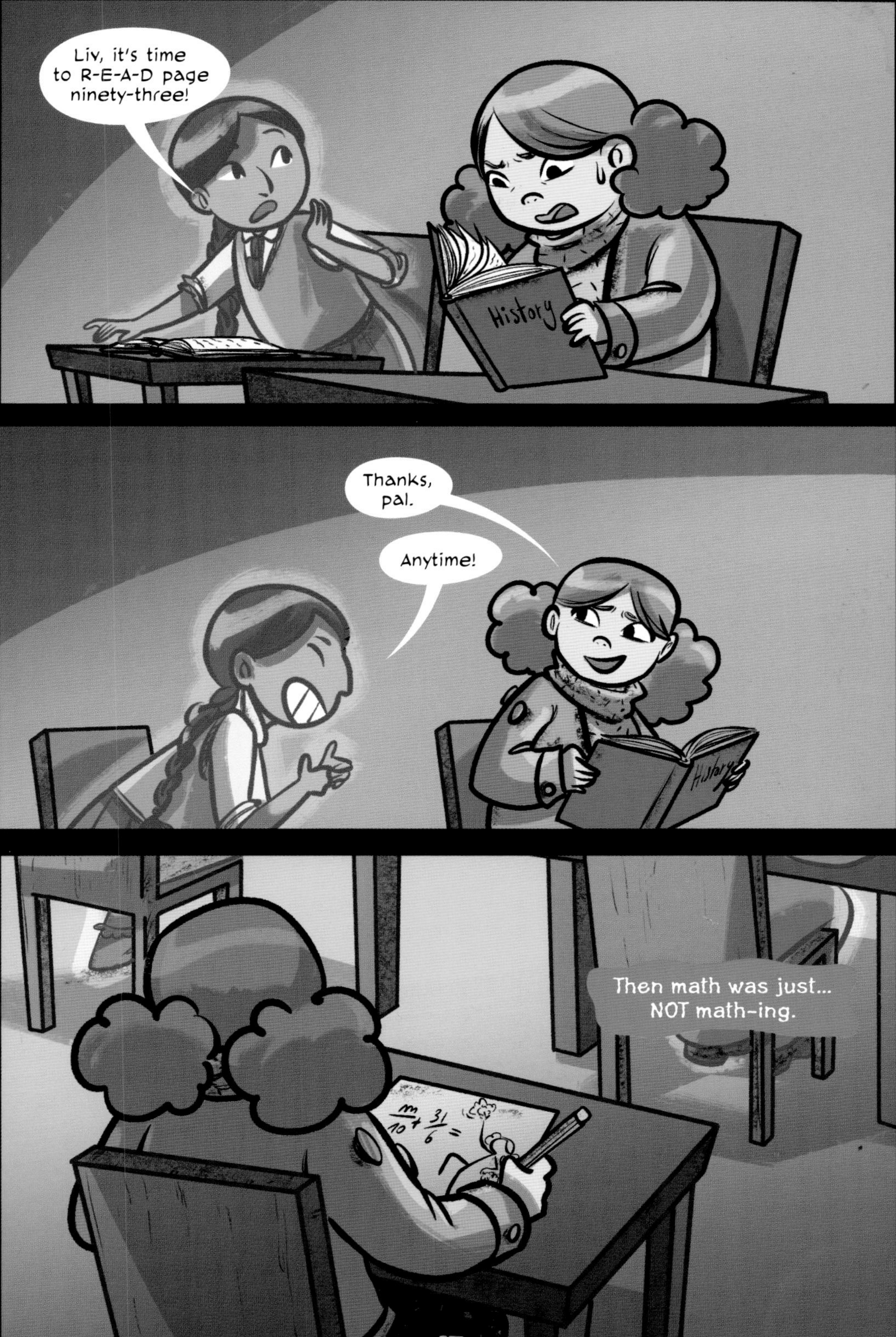
Liv, it's time to R-E-A-D page ninety-three!
History
Thanks, pal.
Anytime!
History
Then math was just... NOT math-ing.

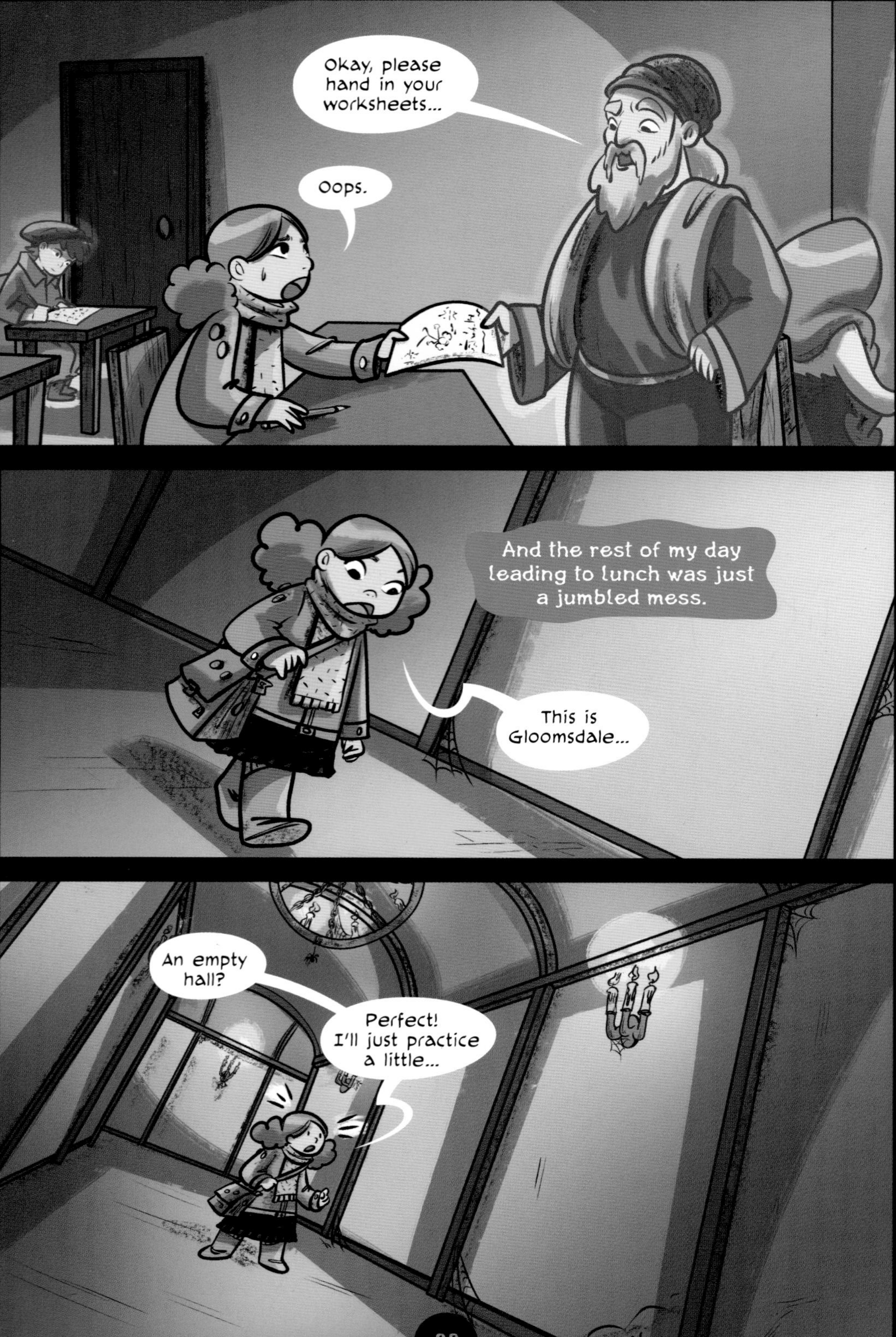
Okay, please hand in your worksheets...
Oops.
And the rest of my day leading to lunch was just a jumbled mess.
This is Gloomsdale...
An empty hall?
Perfect! I'll just practice a little...

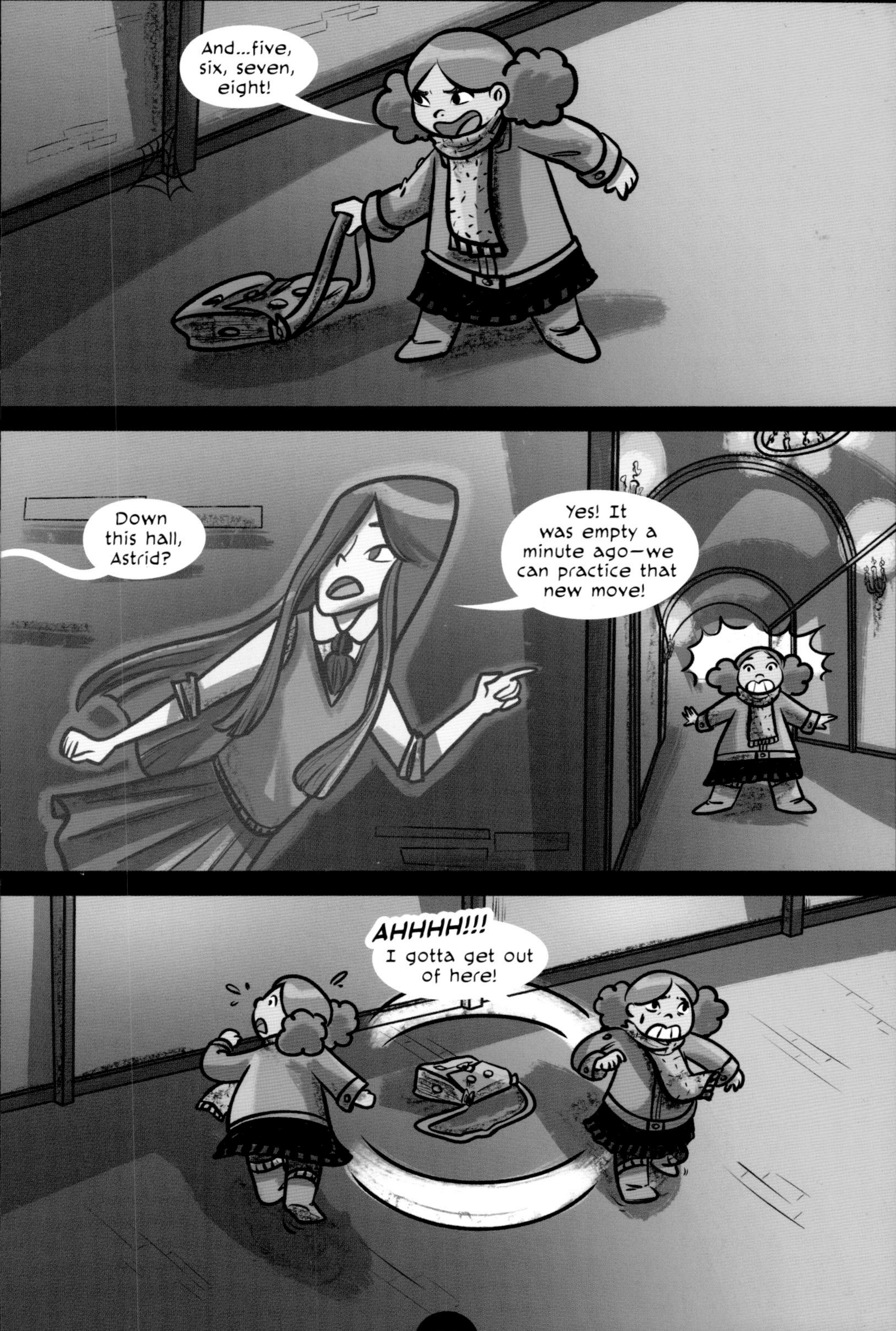
And...five, six, seven, eight!
Down this hall, Astrid?
Yes! It was empty a minute ago—we can practice that new move!
AHHHH!!!
I gotta get out of here!

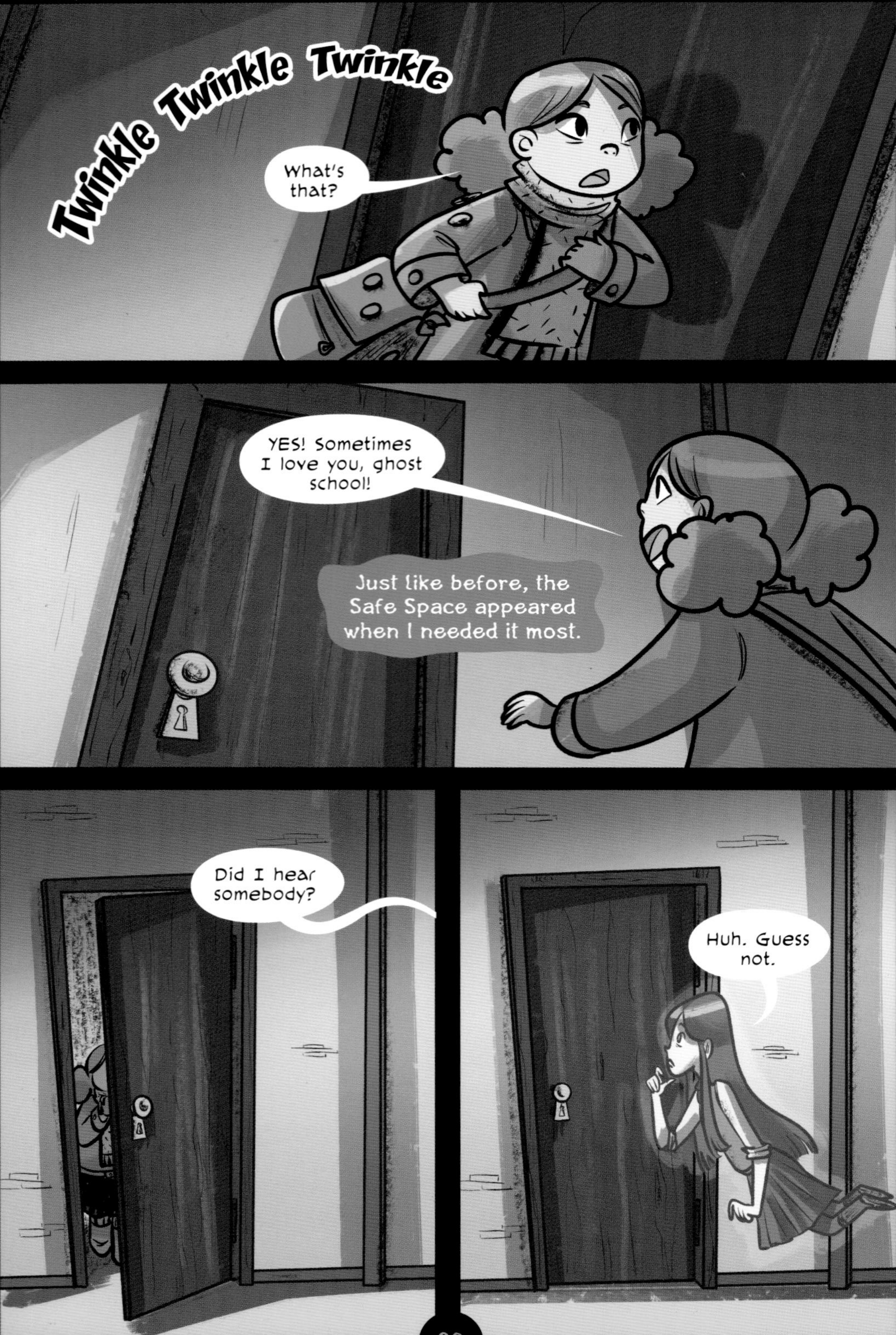
Twinkle Twinkle Twinkle
What's that?
YES! Sometimes I love you, ghost school!
Just like before, the Safe Space appeared when I needed it most.
Did I hear somebody?
Huh. Guess not.

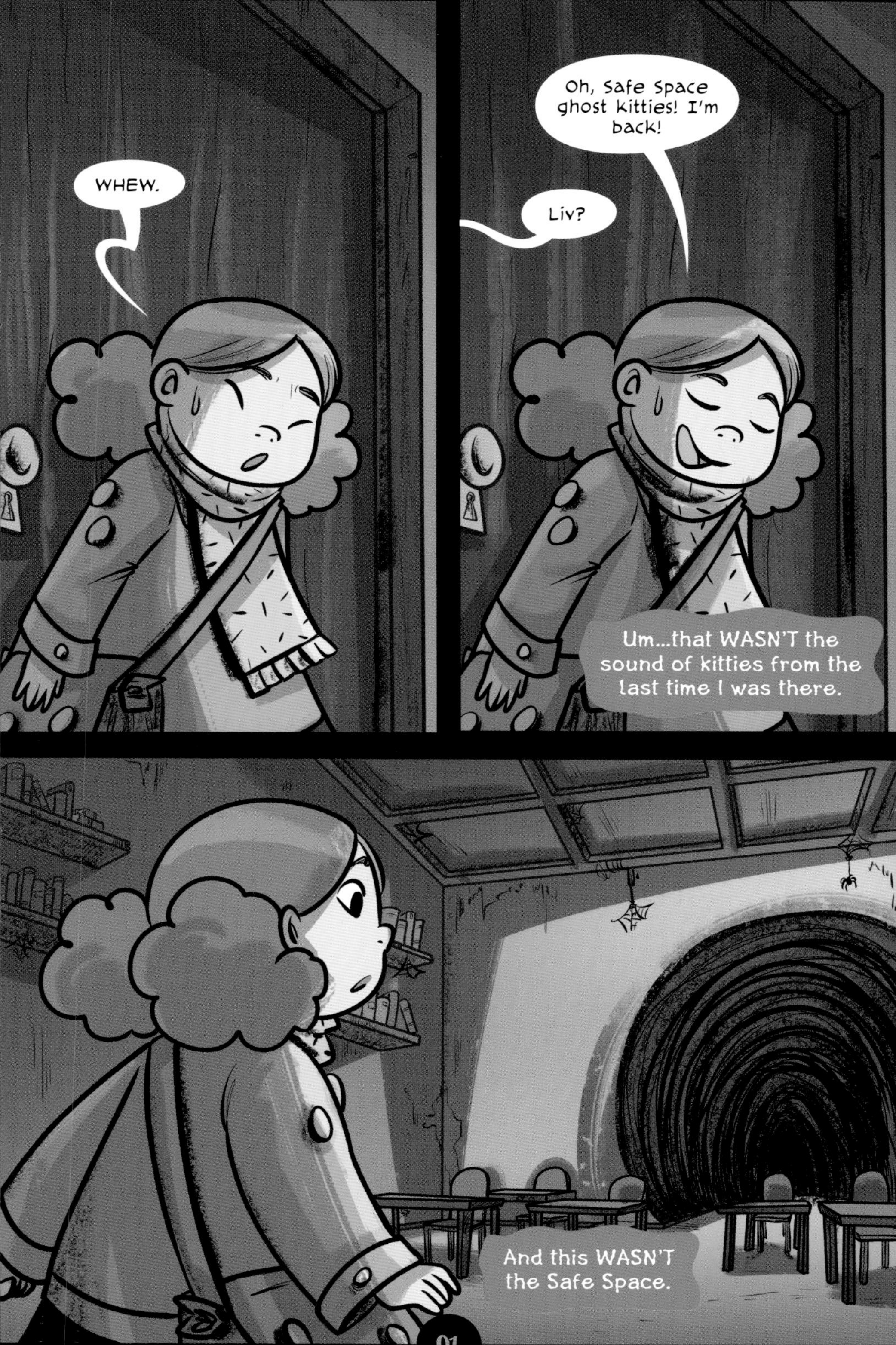
WHEW.
Oh, Safe Space ghost kitties! I'm back!
Liv?
Um...that WASN'T the sound of kitties from the last time I was there.
And this WASN'T the Safe Space.

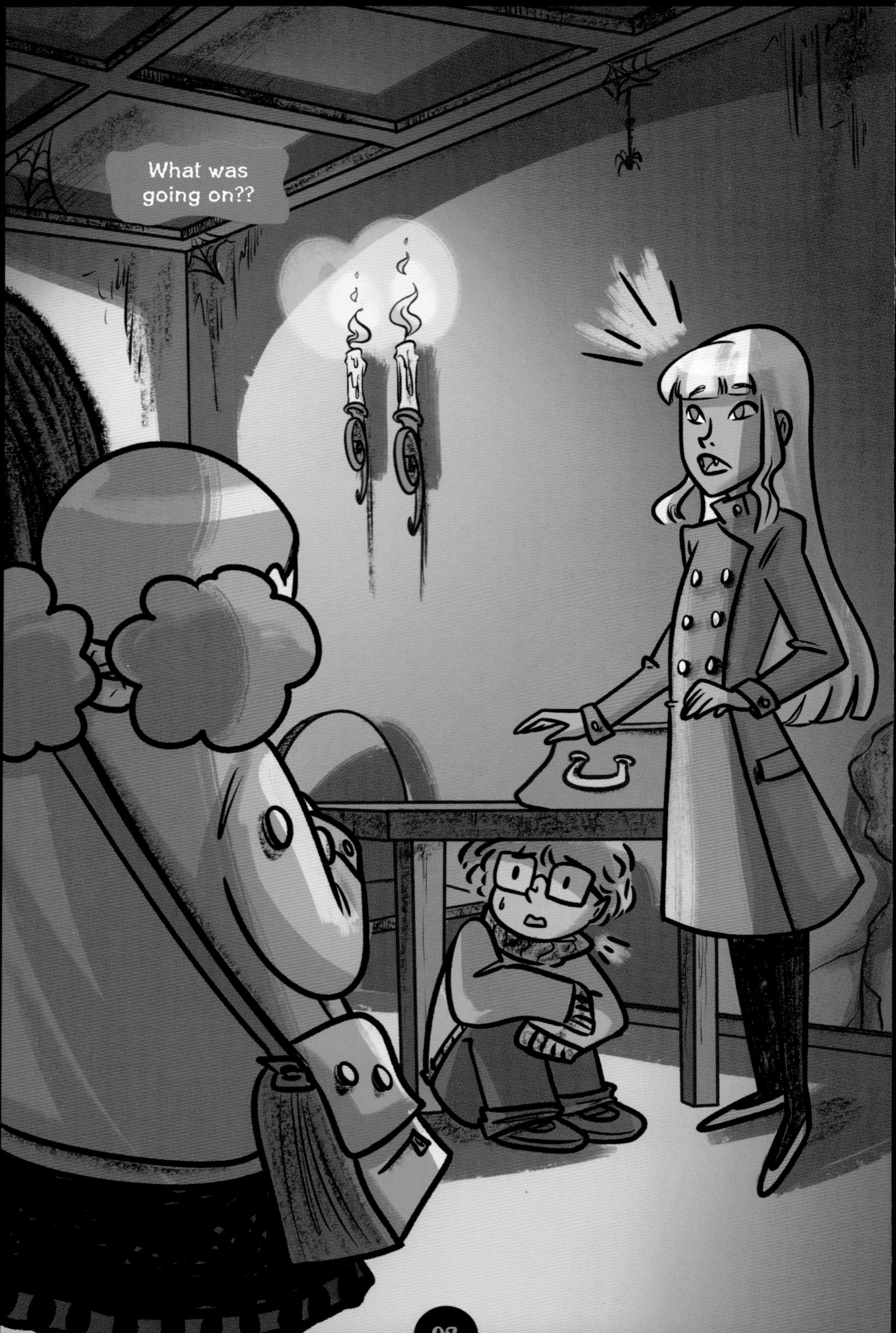
What was going on??

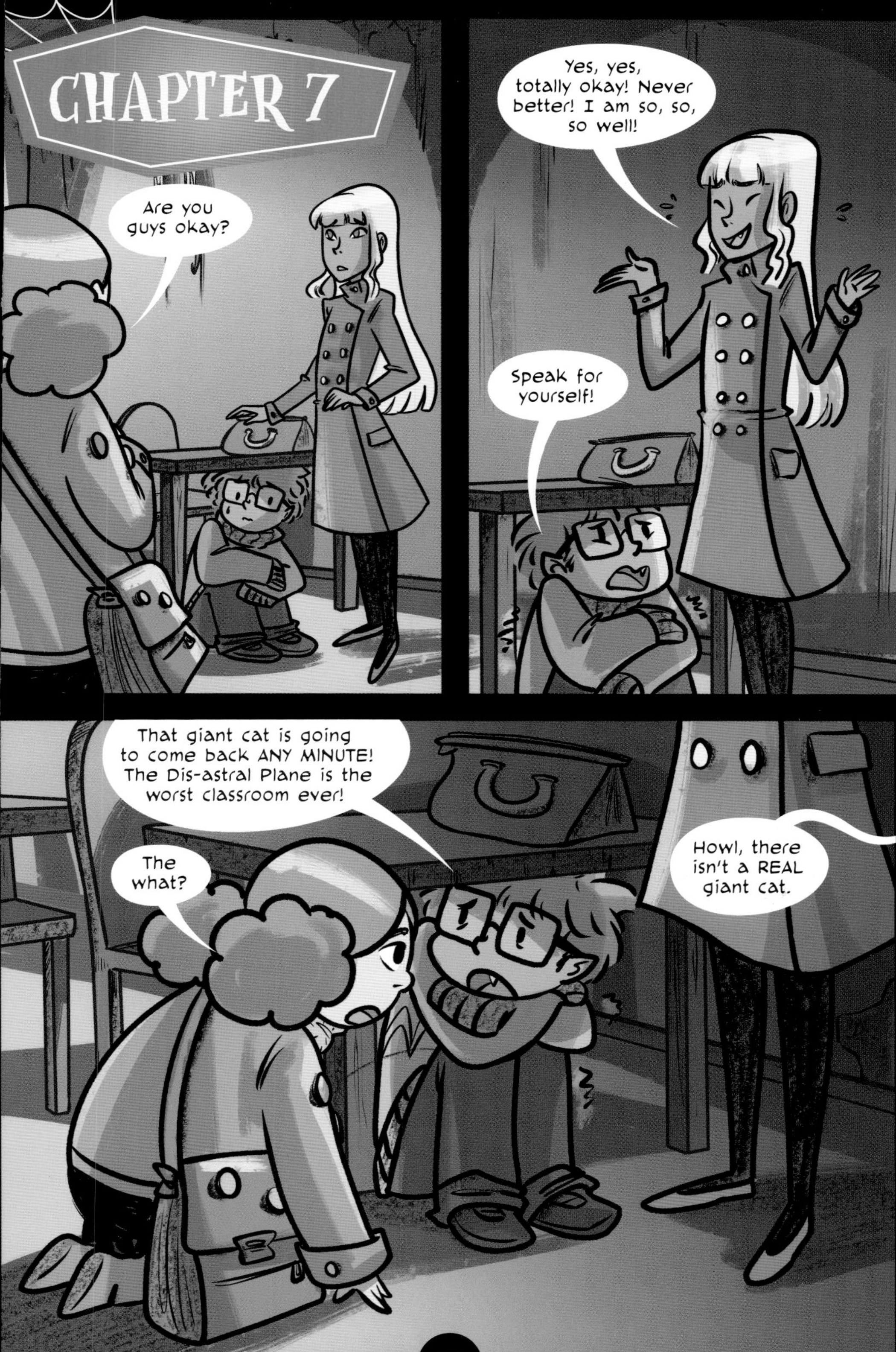
CHAPTER 7
Are you guys okay?
Yes, yes, totally okay! Never better! I am so, so, so well!
Speak for yourself!
That giant cat is going to come back ANY MINUTE! The Dis-astral Plane is the worst classroom ever!
The what?
Howl, there isn't a REAL giant cat.

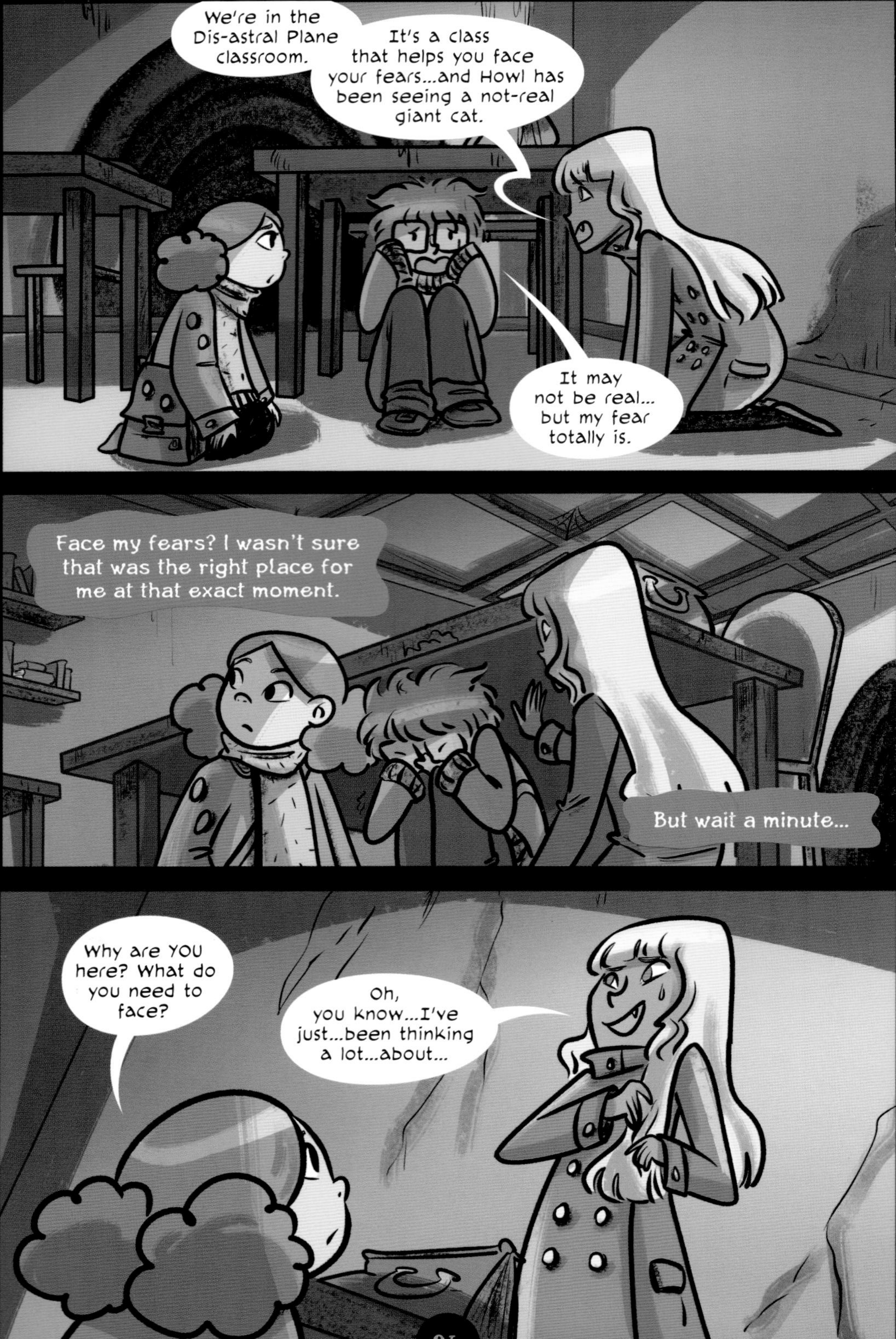
We're in the Dis-astral Plane classroom.
It's a class that helps you face your fears...and Howl has been seeing a not-real giant cat.
It may not be real... but my fear totally is.
Face my fears? I wasn't sure that was the right place for me at that exact moment.
But wait a minute...
Why are YOU here? What do you need to face?
Oh, you know...I've just...been thinking a lot...about...

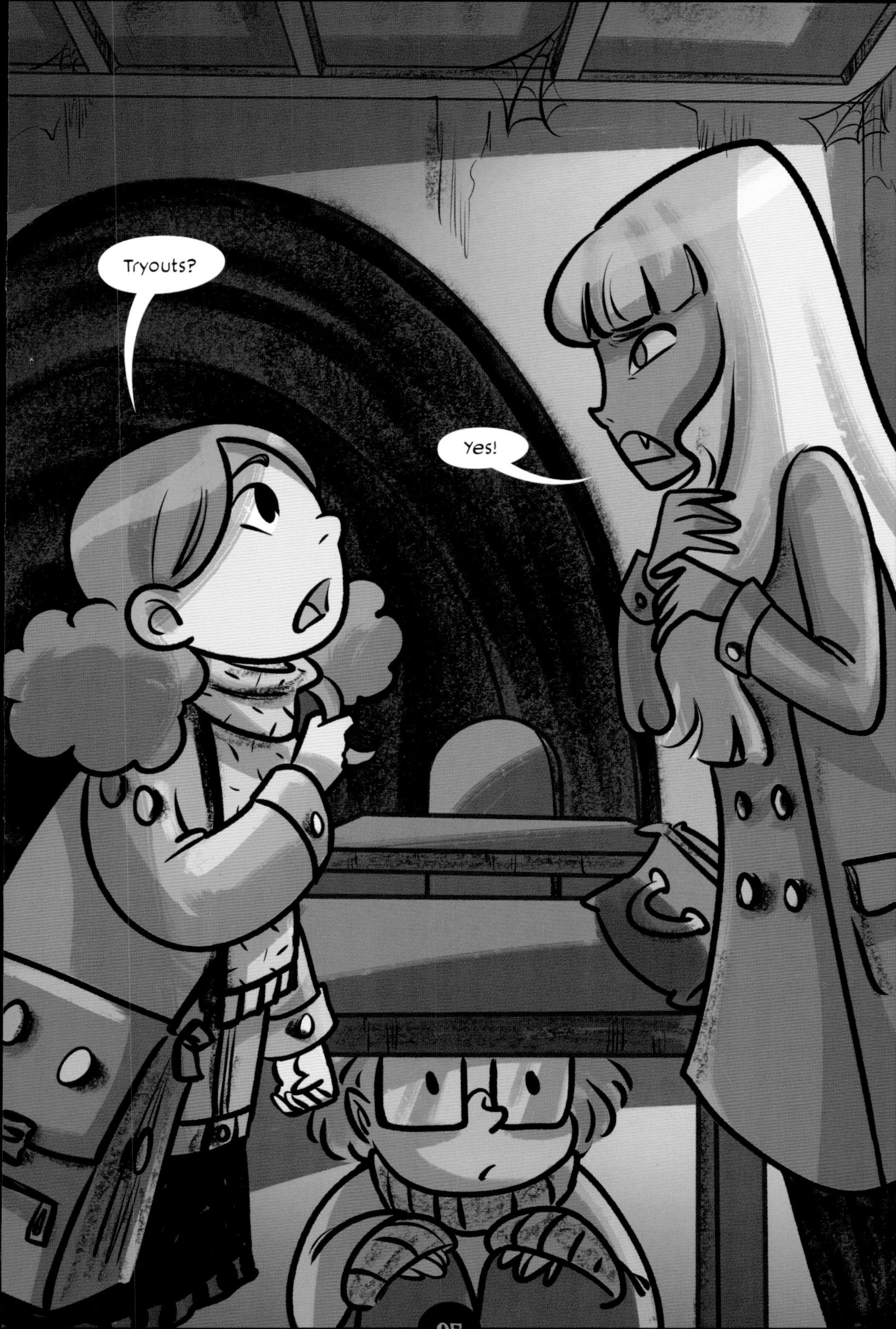
Tryouts?
Yes!

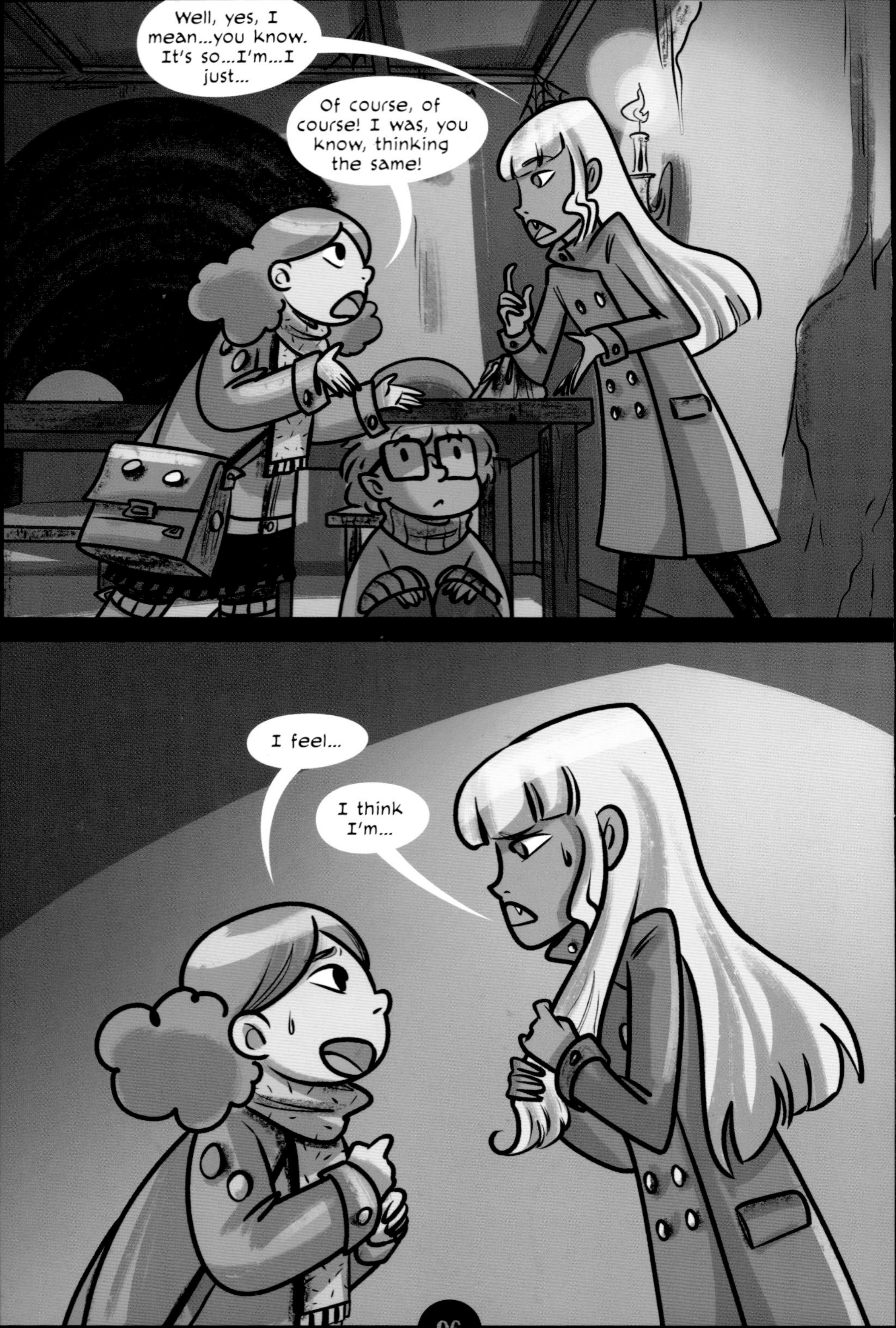
Well, yes, I mean...you know. It's so...I'm...I just...
Of course, of course! I was, you know, thinking the same!
I feel...
I think I'm...

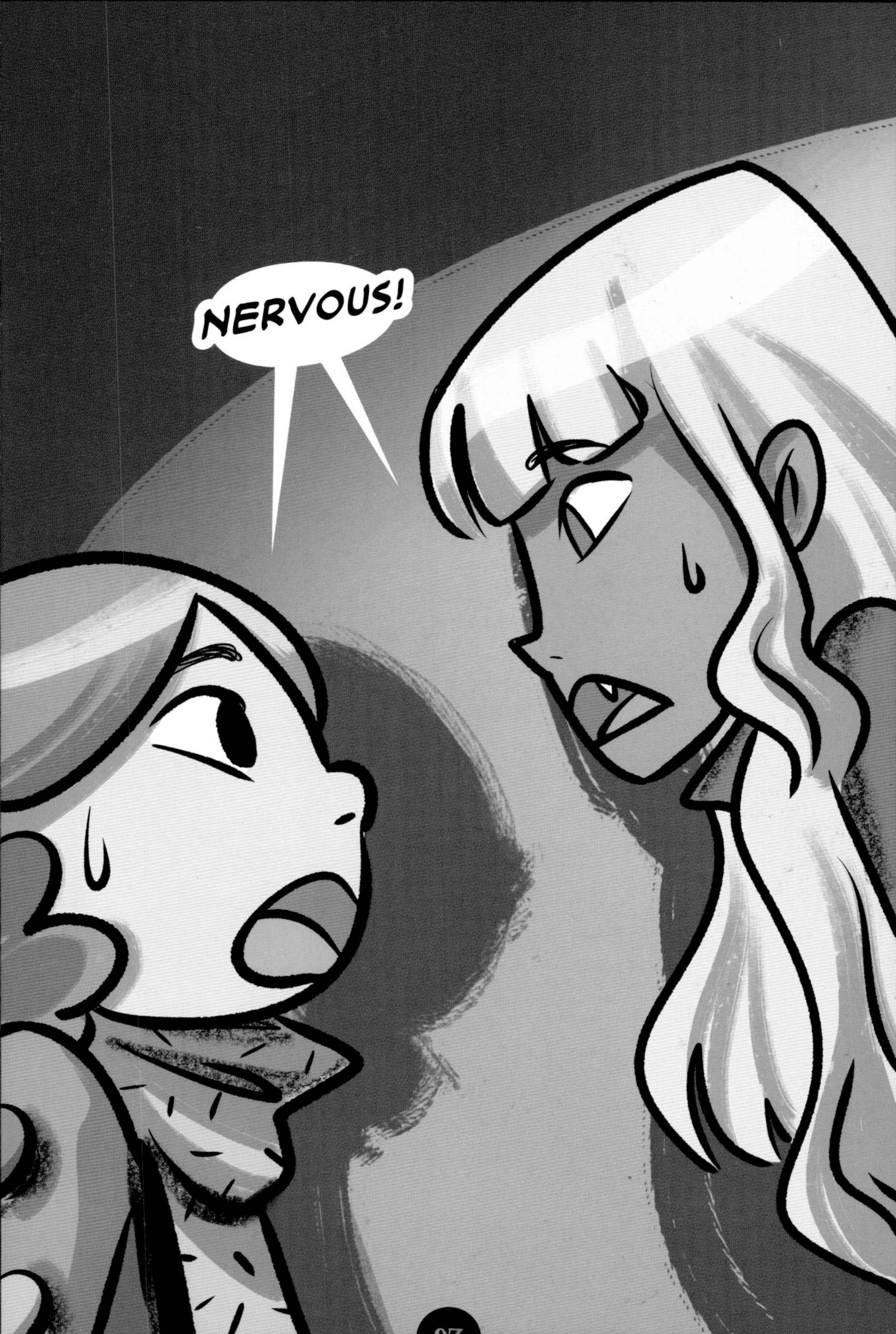
NERVOUS!

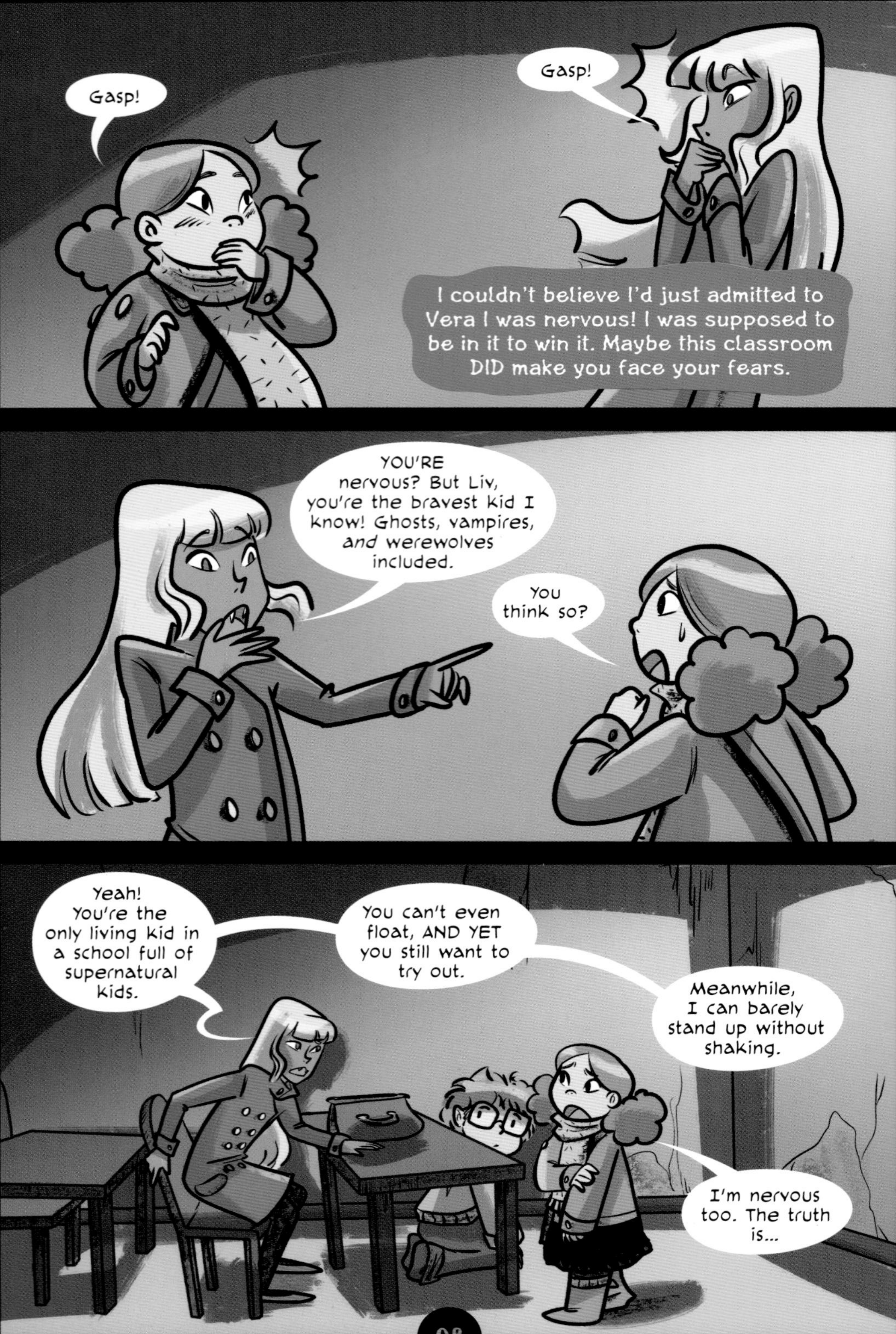
Gasp!
Gasp!
I couldn't believe I'd just admitted to Vera I was nervous! I was supposed to be in it to win it. Maybe this classroom DID make you face your fears.
YOU'RE nervous? But Liv, you're the bravest kid I know! Ghosts, vampires, and werewolves included.
You think so?
Yeah! You're the only living kid in a school full of supernatural kids.
You can't even float, AND YET you still want to try out.
Meanwhile, I can barely stand up without shaking.
I'm nervous too. The truth is...

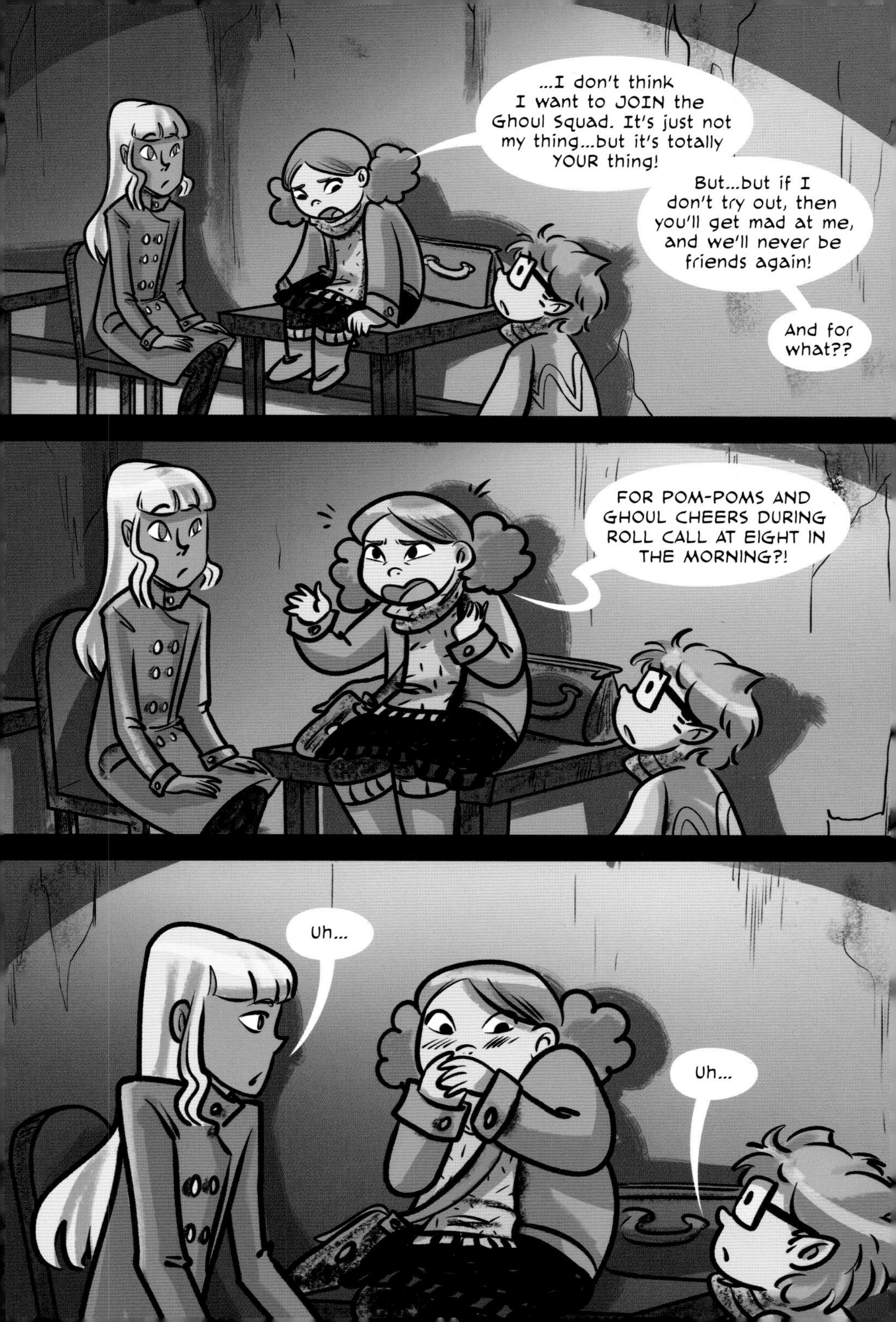

...I don't think I want to JOIN the Ghoul Squad. It's just not my thing...but it's totally YOUR thing!
But...but if I don't try out, then you'll get mad at me, and we'll never be friends again!
And for what??
FOR POM-POMS AND GHOUL CHEERS DURING ROLL CALL AT EIGHT IN THE MORNING?!
Uh...
Uh...

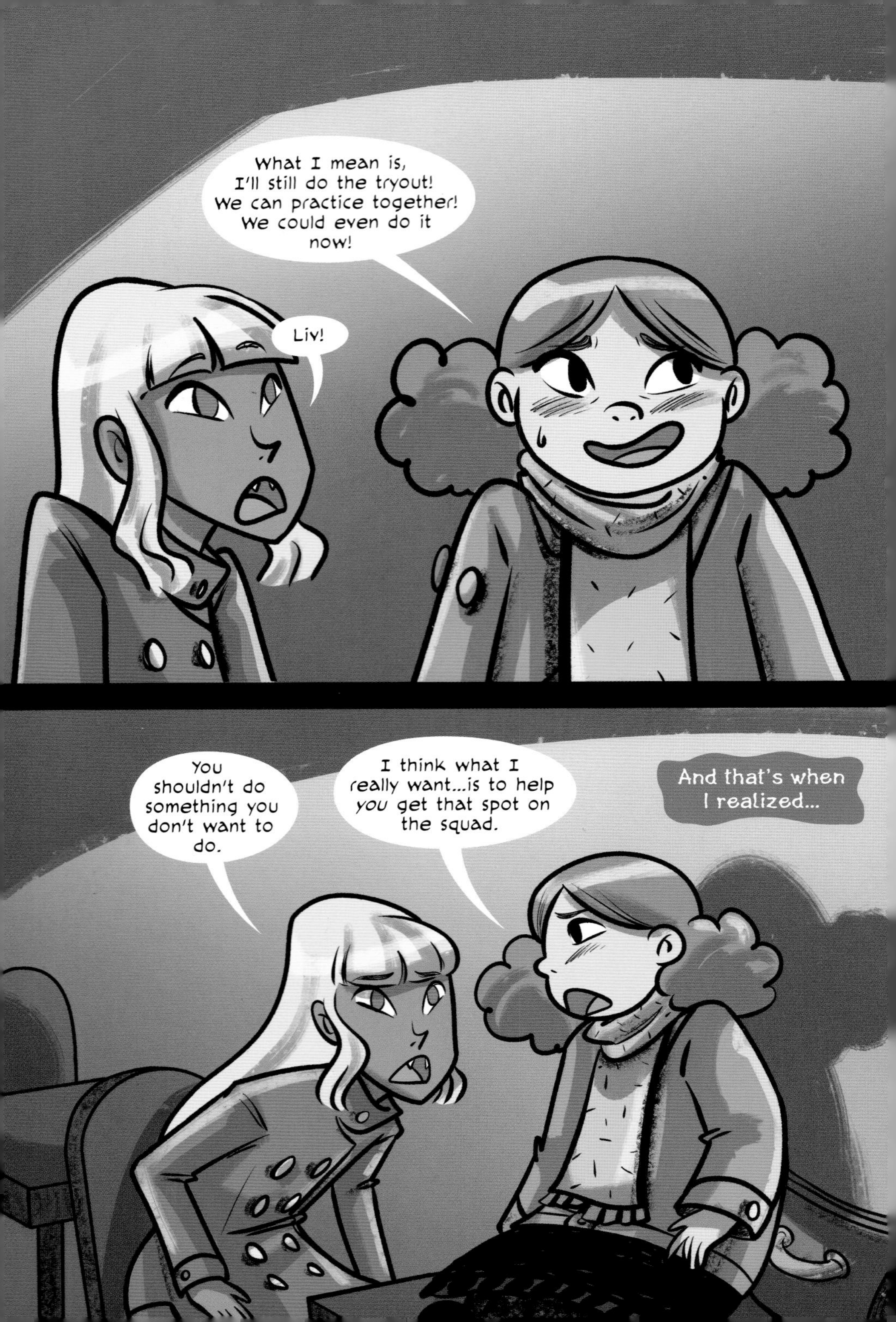
What I mean is, I'll still do the tryout! We can practice together! We could even do it now!
Liv!
You shouldn't do something you don't want to do.
I think what I really want...is to help *you* get that spot on the squad.
And that's when I realized...

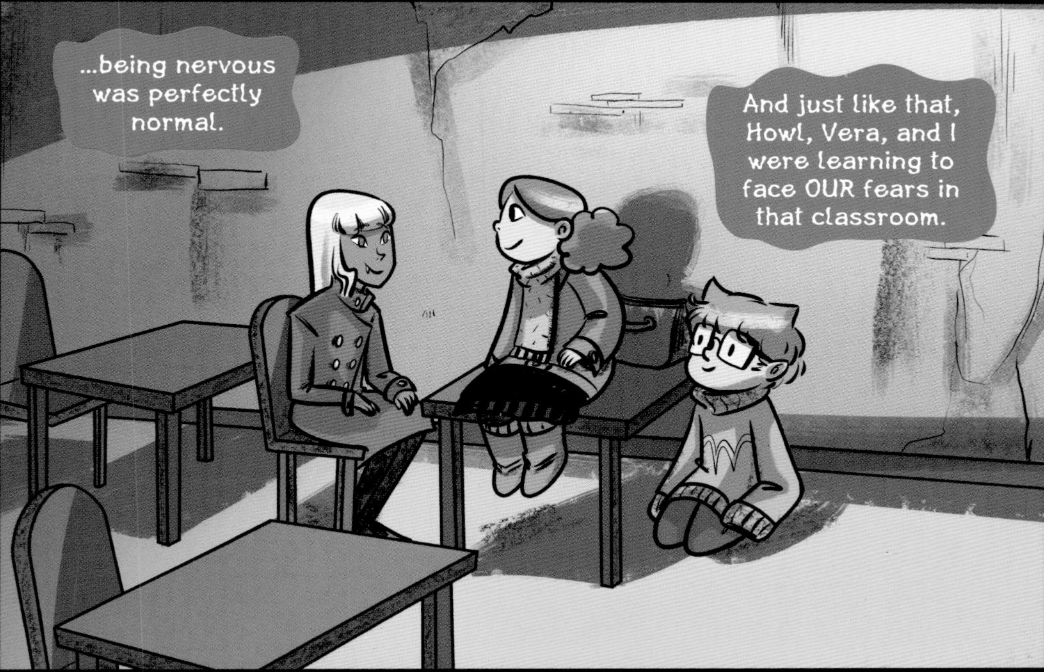
...being nervous was perfectly normal.
And just like that, Howl, Vera, and I were learning to face OUR fears in that classroom.

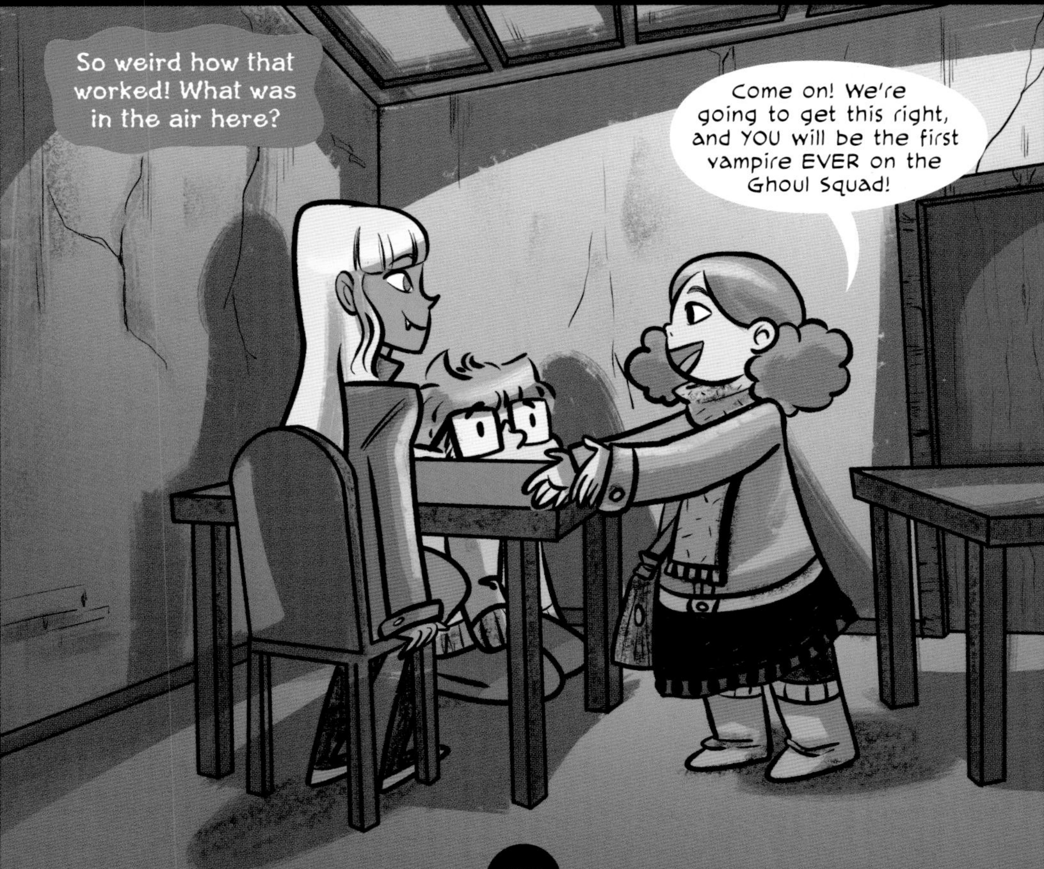
So weird how that worked! What was in the air here?
Come on! We're going to get this right, and YOU will be the first vampire EVER on the Ghoul Squad!

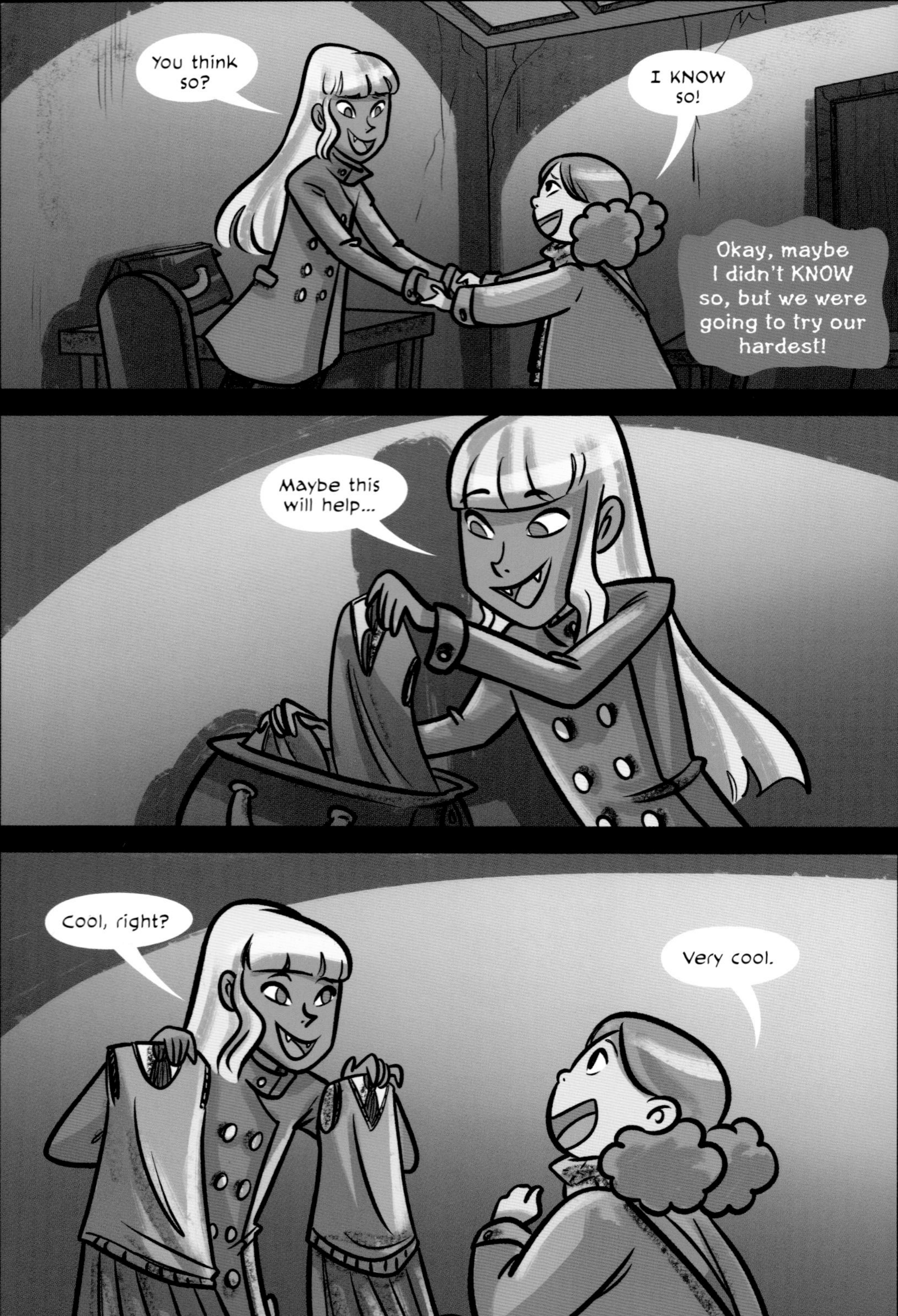
You think so?
I KNOW so!
Okay, maybe I didn't KNOW so, but we were going to try our hardest!
Maybe this will help...
Cool, right?
Very cool.

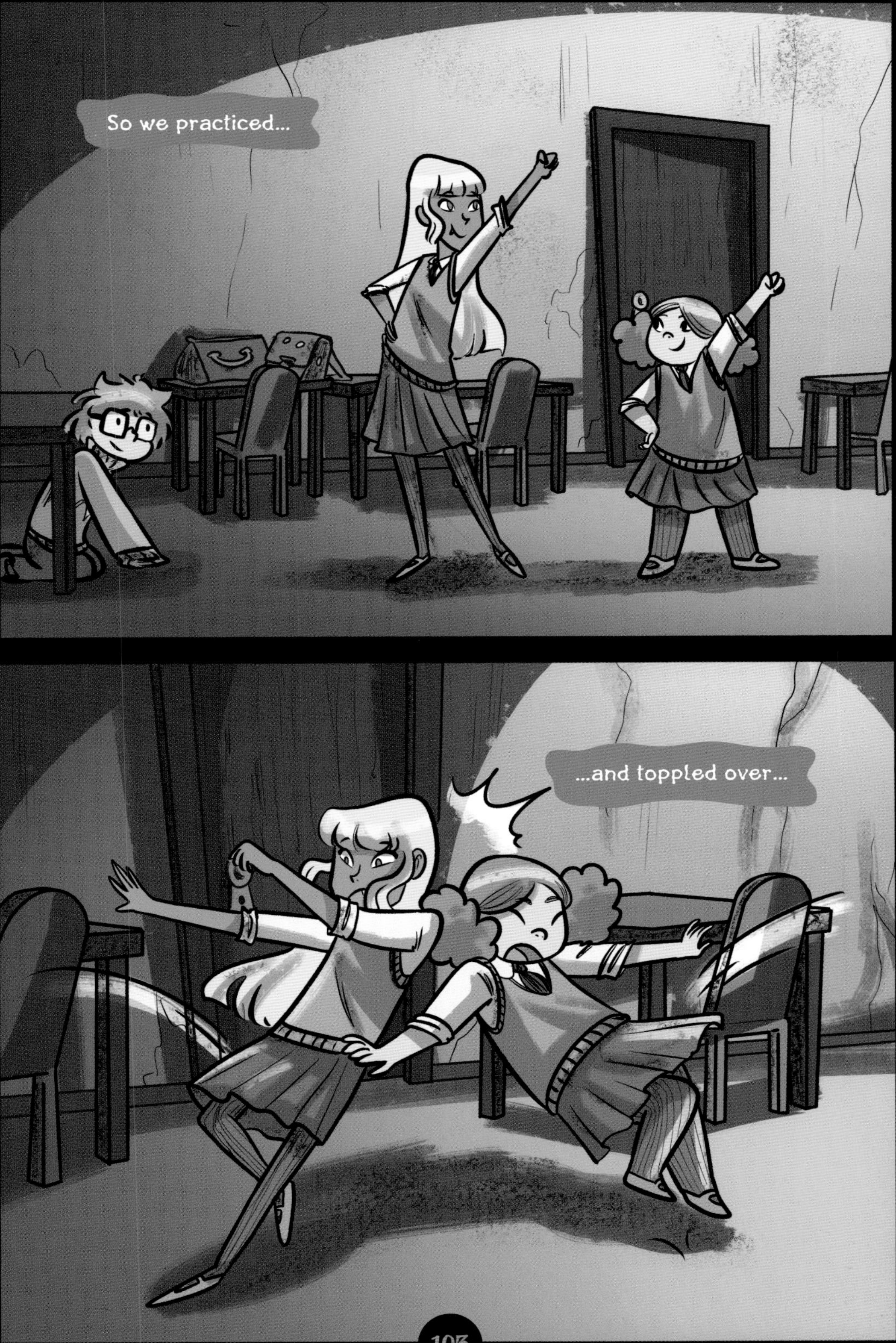
So we practiced...
...and toppled over...

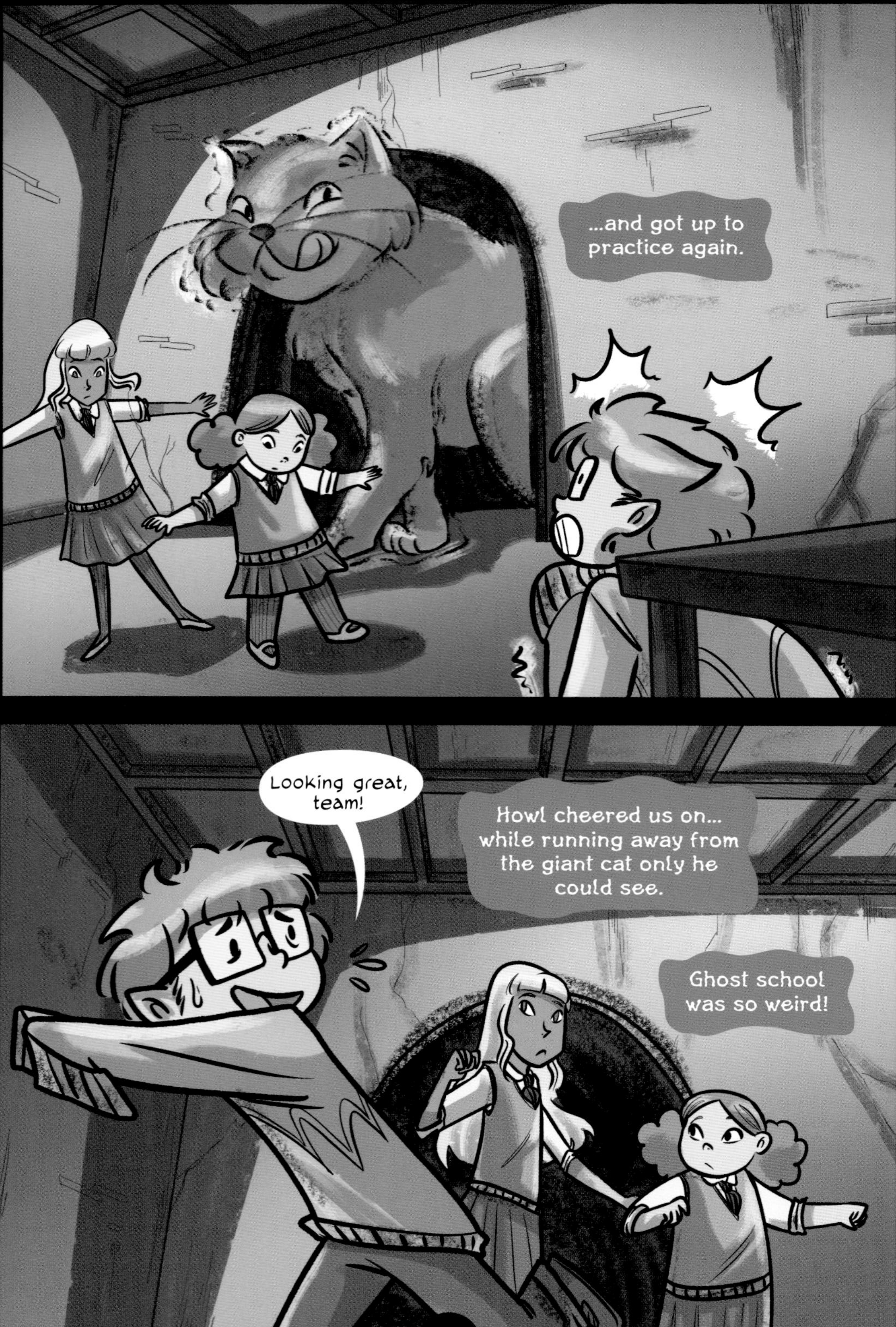
...and got up to practice again.
Looking great, team!
Howl cheered us on... while running away from the giant cat only he could see.
Ghost school was so weird!

CHAPTER 8

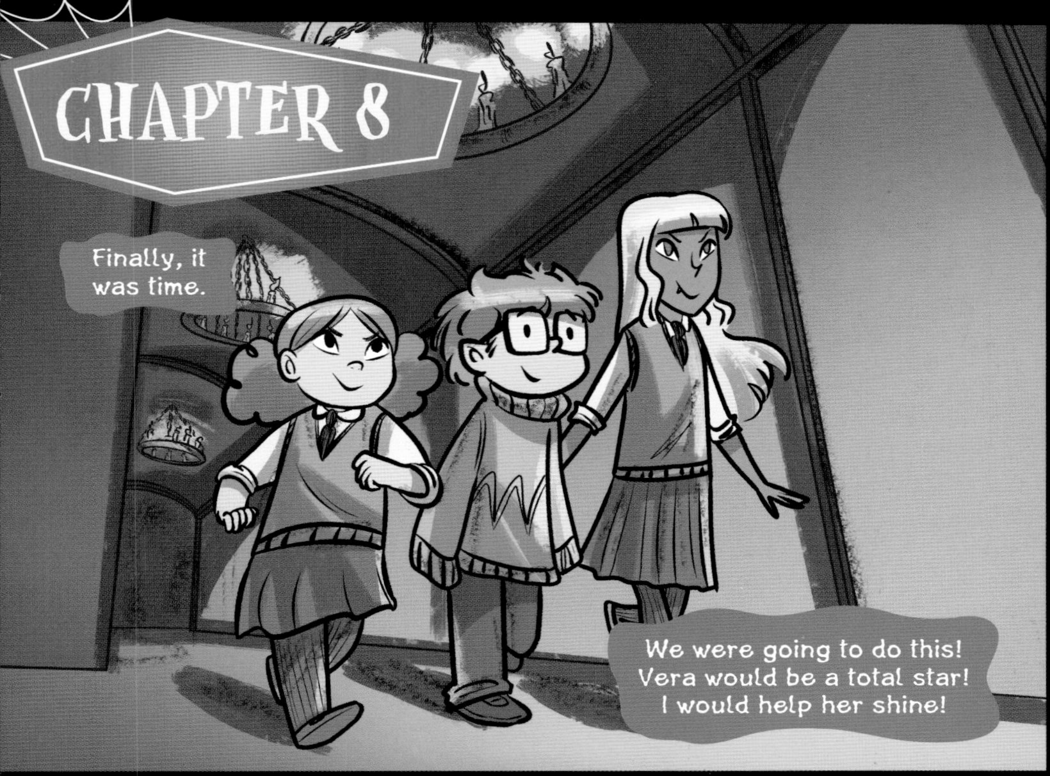
Finally, it was time.
We were going to do this! Vera would be a total star! I would help her shine!

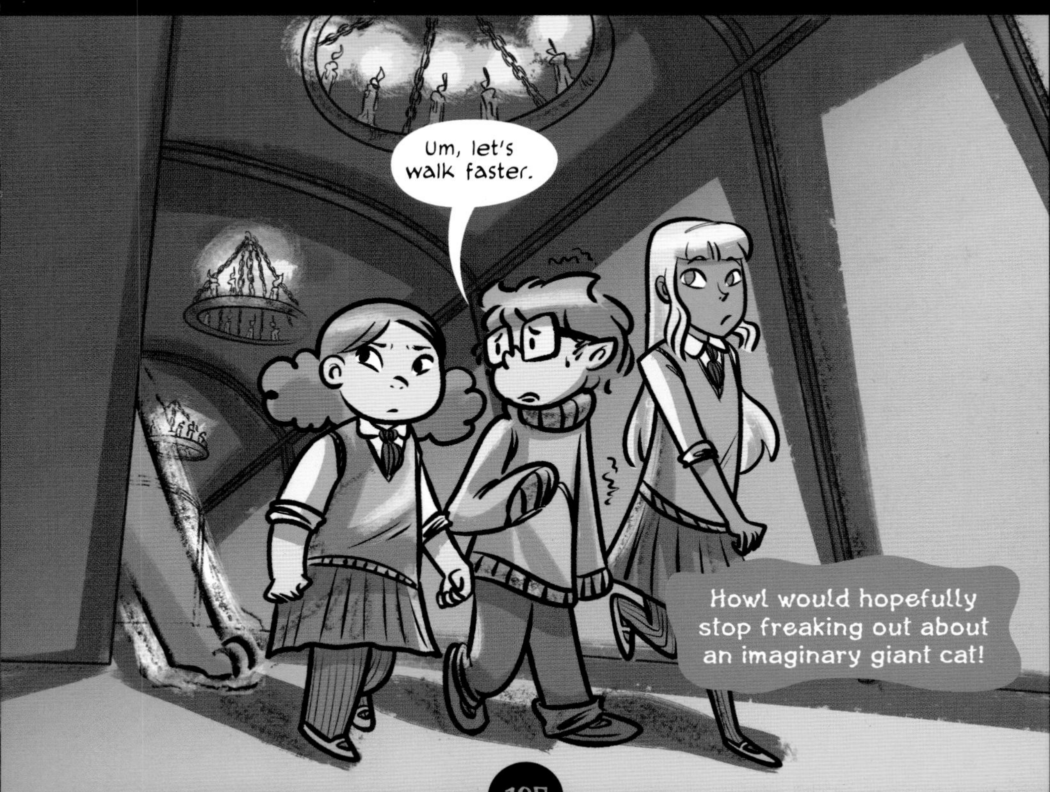
Um, let's walk faster.
Howl would hopefully stop freaking out about an imaginary giant cat!

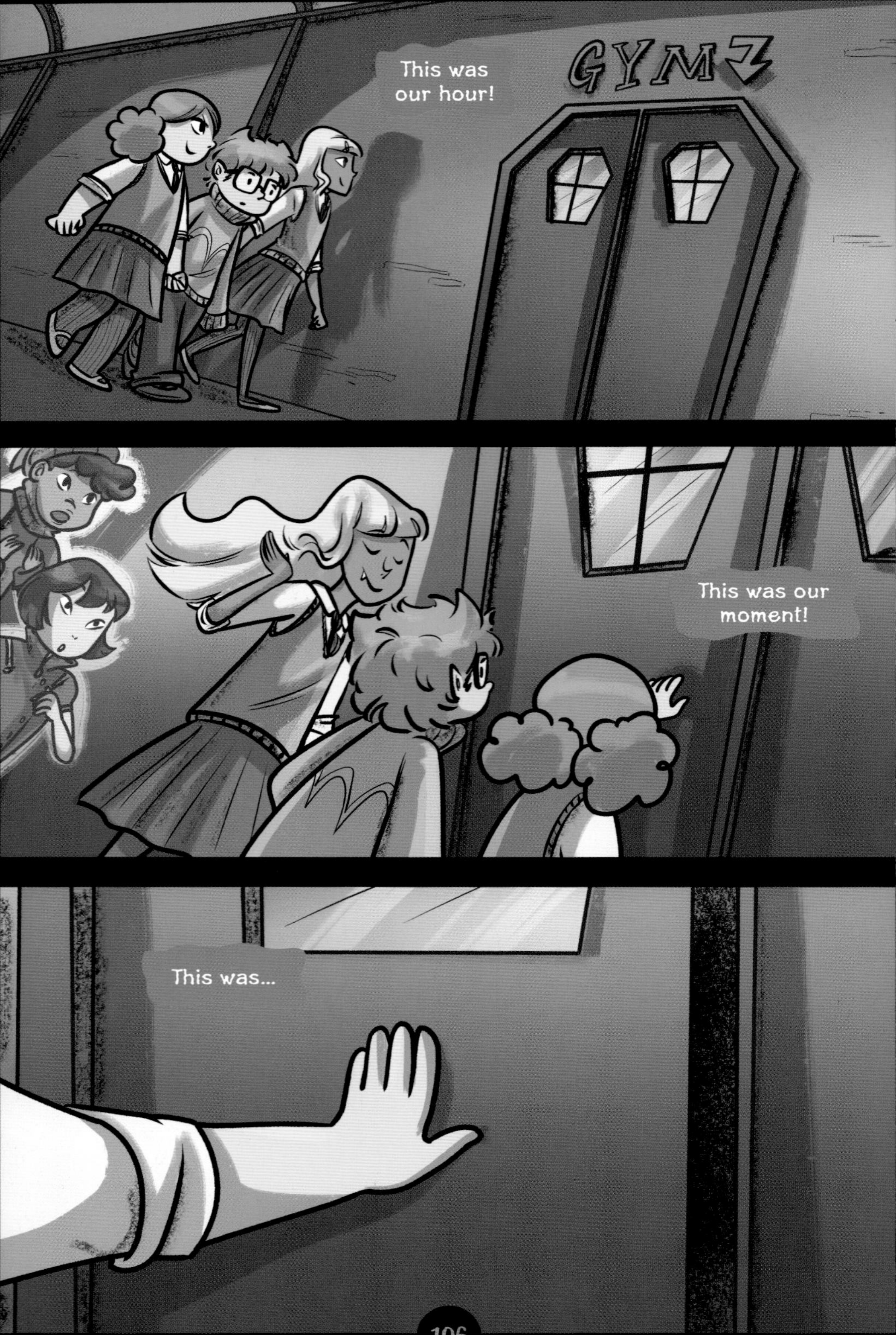
GYM 3
This was our hour!
This was our moment!
This was...

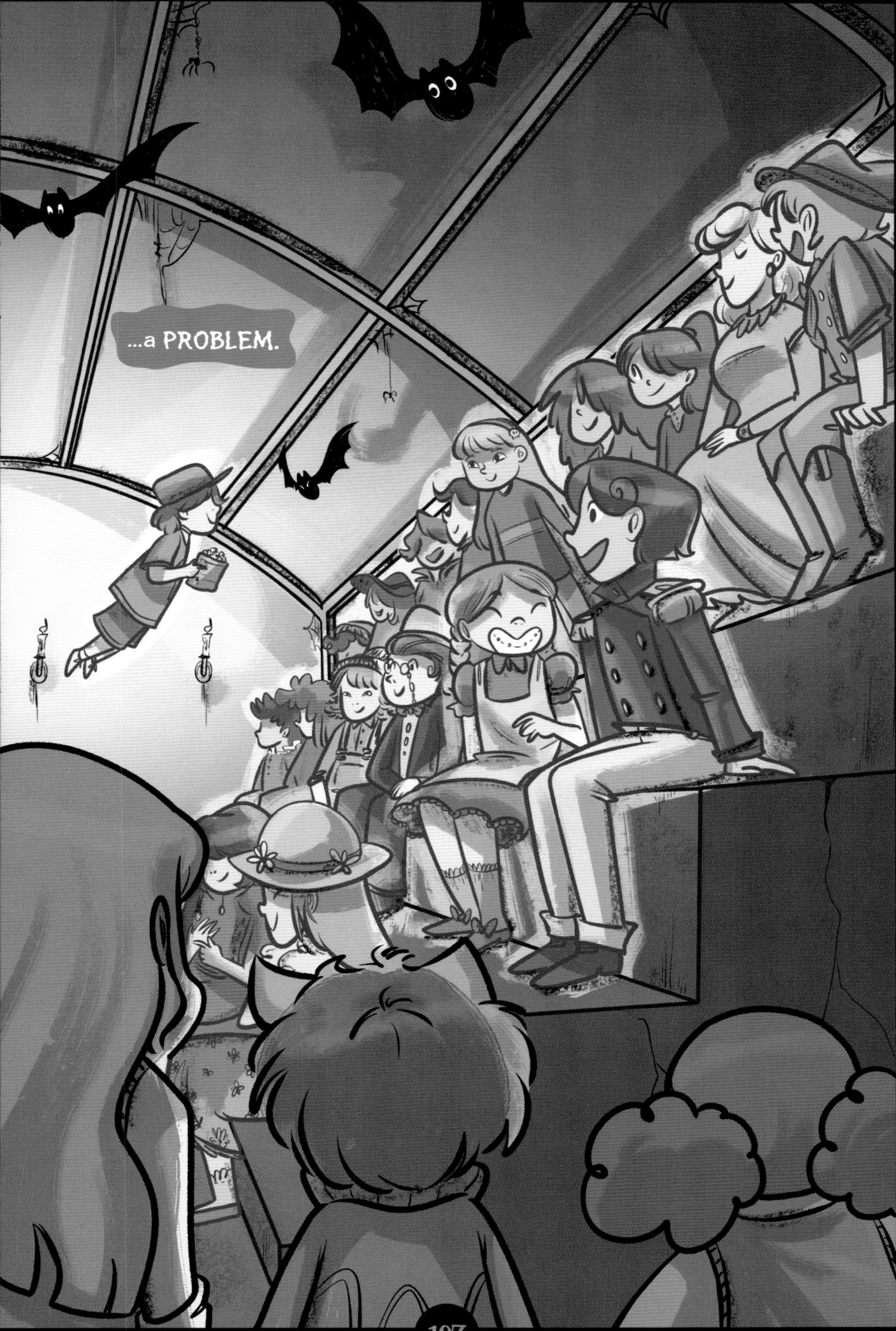
...a PROBLEM.

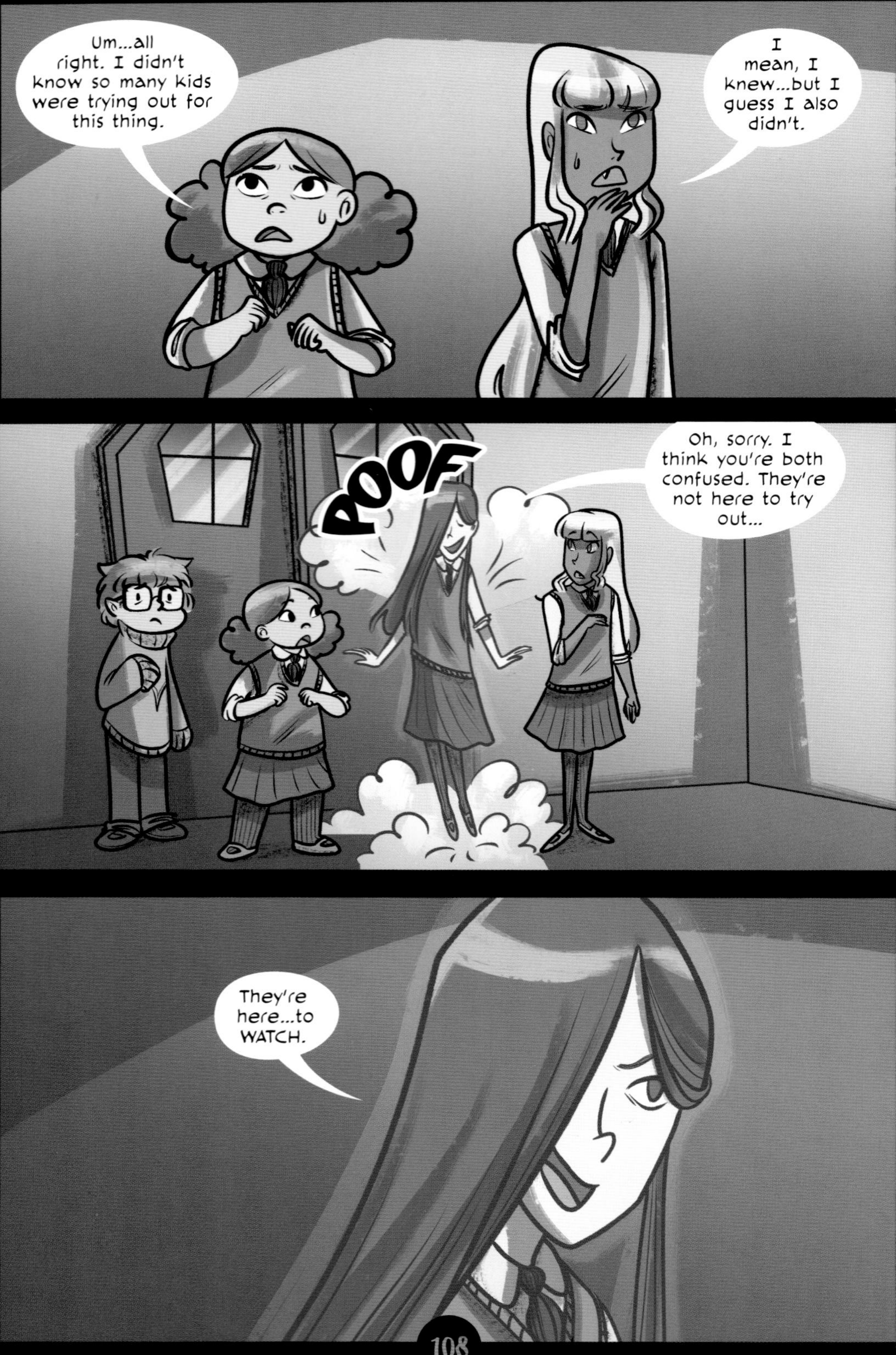
Um...all right. I didn't know so many kids were trying out for this thing.
I mean, I knew...but I guess I also didn't.
POOF
Oh, sorry. I think you're both confused. They're not here to try out...
They're here...to WATCH.

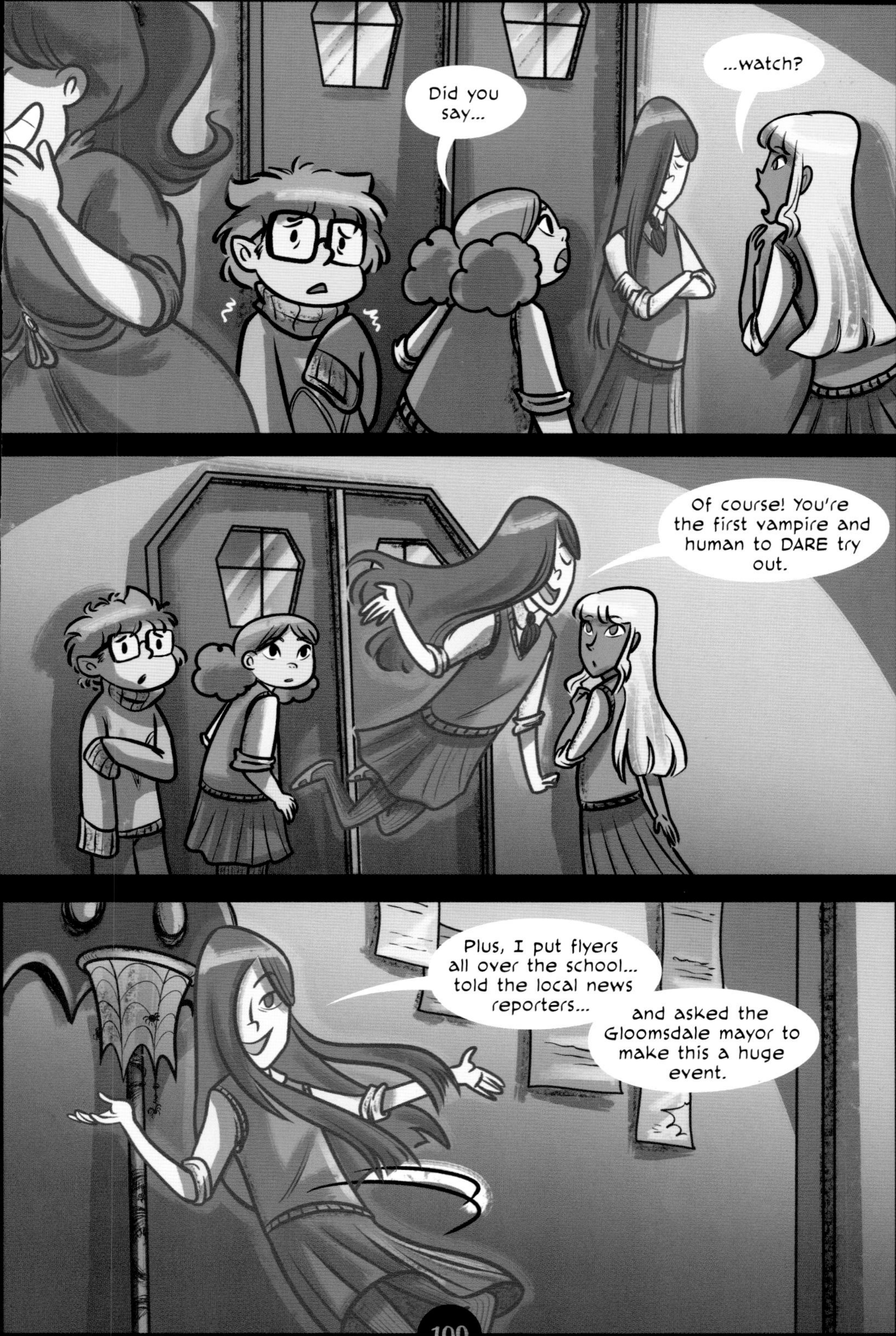
Did you say...
...watch?
Of course! You're the first vampire and human to DARE try out.
Plus, I put flyers all over the school... told the local news reporters...
and asked the Gloomsdale mayor to make this a huge event.

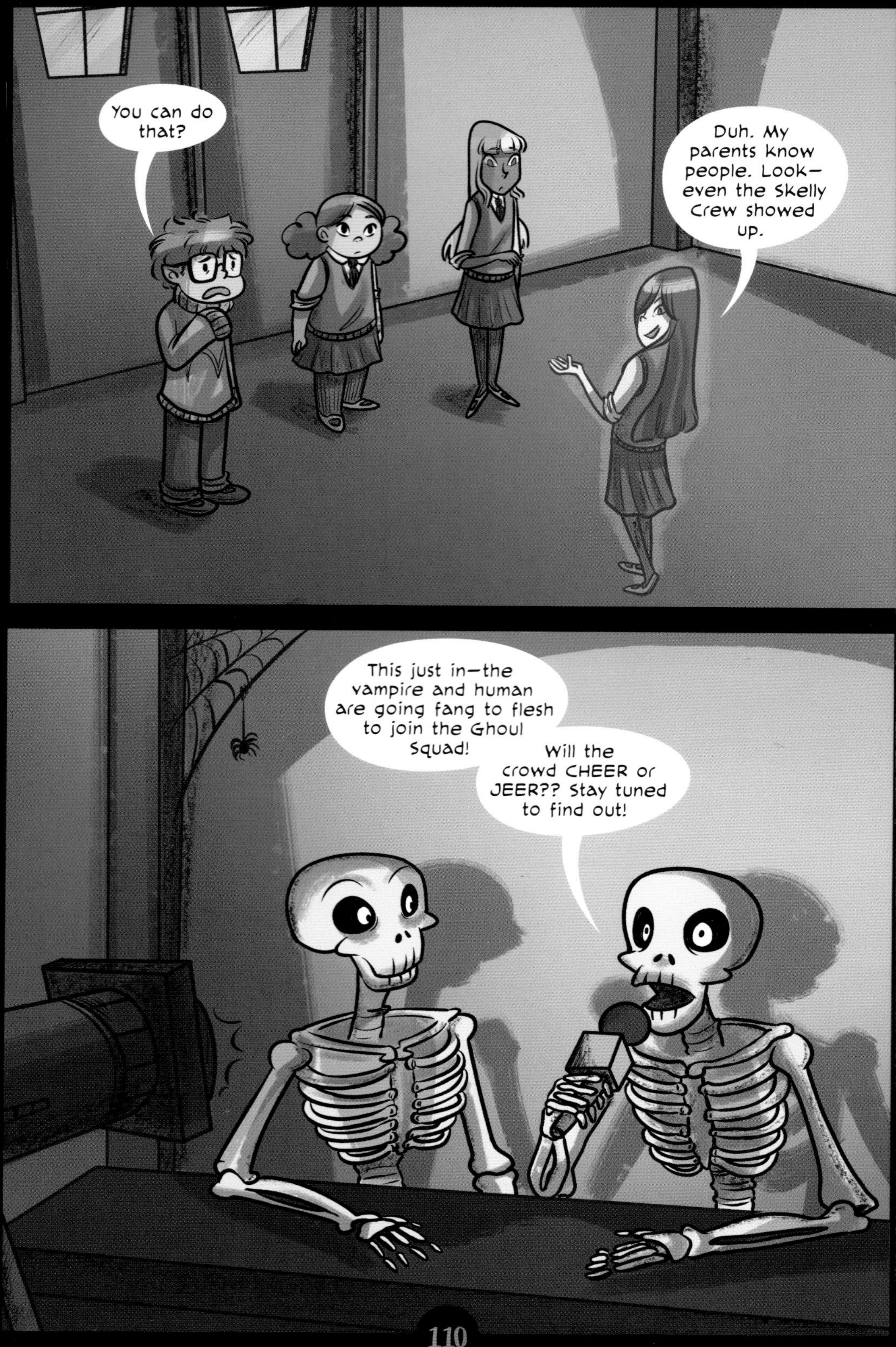
You can do that?
Duh. My parents know people. Look—even the Skelly Crew showed up.
This just in—the vampire and human are going fang to flesh to join the Ghoul Squad!
Will the crowd CHEER or JEER?? Stay tuned to find out!

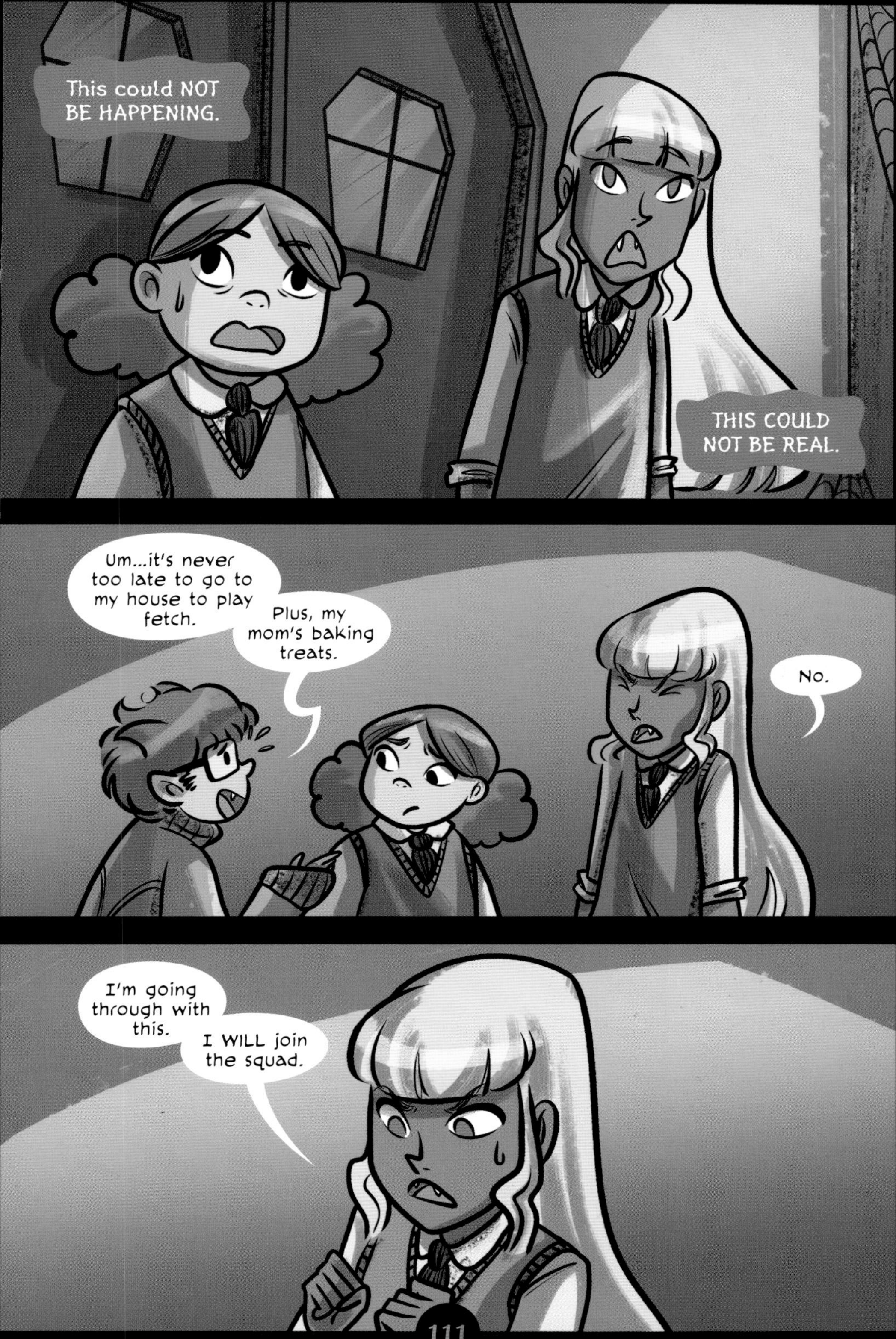
This could NOT BE HAPPENING.
THIS COULD NOT BE REAL.
Um...it's never too late to go to my house to play fetch.
Plus, my mom's baking treats.
No.
I'm going through with this.
I WILL join the squad.

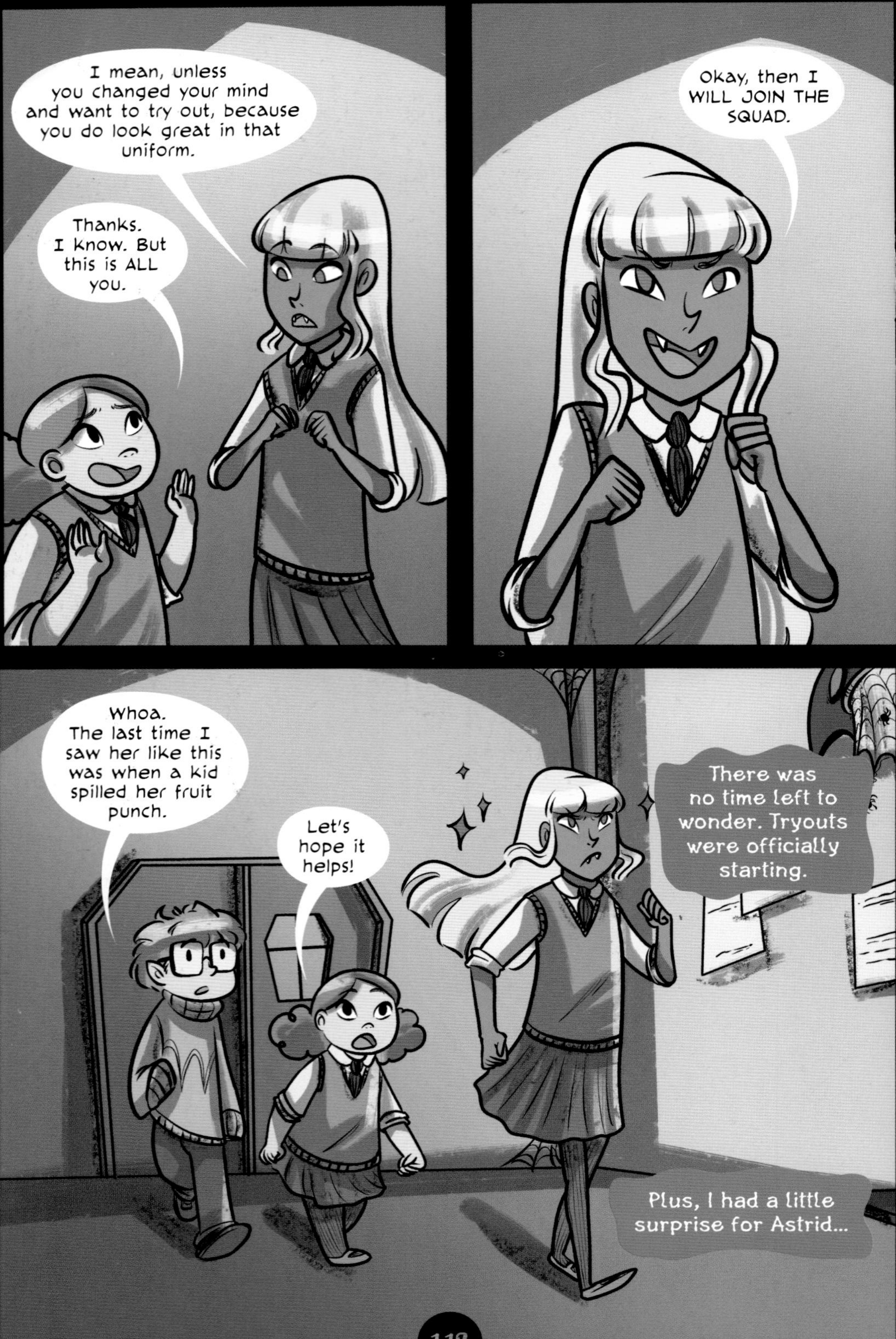
I mean, unless you changed your mind and want to try out, because you do look great in that uniform.
Thanks. I know. But this is ALL you.
Okay, then I WILL JOIN THE SQUAD.
Whoa. The last time I saw her like this was when a kid spilled her fruit punch.
Let's hope it helps!
There was no time left to wonder. Tryouts were officially starting.
Plus, I had a little surprise for Astrid...

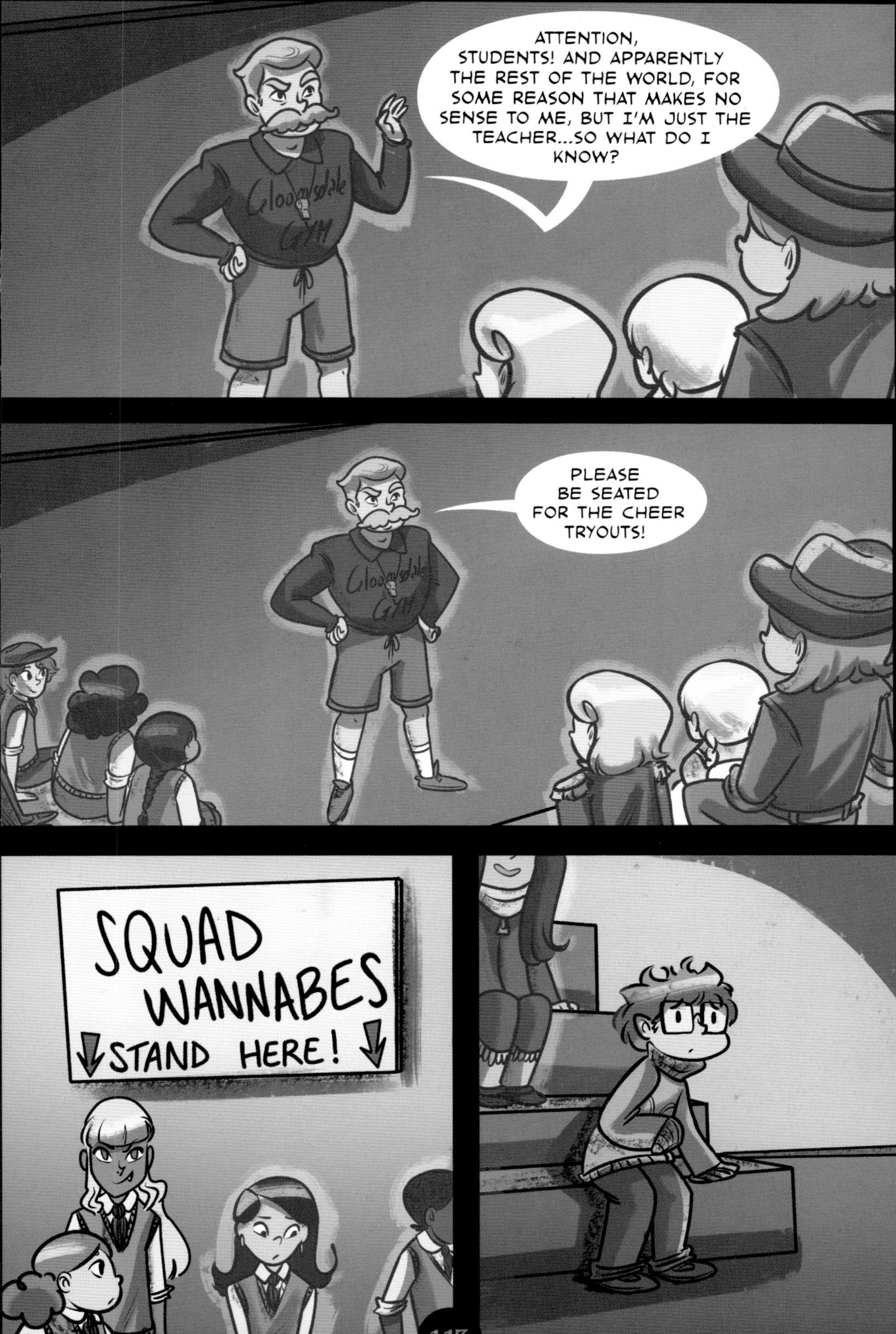
ATTENTION, STUDENTS! AND APPARENTLY THE REST OF THE WORLD, FOR SOME REASON THAT MAKES NO SENSE TO ME, BUT I'M JUST THE TEACHER...SO WHAT DO I KNOW?
PLEASE BE SEATED FOR THE CHEER TRYOUTS!
SQUAD WANNABES STAND HERE!

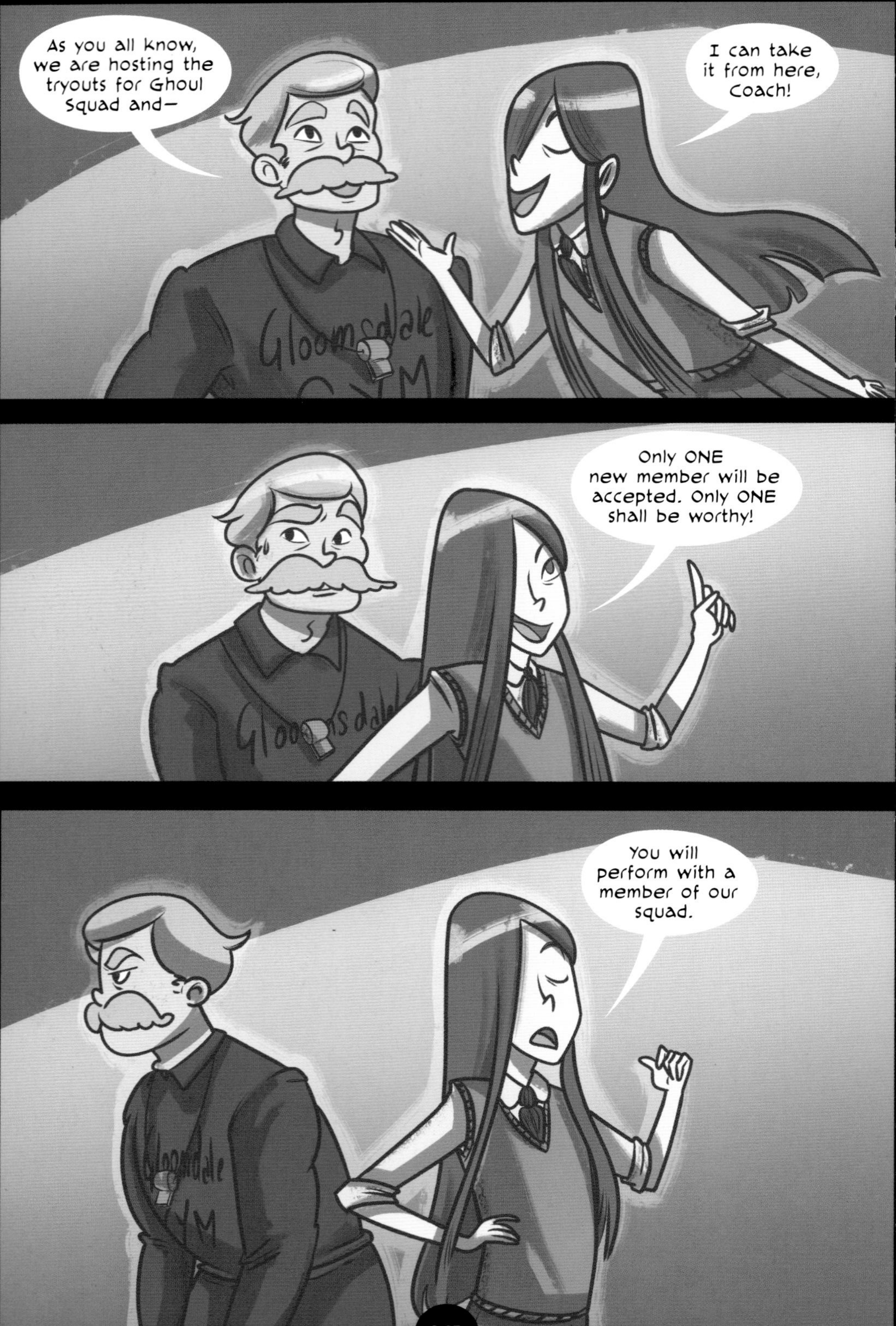
As you all know, we are hosting the tryouts for Ghoul Squad and—
I can take it from here, Coach!
Gloomsdale
Only ONE new member will be accepted. Only ONE shall be worthy!
Gloomsdale
You will perform with a member of our squad.
Gloomsdale
GYM

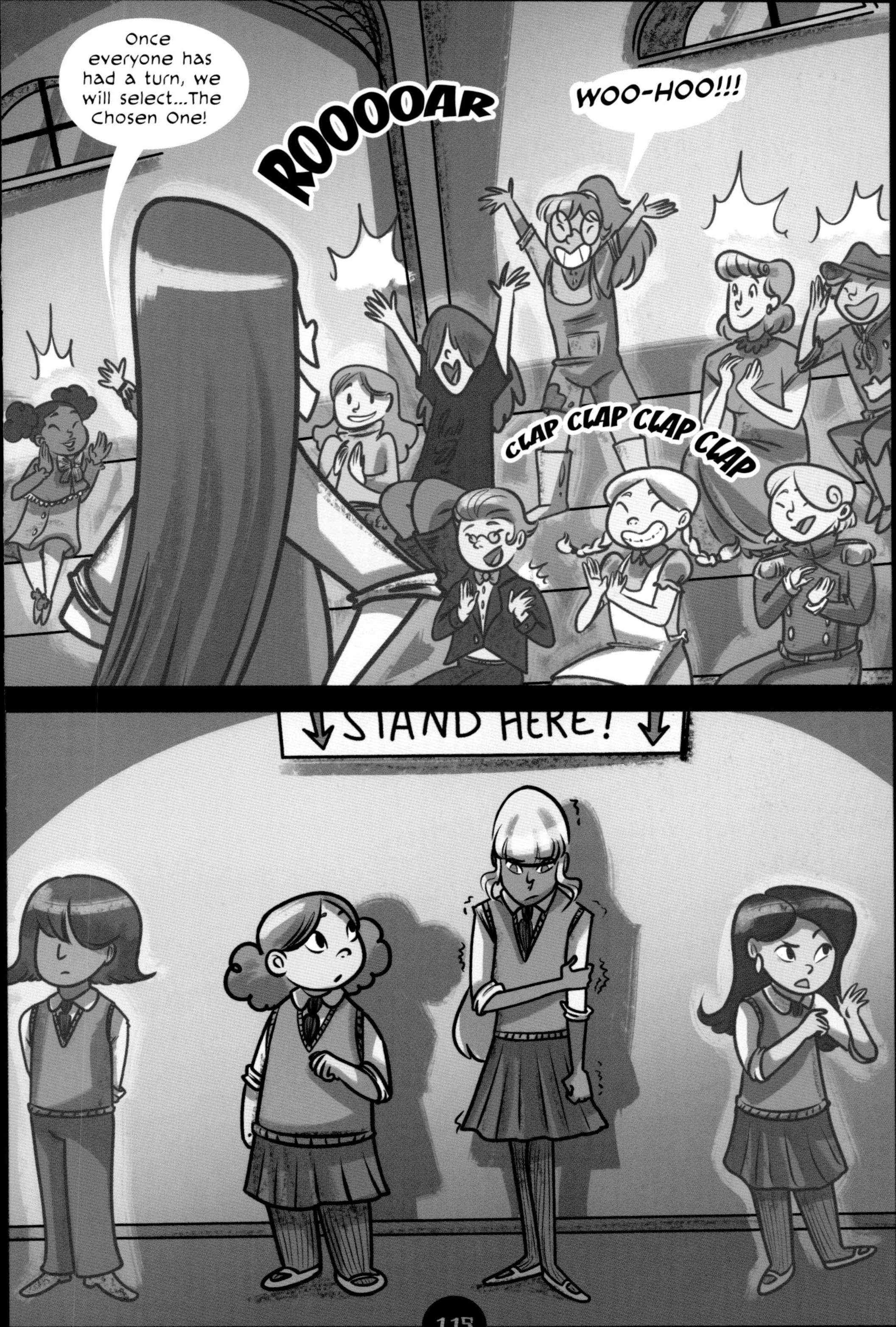
Once everyone has had a turn, we will select...The Chosen One!
ROOOOAR
WOO-HOO!!!
CLAP CLAP CLAP CLAP
STAND HERE!

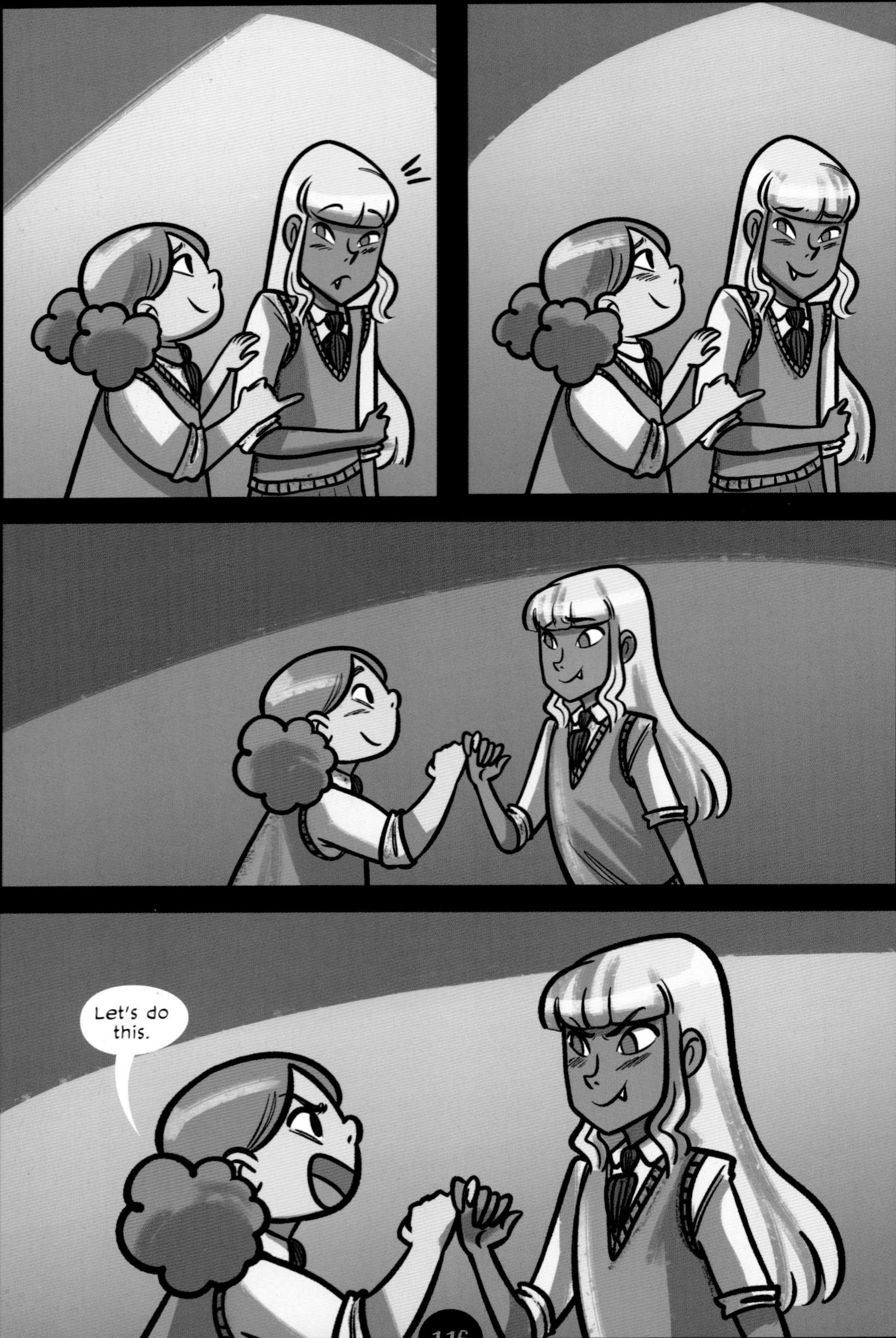
Let's do this.

CHAPTER 9

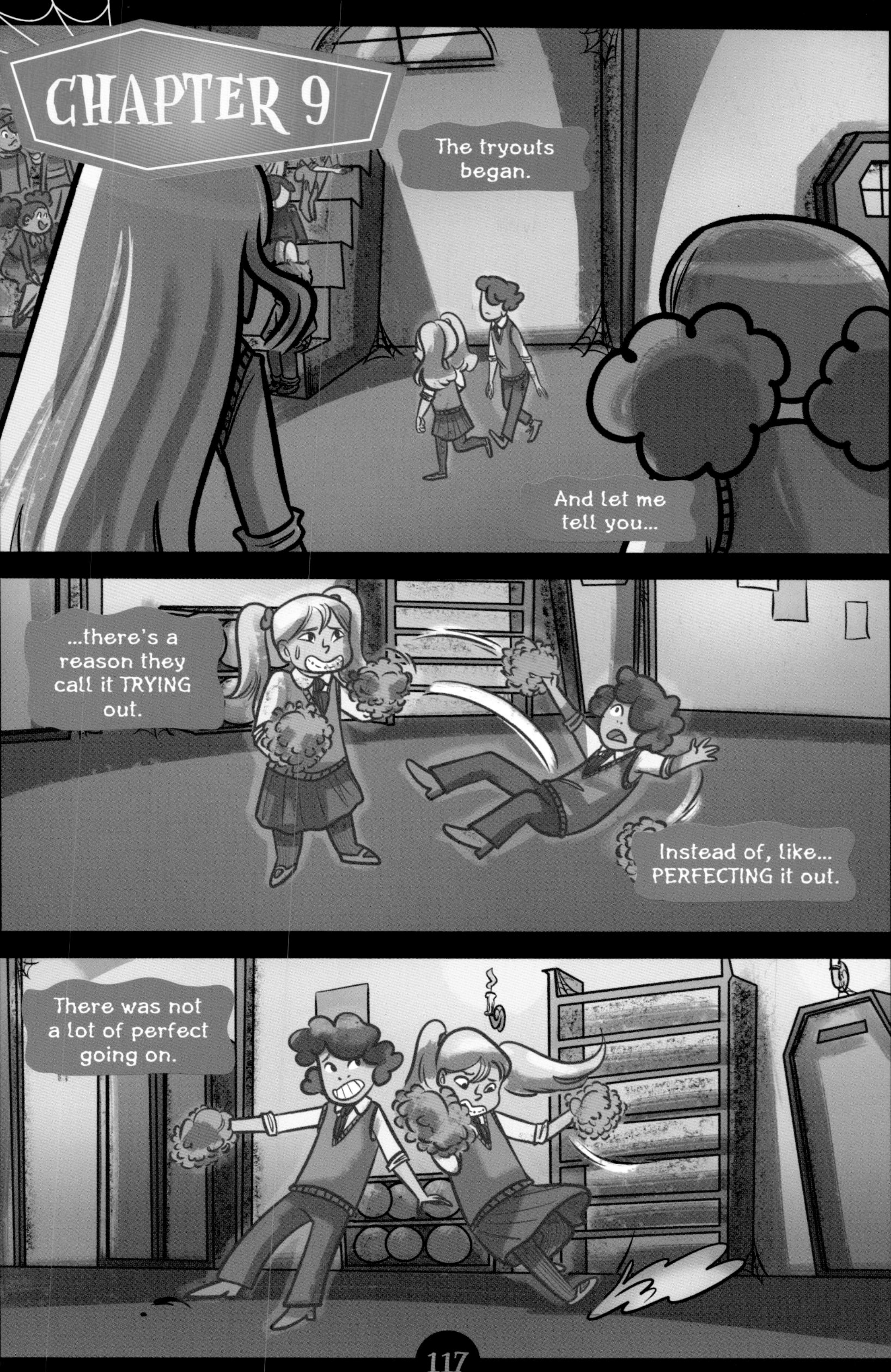
The tryouts began.
And let me tell you...
...there's a reason they call it TRYING out.
Instead of, like... PERFECTING it out.
There was not a lot of perfect going on.

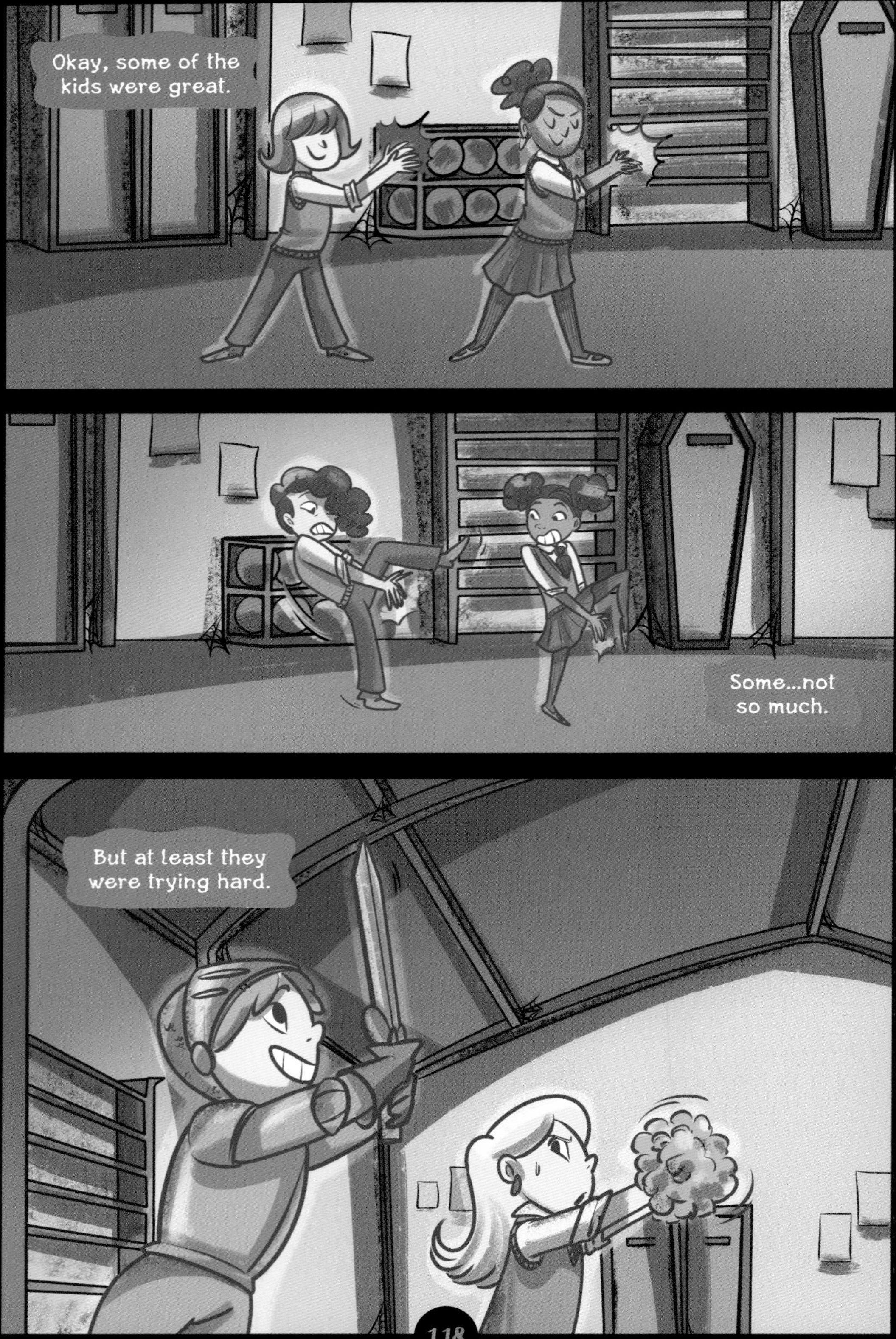
Okay, some of the kids were great.
Some...not so much.
But at least they were trying hard.

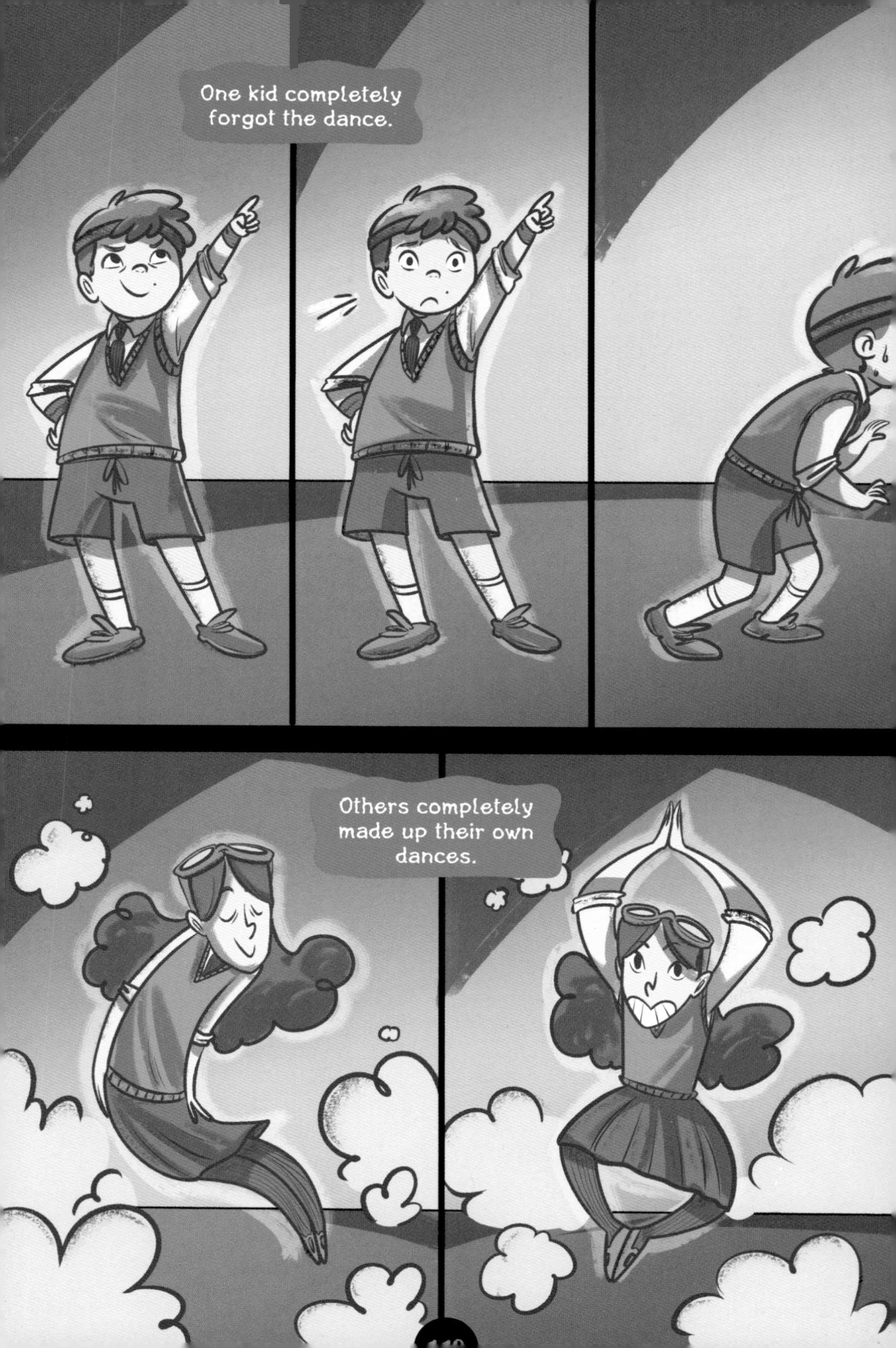
One kid completely forgot the dance.
Others completely made up their own dances.

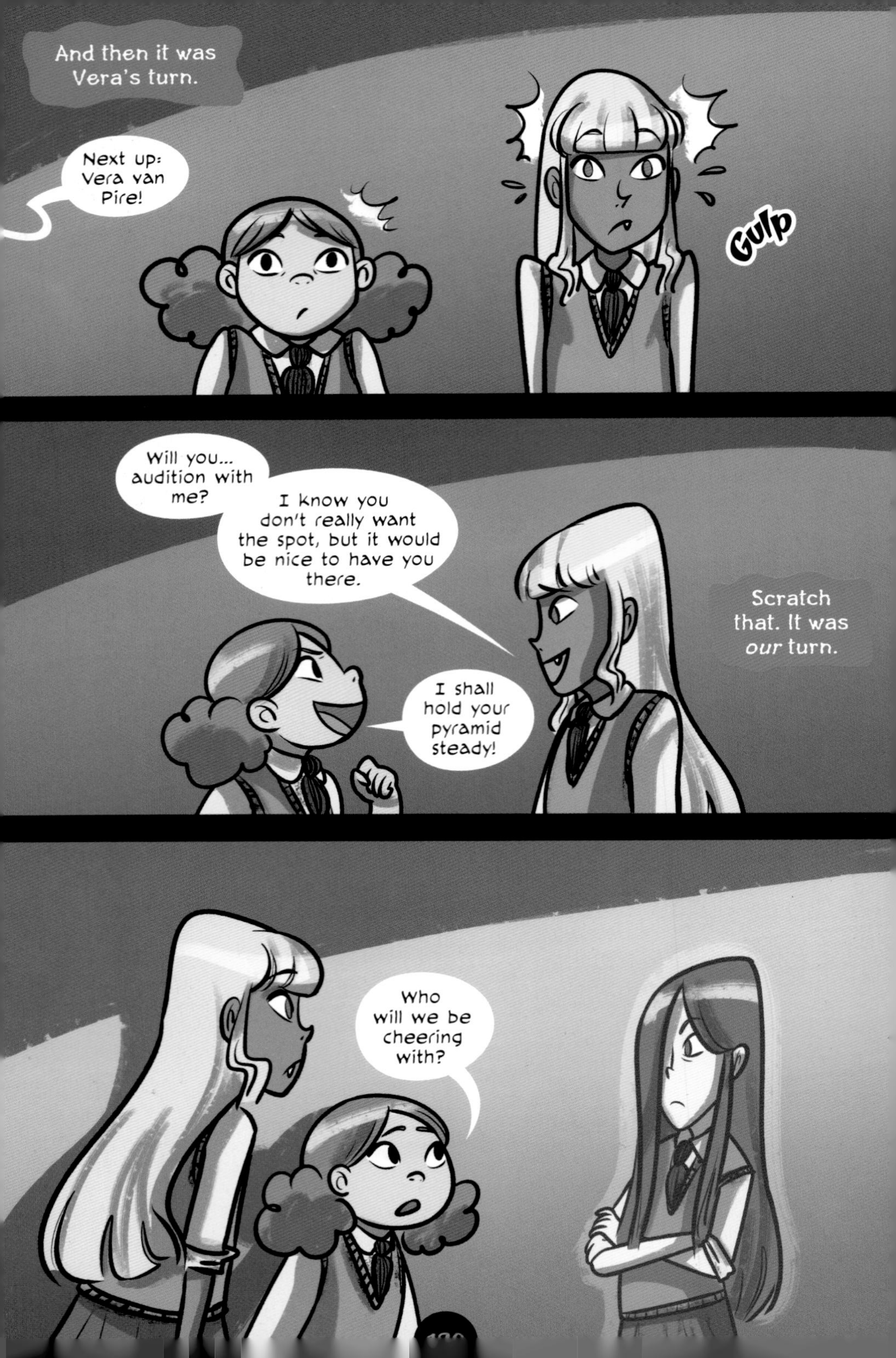
And then it was Vera's turn.
Next up: Vera van Pire!
GULP
Will you... audition with me?
I know you don't really want the spot, but it would be nice to have you there.
I shall hold your pyramid steady!
Scratch that. It was *our* turn.
Who will we be cheering with?

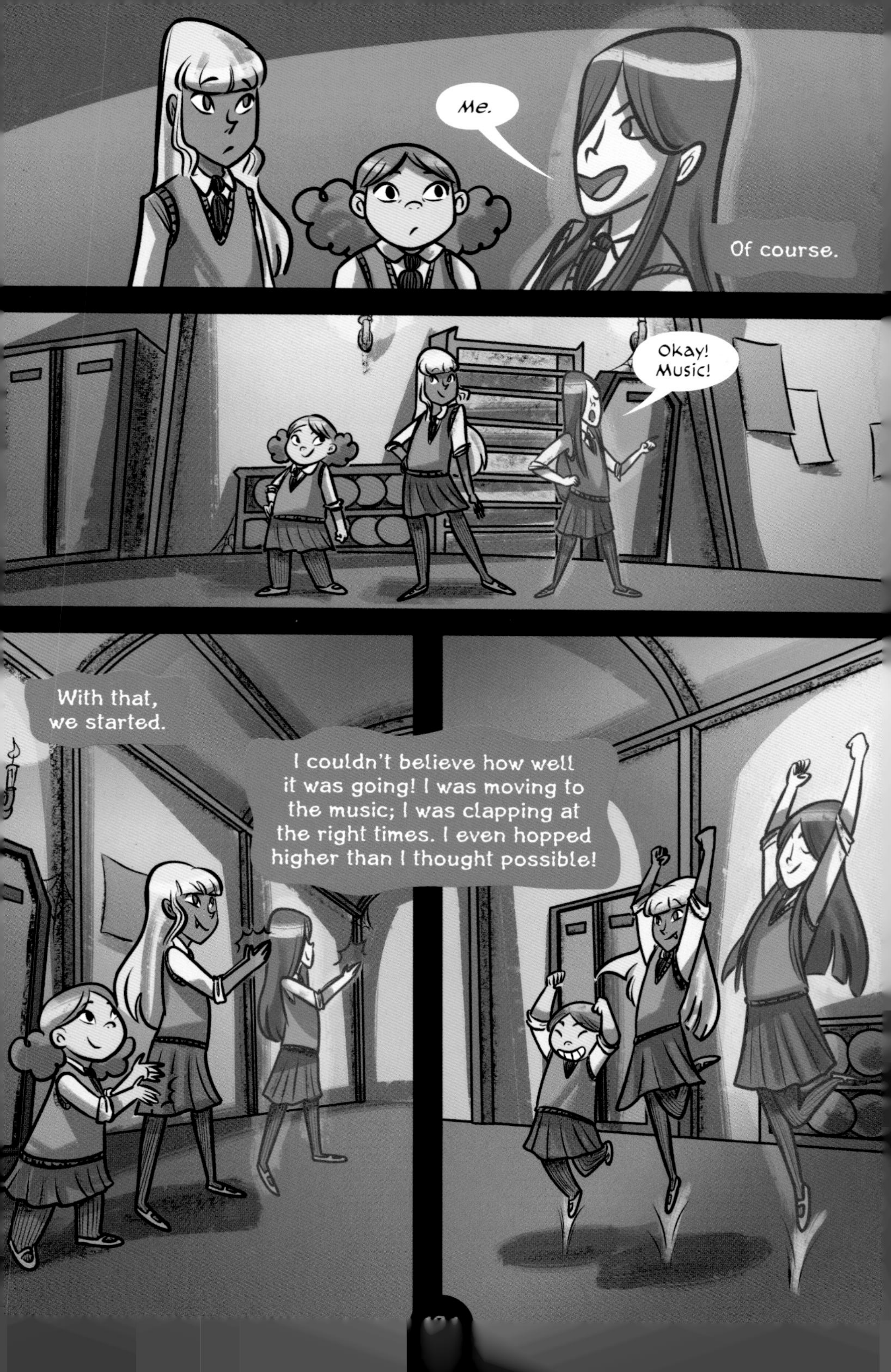
Me.
Of course.
Okay! Music!
With that, we started.
I couldn't believe how well it was going! I was moving to the music; I was clapping at the right times. I even hopped higher than I thought possible!

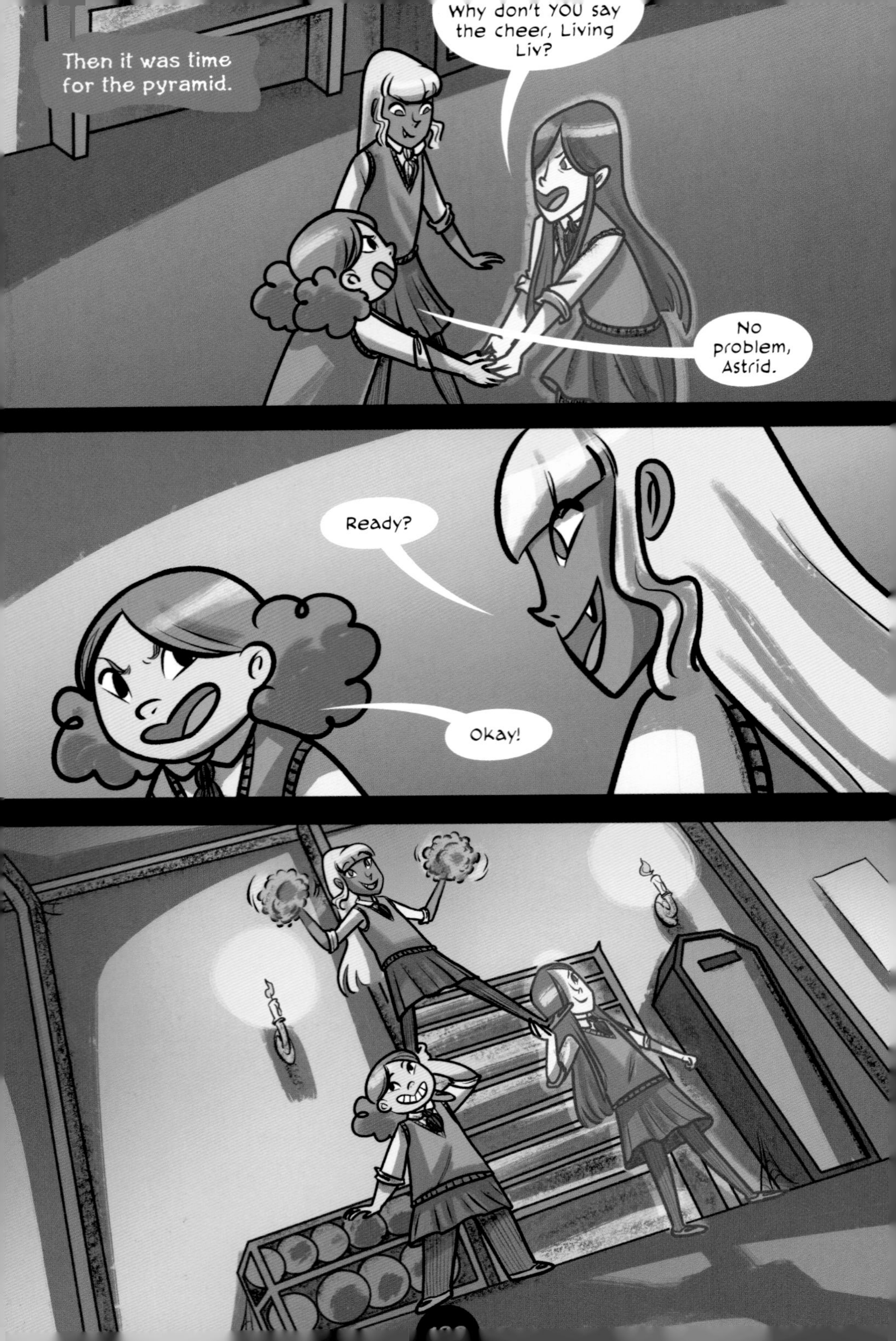
Then it was time for the pyramid.
Why don't YOU say the cheer, Living Liv?
No problem, Astrid.
Ready?
Okay!

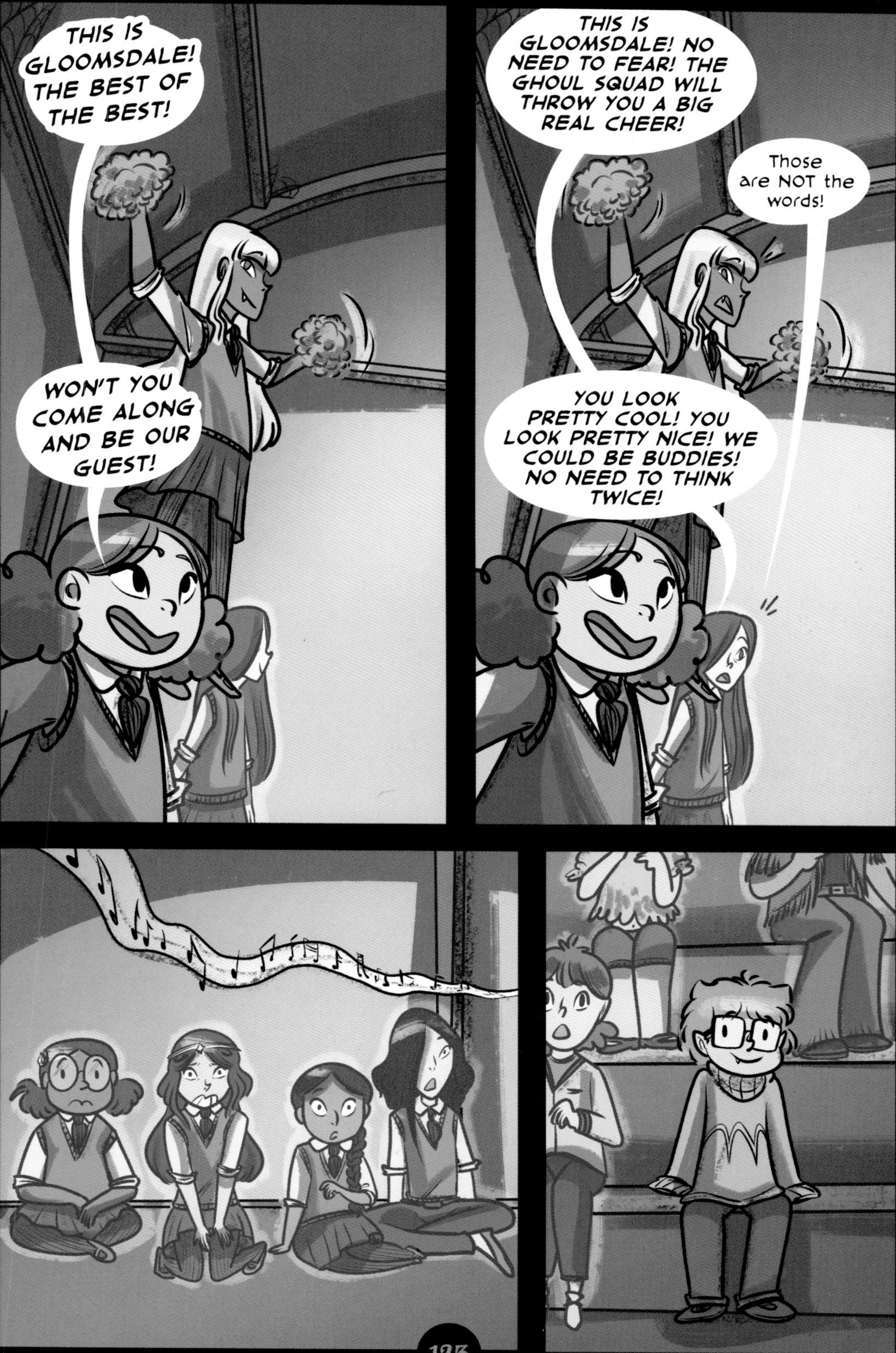
THIS IS GLOOMSDALE! THE BEST OF THE BEST!
WON'T YOU COME ALONG AND BE OUR GUEST!
THIS IS GLOOMSDALE! NO NEED TO FEAR! THE GHOUL SQUAD WILL THROW YOU A BIG REAL CHEER!
YOU LOOK PRETTY COOL! YOU LOOK PRETTY NICE! WE COULD BE BUDDIES! NO NEED TO THINK TWICE!
Those are NOT the words!

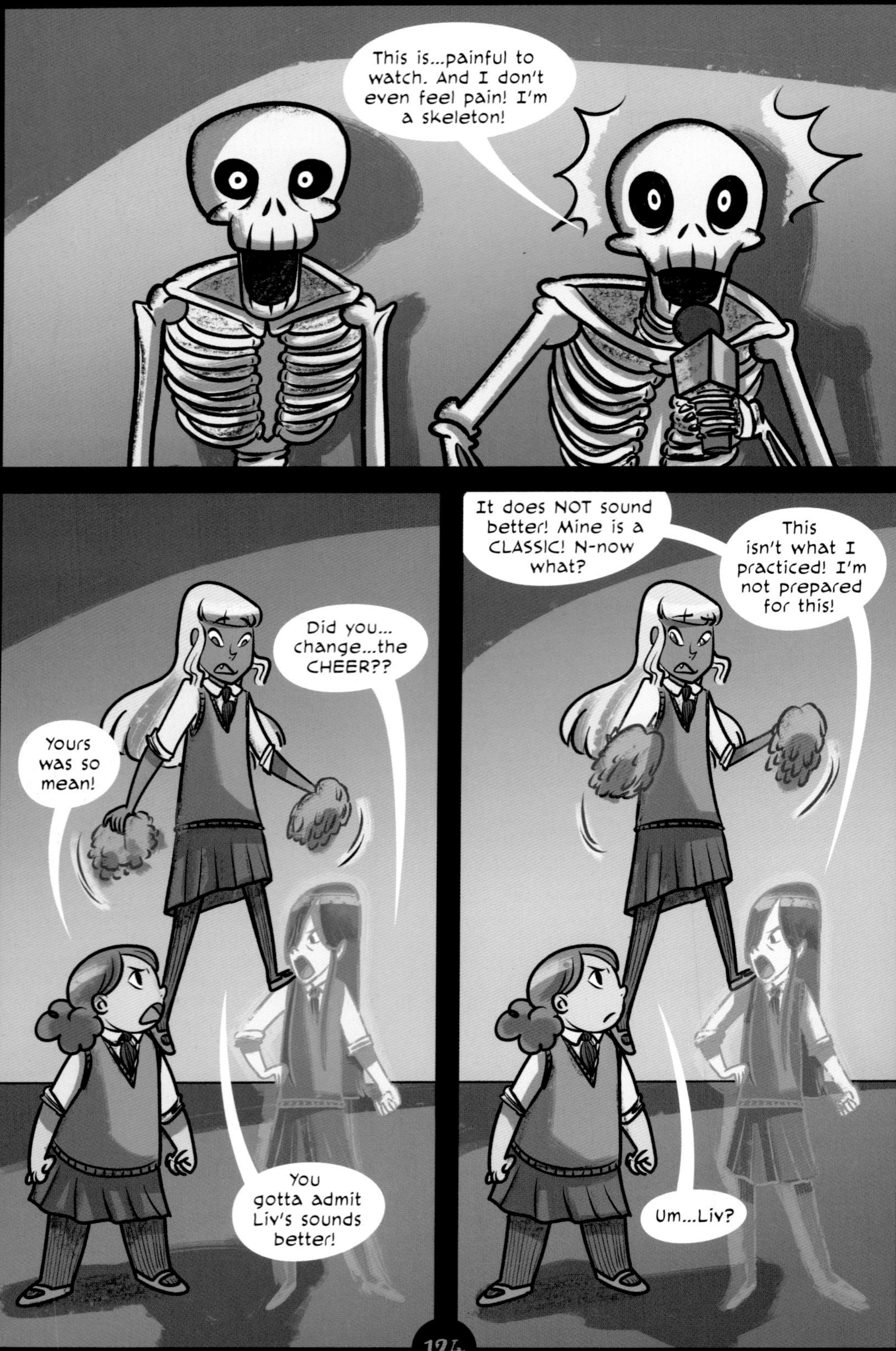
This is...painful to watch. And I don't even feel pain! I'm a skeleton!
Did you... change...the CHEER??
Yours was so mean!
You gotta admit Liv's sounds better!
It does NOT sound better! Mine is a CLASSIC! N-now what?
This isn't what I practiced! I'm not prepared for this!
Um...Liv?

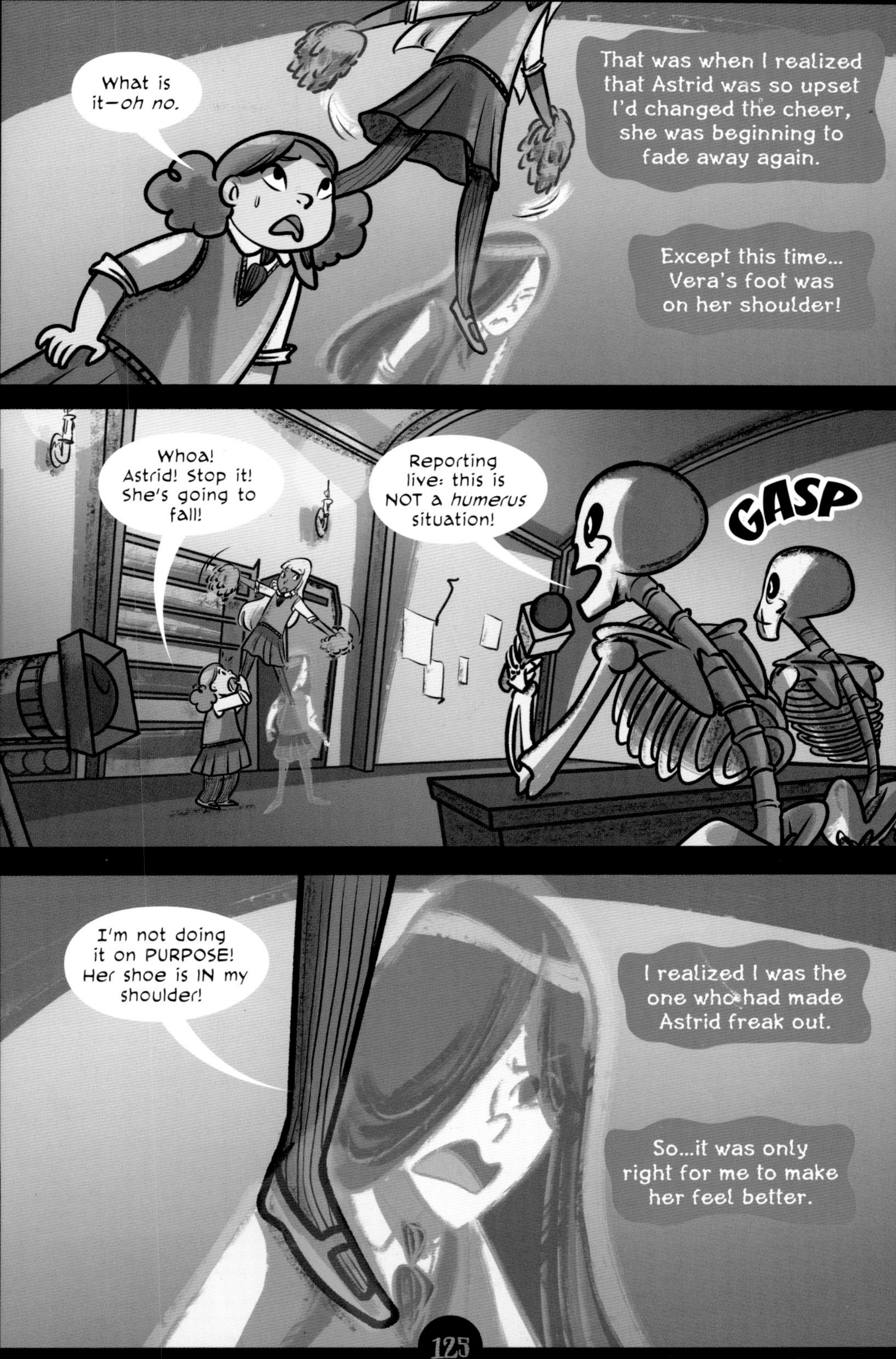
What is it—*oh no.*
That was when I realized that Astrid was so upset I'd changed the cheer, she was beginning to fade away again.
Except this time... Vera's foot was on her shoulder!
Whoa! Astrid! Stop it! She's going to fall!
Reporting live: this is NOT a *humerus* situation!
GASP
I'm not doing it on PURPOSE! Her shoe is IN my shoulder!
I realized I was the one who had made Astrid freak out.
So...it was only right for me to make her feel better.

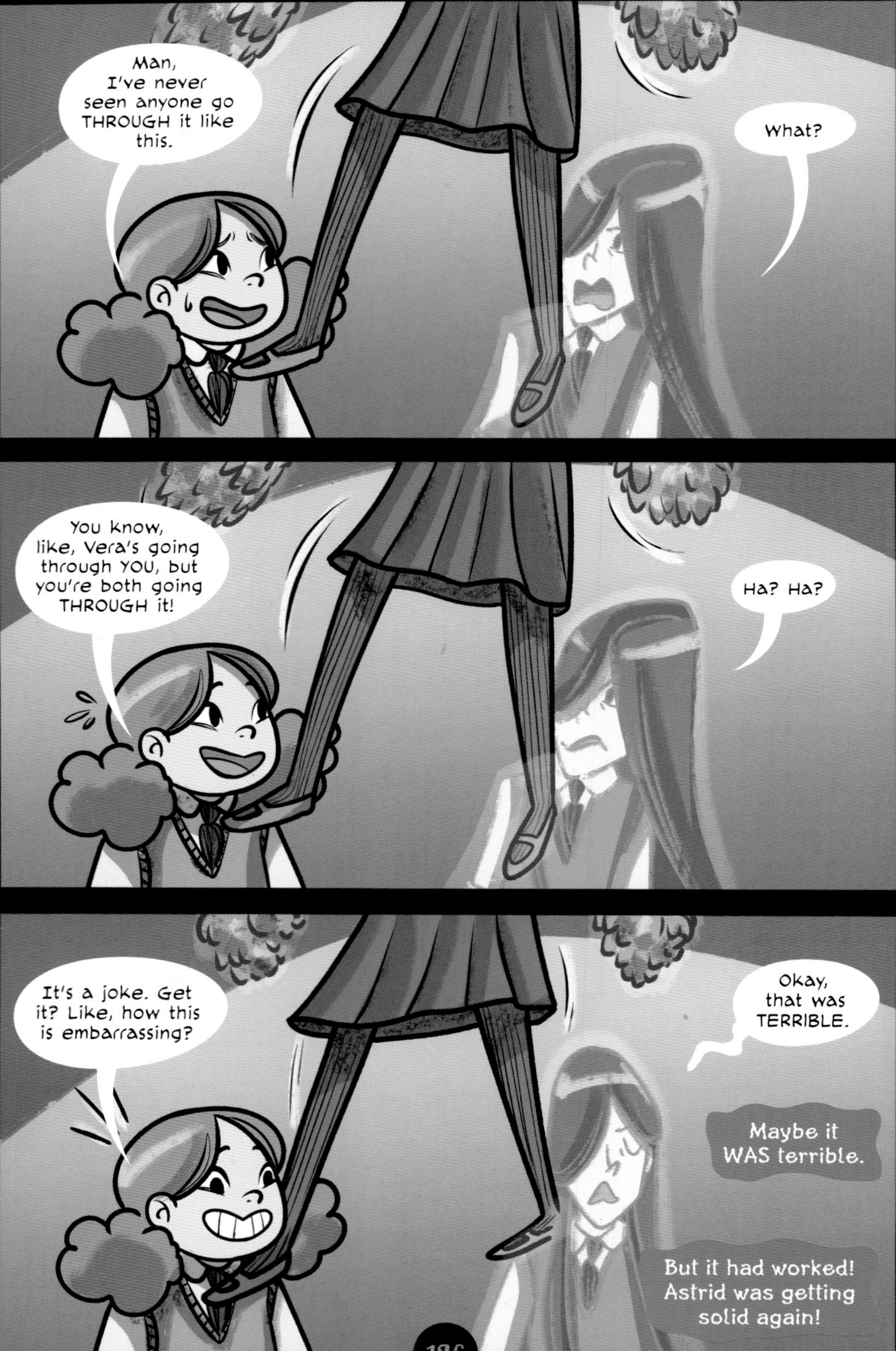
Man, I've never seen anyone go THROUGH it like this.
What?
You know, like, Vera's going through YOU, but you're both going THROUGH it!
Ha? Ha?
It's a joke. Get it? Like, how this is embarrassing?
Okay, that was TERRIBLE.
Maybe it WAS terrible.
But it had worked! Astrid was getting solid again!

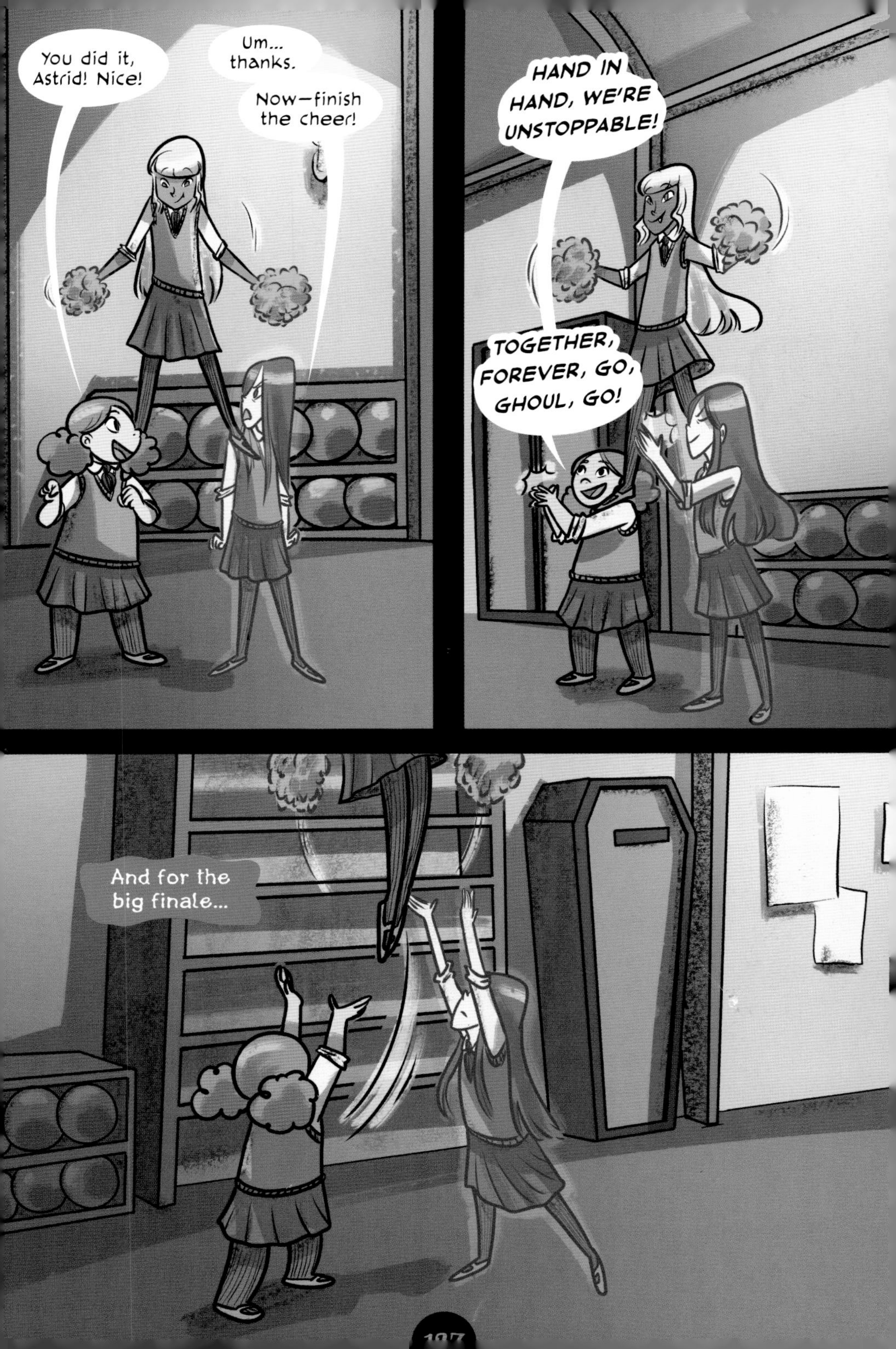
You did it, Astrid! Nice!
Um... thanks.
Now—finish the cheer!
HAND IN HAND, WE'RE UNSTOPPABLE!
TOGETHER, FOREVER, GO, GHOUL, GO!
And for the big finale...

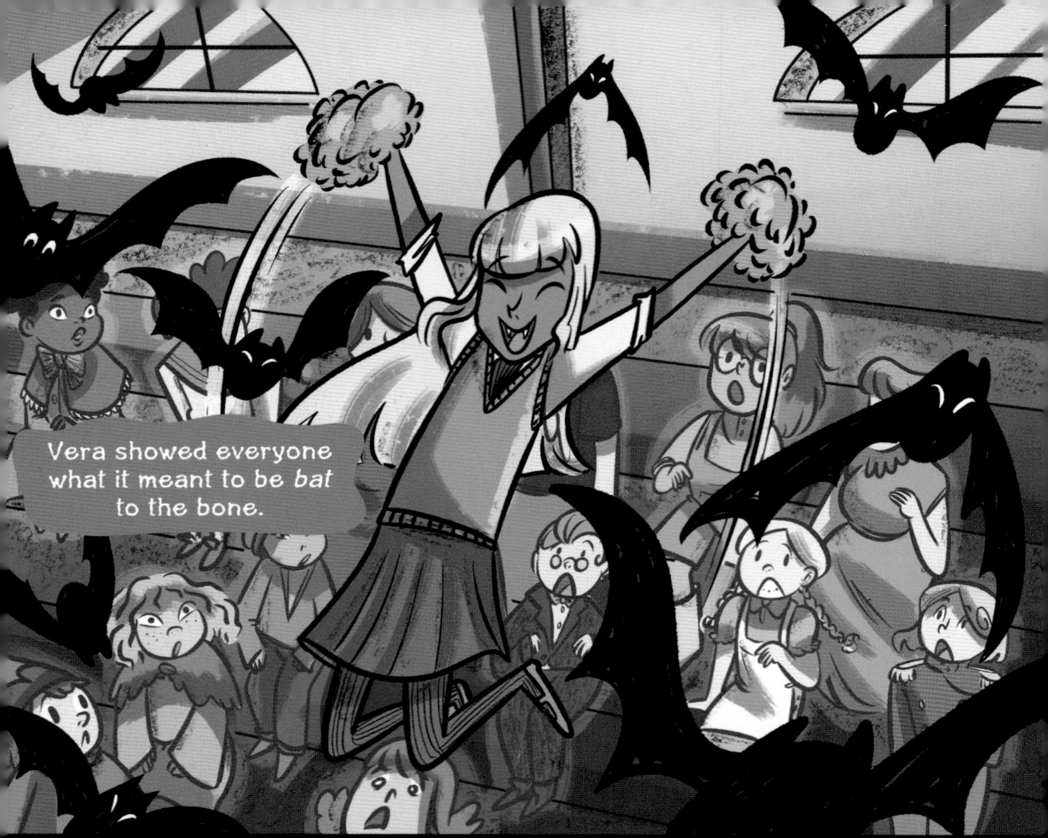
Vera showed everyone what it meant to be *bat* to the bone.

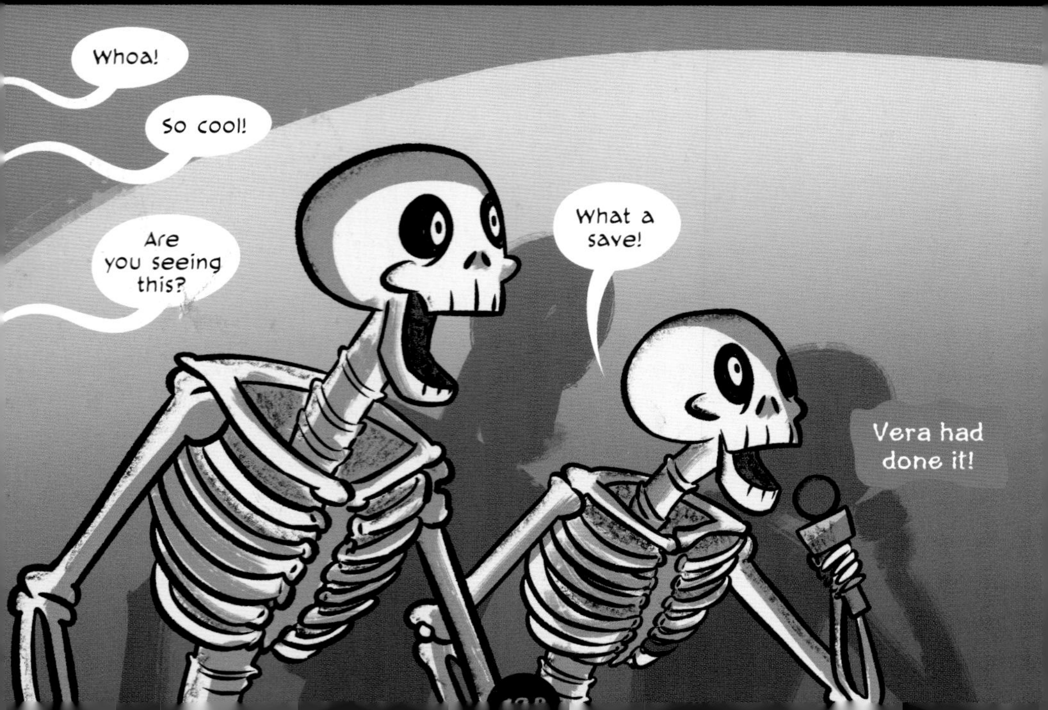
Whoa!
So cool!
Are you seeing this?
What a save!
Vera had done it!

CHAPTER 10

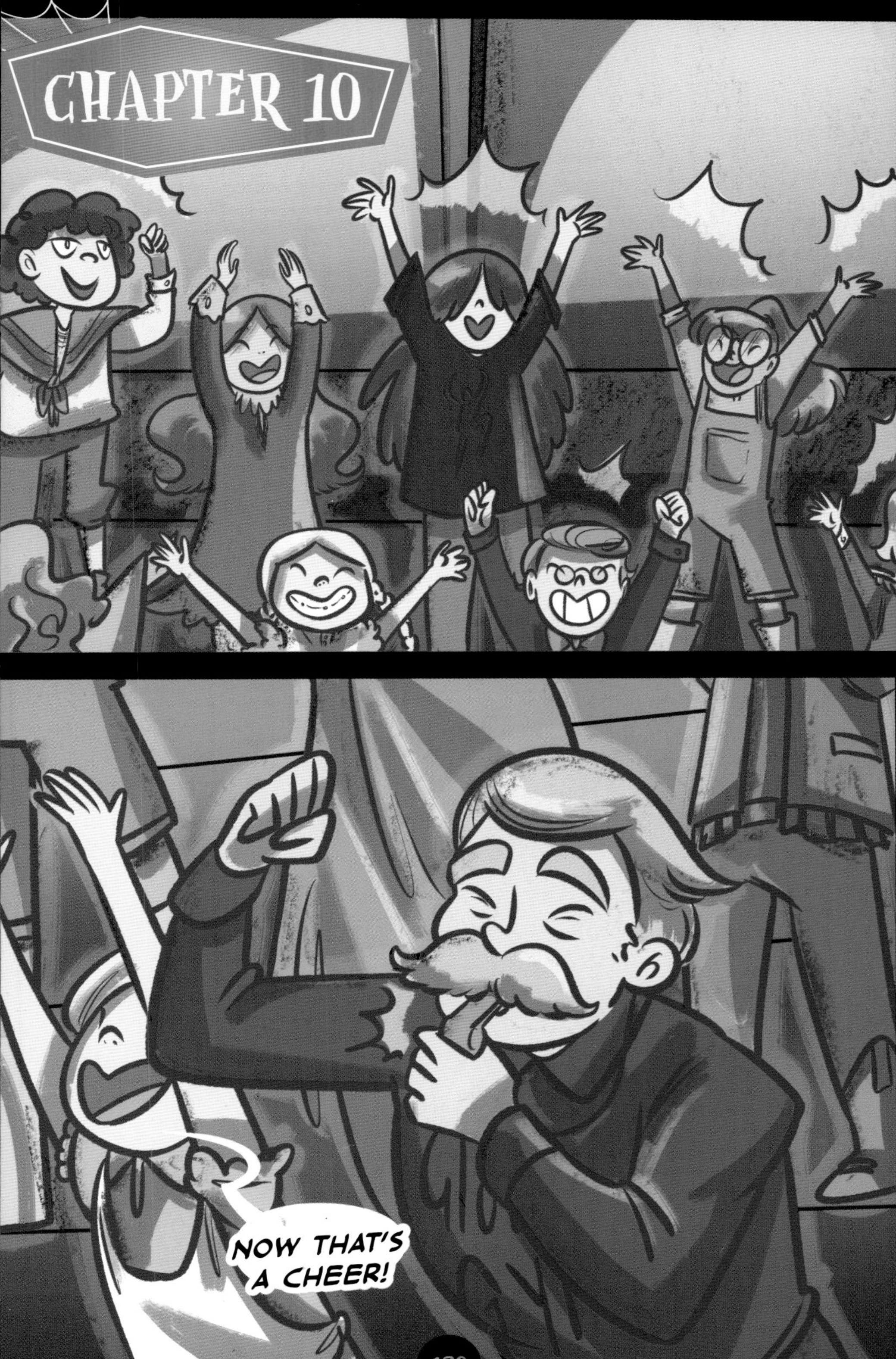
NOW THAT'S A CHEER!

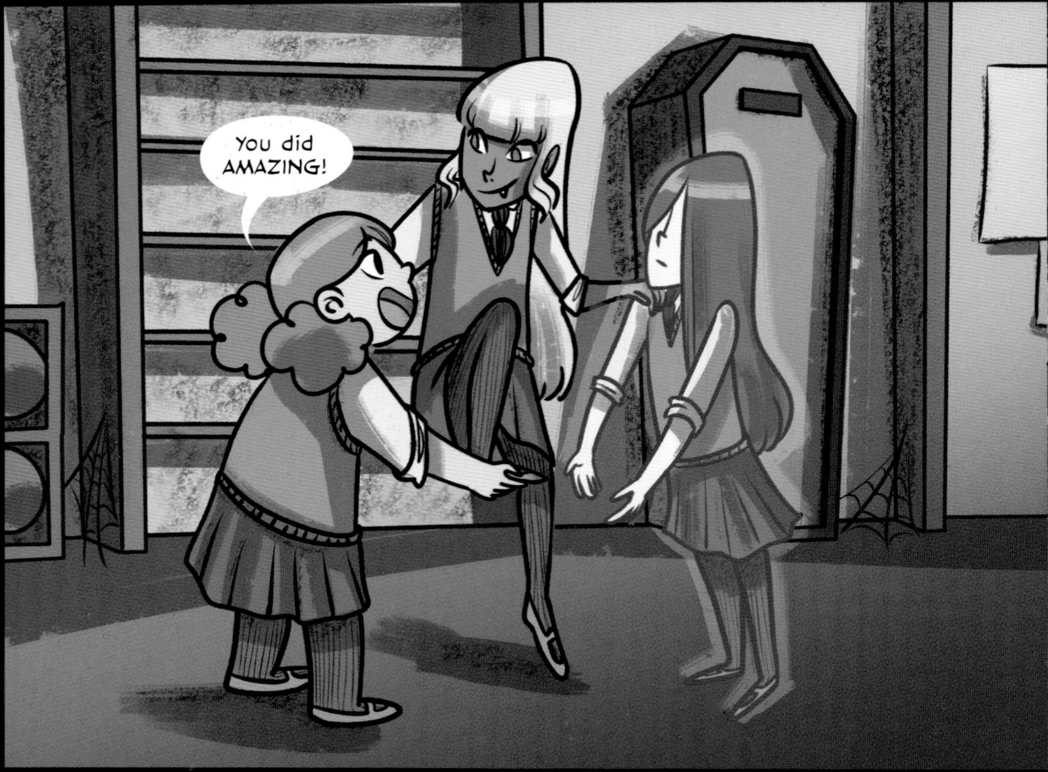
You did AMAZING!

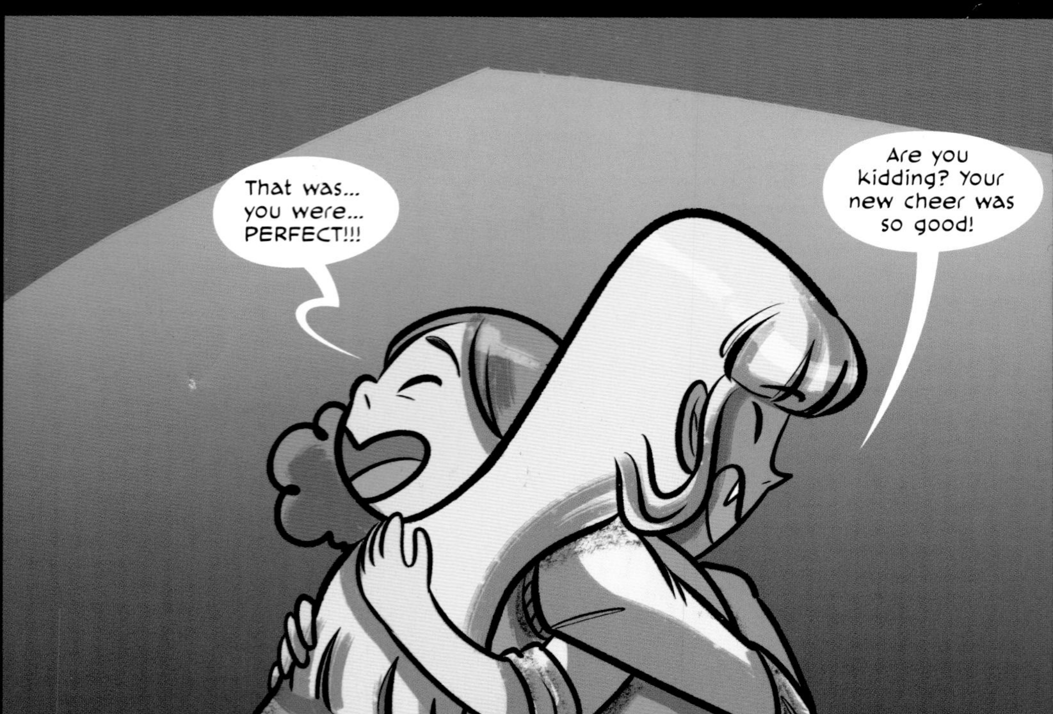
That was... you were... PERFECT!!!
Are you kidding? Your new cheer was so good!

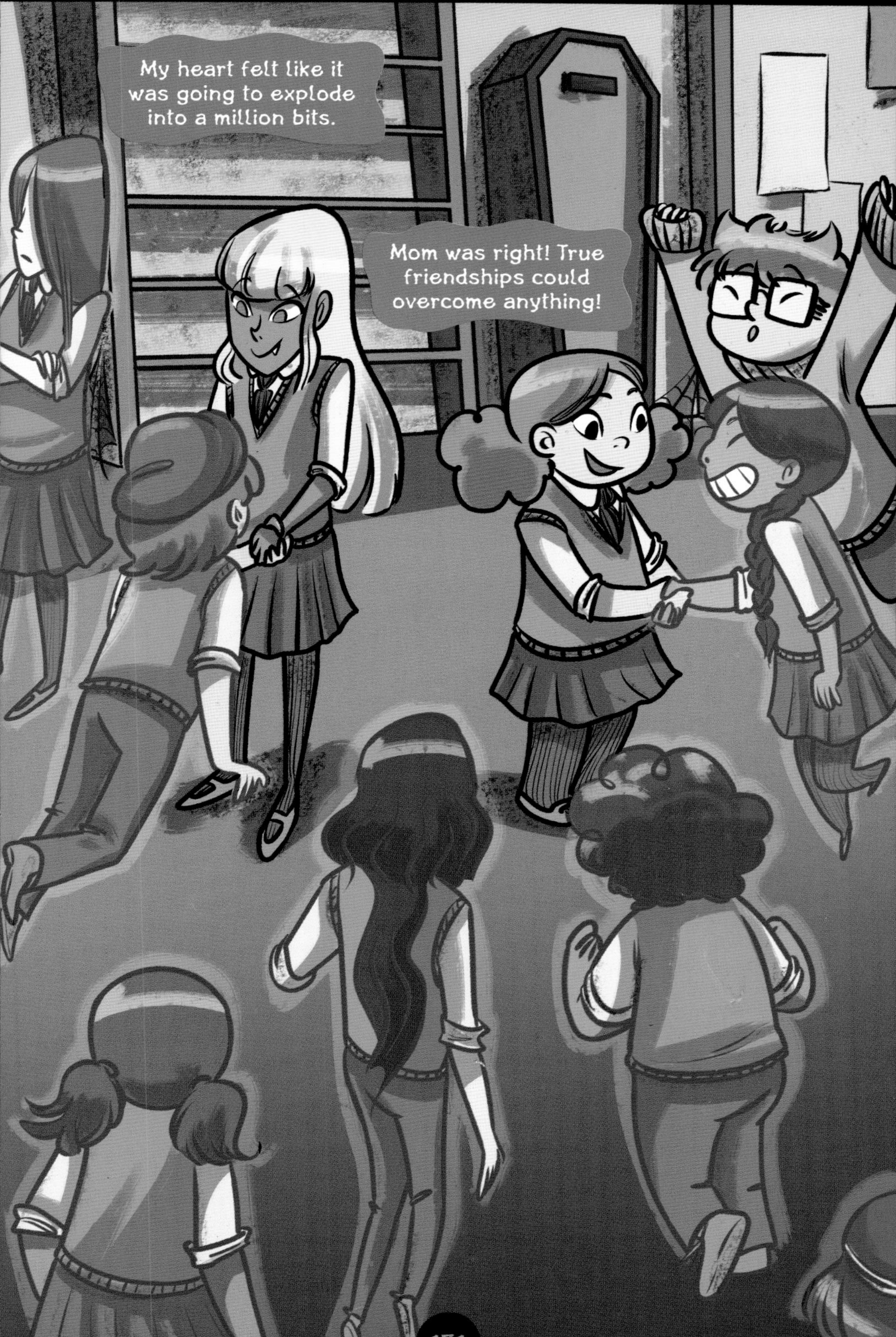
My heart felt like it was going to explode into a million bits.
Mom was right! True friendships could overcome anything!

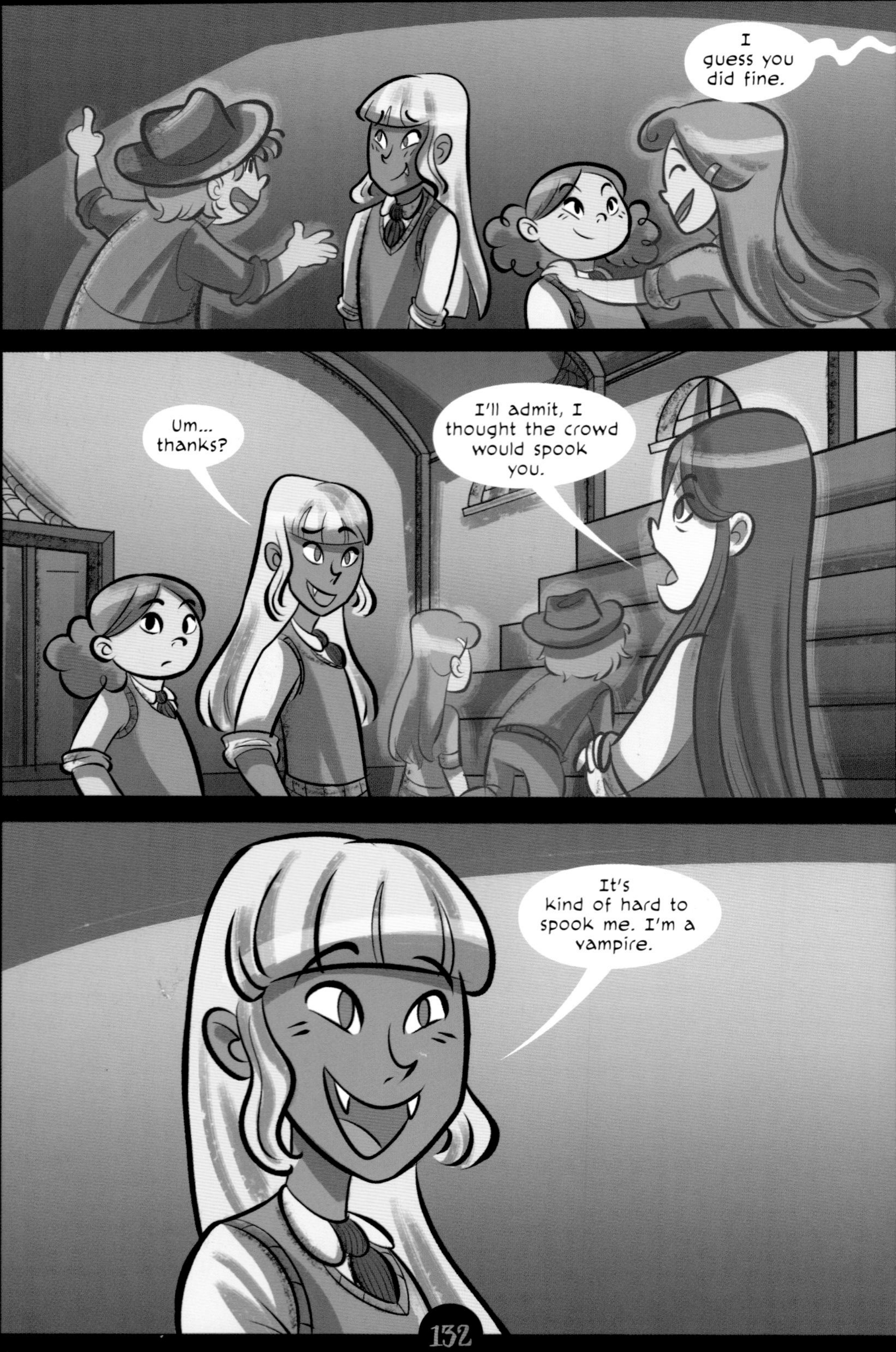
I guess you did fine.
Um... thanks?
I'll admit, I thought the crowd would spook you.
It's kind of hard to spook me. I'm a vampire.

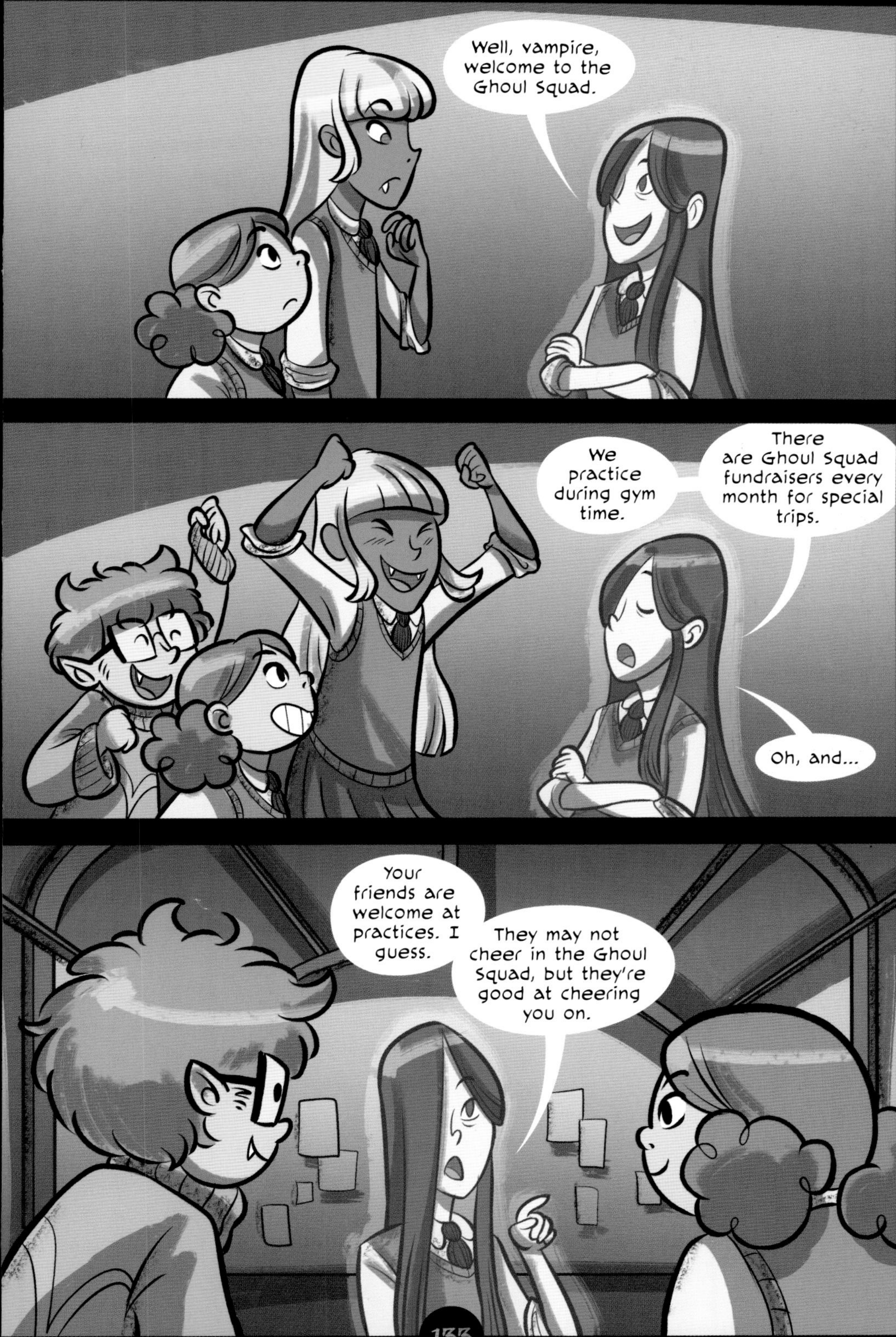
Well, vampire, welcome to the Ghoul Squad.
We practice during gym time.
There are Ghoul Squad fundraisers every month for special trips.
Oh, and...
Your friends are welcome at practices. I guess.
They may not cheer in the Ghoul Squad, but they're good at cheering you on.

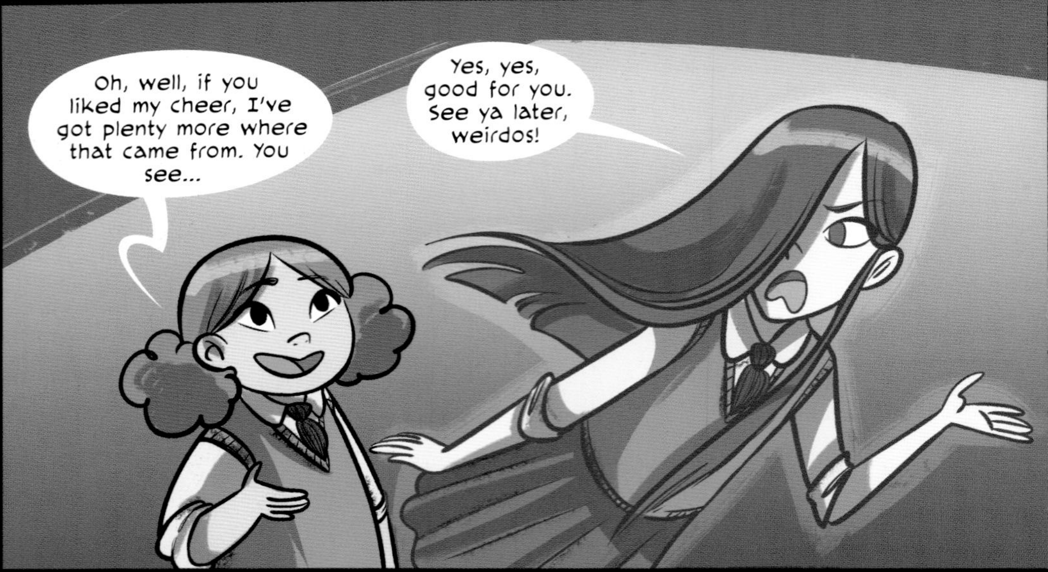
Oh, well, if you liked my cheer, I've got plenty more where that came from. You see...
Yes, yes, good for you. See ya later, weirdos!

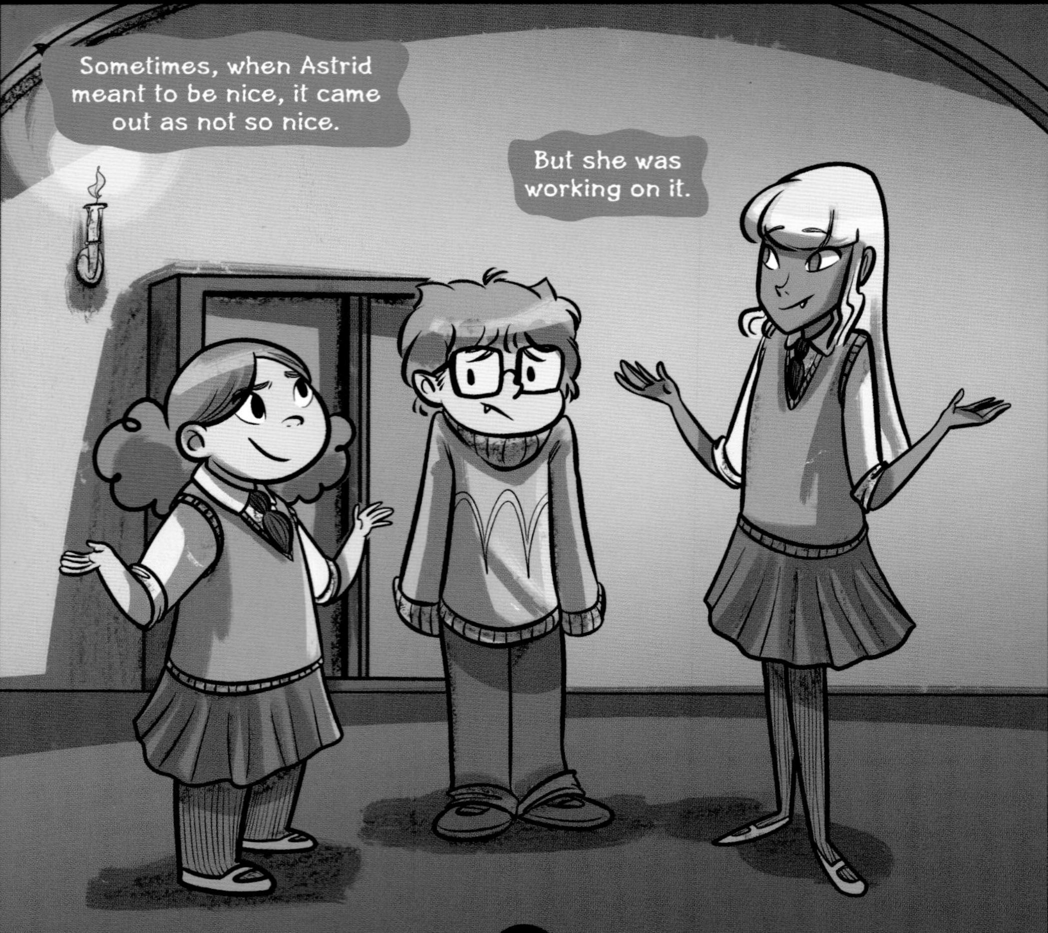
Sometimes, when Astrid meant to be nice, it came out as not so nice.
But she was working on it.

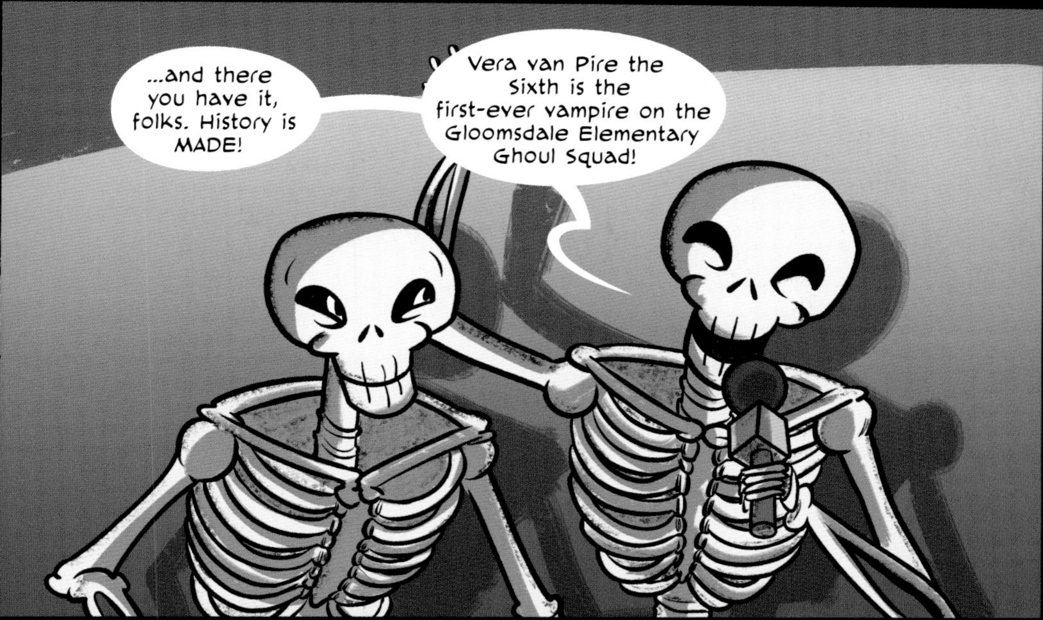
...and there you have it, folks. History is MADE!
Vera van Pire the Sixth is the first-ever vampire on the Gloomsdale Elementary Ghoul Squad!

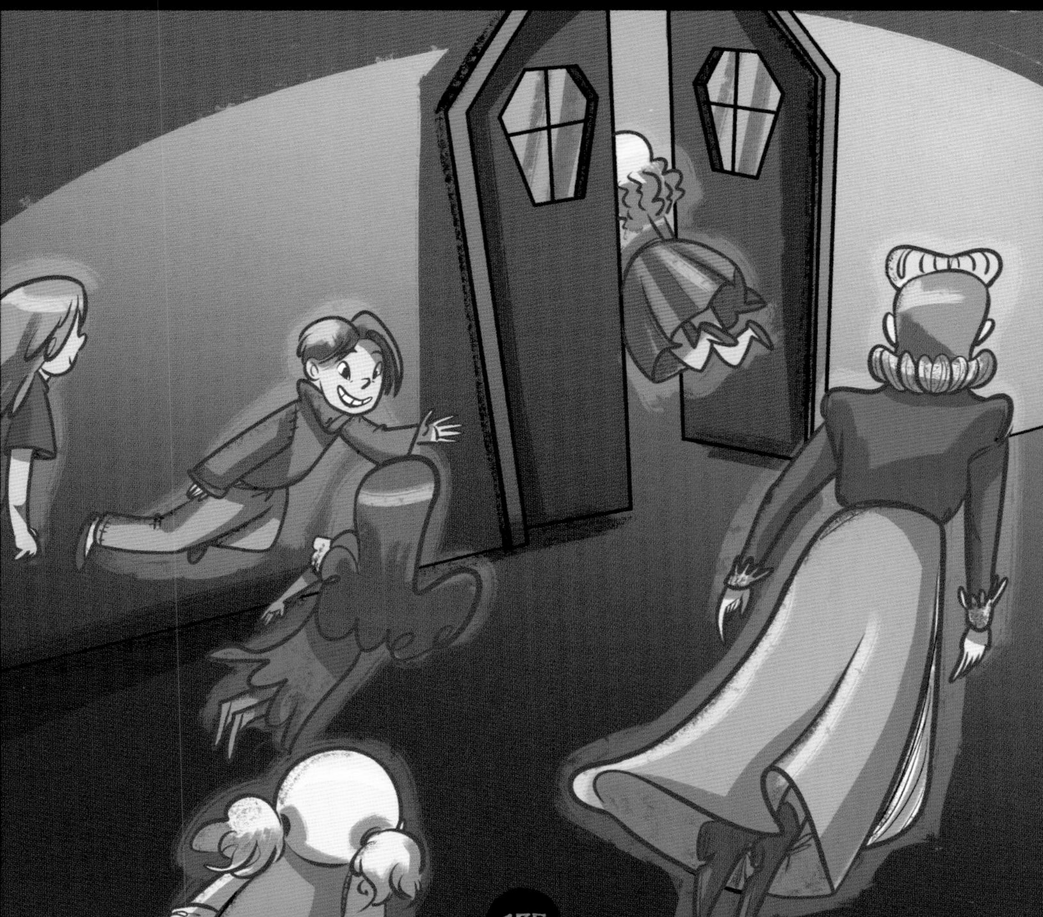

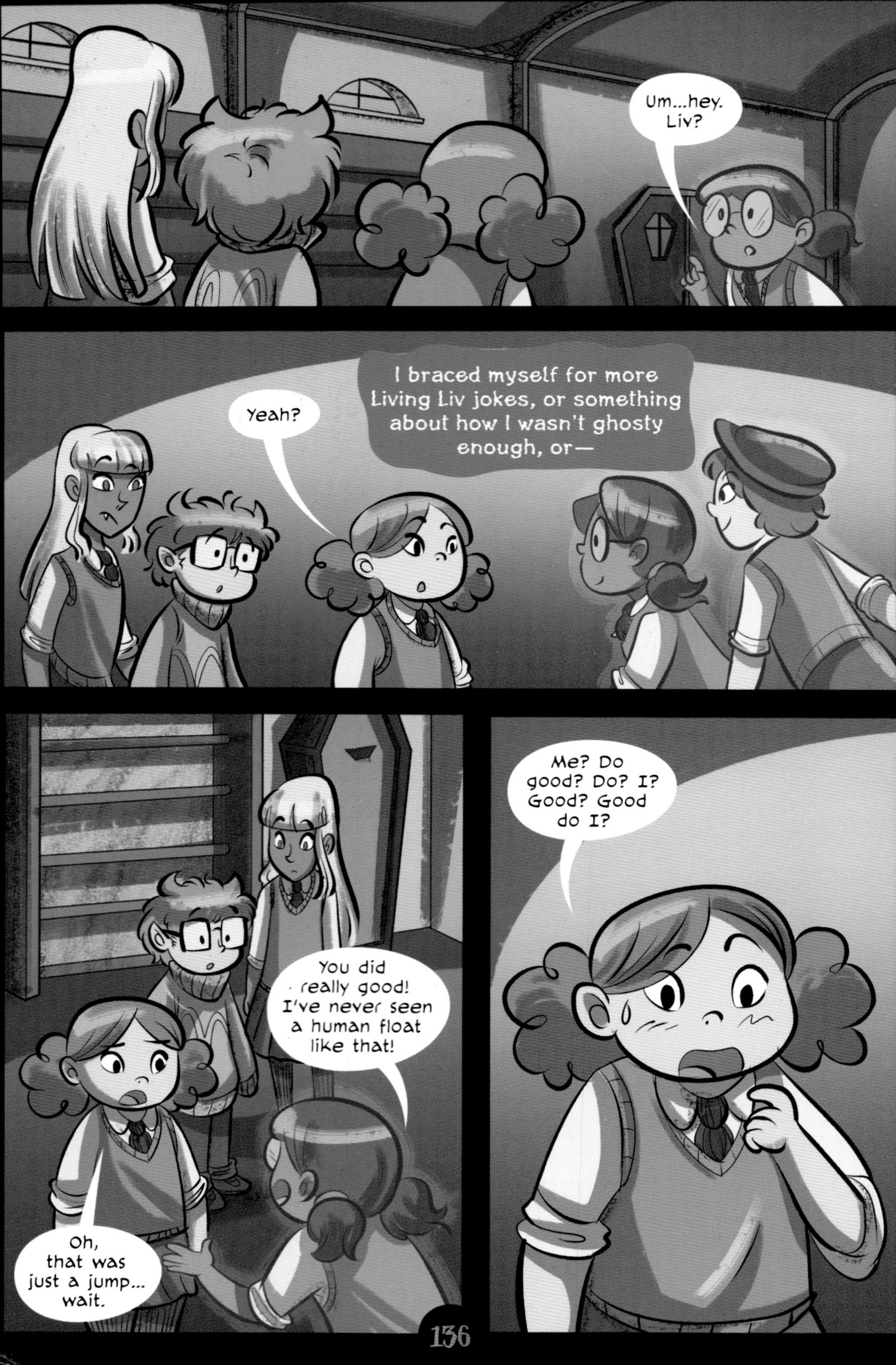
Um...hey. Liv?
Yeah?
I braced myself for more Living Liv jokes, or something about how I wasn't ghosty enough, or—
You did really good! I've never seen a human float like that!
Oh, that was just a jump... wait.
Me? Do good? Do? I? Good? Good do I?

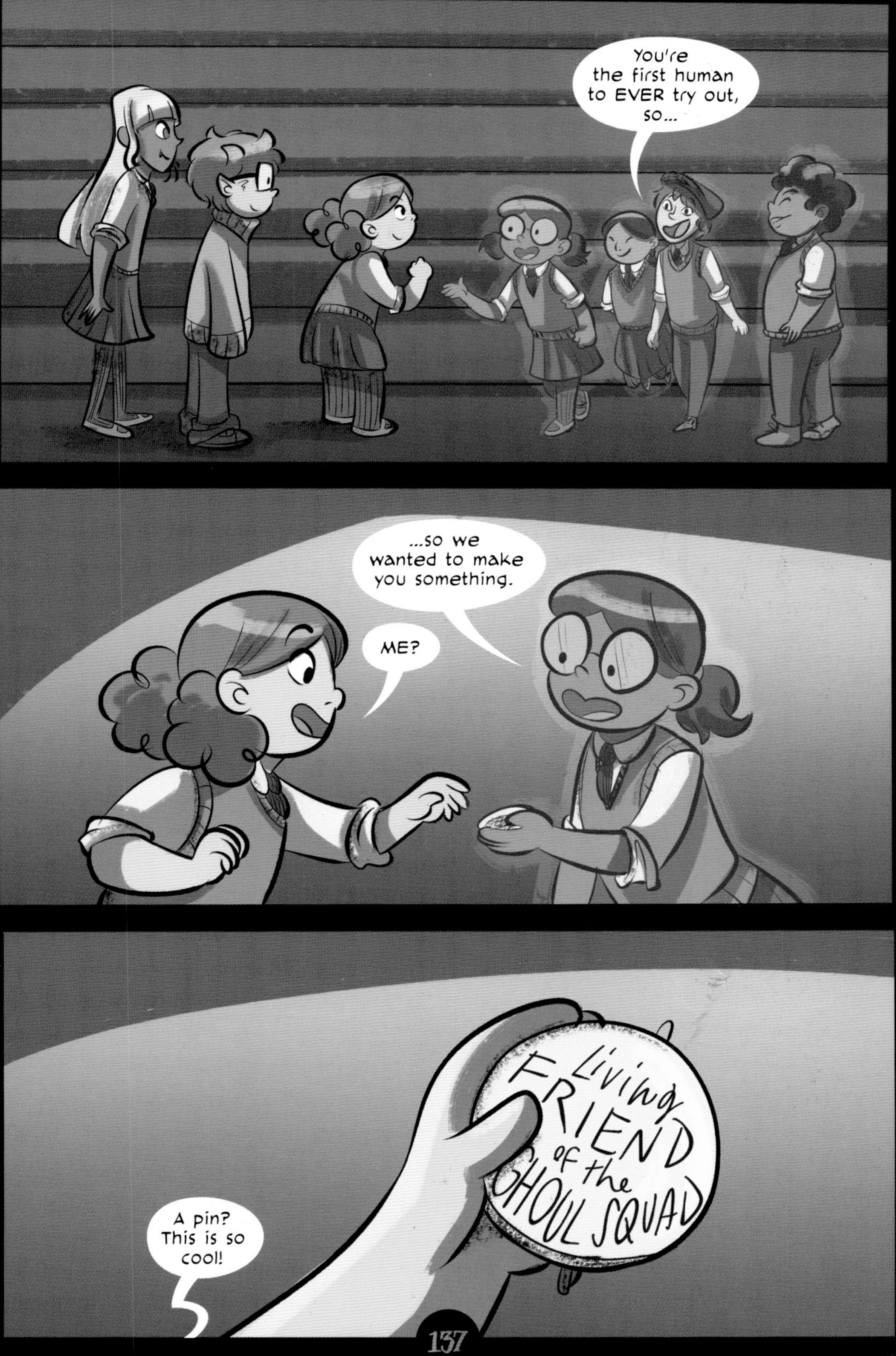
You're the first human to EVER try out, so...
...so we wanted to make you something.
ME?
LIVING FRIEND of the GHOUL SQUAD
A pin? This is so cool!

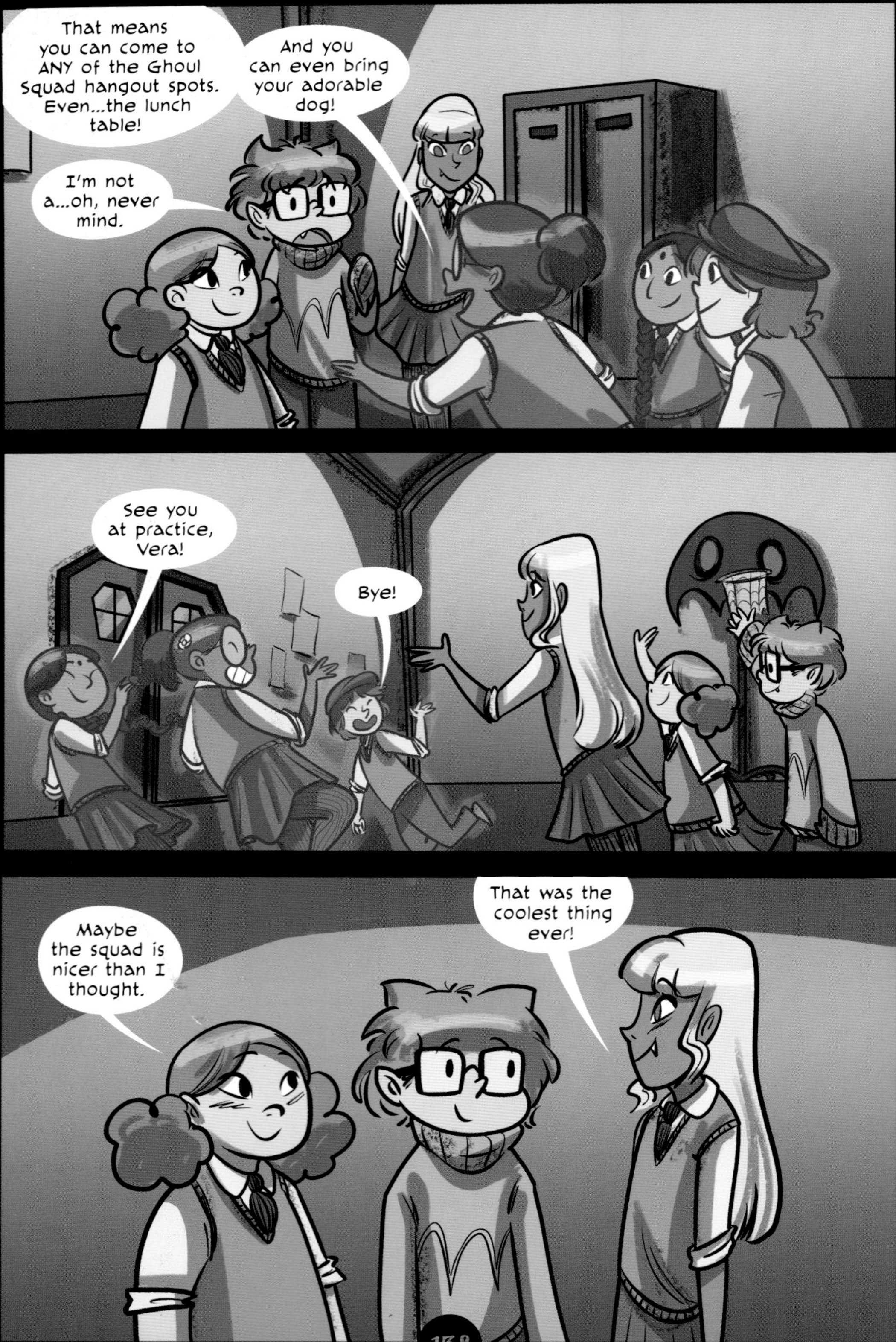

That means you can come to ANY of the Ghoul Squad hangout spots. Even...the lunch table!
And you can even bring your adorable dog!
I'm not a...oh, never mind.
See you at practice, Vera!
Bye!
Maybe the squad is nicer than I thought.
That was the coolest thing ever!

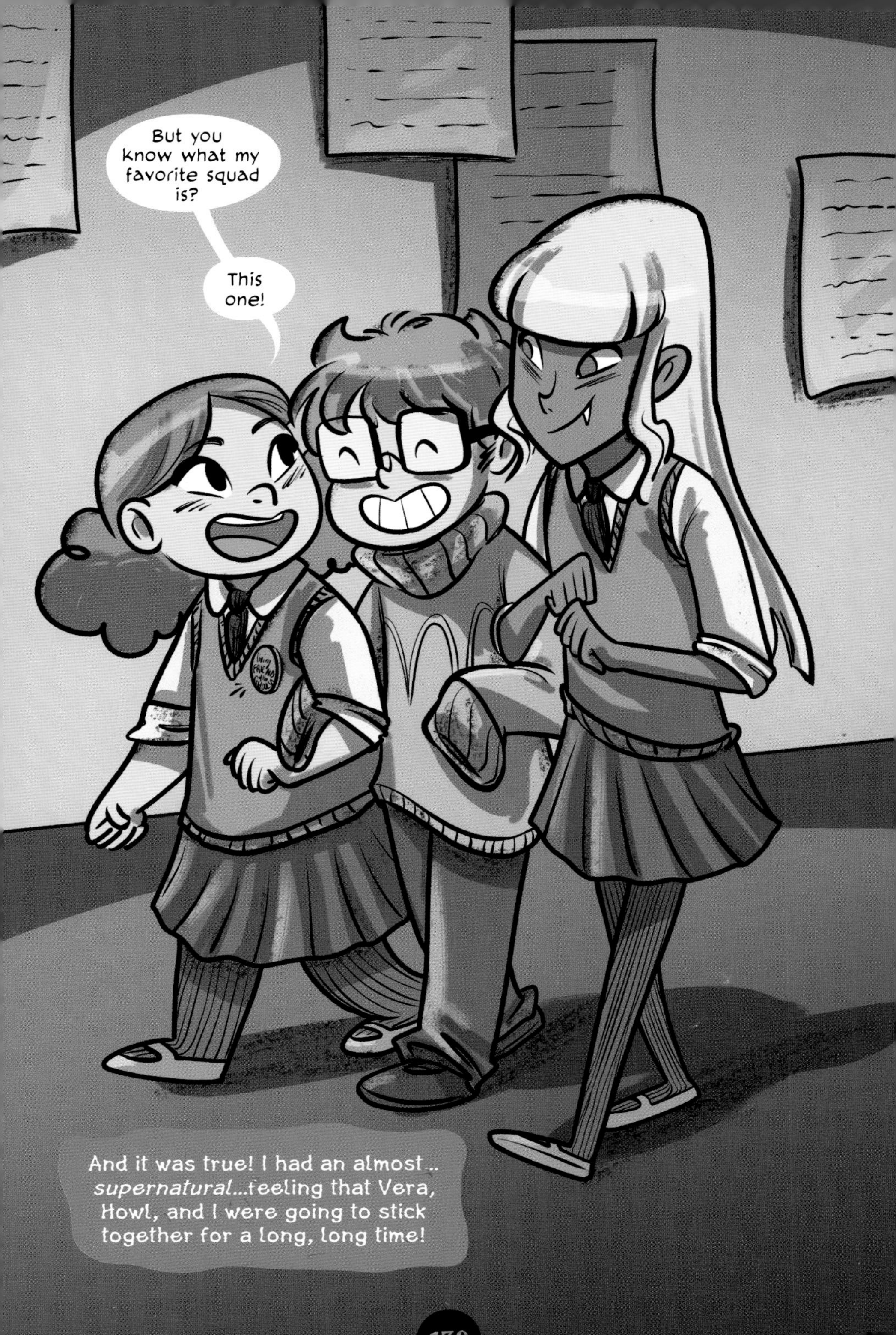
But you know what my favorite squad is?
This one!
And it was true! I had an almost... *supernatural*...feeling that Vera, Howl, and I were going to stick together for a long, long time!

Can't get enough of

Spirited?

Check out the next adventure...

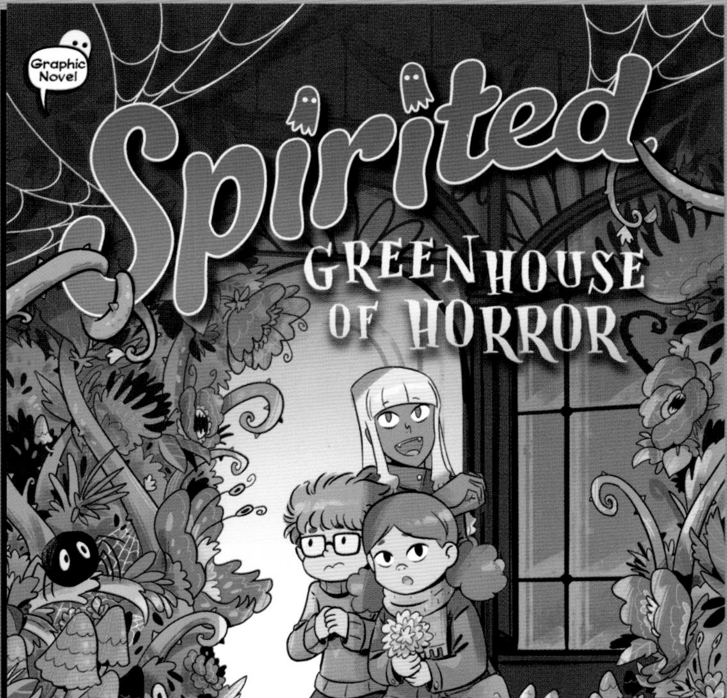
Graphic Novel
Spirited
GREENHOUSE OF HORROR

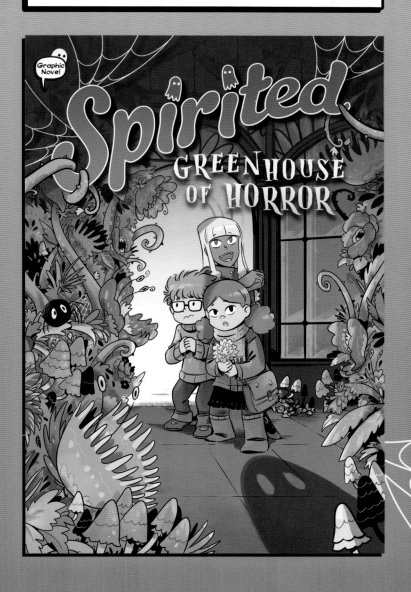